ALL THE LOST LITTLE HORSES

A Desperation Creek Novel

By Janice Kay Johnson

ISBN-13: 978-0-9976638-7-7

All the Lost Little Horses
Copyright 2018 Janice Kay Johnson
All Rights Reserved

Cover Design by Tammy Seidick

PROLOGUE

The rat-a-tat-tat of nails slamming home into the sheet of plywood prevented him from hearing anyone approaching. At the tap on his shoulder, he spun around, the cordless nail gun held like a pistol.

"Whoa!" Bud Coffey raised his hands and backed away. "Boss wants to see you." He smirked. "Right now."

He wanted to flatten the smug little bastard's nose, or 'accidentally' let a few nails fly. He did neither, only nodded a tight-lipped acknowledgement.

Just so the men on site would know he didn't jump the second the bitch summoned him, he finished laying the plywood floor in what would be a living room before he jumped down to the ground and plugged the nail gun in to charge while he was at the trailer that housed the contractor's office. Only then did he walk the half block to where it was parked.

His boss was alone inside. Sharon Jarvis. Fortyish, big tits, big ass, roll around her middle. Going to seed, although she tried to pretend it wasn't happening by dyeing her hair platinum blonde and slabbing on the makeup. Her eyelashes were thick spikes. She looked like a hooker who had to beg for customers.

The men who'd worked for her father hadn't seen much of her until Russ Jarvis keeled over from a heart attack. Looking pleased as punch, she'd pretended to wipe away a tear or two before taking his place. There wasn't a man here who liked taking orders from a woman, and especially not from her, but he'd gritted his teeth and done it so far.

Now he said, "You wanted to see me?"

"Fifteen minutes ago."

"I finish what I start."

She pushed her father's chair back and rose to her feet, holding his gaze. "Not here. Not anymore. You're fired. Collect your things and get off the property. We'll mail your check."

Jolted, he exclaimed, "What? I'm a good worker."

"My father warned you." The bitch sounded condescending. Her lip had an insulting curl to it. "Another incident of domestic violence, you'd be gone. We don't want someone with a hair-trigger temper around here."

Then maybe she shouldn't have tromped on his trip-wire.

He didn't give her a chance to back away, to reach for a phone. He lunged over the desk and closed his hands around her throat before she could scream. She fought, but ineffectually. With his knee planted on the desk, the other booted foot on the floor, he had complete control. He squeezed and squeezed as her face turned red and then blue, as specks of blood appeared in her eyes, as her struggles became weaker. He kept squeezing after he knew she was dead, giving her a hard shake just because he could. And then he dropped her body like the trash she was.

He took a minute to search drawers and the file cabinet, finding a stash of a few thousand dollars that he pocketed. Finally, he pushed the little button to lock the only door into the trailer and left, closing the door behind him.

The rush of pleasure had him looking forward to going home. Two bitches a day, that would be a record. He'd have to take off, of course; that little creep Coffey would be eager to tell the cops who had gone into the trailer last.

But that was okay. He knew who to blame for everything: the reason he was pissed all the time, for being demoted from construction supervisor to foreman, and now fired. And yeah, the reason he'd gotten involved with the airhead who hadn't known how to convince the cops who'd knocked on the door last night that the screaming had been from the TV, not her.

It was past time he took care of his real problem.

CHAPTER ONE

"Hadn't branded the calves yet." Walt Whitney, a tall, lanky rancher, stared straight ahead, his face set in grim lines. "We planned to do it next week. Son of a gun. These bastards chose the prime time to make a move on my herd."

Detective Jed Dawson relaxed in the saddle as the two horses loped across the open pasture. He had a feeling of unreality even though he'd been a cop long enough to know that just about anything could be stolen. Still, this was a first for him, though he'd spent a few years on a ranch in Georgia.

Cattle rustling. Whitney's call had been the second report within the last ten days, besides. Jed hadn't known there was such a thing anymore. In his mind, cattle rustling was classic Old West. Six-shooters, the local sheriff deputizing a bunch of locals to corner the bad guys in a box canyon. The cattle thieves hung, vigilante style.

Turned out he'd been wrong, because here he was, pursuing what he was beginning to think might be a bigger problem than the tip of the iceberg they'd seen so far. Of course, he had an excuse for his ignorance. With his faint southern accent betraying him, anyone would know he wasn't a native Oregonian.

This morning, Whitney had discovered something like twenty-five cows along with their calves missing from their pasture, a fence having been cut to allow the herd to be moved out onto the federal land that stretched for miles beyond the ranch. Where they'd been taken from there…well, that would be Jed's job to find out, along with how they'd been transported.

A lot of people in this rural county on the east side of the mountains ran some cattle, but not many still made a living at it. Whitney was one of those few, his operation at least the equal of the Circle S next door. Jed knew the Circle S all too well after investigating the murder of the owner only a few months back. In fact, the two men now rode parallel to a fence that divided Whitney's land from the ranch still owned by Curt Steagall's widow. From what Jed had heard, she hadn't yet decided whether to sell out or not. Her husband had been the third-generation to work that land, and rumor had it that the baby she was expecting was a boy.

He thought she'd have to sell. She didn't have the experience to run the place herself, and paying for too much help would eat up any profits, and then some. Besides, with corporations swallowing the smaller, family-owned operations, by the time that baby grew up, what were the odds a man could still make a living for his family with the Circle S?

After a brooding silence Jed hadn't broken, Whitney said, "Beef prices are up this year, you know." White-haired, he had the tanned, wrinkled face you'd expect from a man who'd spent a good part of his fifty-six years on earth outdoors beneath a baking summer sun or in bitter cold during the winter and spring. The lines carving his face suggested his expression was most often affable, but he wasn't smiling today. "Should be good news, but for those of us who've been hit, the best prices in the world won't make up for what we've lost."

Jed had learned that although the calves were worth at least $600 each even in a so-so year, they weren't the big loss. It was the cows, who turned out a calf or two a year. They were the working machinery of a cattle ranch, in a sense, and expensive to replace. What's more, Whitney had put a lot of money into shifting his herd to Wagyu from the Herefords he's formerly raised. Kobe beef was in high demand right now, and the stolen animals included his first Wagyu calves and some mighty expensive cows. Unfortunately, the rancher had cut expenses to the extent he could to finance the shift. He'd dropped his insurance.

As they rode, from long habit Jed scanned the landscape ceaselessly, watching for movement, for anything out of place. So far, all he'd seen was sagebrush and more sagebrush, one fleeing jackrabbit, board and wire fences, and cattle, including some red-brown Hereford steers on Circle S land.

"I went online last week," he said, "after the first report of rustling. Suppose you heard about that."

Whitney nodded. "The Harper spread." Like every other rancher in the county, he'd heard within hours of the discovery of missing cattle. If he hadn't, he'd have read about it in the Hayes County Courier, the weekly newspaper owned and run by the sheriff's fiancée, Cassie Ward.

"Read about the problems ranchers had down in Malheur County a few years back," Jed continued.

Whitney grunted, scowling beneath the brim of his hat. "Yeah, the sheriff's department and a coalition of locals and federal agencies did a good job shutting it down, but they never really made arrests. These sons-of-bitches hardly ever get caught."

Jed reined in his borrowed gelding to wait while Whitney leaned over to unlock the padlock on a gate that opened into a back pasture. Once they'd passed through, he left the lock and chain dangling.

"Shouldn't have to lock every gate and door," he grumbled. "Not in these parts. Didn't do a damn bit of good, anyway."

"You can't keep an eye on your herd twenty-four seven."

The rancher's mouth thinned. "I don't have a big enough operation for that."

"You checked with any of your neighbors?" Jed asked.

"Ted Coughlin, to the north." He jerked his head that way. "He had all his cows and calves in close to the barn. He was going to do a count anyway, but he thought he was all right. The Circle S..." He hesitated. "I don't know that fellow Karen hired to manage the place. Have to wonder why she didn't find a local to run it for her."

Having dealt with a number of the local men who might have the experience needed but be available for a job like that because their own spreads were too small or too poorly run to turn a profit, Jed could see why the widow might have looked farther afield. Or maybe he was just a cynic.

"If you were hit, chances are good they were, too," he pointed out.

"Yeah, I'll talk to them."

"I may stop there when I'm done here," Jed said. Not might; would. Jed understood Walt Whitney's suspicion. The new manager and hands next door had been in a prime position to case his operation and know when and how to make off with some pricey beef on the hoof.

Jed was offended to think of someone stealing from a woman still reeling from the trauma of discovering her husband's body. It had been damned ugly. The sight had hit even Jed hard, given his own history.

He was able to shake off the memory for now, but he hadn't slept well since a disgraced military sniper turned serial killer had taken out five people in a matter of weeks this winter. What Jed had seen and done reawakened nightmares he'd deluded himself had been laid to rest.

Live and learn.

Five minutes later, he and Whitney reached the back fence that had been cut not ten feet from a locked gate that opened onto federal land, where Whitney paid to graze his cattle during the summer and early fall. Jed noted that no electric wire topped the fence, one measure that could be effective.

He swung down from the gelding and dropped the reins, then walked a careful grid pattern to study the trampled ground leading through the gap between fence posts. It would have been nice to spot something one of the rustlers had dropped – say, a pack of cigarettes with fingerprints on it. He didn't see a damn thing. Not even a boot print, or so much as a print of a distinctive horseshoe.

"The Harpers had already turned their herd out on the range," he commented.

Whitney grunted his disapproval, which Jed understood even though he hadn't been in Oregon a year yet. The native bunchgrasses were still fragile in May. The more ecologically responsible ranchers in the area protected the land by not turning out cattle until June or July.

Jed continued, "Meant I didn't have a trail like this to follow."

"You want me to come along?"

He shook his head. "No need. Not like I'm going to come up on the gang and have a shootout. They're long gone."

Whitney mumbled something profane.

"I'll stop by the house on my way back," he added.

The older man nodded. "Thanks for coming out. I won't lock the gates."

By the time Jed had led his borrowed bay gelding through the gap in the fence and remounted, Whitney was riding away. Jed tightened his legs, but kept the pace at a slow trot so he wouldn't miss anything. The twenty-foot wide trail left by the cloven hooves of the stolen cattle headed deeper into federal land, topping a rise where the first scraggly junipers made an appearance among the gray-green sagebrush and rabbitbrush, both ubiquitous in this high desert landscape.

He wasn't surprised when, about a mile farther along, he came to a much wider trampled area…and broad tire tracks. Dismounting again, Jed walked around, able to tell from the imprints in the ground that a temporary corral had been set up to hold the herd. His guess from the multiple tire tracks was that a pickup truck and stock trailer had been utilized to move the stolen animals from here. If there'd been only the one truck and trailer, the rustlers would have had to take two or three trips. Maybe more, given that they'd also need to break down the corral and take it at the end, too, as well as loading their horses. If so, Whitney's cows and calves couldn't have been moved any great distance. Chances were good they were still somewhere within the county.

Jed wanted casts of these tire impressions. Given that varying soil compositions, temperatures or types of impressions called for different methods, that took an expert, which he wasn't. He took out his mobile phone and called his boss, Sheriff Grant Holcomb.

When Grant answered, Jed told him what he'd observed so far, and asked that the young deputy who'd recently received training be sent out to do the job. Like every other small, rural county, they were lucky enough to be able to call on the Oregon state crime scene investigators, as they had during this winter's investigation of multiple murders, but Grant had also been working at upgrading sheriff's department capabilities. A newly hired deputy, Erin Brown, had been eager to take classes and handle as much as possible of the CSI tasks. She had a leg up, since she'd been a chemistry major in college before deciding after graduation to go into law enforcement.

As he rode on, Jed thought some about the new deputy, hired to replace a slacker Grant had fired.

He didn't know her well yet, but just hiring Erin Brown had stirred things up around here. She was the first woman ever to work law enforcement in Hayes County, sheriff's department or Fort Halleck P.D. Jed was bemused by the attitude. Rural Georgia leaned to the conservative side, but he'd left his boyhood behind a long time ago. Plenty of women served in the army these days. Even the army Rangers, although not while he was still in.

He glanced up. The day was pleasant, with this being May. Not hot yet, but the broad arch of sky was a rich blue softened by a few thin white clouds. He kept catching aromatic whiffs of sagebrush, and noxious ones when the horse brushed rabbitbrush. To the west lay the low, crumbling remnants of an ancient basalt rimrock, a feature that reappeared throughout the county. With continued erosion, this one might disappear altogether in the next century or so. Not long past it, he got a first, distant glimpse of a straight, two lane country road with a yellow line painted down the middle.

Sure enough, that's where the tracks led him, disappearing when they met the pavement. With the weather having been dry, he couldn't tell which way that truck pulling a stock trailer full of stolen cattle had turned.

He had seen enough tracks during his ride to feel sure that the same pickup had come and gone through this back country several times. All last night? Or would several other ranchers in the same vicinity be reporting missing stock in the next few days? Knocking on doors would be his next task. He made a mental note, too, to contact sheriff's departments in surrounding counties, find out if the same trouble was cropping up elsewhere.

Following the road would make for a shorter trip back, but Jed decided against it. He had no idea how the gelding would react to traffic bearing down fast on them. Besides, with the sun getting higher in the sky, the light would have changed once he turned around. He might see something he'd missed.

Cattle rustling. He shook his head in bemusement, and urged the gelding into a ground-eating lope.

One blessing: the rancher he'd been avoiding since the day he arrived in Hayes County didn't run cattle, so he wouldn't get called out there.

*****

Linette Broussard leaned against the warm, solid body of the stud who was making the reputation of her ranch. El Conde, more familiarly known as Rey, was one of the first Kiger Mustangs she'd adopted during an event held by the Bureau of Land Management, when they offered an opportunity to acquire one of the wild mustangs. The Kigers existed in the wild only in two herd management areas in southern Oregon, the same place they'd been discovered in the 1970s. The BLM still protected them and was careful to ensure they didn't interbreed. Bringing El Conde as a far-from-tame yearling to this land she'd bought only months before had given her joy she'd almost forgotten was possible.

Rey remained skittish with strangers, quiet and well-mannered with Linette's single employee, and loving with her. The promise she'd seen in him then had proved itself when he matured. A dark grulla, almost slate gray, he showed all the desirable qualities that defined the Kiger, descendants of horses brought to the Americas by the Spanish conquistadors. Compact and powerful, he had the classic dorsal stripe down his back, black bars marking his ears and shoulders and a black mask and legs. Faint "zebra" stripes showed on his legs. Just fifteen and a half hands, Rey had the long, lush mane and tail common with the Kiger mustangs. It took work to keep that tail, and a mane that hung nearly to his knees, free of tangles. Fortunately for her, he loved to be brushed and combed, usually half-closing his eyes like a contented cat as she worked on him.

Bright lights in the barn kept the night at bay. With the closest house a mile away, she heard only the whuffle of another of her Kigers blowing out, the faint thud of a hoof hitting wood, the soft hoot of an owl. Rey shook his head, and his mane settled over her like a thick, warm cloak. Laughing, she blew wiry hairs away from her nose.

"Yes, I love you, too," she murmured, before giving him one last stroke and then backing away and letting herself out of the stall that led into a paddock currently open to pasture. Another horse called from a distance, and Rey ambled outside, his deep-gray coat giving him a ghost-like appearance for a few steps until he became lost in the darkness.

She didn't let herself linger any longer. It had to be nine o'clock, and she hadn't yet had dinner. She'd been self-indulgent to stay out here so long this evening. With her horses, she was never lonely. Once in the house, she became aware of how quiet it was, how few contacts she had with other human beings.

That was best for her, she reminded herself. Nothing good had ever come of relationships with men. They either abandoned you, or tried to turn you into a puppet with no remaining will to resist. Good reason to swear off men once and for all. She either had terrible taste, or an inability to make a partner happy. Horses were different. She had an eye for them, and a gift for connecting with them. They rarely let her down. Who needed a man?

She turned out lights, although a motion-activated one at the peak of the barn roof came on as soon as she stepped outside. She hadn't thought to leave on any lights in the house, which meant finding her way through the darkness toward the darker bulk of the plain, two-story farmhouse. Like Rey, she imagined herself disappearing slowly as she left the too-bright circle cast by the floodlight.

Long ago, someone had planted several oaks that had survived the cold winters on this land that lay between the Ochoco Mountains and the barren high desert, where sagebrush thrived. She liked the shade daytimes, the broad, spreading oaks helping keep the house cool during the hot summers. But tonight, broad limbs blocked the moonlight.

Linette climbed the porch steps, her booted feet striking the boards much as Rey's hooves had. Behind her, the floodlight went out. She was reaching for the doorknob when she heard a faint sound. Instinct had her going still, listening. Wildlife, she tried to convince herself. The owl wasn't alone at being nocturnal. Rats, mice, snakes, coyotes. Perhaps something was hunting.

But the fine hairs on her neck prickled. Most night sounds were *familiar*. Whatever she'd heard…wasn't. It made her think of a foot carelessly scuffed against the ground or a rock. Perhaps something brushing the corner of the house.

She couldn't prevent herself from whirling to face the threat, but saw only the dark shapes of the oak trees, shadows. Then her heart jumped. What if the sound had come from *inside* the house? She hadn't locked the door. She never did. Anyone could have walked in.

Linette stayed frozen for an absurd length of time. Gradually, one by one, her muscles relaxed. Yes, she'd read about the recent cattle rustling. That must be responsible for her anxiety. The crime log in the Courier mentioned domestic violence, vandalism, small-time theft, too, but really there wasn't much crime around here compared to where she'd come from. It wasn't as if she had anything worth stealing in the house, and nobody had seemed all that interested in her. Not even the man whose photo she'd seen in the Courier three months ago.

It stretched credulity to think he'd happened to move to Hayes County without knowing she was here. Nine months he'd been here. *Nine months*, and he hadn't so much as called her.

No, not even the man she'd once loved with all her heart was interested in her.

She scanned the yard again, the long drive leading to the paved country road that fronted her property. Nothing.

With a shrug, she opened the door and went inside.

*****

In the next week, Jed found three other ranchers who'd lost cattle. The owner of the largest operation, Arrowhead Creek Ranch, sounded annoyed but philosophical in part because insurance would cover most of their loss. Jed would still be going out to talk to him.

The owner of the smallest of the three, Austin Jackson, was distraught. "I can't afford this," he kept saying, his eyes wild.

Looked like he didn't have more than about thirty, forty acres. The house was small and shabby, but the barn had been rebuilt, the fences were in good repair, and he owned a nice looking quarter horse cross. He'd had a small herd of black Angus, and lost a dozen cows and calves.

"Do you have any idea how hard I've worked to get to this point?" Stocky, brown-haired and probably in his thirties, Jackson looked around. Jed had a feeling he was seeing the magnificent spread of his imagination, not what was in front of him.

"My neighbors promised to sell me some land when I was ready," he said softly. "I was going to expand. Someday quit my job."

"Your job?"

"I work at the lumberyard." He fixed his eyes on Jed in a way that made it hard to look away. "You've got to get my cattle back. Find these bastards. It almost has to be someone local. Most times, it turns out to be neighbors, you know. Damn, I'm tempted to go looking myself."

"I'll do my best, but I'm asking you to stick to your own land. You trespass, I might have to arrest you. I'd be sorry, but I'd do it."

Jed didn't know what else to say. From what he'd read, Jackson was right. Cattle rustling on a small scale was often suspected to be done by locals who could make some calves disappear and later believably express surprise if a cow that carried someone else's brand appeared in their herd. Sometimes the cows reappeared a year or two later, having been used as breeding machines in the meantime.

Jed wouldn't call this small-scale anymore, though. Nearly a hundred and fifty cows and as many calves were gone in his county so far. That added up to enough profit to justify a professional operation having swept in. By this time, the animals could be out of Oregon, hauled to Nevada, Idaho, Montana. If that were the case, tracing them would be a challenge, if not impossible, unless a stockyard somewhere called because they'd found a cow with the wrong brand mixed in with a herd. Even then, the individual selling the animals could deny having any idea where the cattle not his had come from. He could blame the stockyard. And, from what Jed had read, the stolen animals could be sold to feedlots to avoid brand checks, or even straight to butchers. Rump roasts and hamburger didn't carry brands.

Walt Whitney was right. Damn few cattle rustlers were ever arrested.

But the thefts had all been local so far; not a single neighboring sheriff's department had heard from a rancher. In Jed's book, that meant Walt Whitney was right: these men were preying on their own neighbors.

As his department SUV bumped over holes and ruts in Austin Jackson's driveway, he set his jaw. The western way of life was already on the line here, ranchers teetering on the brink of failure. Now this.

He wasn't capable of shrugging and saying, "I did my best." Once he'd gone out to the two remaining spreads that had reported missing cattle, he'd contact every rancher he hadn't yet spoken to, and urge them all to brand their calves now.

Next thing, he'd put in a call to the Malheur County Sheriff's Department for advice. They'd gained cooperation from federal and state agencies, he knew, started patrols. No reason the same thing couldn't be done here…before the rustlers struck yet another ranch.

Right now, he reluctantly made the turn toward Arrowhead Creek Ranch, which lay on the northern boundary of the county. They ran a good-size herd, in part because they bred and trained world-class cutting horses and needed cattle for the horses to work. The route out there would take him right past Linette Broussard's place. The last time he'd been out this way, he'd still been trying to work himself up to knocking on her door. After all, she was the reason he'd come out to Oregon, taken this job.

But things had changed. He should quit the job and move away before they came face to face someday at the gas station or in the grocery store parking lot. But he felt an obligation to Grant Holcomb for hiring him, and he hadn't run into her in the nine months he'd been on the job. From what he'd heard she was something of a recluse. Jed didn't know if that was all his fault or not. These days, his regret was buried deep, though. Sometimes he thought he didn't feel it at all anymore. Maybe today he wouldn't have any trouble keeping his head from turning when he passed the burned wood sign that said, The LB Kiger Ranch.

CHAPTER TWO

Stance combative, Gene Baxter remained on his front porch, two steps above Jed and blocking his way upward. "What do *you* know about running a place like this anyhow?" he demanded, the sneer just subtle enough to allow Jed to ignore it.

He kept his posture relaxed, pretending he hadn't noticed Baxter's need for the high ground. A certain kind of man felt threatened by taller men. So far, Jed wasn't impressed with this, one of many small-time ranches in these parts. Driving in, he'd seen that the fences could use work and the barn roof looked one winter storm from caving in. He was tempted now to say, *I know you start by maintaining what you own*, but he kept that thought, along with plenty of others, to himself. He wasn't here to antagonize anybody. To the contrary, his goal was to build a spirit of cooperation, and ultimately a coalition of Hayes County ranchers, federal agencies and law enforcement officers.

"I grew up on a ranch," he said mildly. Actually, he'd only spent four years in that particular foster home, from the age of twelve to sixteen, more or less, but that meant he'd been old enough to be put to work. He could ride a horse, cut a cow from a herd and rope the same way he didn't have to think about how to ride a bike. As often as he'd been suspended from school back then, he'd about lived in the saddle. "I'm here to pass on a warning, not to criticize," he continued. "Also to let you know we'll be setting up some meetings to come up with ideas to choke these rustlers off before they do any more damage."

Five foot nine or ten and stocky, Baxter spat tobacco juice to one side of the porch. Guess that explained the stained teeth. "I'm surprised you bothered to stop at a ranch the size of mine."

"I'm more concerned about the smaller ranches than the big operations like Arrowhead Creek. They can afford a loss that might put a lot of ranchers under. You know Austin Jackson, don't you? He lost a good part of his herd."

"Huh." His jaw moved, one cheek bulging. He appeared to have dialed back some of the hostility. "Well, happens I already heard from him and branded my calves."

"Glad to hear that." Jed touched the brim of his sheriff's department dark gray Stetson and turned to return to his SUV. "We'll be in touch about those meetings."

Gene Baxter didn't say a civil "thank you" or anything else. He crossed his arms and stayed where he was, still scowling when Jed reached the paved road and turned east.

Jed was able to let a lot slide off his back, but he found he was annoyed by the reception Baxter had given him. Strange he'd been here at all, come to think of it; from what Jed had heard, Baxter actually lived in town and undoubtedly held a job of some kind or other. He sure didn't live off the sale of beef. Although his bottom line might be helped a whole lot if he was part of the recent raids.

Jed had been doing his best to take a look around each place he visited. All those cows and calves had to be held *somewhere*, if only temporarily. When he asked, most ranchers had willingly given him at least an abbreviated tour. He'd learned about a couple of breeds of cattle new to him, got a sense of who was running a serious business, even if it didn't quite provide a living wage, and who kept a small herd for a hobby or because they felt bigger claiming to ranch than admitting they pumped gas at the Shell station in town.

Gene Baxter, Jed thought, hadn't wanted him on his property, which about guaranteed he'd come back at a better time. The guy had a problem with authority, it seemed. He wasn't alone in resenting the concept of paying for the right to graze his herd on federal land – although in his case it was ludicrous since without an allotment – which he didn't have – he had no access to public land even if he was willing to pay for it. Either way, he had been rash enough to have joined Curt Steagall, the owner of the Circle S ranch, in starting up a small militia group meant to imitate the equally hotheaded ranchers who'd staged a rebellion some years back by seizing Malheur National Wildlife Refuge in the southern part of the state and holding off law enforcement with guns and threats.

Baxter's name hadn't seriously come up after Curt Steagall had been murdered in February, although Jed recalled hearing it. He'd apparently attended high school here in Fort Halleck at the same time as the sheriff. On the plus side, Jed hadn't had any reason to arrest the guy in the ten months or so since he joined the sheriff's department. He'd had to pull over several local ranchers for DUIs, and even cuff and file charges on a couple of them, in both cases for bar brawls that got out of hand.

Might be worth asking Grant what else he knew about several of these men whose reactions to Jed's visits seemed off. Grant Holcomb had left home after high school graduation and not come back permanently for seventeen years, but that wasn't common around here. Most people Jed met had grown up locally and were content to stay. From Grant's stories, his former classmates hadn't changed all that much in the intervening years.

Jed glanced at the clipboard on the passenger seat. Next ranch on his list was the Bidwell Cattle Company, a larger operation, and one that hadn't yet reported getting hit by the rustlers. He hoped whomever he spoke to there was a little friendlier.

*****

Ana Rosa was a mess. A yearling, her coat was still a pale silvery shade, and Linette thought she wouldn't end up as dark as her daddy. Of course, she might be somewhat darker when the remnants of her patchy winter coat had been shed.

"You rolled in mud," Linette said with a sigh. A few days ago, she'd discovered a leaking outdoor faucet. Not only did it waste water, it had created an ankle-deep sea of mud. The filly had not only found it, the mud coating her had dried solid. "I'm sure you're a pretty girl underneath." She laughed and ran her hand along the arch of the filly's neck.

Cross-tied in the aisle, Ana Rosa bounced on her dainty hooves and blew out air. Linette suspected she was saying, *And I had a good time, too.*

Mud brush and scraper first, she decided. Grooming tools weren't just set aside here; she kept them in the tack room, in a set of cubbies specifically designed for the purpose. Not even looking, Linette reached for the mud brush and was unexpectedly stabbed. She exclaimed, "Ouch!" and yanked her hand back. Taking a more careful look, she saw a hoof pick, set at just the wrong angle. Her palm was actually bleeding. She wouldn't die from this, but she'd better wash the wound, use some antibiotic ointment and bandage it before she tackled the filthy coat. Damn it, anyway.

And what was the hoof pick doing there? Organized to the nth degree, she had a system, which Troy knew. He should be here any minute, and she'd ask him. But she walked along the double row of small bins looking for the darned mud brush and realized that the grooming tools were *all* in the wrong cubbies. Almost…reversed.

Staring, she felt prickles tiptoe up her spine. Troy wouldn't have thought this was funny, would he? The odds were against her having poked herself enough to bleed. But…Troy? He was quiet and shy, grateful for a job working with horses.

Grabbing a small towel, she went to the deep sink in the barn to wash her hand. She'd just managed to wrap gauze, mummy-like, over a pad on her hand when she heard her employee's old pickup pull up to the barn. It spit and shuddered when he turned off the engine. Ana Rosa rolled her eyes and danced some more, although she didn't really look alarmed. She was just so full of energy, she had trouble staying still.

Troy appeared in the open doorway, grinning at the sight of the filly. "Wallowed in the mud, huh?"

"I'd say so."

Troy was probably six feet tall but still skinny, his feet and hands appearing too big for his body. He wasn't clumsy, though, or Linette probably wouldn't have hired him. She liked that he was soft-spoken and gentle with the horses.

His brown eyes lowered to her conspicuously bandaged hand. "What happened?"

She hesitated. "Well, it was kind of weird. I reached in a bin for the mud brush, but the hoof pick was there instead, point up. I know I should have looked before I reached, but…everything is in the wrong bin."

He walked past her into the tack room. Linette heard only silence for a minute, then he came out.

"I didn't do that." Sometimes he had trouble holding her gaze, but not now. "I wouldn't."

"It's not that big a deal."

"It is 'cuz you hurt yourself." He frowned. "Has anyone else been here?"

The question stunned her, when it shouldn't have. Maybe she'd been trying not to think about who could have moved everything just to toy with her.

"No," she said slowly. "Except, someone must have been."

"Like, a teenager?" His cheeks reddened, because he was a teenager, too. Earnest, though, not the type to commit pranks or deliberately disturb someone. Assuming she really knew him.

Linette shook her head. "I don't know."

"Let me start cleaning up Ana Rosa," he suggested. "Maybe you should check around the barn. You know? Make sure nobody has messed with anything else."

"Yes. Thank you. I'll do that." And should have already.

She started in the tack room, then thought in alarm about the gates. Jogging, she set out to check the nearest ones, then returned shaking her head.

"Nothing. It's just...strange."

As she put out a new salt block, Linette thought of the couple of nights recently when she'd thought she heard something or someone that didn't belong. A couple of times, the hairs at her nape had prickled, as if she sensed she was being watched. She'd convinced herself that she was imagining things, but what if she wasn't? Could a vagrant be sleeping in the barn at night? She hadn't seen any sign – no food wrappers or anything like that. If someone shook out one of the turnout blankets carefully, she wouldn't be able to tell if it was substituting as a sleeping bag nights...which were still pretty cold in this country.

This was the kind of thing Theo would have enjoyed. She froze between one step and the next mid-paddock. Her skin stung at the thought, as if she'd been slapped. He was equally capable of sudden violence, but he could ratchet up the tension for days and weeks, feeding off someone's fears.

No, of course Theo wasn't around. She hadn't seen him in four years. He'd never stalk her; the last time she'd seen him, he'd looked at her as if she was something disgusting at the bottom of his garbage can. In fact, his last words were, "You think I'd chase after a woman? You got it wrong, babe. You're the one who'll be crawling back to me." And then he had walked away. Well, she hadn't crawled back, and she'd never seen him again. Thank God.

Collecting herself, she went back in the barn for a halter and lead rope so she could bring a mare and young foal in for grooming and inspection. Linette made herself shake off the uneasiness. If someone was hanging around, he was trying to go unnoticed. And that was a big *if.* Who knew, maybe she'd sleepwalked last night and done some reorganizing before wandering back to bed.

She made a face. Since she actually had sleepwalked as a child, the unpleasant possibility wasn't all that outlandish.

*****

On Wednesday, Grant waved off the hostess at a café where he and Jed occasionally met for breakfast. They preferred to choose their own booth. In the early days of their acquaintance, they'd raced to it, the winner able to sit with his back to the wall, but mostly now Grant conceded the defensive position to Jed. Only once had he said, "You're the paranoid one."

The fact that Jed hadn't disputed the description had been a statement all its own. Really, all he'd done was confirm some of Grant's suspicions.

Today both ordered without even glancing at a menu. Once they were alone, Grant spoke first.

"I can't believe these sons of bitches hit another ranch."

The call had come in before seven this morning, over two weeks since the first report of stolen cattle. Grant knew that Jed had forgone breakfast and coffee to go out to talk to the rancher and look around. The rustlers hadn't left anything behind he hadn't already seen. All he'd done was shake his head when he got out of his pickup in the café parking lot and saw Grant.

Now he grimaced. "I talked to that old fool two days ago. Says he had a doctor appointment yesterday, just didn't think there needed to be such 'a goldurned hurry'."

Grant huffed out a breath. "We've been spoiled around here. And I've got to tell you, I'm glad Jack of all people didn't hear something during the night and go out to see what was happening."

"Or wave a gun around," Jed said. "He proudly showed me a shotgun as old as he is."

"I think I went to school with one of the Bakers' granddaughters." Grant nodded his thanks to the middle-aged waitress who delivered their drinks.

"Yeah, meant to ask you about some of the ranchers who are around your age. I understood when Rob Fullerton wasn't happy to see me—"

The two men shared wry smiles. Unlike Gene Baxter, Fullerton had been a person of interest during the killing spree this winter. They'd had good reason to think the perpetrator was ex-military and very possibly sniper trained. Fullerton's dishonorable discharge had caught their attention, although neither of them had thought he had the patience or the self-control to have trained as a sniper or commit several murders and leave behind no trace of his presence. Truth was, Fullerton was just an asshole. Grant had always known that.

As it happened, Jed hadn't been on the job here more than a few weeks when he'd joined a uniformed deputy in breaking up an ugly bar fight. Jed had sported a black eye the next day after bringing Rob down. The guy was lucky not to face the additional charge of assaulting an officer of the law.

"Did he at least listen to you?" Grant asked now.

"Fullerton? Don't know. He said, 'I hope they do show up at my place.'" Jed rubbed a hand over his jaw. "I told him to call us and not confront anyone on his own, but I think it's safe to say he didn't hear that part."

"No." Grant rolled his shoulders. "I keep thinking—" He broke off, in part because the waitress was approaching with their meals, but also because he didn't want to put into words what he guessed Jed, too, had been thinking. For any cop, logic led only one way.

This gang had gotten away with a lot of meat on the hoof. They had to know law enforcement was involved and that the ranchers were talking to each other. This would be a smart time to stop. If they were outsiders, Grant would expect them to move their base of operations somewhere the alarm hadn't yet been sounded. Instead, they were still willing to take their chances. People were mad as hell about these thefts. If the rustlers didn't back off, a confrontation was inevitable. Grant knew damn well there wasn't a rancher in the county who didn't own at least a couple of rifles and probably a handgun, too. The only question was who'd die: a good guy, or a bad guy?

He knew which way he'd vote, but wasn't happy about either possibility.

As they ate, he steered the conversation to other business. The county was rural, the population sparse, which meant tax money was limited and the sheriff's department inadequately staffed. Grant had scraped up some additional funding to pay for more training, but Jed remained the only detective, and Grant too often had to take patrol shifts, when as sheriff his time could be better spent.

He mentioned that his parents would be back from wintering in Arizona any day. "Cassie met them, but now she's panicking," Grant said with amusement. "She's not used to family. It's going to take her some time."

"I'd panic, too." Expressionless, Jed shrugged. "People like you who grew up feeling secure don't really get it. Mother? Father? What's that?"

Jesus. Grant hadn't for a second regretted hiring this man. He and Cassie would both be dead if not for Jed. Grant considered the detective to be a friend, but he'd always known Jed bore deep scars.

Never much for poetry, Grant had made an exception for John Donne's reflections on why no man is an island, entire of itself. He wondered whether Jed would agree. Jed was a loner, all right, but also a man who wouldn't hesitate to sacrifice himself for someone else. He'd been in one way the ideal personality for the army to train and field as a sniper. But if he clung to even a shred of belief that any man's death diminished him, he must be nearly crushed by the guilt of how many deaths he had caused, and while seeing each face.

And Grant had added one more to that toll.

"Cassie had her father, at least," he said.

"Not sure that's saying much."

"No." Henry Ward had been an angry, bitter man whose temper had soured even more when he'd needed to ask his daughter to come home after he had a stroke. She'd not only taken care of him, she'd kept the local newspaper going in hopes he'd be able to return to work. Even she'd never been sure whether Henry appreciated anything she'd done for him. He'd died without ever answering that question.

"You've never said anything about your own family," Grant commented.

Jed moved his shoulders uncomfortably. "Don't have one."

Well, shit. Grant could have guessed as much. Now what should he say? *I'm sorry?* That wouldn't go over well.

After a minute, Jed did surprise him. He pushed his plate away and said, "Don't know who my father was, barely remember my mother." Pause. "I wasn't quite what people had in mind to adopt."

"You've turned into a good man, starting from a hard place."

Jed stared at him for a long minute. Grant had a feeling that Jed was stunned, even though he never let his expression change. At last, he dipped his head. "Thank you. Not so sure which way I'll be going when the time comes, though."

What a strange and unexpected conversation.

Voice low, scraped raw, Grant said, "I've killed my share of men, too, you know."

Desperate eyes met his. "It's not only that. You can't—" He broke off and shook his head, said brusquely, "Let's drop it."

Grant could only nod. For once, he didn't mind when his phone rang. Dispatch.

"Holcomb."

"Sheriff, Cliff Avery called in a murder."

Jed had stiffened.

"Did he say who the victim is?"

"Gary Webb."

"Oh, hell." Gary's son Hayden had been a good friend of Grant's when they were kids.

"Ah...do you know where Detective Dawson is? He's not answering his phone."

"Yeah, he's right here with me." Grant pulled out his wallet. No time for pie. "You let Cliff know we're on our way." He ended the call.

Jed produced a twenty and dropped it on the table, too. "Who is it?" he asked.

When Grant told him, Jed muttered an obscenity. "I was going out there this afternoon."

"This isn't necessarily related."

Grabbing his hat from the bench seat, Jed said, "What are the odds of that?"

"Probably zero," Grant conceded, sliding out from behind the table himself. "Cheryl says she tried to call you."

"What?" Jed patted his pockets. "Damn, I think I set my phone in the cup holder."

They walked out, Grant nodding a greeting at a few people on the way, Jed thanking their waitress. Outside, they split up to drive separately. Whatever Grant had said, he had no doubt that Gary had heard cattle lowing in agitation or voices that didn't belong or who knew what and stormed out during the night to threaten the intruders. If only he'd called 911 instead, they might have had a chance to arrest these SOBs – and Gary would have been able to see his grandkids grow up.

Grant turned on the rack of lights but not the siren, speeding out of town, Jed Dawson's department-issue SUV right behind him.

All Grant could think was about the phone call he'd have to make to Hayden. The one where he said the most useless words he knew: *I'm sorry for your loss.*

CHAPTER THREE

Jed squatted beside the body of a gray-haired man who reminded him more than he liked of Walt Whitney: build long and lean, skin weathered and wrinkled, wearing faded jeans and denim jacket. When Jed nudged the jacket open, however, he saw not the usual flannel shirt a man like Gary Webb would wear, but instead a pajama top.

So he'd either been getting ready for bed, or already in it when he heard something outside that he felt compelled to personally check out versus calling 911. The lowing of confused cattle, men's voices, the rumble of a truck engine. That was something they'd never know, but Jed felt sure they'd find the WBB Ranch had lost some cows and calves during the night.

He glanced at Grant, who had a pained expression on his face as he stared down at the blue-and-white striped pajama top.

"Did you know him well?"

Standing above him, Grant said tightly, "His son Hayden wasn't one of my closest friends, but we played football together, did some local rodeo riding together." His shoulders jerked. "He was always up for a party at the butt crack."

Jed winced. The crazed sharpshooter and serial killer who had kidnapped Grant's girlfriend had set up what he hadn't known would be his final hurrah at the rimrock that had been a gathering place for teenagers in Grant's day – and, from what Jed had heard since, was still a favorite hangout despite the bloody events of a few months back.

"Gary and my father have played a weekly poker game as far back as I can remember. After Dad started wintering in Arizona, I don't know if Gary and the other two men found a substitute, or didn't play unless Dad was in town."

That poker game would never be the same.

"He the kind who wouldn't think twice about grabbing his gun and coming out to stop what he had to guess were cattle rustlers?"

"Oh, yeah." Grant dropped to a crouch beside Jed. "What's that under his arm?"

Since he'd snapped on latex gloves and Grant hadn't, Jed lifted the slack arm slightly. "Phone. Wonder if he'd started dialing?"

Grant scowled and rose to his feet again. "I really don't want to think these sons-of-bitches are locals. If they are—"

Chances were good they were Grant's generation rather than his father's. They might have been in classes with Hayden Webb, too, drank from kegs of beer he'd bought, possibly played on sports teams with him…and hitched rides from his father. They could be younger, of course – Grant was thirty-six years old – but the guys who were much younger were unlikely to own ranch land where they could keep the stolen herds out of sight.

The Oregon State Police CSI van pulled in. Jed walked to meet the investigators, leaving Grant to brood over the body of yet another man he'd known well. Shit, Jed thought; dealing with death was an ugly enough business when the victims were strangers. He wondered if his boss was regretting his decision to return to his home town as county sheriff.

"Didn't expect to see you so soon," Karin Engstrom said. A sleek blonde in what he guessed was her early forties, she was already suited up to avoid contaminating the scene. Speaking briskly, she asked, "Do you have an identity?"

"Seems we've become murder central." He turned to walk with her. "The dead man is Gary Webb, the rancher who lives here and owns the land. You've heard about our cattle-rustling problem?"

"Caught my attention."

"Once we have permission from the victim's son, Sheriff Holcomb and I intend to find out if the WBB is short on cattle. It's the most probable scenario. The M.E. could surprise us with a time of death that doesn't fit, but to all appearances Mr. Webb came out during the night because he heard something that didn't belong."

She surveyed the dead man, her gaze pausing on the evidence that he wore pajamas beneath his jacket, then on the rifle lying a few feet from his hand on the hard-packed earth outside the barn. "Let's see what we come up with."

Jed watched as they set up a perimeter while the photographer started with the body.

"Crap," Grant said. "I've known the Webbs since I was a kid. Assuming the door is unlocked, I'm not waiting for a warrant to go in the house. The least I can do is call Hayden." He raised his eyebrows at Jed. "Unless you want to do it?"

"No."

Grateful his boss was willing to do the notification – probably Jed's least favorite part of the job – he lingered in the barnyard to oversee the CSI crew. He saw Grant go in through the back door.

Twenty minutes later, Grant reappeared. He'd found the phone number and talked to the dead man's son, who had given permission for any and all searches on the property that he and his sister had jointly inherited.

"He's in software, works for Apptio up in the Seattle area." Grant shook his head. "I think she's in the D.C. area. I don't suppose either will be interested in coming home to ranch. They may have trouble even selling the place unless one of the neighbors wants to expand."

Despite booming real estate prices in urban areas on the west coast, much of eastern Oregon was a stark contrast. Competing with enormous corporate cattle ranches, family ranches on the scale of the ones in this county were less economically viable than they'd been a generation ago. And what were the other choices? A city as small as Fort Halleck had limited jobs available and the two other incorporated towns in the county even less so. Retirees were moving east of the Cascade Mountains for the lower cost of living, recreational opportunities and low rainfall, but they mostly settled in Deschutes County around central Oregon's largest city, Bend, and Mount Bachelor, famous for powder snow and world-class skiing.

Grant was right; Jed could think of half a dozen small ranches already up for sale.

The morgue crew – i.e. a couple of employees from the town's only funeral home – arrived to transport the body. By the time they loaded the body bag in the back of the hearse, Grant had saddled two horses he found in the barn.

Before they mounted, Karin led them to a wide swath of trampled ground and some tracks that Jed was damn sure were made by a stock trailer. With the weather as dry as it was, even she didn't suggest trying to make casts of the impressions.

Leaving Karin and her crew to lay out a wider grid and go over the area with meticulous care, Jed and Grant rode the property. They found some steers and a few cows that probably hadn't come up pregnant, but not a single calf and none of the mommies, either. Both the back fence and one that bisected the land had been cut. Apparently Gary Webb had taken heed of the news and brought the most vulnerable part of his herd into the pasture nearest the house. Whether he'd branded the calves, Jed didn't know. With luck, a neighbor would.

Back in the barn, Grant dismounted, freed the cinch and hefted the saddle from his borrowed mount's back, placing it on a stand. "We need to find out when he moved his cows and calves. The raid would make more sense if he did it in the last day or two."

"It would." Jed led his borrowed gelding to a stall. "I can't believe they thought they could drive those cattle through the cut fences and out onto federal land without Gary hearing something."

"They came armed, which means they were willing to kill if they had to. You'd think if they were shaken by what one of them had done, they wouldn't have driven their damn trailer right past his body and loaded the animals this close to the house."

"That was cold, all right. They had to know he lived here alone."

"If that's true, they also knew he had kids. What if Hayden or his sister had been home for a visit?"

Jed didn't have to answer what wasn't really a question.

Grant had already told Jed that Webb's wife had died some ten years back and that neither of their two children lived in the state anymore. Now he opened a stall door and unclipped the lead rope as the horse he'd ridden headed for his manger.

"We need to catch these fuckers," he said grimly.

Waiting in the aisle, Jed only said, "Amen." He hadn't known Gary Webb or his son or daughter, but he was as angry as his friend and boss.

*****

After a quick shower, Linette braided her wet hair with the ease of long practice. She thought how much easier it would be to cut it short, but the southern girl in her insisted she hold onto some last evidence of femininity. She had memories from when she was a child of her mother sitting on the bed beside her brushing her hair. The bristles felt so good on her scalp, the even strokes soothing. It was the time of day when Mama was her softest, too. Linette could say things she wouldn't dare when Mama was snapping out orders and expecting her daughter to jump to her bidding.

And then there was Jed. He'd loved her hair. Running his fingers through it, he'd more than once begged her never to cut it. Her scalp tingled at the memory of his rough fingertips massaging her scalp, his hands gentle when he unbraided her hair with an expression of fascination on his face.

She made a soft sound.

Linette snapped back to the present to meet her own eyes in the mirror. What, she was mooning over a man who had no interest in every touching her again?

Jed was all the more reason she should march into the salon in town and have the whole mass chopped off. She could donate it to be made into a wig for a cancer survivor. Her good deed, and just think! All she'd have to do in the morning was finger-comb her hair and be done with it. She'd feel light besides, all that weight gone.

Trying to believe she'd actually do it the next time she had to go to town, Linette went downstairs already thinking about the day's chores. She'd make her breakfast quick, since Troy would be here anytime. Her only excuse was that she'd had trouble falling asleep last night. Too often these days, she found herself unable to settle down easily, instead straining to hear any sounds in the night. Of course, then she'd sleep like a log, which made dragging herself out of bed a whole lot harder.

Seemed like every morning she expected the kitchen to have improved during the night. Every morning, she was disappointed. Like the rest of the house, the kitchen hadn't been remodeled since the 1970s and badly needed an update. It and the bathrooms looked the worst. Well, it could all wait. She had her priorities.

Linette frowned at the strong smell of manure. Apparently, she'd left the sash window above the sink open a few inches, as she often did. The house was rarely downwind from the manure pile, but it happened. Lucky she'd spent enough time shoveling horse shit, she could ignore the stink while eating a quick breakfast.

Like so much in her life now, she always went about her tasks in a certain order. She filled her tea kettle and put it on to boil first – she'd never learned to like coffee – took a mug from the cabinet and a teabag from a canister, then added a spoonful of sugar to the mug. Now when the water boiled, she could just pour.

Some days she scrambled or poached a couple of eggs and had them with toast. Instant oatmeal was faster, especially since she was already boiling water. She dumped a couple of packets into a bowl and took a spoon from the silverware drawer before going to the refrigerator for milk. She took a second longer than she should have to see what was inside her formerly spotless refrigerator.

Manure. Several shovelfuls of it. Spilling off shelves, pungent yellow-green liquid dripping down the white sides of the refrigerator.

Linette gaped, letting the cold air pour out. It took the shrill of the tea kettle to yank her from her shock. She thrust the door shut and whirled to lift the kettle with a hand that shook and pour boiling water into her mug and bowl. Then she closed her eyes and willed anger to replace the shock. That was one of the most useful things a psychologist had taught her. She didn't have to *accept* having shit thrown at her – and wasn't that a fine way of thinking about it. She could fight back.

After a few deep breaths, the anger settled in, available if she needed it.

Unfortunately, now her kitchen smelled like a barn.

Where was the food that had been *in* the refrigerator? she wondered belatedly. On the manure pile near the barn? Maybe, but it would have been easier for someone who'd sneaked into her house to—

Linette opened the oven door to find it crammed full with a carton of milk, a pitcher of lemonade, margarine, leftovers in containers, fruit and veggies, meat she'd been defrosting and the condiments that tended to take over the shelves on the door.

Nobody could have climbed in the window, she knew that; the wood casing was so swollen, wrenching it up two or three inches was all she'd managed. She closed the oven and went straight to the back door. Unlocked. She'd checked all the locks last night before she went to bed, she'd swear she had. As paranoid as she'd been this past week, she wouldn't have skipped making those rounds. She'd known how worthless push-button locks were, though, and should have already added a dead-bolt on this door. *Would* have added one, if she hadn't been trying so hard to convince herself she was imagining noises in the night that didn't belong or the skin-crawling feeling of being watched.

She marched through the entire downstairs, re-checking all the windows and the front door locks.

The worry that she'd somehow done this when sleepwalking came and went. It was all too…too elaborate. Too nonsensical.

An icy chill crawled down her spine, reminding her that this "prank" was more than nonsensical. Along with being creepy, even threatening, it was just plain disgusting.

Maybe she ought to wish she *was* responsible. Because otherwise, someone had been in the house last night while she slept, utterly vulnerable.

This time, she was calling the cops – and trusting that a deputy would show up, not the one and only detective in the sheriff's department.

*****

Jed didn't love fast food, but he stopped for a burger and fries anyway on his way back to town. It gave him time to think back over the couple of hours he had spent canvassing Gary Webb's neighbors.

Chet Jones to the east of the WBB hadn't heard a thing, but he did shake his head when Jed asked about the branding.

"He was aiming for later this week. Needed to get some help in."

The first report of cattle rustling had come in late April, the second days later, in the first week of May. Word of both incidents had spread fast. Gary Webb had been killed a week after Walt Whitney's ranch had been hit. Damn it, how long did it take to hire the same men Webb would have used whenever he did the branding?

Walking Jed out to his pickup truck, Chet said, "Can you get me Hayden's phone number? I'll take over feeding what herd is left along with the horses, but I'd like his permission. Or is he coming home right away? Do you know?"

"I don't." Jed hadn't thought to ask Grant. "I'll call you later today with the number. It's good of you to take charge of the animals for now."

Chet only shrugged. That's what neighbors in these parts did.

The driveway almost directly across the road from the WBB belonged to a local veterinarian who moonlighted breeding and training dogs for search and rescue. Jed had heard that Dr. Knappe only worked part-time at his clinic now, although he still owned it. He and some volunteers who owned S and R dogs were available any time when the police in a several county area needed their services. Dr. Knappe himself and a yellow lab named Snoopy had found a three-year-old girl who'd wandered away from a campground on Desperation Creek last summer, shortly after Jed's arrival in town.

An energetic, fit man in his late fifties, Knappe must have heard Jed's truck because he had walked out of a barn converted into kennels to meet him.

"Detective Dawson. I might not remember you except that you seem to make it into the Courier pretty regularly."

Jed winced. "I think Cassie Ward knows how much I hate having my picture in the newspaper, so she thinks of excuses even more often."

Knappe grinned, but then sobered right away. "I saw the activity over there." He nodded toward the road fronting his property. "Figured Gary got hit by these sons-of-bitches stealing cattle."

"He did, but it's worse than that. He was fatally shot. Our best guess right now is that he heard something he didn't like, grabbed his rifle and went out to confront the trespassers."

"Jesus." The veterinarian rubbed a hand hard over his jaw. "He's *dead*?"

"I'm afraid so."

On being questioned, Knappe admitted that the barking of his dogs had awakened him at just after four a.m. Regret deepened the lines on his well-used face. "They were carrying on, but I didn't hear anything else. My wife always said I sleep like the dead."

"May I speak to her?"

"No, she's gone now. Almost three years ago."

After offering his sympathy, Jed left his card in case Dr. Knappe remembered anything else

No one else within a mile either way of the Webb ranch had heard a thing or noticed any traffic.

Having pulled over in the burger chain parking lot to eat, he now wadded up the wrappings and stuffed them in the bag. He intended to stop at several more ranches this afternoon, but wanted to switch to a department vehicle from his own pickup. He'd update Grant while he was at headquarters, too.

As he was crossing the parking lot behind the sheriff's department, the back door swung open and a young deputy he didn't much like came out. Far as he knew, Chris Jarman hadn't actually screwed up, but his chronic smirk rubbed Jed wrong.

"Kiger horses," he said, seeing Jed. And there was the smirk. "That's something I never heard of."

Jed stiffened, although from long practice he kept his expression neutral. "Kiger mustangs are descendants of the horses the Spanish conquistadors brought to America. It's a registered breed, discovered right here in Oregon. What brought them to mind?"

He didn't much like Jarman's shaved head, either, he realized. Or the way he liked to keep his hand resting on his belt right beside his holstered service weapon.

"Took a call out to a *Kiger* ranch." His grin grew. "Lady out there got up to fix breakfast and found a whole lot of shit in her refrigerator."

"Shit? Literal?"

Maybe his self-control had slipped, because Jarman's smirk died. He looked wary and not as if he liked the feeling.

"Manure. Her food was all in her oven, and some horse shit found its way into the fridge. Hell of a cleaning job she'll have." He shrugged. "Looked like a practical joke to me. She has a kid working for her. He says he didn't have anything to do with it, but he's likeliest. Can't blame him for being pissed if she shut him down. She's one hot woman."

Jed's molars were going to crack any second. "Did you ask Deputy Brown to take fingerprints?"

"For something like that? I told the woman, no harm, no foul, and advised her to do a better job locking her doors." He grinned. "Foul. Get it?" Without waiting to see if Jed was amused, Jarman said, "I gotta get back out on the road." He flipped a hand and swaggered over to a patrol car.

Jed didn't know what stupid thing he might have done if he hadn't gotten lucky just inside and saw their young woman deputy slash budding crime scene investigator in a small conference room poring over what appeared to be a textbook while she ate a salad from a plastic bowl.

He walked in and she immediately looked up, her eyes widening. He guessed he must have crossed over from impassive to implacable where facial expressions were concerned.

"Deputy Brown, I wonder if you could do a favor for me. This…is a little above and beyond…"

"What is it?"

He explained what Linette Broussard had discovered this morning in her kitchen. "Detective Jarman chose to dismiss it as unimportant. I'm concerned that someone got into a single woman's house during the night to do this. It may be too late, but I'd appreciate it if you'd call Ms. Broussard and, if she hasn't already scrubbed her refrigerator and stove, go out and do some fingerprinting."

"Oh." Erin Brown beamed at him. "Sure! Except…" She hesitated.

"I'll clear it with the sheriff."

"Okay!"

She opened her laptop to look up the number for the LB Kiger Ranch. Jed continued down the hall to the sheriff's office, no larger than his own.

Even before he reached it, he heard Grant talking to someone. The tone was polite, but his expression when Jed stopped in the doorway was anything but. He grimaced and waved Jed in.

"I do understand your point of view—" He listened for what had to be a minute before he said, "I'm sorry you feel that way, but I don't think you're hearing me, either."

Jed sat in the comfortable chair across the desk from his boss and quit listening. Instead, he did battle with the instinct that wanted him to get out to Linette's place *right now*. Fighting it with reason didn't help. Tension vibrated through his body. Some creep had been in her house during the night, playing a nasty trick on her while she was asleep. Had he gone to her room and watched her sleep? Did he smirk, too?

Jed closed his eyes, remembering how often he'd laid awake just to watch Linette sleep. She was always beautiful, but sleep softened her face, easing wariness or worry he hadn't consciously recognized then, but in retrospect had identified. Whatever the cause of those shadows, he wouldn't be around long enough ever to see her free of them. Knowing that had made his heart hurt. Now, thinking about how vulnerable she was in her own home felt like an iron-shod hoof smacking his breastbone.

"Detective Dawson?"

He stood and went out into the hall, where Deputy Brown hovered.

"I spoke to Ms. Broussard, and unfortunately she'd already scrubbed her refrigerator and stove. Although she's afraid she may have to throw out the refrigerator."

Jed could imagine. "Thank you," he said.

She nodded. "Ms. Broussard also said her back door was locked when she went to bed. Oh, and that this isn't the first weird thing that's happened." Her lips parted again, then closed, and she shifted as if she wanted to say more but wasn't sure she should.

"What are you thinking?" he asked.

"Well, more wondering. Would I be stepping on toes if I stopped by to talk to her?"

Relief brought him back from the edge. "If you don't mention it to Jarman, I won't either. I imagine she'll prefer talking to another woman."

Her face brightened again. "I'll do that this afternoon then. Thank you, sir."

She bustled away. As he watched her go, Jed became aware of the silence in Grant's office. His boss raised a dark eyebrow when Jed returned to his seat.

"Are you sure she's not eighteen?" Jed asked.

Grant laughed. "Driver's license says twenty-four. Old man."

"She's so…hopeful." That was the closest he could come, however unfamiliar he was with that particular emotion.

"She's doing a fine job. People react favorably to her."

"They do to kittens and puppies, too. What if she gets into trouble?"

"Happens to every cop sooner or later." Pause. "You want to tell me what that was about?"

God, no, was Jed's first reaction. But he just about had to, in case Jarman made trouble.

He explained about his conversation with Jarman and his discomfort with the deputy's attitude and how little good he'd done a woman who called 911 because she'd been scared. He didn't say, *I know the woman.* He especially didn't say, *If I've ever loved anyone in my life, it was her.* Because Grant would then want to know why the hell he wasn't burning rubber on the way out to her ranch right now.

Because I'm not good for her.

The answer was familiar. It just sounded a little weak right now.

Grant's studied him, expression unreadable. Finally, all he said was, "You know I need to talk to Jarman about this."

Jed shrugged. "If you're asking whether I mind you telling him I'm the one who ratted on him, feel free. I can handle him."

The sheriff nodded. "What's up with Deputy Brown?"

Jed told him that, too, and wasn't surprised when Grant nodded his satisfaction.

"If somebody is set on scaring the hell out of a woman who lives alone, we need to nail him."

Jed could not agree more.

CHAPTER FOUR

"If we'd just have some rain," the young female deputy complained, "we might have found footprints. At least that would have been a clue."

Linette appreciated Deputy Brown's visit and her evident enthusiasm for doing her job, but couldn't see that a boot print by the back door would have been much help. As it was, she'd already called a locksmith to come out and replace the house locks on the front door and add a deadbolt to the back door. She was more concerned about her horses, and while she did use chains and padlocks on gates, she knew how easily those chains could be cut – or the whole gate removed. Oh, hey – how hard would it be to bypass the gate altogether and knock down a section of fencing?

The two women reached the patrol car. Linette saw Troy watching from the shadows of the barn, but when he realized she'd seen him, he backed out of sight.

"I feel better now that you dusted for fingerprints," she told the deputy, although she suspected the only fingerprints on the doorknob or handle of the shovel would be hers. Still, people didn't always think. "You'll let me know if you get a name?"

"You bet." Petite, with her light brown hair cut pixie short, Deputy Brown made a face. "I wish I could tell you there's any likelihood we'll identify him from his fingerprints, but really it's a long shot. Even if the intruder didn't wear gloves, he has to have committed a crime before or there won't be a match. Or we might get a match to another crime, but no name because he wasn't caught."

If Theo was responsible for these tricks, there'd be a match. Linette was sure the police in Georgia would have taken his fingerprints when he was convicted of 'family violence' after beating her. He'd served five months in jail for that. Not enough, in her opinion, but sooner or later he'd do the same to another woman, and that would be counted as a felony and earn him something like five years in prison.

Maybe he was in prison right now. Deputy Brown would be able to find out, Linette assumed. But the chance that he'd followed her out here so many years after they'd parted ways was so low, she couldn't bring herself to admit she'd been a battered woman.

She did say, "I had the impression the deputy who responded this morning considered my call a nuisance. I'm surprised but grateful that he sent you out here."

An uncomfortable expression showed on a face that seemed too open for a police officer. "I actually haven't spoken to him," Deputy Brown said. "Detective Dawson heard what happened and asked for fingerprints."

Electrified by the casual mention of Jed's name, Linette wasn't sure why she felt so much. When she first saw his face in the weekly newspaper, she'd been stunned. Angry, hopeful and everything in between. He'd followed her here; that was the only explanation for his appearance in a sparsely populated county far from their native south. Even now, she felt a painful clench in her chest.

She forced herself to say pleasantly, "Well, pass on my thanks to him instead, then."

All but paralyzed, she stood stock still as the deputy drove away.

Jed Dawson had heard what happened and insisted the department go the extra mile to reassure her. But he hadn't called, hadn't come out here himself. In fact, it appeared he'd sent a message by doing his job but not making any personal contact.

Don't expect to hear from me.

Yes, she thought that was exactly what he'd intended to convey. In fact, he had made his point rather bluntly.

And that was why she felt so sick. She hadn't known she had held onto any hope at all, but the treacherous emotion had apparently hidden itself in dark corners of her psyche.

Well, no longer. Feeling a chill that would eventually result in numbness, she turned and walked toward the barn. It wasn't as if she'd wanted ever to see the man again.

*****

Jed attended Gary Webb's autopsy the next morning. Grant had offered to go in his place, but as much as Jed dreaded the duty, at least he hadn't known the guy. He could better focus on the science and block out the humanity.

Since Hayes County didn't boast a hospital large enough to have a pathologist, the round-trip drive ate up half Jed's day.

The instant he walked into Grant's office to report on the results, his boss grimaced.

"Maybe it's my imagination, but I just got a whiff of eau de morgue."

Jed lifted his arm to take a sniff of his shirtsleeve. "My sense of smell hasn't come back yet, but I'll take your word for it and make a stop at home for a shower and change of clothes."

"Good idea. Did you learn anything?"

"Nothing unexpected. There was a lot of plaque in his arteries, but otherwise his health was good. Gunshot wound killed him. It nicked his heart, and he bled out fast."

"I want to catch this guy," Grant said grimly.

"You and me both." Tension gripped Jed's neck and shoulder muscles. Maybe the hot shower would help with that, too. "Did Deputy Brown submit those fingerprints from Ms. Broussard's house?"

"Most were the homeowner's. There were a few partials that probably belonged to people who lived in the house previously. Which suggests the intruder wore gloves."

"Because he knew his fingerprints *would* have popped."

"Very possibly," Grant agreed. "You have a special interest?"

Jed ruthlessly schooled his expression. "Jarman's attitude irritated me."

"Uh huh."

Aware he hadn't convinced Grant, Jed threw out a smoke screen. A couple of weeks ago, he'd asked the deputies to pull over cattle trailers that stood out for some reason, night or day.

"Aguilar stopped a pickup pulling a stock trailer at four this morning. The driver was an Oren Calderon, who apparently has a spread in Crook County. Said he always got an early start when he made a trip to the stockyard. Got huffy when Aguilar wondered if he could look at the brands, so he backed off."

"Don't know the name. You ask around about him?"

"Not yet. I figured you know all."

Grant flashed a grin. "Only within my own county."

"Gotcha." Jed stood. "I'm off to shower and have lunch." In fact, on his way out of the building, he called Walt Whitney.

"Oren? I've met him at Cattlemen's Association Conventions," he said immediately. "The name kind of catches your attention. Older fellow?"

"So I'm told."

"I was stuck at his table during one of the banquets. He did a lot of complaining. Said he has a big spread, but then bitched about the calves he's lost to a local wolf pack. He insisted the damn wolves were about to put him out of business."

"That doesn't seem likely."

"No, it doesn't. Nobody likes losing a calf, but he sounded as if he has a pack denning on his land, dining freely at his expense."

Jed slammed the car door and reached for the seatbelt. "Anything else occurs to you about him, I'd appreciate a call."

He talked to two other local ranchers during the short drive to his rental house. The more helpful was Alex Burke of the Arrowhead Creek Ranch. After his older brother, Travis, had been killed this winter, their father came back out of retirement, at least for the short term, and was living in the big house at the ranch, but it was Jed's impression that Alex was the acknowledged head of the operation now. Travis had focused on the horse breeding and training side, while Alex always had been in charge of the cattle.

"Oren? Don't like him," he said without hesitation. "I wouldn't have taken him for a man who'd steal from his neighbors, but..." The silence hummed before he continued, "It wouldn't totally surprise me, either. Farmers and ranchers aren't often happy, you understand. Today might be sunny, but we're all too well aware that a blizzard tomorrow might wipe us out. Even so, Oren takes it to an extreme. He's one of those guys who never accepts responsibility when things go wrong."

"Doesn't have any shortcomings himself, I take it."

"Not to hear Oren tell it. Still…damn. He's got to be in his sixties. Is he really sneaking around in the middle of the night cutting fences and herding cattle in the dark?"

Jed agreed that seemed unlikely, although privately he speculated that Oren's role might be providing pasturage for stolen cattle, maybe hauling some to stockyards. His chronic discontent could easily have drawn the attention of the conspirators. If he weren't directly involved in stealing the cattle, he could convince himself what he was doing wasn't so bad.

When Jed parked in his driveway, he decided he'd call the Crook County Sheriff's Department and find out if somebody would pay a visit to Calderon's ranch, possibly take a look around. It would be almost impossible to recover the stolen calves that hadn't been branded. Altering a brand wasn't easy, however, and was one of those things employees at reputable stockyards watched out for. Crook County undoubtedly had a deputy who'd know what kind of anomalies to look for.

Jed felt a surge of satisfaction. Finding one person involved in these thefts would lead him to the next and right on up the line.

Still, it wasn't cattle rustling he thought about while he stood in the shower with hot water pounding down on the back of his neck. If Linette had any more trouble…he didn't know if he could stay away.

*****

Craning her neck to see ahead over the line of parked cars, Cassie said, "That doesn't sound good."

With his greater height, Grant had already focused on a cluster of men in the parking lot outside Ralph's Steakhouse. This being Saturday, it had seemed reasonable for him to take off the afternoon and evening. With their wedding scheduled for June, barely a month away, the two of them had taken a second look at a house for sale they'd both liked at the first go-through. He was not in the mood for trouble, but there it was, right up ahead.

"Don't feed me that bullshit!" a man snarled. "A month ago, you couldn't have afforded to walk onto the car lot and *look* at a fifty-thousand dollar truck, and now you own one?"

Several men chimed in with, "Yeah! You better have an explanation."

"Or I'm taking the value of my cattle out of you in blood," the first speaker threatened.

"God damn it," Grant muttered. He grabbed Cassie's wrist and waited until she met his eyes. "You stay back."

He saw the unwillingness on her face. Insatiably curious and reckless despite her near-death experience in February, the woman he loved, a journalist to her bones, never held back.

But after a reluctant moment, she nodded.

"Gun," somebody called in warning.

"Wonderful." He jogged the last few feet and said, "There'd better not be a gun out here."

He wouldn't have been surprised to see Mason Thayer or his buddies Gene Baxter and Brian Warring, given their usual belligerence, but the apparent owner of a new pickup truck was Duane Hathaway, whose sister Grant had dated sophomore year in high school.

The men surrounding him were even more unlikely. Blair Greenough ran some cattle on his acreage, but was also an auto mechanic and married man with two kids. Denny Everson was a firefighter, Bill Pollard a county employee in the roadworks department. Neither had been hotheads in Grant's memory. He didn't know several of the men, but was less surprised to see an angry Austin Jackson.

"Duane, you put that gun away or I get the cuffs out," Grant warned.

Face flushed, he held his ground. "These dickheads threatened me."

"I'm not repeating myself."

Jackson said urgently, "You make him tell us where he got that much money. All we did was ask a simple question."

And all Grant wanted was to sit down to eat dinner with his fiancée and take a look at the photos Cassie had taken with her phone of the house they were considering buying.

"Back off!" he snapped, turning an icy stare on each of the other men in turn before focusing again on the one with a revolver cocked and ready to fire. "Last chance."

Duane holstered the gun in a short, violent motion. "It's none of their fucking business how I bought a new truck!"

Grant relaxed only slightly. Two of the other men were carrying in plain sight, handguns in holsters at their hips. From long practice, he noted lumps under denim jackets that told him two of the strangers were armed, too. For all he knew, they might all be.

"You and you." He pointed at the two who seemed to be wearing shoulder holsters. "Let me see what you have under your jacket."

They didn't like it, but followed his order.

Sure enough.

"Now I need to see your driver's licenses and concealed carry permits."

A few guys on the edges of the group were easing away. Since he hadn't heard any of them speak out, he decided to let them go.

"Ah…" one of the two began. "I don't know if I have it on me."

"Start with the driver's license."

Both presented them. The second guy did have a Washington state concealed weapon permit but an Oregon drivers license.

A Fort Halleck PD car rolled up a few feet away and an officer Grant recognized but didn't know well climbed out and sauntered forward with his thumbs hooked on his heavy belt. "What seems to be going on here?"

Grant identified himself and gave a terse summation. He let the officer – Bill Wheeler – decide whether or not to confiscate weapons and/or cite anybody, while he led Duane Hathaway to one side.

Vibrating with hostility, Austin stepped right in front of them. "You're not just letting him go, are you? He hasn't lost any cattle, but he's suddenly a whole hell of a lot richer? That suggests he's one of these fu—"

"Out of my way," Grant snapped. "If that's a question I need to ask, I'll ask it, and if it's not, I won't. You go home."

Their gazes locked, Austin's gaze breaking away first, settling as a glare on Hathaway. "You intend to stay around here, you better have an explanation."

Grant moved fast, shoving Austin against the side of an SUV, getting right up in his face. "Was that a threat?"

"You know I'm right!" he yelled.

"*Was it a threat?*"

"No!"

Grant shook his head in disgust and stepped back. "Go home. If anybody gets hurt, I'll look at you first. You understand?"

With an inarticulate sound of rage, Austin Jackson flung himself to one side. His boot heels rapped hard on the asphalt as he stalked away. Instead of veering to avoid Cassie, he bumped her with his shoulder in passing.

On a spike of fury, Grant started forward, but she shook her head at him. He stopped, took some deep breaths, and turned back to Duane.

The guy wasn't quite as skinny as he'd been back in high school, but his Adam's apple was still too big and he might have been ten years younger than Grant knew him to be. His voice shook. "I'm lucky you came along."

"Yes, you are." Grant sighed. "Until we make some arrests, tempers are going to stay hot." More so than he'd realized. He needed to call Chief Seward and suggest his officers keep a closer eye on the bars and taverns in town.

"I'd be mad if those damn thieves had hit me," Duane said fairly.

Grant nodded. "I think you'd better tell me about the truck."

"My old one was a '97. Falling apart, you know." He looked down at his cowboy boots, old but buffed to a shine. "Thing is…my dad ran out on us when I was eight. I didn't see much of him after that, but he got in touch six months or so ago and we've been talking." He swallowed, the effect startling with that skinny neck. "After a lot of hard years, he's doing real good. He said he wanted to buy me the truck and it wasn't a bribe. Kathy and her husband couldn't buy a house because they didn't have the down payment, and he handed them a check, too." Finally he lifted his head, his expression strained but the honesty painful to see. "I haven't been saying much about it, because maybe I shouldn't have taken anything that expensive from a man who left us that way. But life's been hard, and Mom… Well, you wouldn't know, but I wished I didn't have to live with her, either."

Grant said, "You have nothing to be ashamed about. He owed you and your sister, and he must know it. Maybe part of you is glad to see him, while part of you wants to spit in his face, but I don't see any reason you can't enjoy the truck, and to hell with that crowd."

Duane's fleeting smile was quickly replaced by what Grant suspected was more usual anxiety.

"Will you get the word out that I didn't steal anything to get the money?"

"I will." Grant clapped him on the shoulder. "You on your way in or out?"

"Out."

"Well, I need to feed my fiancée."

"Ah…thanks again." He retreated, nodded in Cassie's direction then hurried to a shiny red crew-cab, full-size pickup.

Cassie joined him to watch the guy back carefully out of the parking spot and make his way to the street. She tucked her hand in the crook of his arm. "Well, that was fun. Nice to know half the citizens are carrying guns these days."

He shook his head as they walked toward the restaurant door. "Don't piss anybody off right now."

She laughed. "Now come on. You know that's my specialty."

Grant groaned.

*****

Even at night, the treehouse was perfectly situated for surveillance. So perfectly, Linette had to wonder whether the child for whom it had been built had wanted to be able to keep an eye on both the house and the barn.

No, she already knew that, while an adult had helped build this fort, the child had done part of the work. She'd climbed up here when she first moved in, although not since. There'd been so much to do to get set up, she had barely given the treehouse a thought. But she remembered that many of the wood cuts were sharp and professional while others were ragged. Most nails had been driven straight in, but others were bent. For some reason she pictured a father and son doing the work, the father patient, explaining each step, accepting of mistakes.

She gave a soft snort at what was probably a fantasy she'd acquired via a family sitcom or movie of the week. Her life might be different if she'd had a father like that, one who'd have given her a standard by which to measure other men. She'd have still been fine if Jed had grown up loved by a good man who taught him to believe in himself. Maybe even if Theo's father hadn't been brutal...but she had trouble believing that. Despite Jed's sad upbringing, he had become a man who lived by a code of honor and even chivalry. He just didn't know how to love – or didn't love her. Theo... No. He took too much pleasure in other people's pain.

With both men...she'd been the fool, and Linette couldn't forget that.

An owl hooted. Several whuffles came from the darkness in response. There were small rustling sounds, a clunk of a hoof on the hard floor in the barn.

Her perch was surprisingly comfortable. So comfortable, sleep beckoned. It didn't help that she felt safer up here than she would have in her bedroom. Her mistake had been hauling the foam pad and the sleeping bag up with her. The pillow was the last straw. Linette made herself sit up, moving slowly until her back rested against the trunk of the enormous oak tree.

An alien, droning sound came from a great distance but gradually drew nearer. At last she saw several lights in the sky. She'd heard or seen a small plane circle overhead almost every night lately. The flights almost had to be part of the law enforcement response to the cattle rustling. Somebody up there was watching for movement or road traffic that didn't belong. Linette found the sound to be reassuring. She wondered who was actually in the plane looking down. For a moment, she imagined Jed searching the dark land below with binoculars – but that was silly, of course.

The plane drifted away, east over the Arrowhead Creek Ranch, then south, she thought. The moon rose higher in the sky.

This was stupid, she thought some time later. The intruder would undoubtedly be back, but probably not two nights in a row. And she couldn't stay on watch night after night. She had to sleep sometime. She wished she knew what time he – or she, although that seemed unlikely – had slipped into her house last night. If it had been almost morning...she had hours to wait.

The far off sound of an engine roused her. Was the car coming her direction?

Yes, but it never got as far as her ranch. A neighbor coming home late, that's all. Maybe a teenager who'd been partying with friends.

Linette's eyelids grew heavier. To keep herself awake, she thought about what she had to do tomorrow…but it felt too much like counting sheep.

A horse screaming awakened her with a painful jolt. Her head shot up. Thrashing not far away was accompanied by muffled swearing.

Snatching up her flashlight, she flung herself down the boards nailed to the tree trunk with such haste, she fell the last six or eight feet and landed with a jarring thud. No time to lie dazed. Linette scrambled to her feet, turned on the flashlight and swept it back and forth until the beam illuminated the horrifying scene of a huge dark man whipping at the rump of a foal he had on a lead line. The dam was racing back and forth on the other side of the fence, screaming her distress.

That dirt bag was trying to steal a two-month-old foal.

Over her dead body. She grabbed the baseball bat she'd left on the ground and, with an enraged yell, ran at him.

CHAPTER FIVE

"Ma'am? Are you all right?" a man kept saying. "Talk to me. I've called for the cops and an ambulance. They should be here any minute."

Linette pried open her eyes. The darkness didn't lessen. Was she blind? She blinked a couple of times, a memory sneaking through a crack. No, this was night, and an especially dark one.

She heard herself make a croaking sound, and the man kneeling at her side bent closer.

"You with me again?"

Had she ever been with him? she wondered. His voice seemed familiar, though. She tried to moisten her mouth. "Who…?"

"I'm Alex Burke from the Arrowhead Creek Ranch. Lucky I was driving home when I did. I glanced up this way and saw some SOB knock you down."

On a gasp of alarm, she struggled to sit up. "Foal?"

"Looks fine. She huddled up to the fence as close to her mommy as she could get. I didn't even have to chase her." He paused. "Padlock was cut on the gate. I released her back in the pasture."

Pasture was a nicer description than Linette's raw acreage deserved. Still, this being spring, the bunchgrasses were green and healthy. Her intent was to allow the horses to roam in a wild environment, however limited. She supplemented with oats and hay.

The wail of a siren was joined by a second one.

"I don't need an ambulance," she said petulantly. Yes, she felt foggy, her thoughts wandering unpredictably, but she didn't want to go to the hospital.

Her fellow rancher shook his head. "Beg to differ. You were unconscious for a good ten minutes. You need an MRI or CT scan."

"I can't leave—"

He must have heard her panic, because he took her hand in his. His calluses were reassuring for some absurd reason, and so was his voice.

"I'll stay here for the night. I already grabbed my rifle." The grimness came through. "Nobody will be getting away with a horse tonight."

He'd lived through hell when his older brother was murdered a few months back. It was the older brother, Travis, who had stopped by her place shortly after the For Sale sign went down and the LB Kiger ranch sign went up. He'd told her to call on them any time, whatever she needed.

A few weeks after the murder, she'd encountered Alex at the feed store and awkwardly told him how sorry she was about Travis. That was the only time they'd met, although now and again she'd waved at one brother or another driving by in pickup trucks. They looked enough alike, she'd never been sure which was which. Until…well, one of the two was dead and buried.

All she could say now was "Thank you."

A squad car rocketed up the lane first, slamming to a stop behind Alex's pickup truck. Linette braced herself, but she didn't know the deputy who strode toward them. He was young, like the jerk who'd been out here last week, but darker skinned and had an earnest, serious expression.

He nodded, said, "Burke," then squatted to her level. "Ms. Broussard? How are you feeling?" He actually sounded as if he cared.

"Not too bad—" Abruptly, she clapped a hand over her mouth. She twisted away from the men and heaved, not bringing up an awful lot, but tasting the bitterness of bile.

Once done, she discovered two EMTs stood above her. They asked questions. She admitted her head hurt, lifting her hand to tentatively touch where she'd been struck.

"I think he hit me with the butt of a pistol."

The deputy jumped in. "Did you see your assailant?"

"Not his face." She'd give just about anything to be able to identify the man. "It was too dark. He was…wearing all black, I think. Maybe even over his face?"

"Like a balaclava?"

That didn't sound quite right. "Or a bandana?"

"What about size?" It was Alex asking.

"Big," she said slowly. "Not fat. Tall. Muscular." She made a face. "I can't be sure. That's just my impression."

Her impression made her reluctantly think about the two men she'd run from. Jed was definitely a large man, lightning fast, strong. Theo worked construction and had the powerful body to show for it. Remembering how fast he moved when he was angry, she winced.

Of course, she'd seen or even met plenty of other big, strongly built men here in Hayes County. The county sheriff, Grant Holcomb, fit the description to a T. Alex was more tall and lean, but he was also younger and had the shoulders of a man who would put on more bulk in the coming years. A lot of men in this rural county worked hard for a living and their physiques showed it.

In other words, her observations were next to worthless. A thin man might have been wearing a bullet-proof vest. If he was one of the rustlers, he'd have every reason to expect a rancher to come after him with a rifle. Plus, she'd read that victims of crimes often exaggerated the size of their assailants. Who ever said, *Well, he was a scrawny guy but he overpowered me anyway?*

Alex walked beside the gurney, his hand resting on hers until the EMTs loaded her in the back of the ambulance. Then she tried to sit up again but didn't get far with the EMT pressing her back down.

"Alex!"

"Yeah?"

"There's a treehouse in the big oak in front of the house. Sleeping bag, pad and pillow. That's where I was keeping watch."

"Keeping watch?" the deputy asked sharply.

"You can talk to her at the hospital." The older looking EMT hopped out and slammed the doors shut.

Linette let her heavy eyelids sink closed. There was nothing she could do right now. She might as well go along for the ride.

*****

Jed considered another cup of coffee but decided he couldn't afford any more caffeine if he intended to hit the sack. Since it wouldn't be a surprise if he were called out in the middle of the night – especially a

Saturday night – he should take advantage of a chance to sleep when it came along. Still, insomniac enough to know he'd have trouble nodding off in the immediate future, he stayed where he was, slouched on the sofa that had come with the house. It had shit for springs and sagging cushions. Every few days he thought about replacing it. Ditto for the scarred, fake early American coffee table where he'd stacked his sock-clad feet. In fact, this place really was a dump. Clean and tidy, because he'd spent too long in the military, but not homey. He really should decide whether he was going to stay or go. If he committed, he'd buy a house.

He'd been telling himself that for heading onto a year now.

Jed was in the middle of a Larry McMurtry novel that wasn't quite within hand's reach. He eyed it and debated whether he should sit up and grab it or just zone out.

He hadn't made up his mind when his phone rang. Mumbling some profanities, Jed put his feet on the floor and snagged his phone from the coffee table, taking in the phone number. Dispatch. Did this qualify as a presentiment or what?

"Dawson."

"Detective, Deputy Aguilar asked me to call. A woman was assaulted tonight during what he thinks was a rustling incident. Horses, not cattle."

Jed snapped to attention. *This* was a presentiment. Despite reason telling him there were plenty of women ranchers in this county, he knew who she'd turn out to be.

"Where's Aguilar?"

"Still cruising the area in hopes of spotting a vehicle." She gave him the gist: Alex Burke from the Arrowhead Creek Ranch had been driving home, happened to glance toward the LB Kiger Ranch and saw a struggle. "The man had a foal on a lead rope," she continued. "He ran when Mr. Burke turned in. Mr. Burke said he would have given chase, but chose to stay with the injured woman."

"And Linette? Ms. Broussard? Where is she?"

"On her way to the hospital in Madras, with a head injury."

"Tell Aguilar he can reach me there." He cut her off, found his shoes, grabbed his weapon, badge, wallet and keys, and went out the door.

He'd done his damndest to stay away from Linette, but he knew when he was beaten.

At this time of night, there wasn't much traffic. If there had been any, he'd have cleared his way with lights and siren even though that wasn't completely justified. As it was, he stayed about ten miles over the speed limit, headlights on high. The only danger was the chance of wildlife crossing the road in front of him. He tried to keep his attention sharp even as he brooded.

He should have asked more about the head injury. Was Linette in a coma? Had she suffered a skull fracture?

His hands flexed on the steering wheel.

He should have been there. She shouldn't have had to depend on a passing stranger to save her. Or was Alex a stranger? What if he'd turned in to see Linette? He was a good-looking guy, personable, wealthy by more than Hayes County standards. There were only four ranches out that way. They must be acquainted, at least.

Jed let out a disbelieving laugh. He was jealous. He'd had her, and let her go. Now the idea of her with another man stung. No, it hit him like a two-by-four to the chest. And he had no right at all.

Then he relapsed to worrying about whether she might be in a coma. What if he got to the hospital to find she'd *died*?

No, someone would call him.

He reached the hospital, a low-slung, modern brick building, parked in a spot marked for emergency vehicles and walked into the ER. No surprise to see the place was busy despite it being after one in the morning. A baby sobbed as a woman walked in circles jiggling her. A teenage boy curled forward in his chair as if his stomach hurt. A man whose pallor looked worrisome was being comforted by his wife.

Jed went straight to the receptionist, who called back and said someone would be out to talk to him. Waiting, he paced the hall, senses locked on the doors leading into the treatment area. It seemed like an eternity but was actually only ten minutes before a plump nurse in neon pink scrubs called his name.

Ms. Broussard was conscious, but currently having a CT-scan. That had been delayed while they called a technician in. "I'm afraid we're a small hospital," she explained.

"I understand." And didn't like it. Home in Atlanta, Linette would have had an MRI by now. "I'd like to wait in her cubicle."

"If you're here to ask questions…"

"I am," he said, "but I've known Linette for many years. I'm as close to family as she has in the area."

She grudgingly decided to take him at his word, warning him as she led him in back not to press Ms. Broussard for answers yet.

"Head injuries can be tricky."

"I won't." His fear for Linette outweighed his painful need to catch the bastard who hurt her.

Once in her cubicle, he sat for about thirty seconds before shooting to his feet again. He wanted to go out and pace…but the ER wasn't very big. All he'd be doing was stalking back and forth in front of the nurse's station. He couldn't risk someone questioning his presence.

Christ. He'd been mostly numb for so long, this storm of emotions crowded inside him like a jumble of broken bones. How would she react when she saw him? What if she asked for him to be removed?

Nothing I can do, he knew, feeling sick now, too.

Jed had just made himself sit down when a cheerful man's voice and the faint but distinct sound of rolling wheels approached. Without thought, he was on his feet again when a young guy in scrubs steered the bed into the room.

Jed backed out of the way. His first sight of her scared him again. Her face had no color at all. The man in the waiting room had nothing on her. Her eyes were closed, her rich brown hair a mess. Blood matted it above her right temple. A bruise had already crept down her forehead and slid like a purple shadow beneath her eye.

Jed made an involuntary exclamation as he stepped forward. She opened her eyes and saw him. Damn, he'd forgotten how beautiful those eyes were, green-gold. She didn't so much as blink. He didn't either, not wanting to miss even a flicker of a second, unable to look away.

*****

Jedediah Dawson, in the flesh. As stunning as ever. Too bad he hadn't acquired an ugly slash on his face during one of his last deployments. Instead, he might be even better looking, classically handsome with sharply angled cheekbones, a thin nose, sexy mouth and eyes of a rare crystalline blue rimmed with navy. Haunted eyes. His wheat colored hair had darkened. The strong neck exposed by the open collar of his shirt told her he hadn't lost muscle tone. He was tanned, and all that extraordinarily expressionless face revealed was wariness.

Whatever Linette had expected of a first meeting, numbness wasn't it. Truthfully, it came as a relief. She hadn't *wanted* to feel anything. Why should she?

"Jed," she acknowledged. "I suppose you have questions."

"I told the nurse we're friends. That's why she let me back."

"You lied."

A nerve ticked beneath one eye, an astonishing betrayal of emotion for a man who didn't feel any. "No," he said quietly.

Weariness sapped Linette's ability to deal with him. She turned her head on the pillow so she could no longer see him.

"Ignoring me won't make me go away." His voice was the same, too, low, dark, still carrying a hint of the south.

"Why not? You're good at going away."

The silence made her hope he had walked out. She knew he could do so without so much as a scuff of a boot sole. Then she heard a scrape across the vinyl floor. A chair. He'd just pulled up a chair.

So what?

Her head ached fiercely. The doctor had said they'd give her something once she had the CT-scan. With her eyes closed, she felt herself swinging the bat, connecting with a shoulder instead of the man's head. Too bad. He'd been fast, recovering quicker than she could get the bat back for another swing. He'd seized it, wrenched it from her grip and flung it away. Then he grabbed something from his hip – it had to be a gun. She remembered *his* swing, the agony, her falling into darkness.

"Don't," Jed said from the side of her bed.

"Don't what?"

"You're reliving what happened. Your muscles are twitching. You moaned."

"I did not!" Despite herself, she rolled her head to see him.

He's risen to his feet and was looking down at her, his forehead creased. "Yeah, you did. Damn it, Linette—!"

Perplexed at the vehemence in that usually even voice, she didn't hear approaching footsteps. He did, because his face went blank again and he turned before the curtain twitched aside.

Doctor… She couldn't recall his name, couldn't focus her eyes well enough to read the pin with his name on his chest.

He smiled at her. "Ms. Broussard." Then, eyebrows raised, he looked at Jed. "And you are?"

"I'm a long-time friend of Linette's," he said easily. "Also the investigating officer. Detective Jed Dawson." He held out a hand.

The two men shook.

"Dr. Carson." He shifted his attention back to her. "Well, we don't see anything too worrisome on the CT-scan, but I want to keep you for the night and evaluate how you're feeling in the morning," he said, expression kindly. "The fact that you were unconscious for as long as ten minutes is always of concern."

He talked a little more, promised some pain relief and told her she'd be moved to a patient room in just a few minutes. He'd barely stepped out of the room than a nurse nabbed him to see another patient.

Gaze steady, Jed lowered himself onto the plastic and metal chair again.

She blinked woozily at him. "Go ahead. Ask your questions."

"You're in no shape for that." He sounded angry. "I'll only ask you one thing. Did you see enough of this guy to identify him?"

"I wish," she mumbled.

"Any distinctive smell?"

Surprised, she gave that some thought. "No. He kind of stunk, but it was just underarm odor."

"Like he hadn't showered in days?"

"Maybe." Linette frowned. "Or had just worked hard all day in the sun."

"Okay," he said gently. "I hear Alex Burke is staying on guard at your place tonight."

"He could get hurt."

"Burke said the guy took off at a dead run. Unless he's stupid, he'll guess that at the very least, we'll be doing frequent drive-bys."

"I don't understand any of this."

"No." There was the gentleness again. "Let's not worry about that until tomorrow."

I can worry all I want, she thought on a flare of defiance. But of course that was dumb, because she couldn't *do* anything.

And where were those pain meds?

*****

Linette was asleep by the time they allowed Jed into her room. Probably just as well, he tried to convince himself, considering the lack of warmth in her reception of him. Forgiveness didn't seem to be in the near future.

Not that he deserved it. A few hours ago, Jed would have told himself he didn't want anything from her, but even then he'd been lying.

He set his phone on vibrate and settled down at Lisette's bedside. At least the chair was reasonably comfortable, since he planned to stay the night. It beat out his sway-backed sofa.

While he'd waited in the hall, he texted Grant to let him know where to find him. He surely did hope nobody stole any cattle tonight, and even more that no homeowner got it into his head he could scare the bastards away all on his own.

Sitting where he could see Linette's face, Jed wished he had the right to stretch out in bed beside her. Shelter her with his body, keep her warm.

He yanked himself back with a reminder that his first priority had to be keeping her safe. The darkness, the quiet, were perfect for brooding about whether her assailant belonged to the ring of cattle rustlers. It seemed likely, even though there were so many differences in how this had happened. In other instances, there had to be several men working together, for example. From what little Jed knew at this point, at her place it appeared that the object had been to steal only a single foal.

How old was the foal? He made a mental note to ask Linette how much the foal was worth, too. Potentially, a lot more than one cow or calf. Still, why not take the dam, too? Put her on a lead, and the foal would have trotted right along, cooperative as could be. Or had they been separated for some reason? But either something had awakened Linette, or she'd been awake or even standing guard after the bizarre episode a couple of nights ago. Hard to imagine a woman snuggling down to sleep like a baby after an intruder had been inside her house that recently.

His thoughts drifted as he slouched low in the chair. He didn't expect to sleep, but he wouldn't fight it off if it came. He'd be awake in an instant if he heard someone come into the room.

The next thing he knew, his eyes snapped open. A whimper, that's what he'd heard.

Diffused light from the hall let him see that Linette was flailing at something unseen. The whimper became a raw sound that brought him to his feet.

"Sweetheart." Jed sat on the edge of the bed, catching one of her hands. "Wake up. It's okay. You're safe, I promise." He had to repeat himself several times. He was smoothing her hair back from her forehead when her lashes fluttered, letting him see the gleam of her eyes. "You had a nightmare," he said quietly.

"Wot…" She worked her mouth. "You doing…?"

"Why am I here?"

Jed took the sound she made for assent. "I'm staying the night, just in case he thinks you might be able to identify him." Not the entire truth, but good enough. "A hospital isn't secure."

Come to think of it, one as small as this was probably more secure than a large city hospital. People who worked here knew each other, would notice strangers. Didn't matter. He'd have stayed even if a deputy had been stationed outside the door of Linette's room.

"Here," he murmured, putting the button in her hand. "It'll help you go back to sleep."

With her eyes fully open now, she had the look of a bewildered, fledgling owl. In fact, he was always surprised by how young she looked. With him thirty-five now, she had to be…he counted. Thirty. Almost thirty-one. At first glance, she could have been a teenager. It might be the scattering of freckles. Up this close to her, Jed saw crinkles beside her eyes from squinting against the sun. Not much of a tan, despite her outdoor occupation. Her skin was too white to take the sun well.

Still watching him, she did squeeze the button then let it fall to the bedcovers. "There must be something more important you could be doing."

She really was awake.

"No."

"Like sleeping."

He smiled faintly. "I was asleep."

"Have you heard anything?"

"Not a word."

"So they didn't catch him."

"Odds were against it."

Her gaze slid away. "You know about the other episodes?"

"Yeah." He cleared his throat. "Unless there's something you didn't tell Deputy Brown."

She looked back at him. "There've been a few times I thought someone might be lurking. Stuff was moved around in the tack room. I'd hear a sound that didn't belong, get these prickles on the back of my neck for no reason."

"You sensed someone watching you."

"It might have all been in my head. I stay in the barn until full dark a lot of the time. Just recently I started locking the house. I'm used to being by myself, but…it can be creepy."

The muscles in his jaw spasmed. Given subsequent events, he thought someone *had* been lurking. Watching her. Angry, if the horse shit in her refrigerator was any indication. What Jed didn't know was whether the attempted theft of one of her Kiger foals was connected to the other things that had been happening.

"You can't stay alone out there." Even to his ears, he sounded brusque.

"That's ridiculous! It's my home."

"Someone has been toying with you. He found a way through a locked door. Tried to make one of your foals disappear."

"I'll be alert—"

"You were alert." He stood, afraid he'd put his hands on her unless he opened some distance. "If Alex Burke hadn't passed, you might be dead."

Of course she argued. "There's no reason to think—"

"There's *every* reason to think," he said from between clenched teeth.

The mutinous set to her chin and mouth didn't ease an iota.

CHAPTER SIX

It took everything Linette had to refuse Jed's offer to stay nights in her farmhouse. She wanted with an ache that terrified her to accept, to go to bed knowing he was close, wake in the morning to find him in the kitchen brewing coffee.

But she knew better. He was a decent enough man to feel some guilt where she was concerned. When he announced he was done with her, he'd known she was madly in love with him. He could redeem himself now, let go of any lingering regret.

Having him living in the house wouldn't be comforting, it would savage her. Call it the difference between truly having a lost lover back or discovering he'd died and his ghost drifted through her house. The one would offer joy, the other grief and longing. She could easily imagine the razor-sharp pangs at every movement seen from the corner of her eye.

No.

She finally blurted, "Given our past, I'm just not comfortable having you here."

He had just delivered her home in his gray Silverado pickup truck, a change from the old Dodge Ram he'd owned during their too-brief relationship.

Troy was hovering in the opening into the barn when she got out quickly so she didn't have to see Jed's response to what she'd said. She certainly wasn't about to wait until he could come around to help her.

When Linette called a greeting, Troy lifted his hand in a wave and smiled tentatively. Arriving at her side, Jed glanced Troy's way, a cold glint in his eyes. Or maybe the ice was for her.

"I wonder if Troy would be willing to stay nights for a while," she suggested.

Jed turned an incredulous look on her. "He's a kid."

"He's stronger than he looks, and a good employee. At least I wouldn't be alone."

"You'd kill any social life he has." There was another, assessing glance. "If he has any."

"That's just mean." Although she suspected he'd summed up her young employee accurately. Troy might well be too shy to ask out a girl.

"You're willing to put a teenager up against the man who slammed your head with the butt of his gun."

If Jed hadn't sounded so disgusted, Linette might have weakened. As it was, she snapped, "Maybe I'll call Alex Burke."

Jed's face darkened before going blank.

"Fine." He circled back around his pickup. Over the hood, he gave her one of his patented impassive looks. "Give us a call if you have any more problems," he added with what sounded like complete indifference. Then he got in behind the wheel, started the engine and, in moments, made a U-turn and drove down her lane.

She stood there with her heart thudding and watched him turn toward town and pass out of sight.

Oh, dear God, what had she done?

*****

Son of a bitch. Jed knew he hadn't handled that well, but he was still shocked that Linette had shut him down without any hesitation. She'd rather get attacked in her own home than accept anything at all from him.

You're surprised?

Yeah, he realized to his dismay. A part of him had thought whenever – if ever – he approached Linette, she'd accept his apologies and open the door to him. When they were together, she had accepted him even in his blackest moods, seeming to understand that he had demons that would never leave him alone.

Jed focused on the steering wheel long enough to see that he was doing his best to strangle it. Chagrined, he deliberately relaxed his hands even as he wondered why, back then, he hadn't pushed himself out of his comfort zone and tried talking to Linette. But he knew, of course. By the time he was eight or ten years old, the shell that enclosed him had hardened. A bullet might penetrate it, but not much else. When a man had never been loved, never loved anyone, how was he supposed to know how?

He didn't.

She'd made the smart decision last night and this morning. All he could offer her was another round of the same thing. Great sex, an illusion of companionship, more great sex.

They had chemistry together that was like nothing else he'd ever experienced. And that's all it was: pheromones.

Easy to say, but his body had gotten excited by the memories he'd involuntarily called up. He had to shift in his seat and reach down to adjust himself. Problem was, he hadn't had sex, even mediocre sex, in a long time. Since he got here, he hadn't been looking. All he had thought about was Linette. Then after watching Rick Oberg's head explode – since he'd blown up Oberg's head – he hadn't been capable of responding with any warmth to a woman, even if he'd seen one who pushed his buttons.

He should start looking.

That wouldn't be happening, not now that he'd set eyes again on Linette Broussard. Hating this emotional whiplash, he groaned.

*****

Gary Webb's son Hayden looked as grim and tired as you'd expect for a man who was in town to deal with his murdered father's affairs. The resemblance to his father was immediately apparent, although the differences were striking. That he'd chosen a different kind of life showed in the lack of a deep tan and weathered skin.

Shortly after Jed arrived at headquarters, he'd joined Webb and Grant in the small conference room. Grant and Cassie had taken the guy to dinner last night in the name of a long ago friendship. Jed had no doubt they had discussed the investigation. He wished he could tell the man anything Grant hadn't already. He'd be happy just to be able to say, *We're following up on some leads.* Unfortunately, he'd never seen the use of lying.

"We have the bullet," he said. "We can match it when we catch these cattle rustlers. I promise you we're giving that everything we have.

Committing murder to get away with your father's herd, they crossed a line."

And they had to know it. That knowledge could make them more cautious…or more dangerous.

Hayden nodded in acknowledgement. "If Dad had just dialed 911 instead of grabbing his rifle and going out there himself, he wouldn't be dead."

"If he'd even called 911 *before* he went out, it would have been a help," Grant said. "We might have had a unit close enough to intervene."

In fact, they now knew that a deputy, Ben Fischer, had been less than a mile away at roughly the time of Gary Webb's death. Sally Ostlund, a perennial annoyance, had been sure she had an intruder. Every couple of months, she called, voice shaking, because she heard breaking glass or footsteps downstairs in her old farmhouse. Jed hadn't met the woman, but had heard plenty about her. Unlike with some local irritants, everyone felt sorry for her. Grant had tried suggesting that, with her husband now gone, she sell the place and consider moving into town or even to LaGrande to be near her daughter, but she wouldn't hear it. This had been her home since she got married at twenty, and by God she wouldn't be driven out.

Aguilar, also on nights right now, had shrugged tolerantly. "She breaks up the night. Now, if she had a gun, that might worry me."

Nobody laughed.

Gary Webb getting murdered on his own place, so close to hers, would make her even more afraid.

Jed was itching to escape the conference room when his phone rang. Dispatch.

"Cheryl," he murmured, and stepped out into the hall.

"Gene Baxter just called to report a stolen stock trailer,' she said.

"Okay. I'll go talk to him."

Before he left, he stuck his head back into the conference room to tell Grant. Grant's eyes met his and he said only, "Let me know," but Jed knew they were thinking the same thing. Baxter was high on Jed's list of potential cattle rustlers, along with his buddies Mason Thayer and Brian Warring. If he had some reason to think his trailer might have been spotted, claiming it had been stolen might seem like an out.

Last year, those three had joined with Curt Steagall of the Circle S to try to form a militia out of anger at the amount of land here in the west owned by the federal government. They were talking about a controlled burn on some of that federal land, a highly illegal act. How controlled it would have been with their small numbers and lack of smarts was the scariest part of it. Interestingly, Curt was the only one who held an allotment to graze cattle on federal lands. The others called themselves cattle ranchers but had small operations and held other jobs. In fact, they had no justification for the animosity they felt for the feds.

Grant and Jed had initially wondered if Curt's murder had something to do with the same festering resentment felt by cattle ranchers that had resulted a few years back in the takeover of the Malheur Wildlife Refuge in southern Oregon. Turned out they were wrong, but Jed hadn't much liked any of the three men. They all harbored resentment because they wanted to be more important, richer than they were. Mason seemed to be the most belligerent of the three, but all of them had bad attitudes and anger at any authority – including cops – who got in their way.

Problem was, Jed believed these three could well be the muscle of the cattle rustling organization, but not the brains behind it. So far, the operation had been nearly seamless but for the murder, and even then they'd left behind no clues and no witnesses. Jed had not so much as a niggle of an idea who the ringleader could be.

Once he'd talked to Baxter today, he intended to drop in on the other two as well, since their spreads were east of town, too. If he was real lucky, neither of them would be home. Both had been unwelcoming enough to make him wonder what they were hiding. As a direct result, he'd been itching to get a look at their places on his own.

He'd made it halfway across the parking lot to his vehicle when he heard footsteps and turned. Expression enraged, Chris Jarman stormed toward him. Apparently he'd had his sit-down with Grant, and now knew who to blame.

Hands fisted at his sides, muscles bunched, the deputy stopped a couple of feet from Jed. "What goddamn right do you have to claim I'm not doing my job?"

"You told me yourself that you hadn't. Remember? 'No harm, no foul?'" He let his anger show. "An intruder gets into a house where a single woman lives, may even have strolled into her bedroom to watch her sleep before filling her refrigerator with *shit*, and you shrug and say, Hey, call us if he comes back to rape you? When you wake up to find him standing over you with a knife? Is that your idea of *doing your job*?"

Jarman backed up a step. "It was a prank!"

"It was a threat."

"You weren't there. You don't know what I said. So I joked about it! That's called cop humor." He glared at Jed. "Now, thanks to you, I'm on probation. All I can say is, don't expect any favors from me."

Jed had half hoped the SOB would issue a threat. Too bad he was smart enough to refrain from quite crossing that line. So Jed said, "Never expected any," and to express his contempt and disdain, deliberately turned his back on Jarman to continue the last few feet to the SUV.

Didn't mean he wasn't listening for any movement, but the deputy still stood where he had been when Jed got in and fired up the engine. When he backed up, Jarman had to step aside quickly. Jed took care not to make any eye contact. For a guy like Jarman with an ego problem, being dismissed would sting more than any hard words.

Jed had been driving ten minutes before fear sliced into his belly. What if Jarman's pride drove him to retaliate? He was the kind to go for a soft target. Linette.

Jed ground his teeth, angry he hadn't considered the possibility. Too late.

What he knew was that if she came to any harm at all, Jarman would be sorrier than he'd ever been in his entire, worthless life.

*****

Once Jed turned in Gene Baxter's long dirt drive, he slowed to a crawl and forced himself to focus on his job. Rutted and rife with Jacuzzi-size holes, the driveway threatened the suspension on Jed's truck. Thank God it wasn't winter.

A few steers grazed desultorily on a ragged pasture to the right. A rusting single-wide trailer apparently stood in for a house on the property. No wonder the guy lived elsewhere.

He drove past the single-wide and parked in front of the barn. Interestingly, pale wood here and there showed that repairs were being made. Baxter hadn't tackled the sagging roof yet, but a pile of shingles showed that he'd be starting soon. Had he come by a fresh infusion of enthusiasm? Or was it cash?

Getting out, Jed saw a small herd of cows and young calves behind a barbed wire fence not twenty feet from the barn.

"Who's here?" a voice called. Moments later, Baxter appeared from the dim interior of the barn.

Jed greeted him with a nod. "I hear you've had a theft."

"Detective." Baxter walked out into the sunlight. Stocky and nearly a head shorter than Jed's six foot two, he wore jeans, scuffed cowboy boots and a sweat-soaked T-shirt. He pulled off leather gloves as he approached. "Yeah, shit, I had a decent stock trailer. Had it parked in that shed—" He nodded to his left. "Gave it some protection. You know."

Jed walked closer to the shed, scanning crumbling cement floor. Bits of hay or straw littered it along with clumps of long-dried mud. He didn't see anything that would prove or disprove the existence of the trailer.

"It was a Featherlite, 1995," Baxter told him. "Twenty-two foot, rubber mats on the floor and walls. Even had a roll-up door."

He claimed to have paid eight thousand dollars for it and since done some work on it to bring it up to par. "Bet I could get more like fifteen thousand now."

That seemed optimistic to Jed, but he jotted it down as an estimate.

Unfortunately, stock trailers didn't have to be licensed by the state in Oregon. So what made Baxter think his would stand out if a witness described it loaded with stolen cattle?

"Any distinguishing features?"

"It's got a pretty bad dent in back," he admitted grudgingly. "Jackass in a fancy SUV rear-ended me. His truck suffered more damage than the trailer did, though, and it was his fault. I collected some insurance money, but I needed it more for something else at the time. Thought I could hammer the dent out pretty good myself, but I haven't gotten to it."

A receipt to prove his ownership of the trailer? Well, he'd have to hunt for that. Was it important?

"It would be helpful," Jed said in cop-neutral. "Is the trailer insured?"

"No, that's what makes this so bad." Baxter scowled. "It was too long for the shed, so I couldn't lock it up, but nobody could see it from the road. So how'd they know I had it?"

Good question, if it really had been stolen. If it hadn't been stolen, where was it currently stored?

"Well, let me sign this, and you keep a copy. If you have a photo of it and can get it to us, that would be helpful." He tore off the top sheet of the pad he'd been using and handed it to Baxter, then looked toward the visible herd. "I hope you've got those calves branded, seeing as how you're not here nights."

"How'd you know that?" Baxter snapped.

"You told me when I talked to you about the rustling problem."

"Oh. Oh, yeah. I guess I did."

"You hold a job along with your ranching?"

"Yeah, I'm working out at the Circle S right now. This is one of my days off."

Interesting.

"They got hit pretty bad by the rustlers," Jed commented. "Seems especially ugly to steal from a widow trying to hold onto the ranch for her son."

"Yeah, it was hard on her. I doubt she can stick it out."

Was that an excuse for preying on the Circle S? Karen Steagall wouldn't be able to hold onto it for the long haul anyway? Did the manager and hands working for her curl their lips behind her back? Maybe because she was ignorant, never having been involved in the ranching, not just because she was a woman?

"How much acreage do you have?" Jed asked, going for conversational.

"Twenty. Not enough to run many cattle. It would help if I had an allotment."

Jed raised his eyebrows. "Would you pay what the BLM asks per head for grazing rights?" The charge for use of public land was dirt cheap, in Jed's opinion. Of course, that wasn't the real issue; it was only a way of protesting federal ownership of so much land.

Baxter's jaw worked for a minute. Couldn't be good for those molars. "If I had to," he said finally, bitterly. "Don't have that choice, do I?"

Jed tucked away the notepad. "Well, it's a shame the trailer wasn't insured, but when we arrest those rustlers, I won't be surprised if we don't find it, too."

Stone-faced, Baxter didn't say a word.

Jed brushed a finger on the brim of his Stetson. "Good day."

He got into his pickup, did a three-point turn and drove away, seeing in his rearview mirror that Gene Baxter still hadn't moved.

*****

Spotting a white pickup parked by the barn at Brian Warring's place, Jed drove on past. If he'd wanted to do any reconnaissance here, he should have remembered this was Sunday. Same reason Gene Baxter had been available midday.

Still worthwhile to check on Mason Thayer.

Fifteen minutes later, he made a slow approach on a rutted dirt driveway to the run-down ranch. Jed hadn't made it past Thayer's concrete front doorstep the last time he was here. He'd seen enough to know Mason wasn't putting a lot of work into the place.

The house was a basic clapboard box that might date back to the 1930s or 40s. It had once been painted white but was in the process of peeling down to weather-grayed wood. Seeking Thayer for a quote for an article she was writing, Cassie had come out here once and gotten a look in a window in back. She said if Thayer had been there that day and actually let her in, she'd have had to go straight home and scrub herself from head to toe to decontaminate.

Jed parked in back, went around to ring the doorbell in front, then strolled back around to rap on the kitchen door and peer in. He wasn't quite as squeamish as Cassie, but he wouldn't want to eat a meal prepared in that kitchen.

When he saw no movement inside, he headed for the barn.

"Mason Thayer?" he called. "You here?"

A soft nicker answered him.

The barn was deserted, a horse lipping at hay the only thing moving except for a swallow flitting through. Interestingly, despite the small size of his operation, he did own a stock trailer, what looked like a fourteen-footer. Shabby and dented, in keeping with its surroundings. Probably not big enough to be useful during those nighttime operations.

The maybe/maybe-not stolen trailer Gene Baxter claimed was another story, though.

As tempted as he was to vault the fence and see what he could find in the pasture, Jed decided to move his truck to the next property over, currently uninhabited. He was told it had been for sale for four years now, which was why the barn appeared derelict and the house not much better. It went to show what Hayden Webb might face, although his father had owned enough land to make his living as a rancher. A grazing allotment would go along with the ranch when it sold, too, which was a big plus.

Dust rose behind his truck after he turned past the For Sale sign and followed the dirt track to the buildings. No serious potholes, he noted. Of course, who knew how long it had been since anyone had driven in here?

After parking behind the house for cover from the road, and where the sagging barn would hide his truck from Thayer should he suddenly show up, Jed jogged toward the back of this acreage. On his agenda was checking out vacant places where stolen cattle could be concealed. Might as well start here. He didn't expect to find any, however. Long grass wasn't flattened from tire tracks. The second gate he came to slumped from its hinges. The absolute silence sent its own message.

Fencing that separated this tract from publicly owned land was in bad shape. No, the rustlers wouldn't be stashing a herd here.

Ducking through the barbed wire fence onto Thayer's property, Jed got snagged and ripped the shoulder of his shirt. From the sting, he could tell he'd scratched himself, too.

Some cows that probably hadn't come up pregnant this spring grazed without much interest in him. Jed checked brands, finding all had the same one, a play on the capital letter T. What he most wanted to get a look at were the cows and calves closer to the house. If Thayer hadn't wanted him on his property during that earlier visit, they might be the reason.

Jed reached the fence that bisected the property. Only as he swung himself up on the metal bar gate did he registered the sight of dust rising near the house.

Swearing, he dropped back to the ground and sprinted for a galvanized water tank too far away.

CHAPTER SEVEN

Out of breath, Jed lay sprawled behind the galvanized water tank. Thank God it was there, because there wasn't any other cover at all out here. He drew up his knees to be sure his lower legs and booted feet wouldn't be visible.

Damn, he hoped Thayer didn't get it in his head to come out here to check on the cattle in this pasture. Getting caught trespassing would be embarrassing at the least, creating trouble for Grant and the department if Thayer was enraged enough. There was a good reason Jed hadn't gone for a warrant; he had zero justification for one.

Rising to a crouch but staying low, he peered around the curved side of the tank. Yeah, that was Mason Thayer, all right, striding toward the barn. A minute later, he hauled a hose across the barnyard and appeared to be filling the nearer water tank. It didn't appear that it would happen fast.

"Shit," Jed muttered. He was pinned down here until Mason decided to leave. Except...the guy lived here. Even if he disappeared into the barn or house, could Jed count on him staying inside? Or not looking out a window?

His phone vibrated. He didn't offhand recognize the number, but it was local, so he answered.

"Alex Burke here, from the Arrowhead Creek Ranch. I'm told you're investigating the assault on Linette Broussard?"

"That's right." Hey, this was one thing he could do squatting in the pasture: take phone calls, as long as he kept his voice low.

"I just called to check up on her. She said she's fine."

"So fine, they kept her overnight for observation."

"Yeah, that's kind of what I thought. I offered to spend the night again to keep watch."

Jed tensed.

But Alex sounded aggrieved, not pleased to be making progress with a beautiful woman. "She has a treehouse that lets you see the driveway, pastures, barn, front of the house. It's not like I'm asking to stay inside her house."

"I take it she declined your offer and assured you that she really didn't need you?"

Pause. "Sounds like she said the same to you."

Jed didn't feel inclined to admit he was in the same boat. "I intend to be out there tonight, somewhere." And every night until he became less convinced she was a target, not just one of many ranchers who'd been hit by the rustlers.

There were too many discrepancies. And what were the odds that one person had committed the acts of vandalism, while another, only days later, tried to steal one of her horses?

"That's good to hear," Alex said. "I was thinking I might do the same thing, except when a woman says no..."

A *woman* says no? Had he couched his offer in terms that implied something more than mere neighborliness? But Jed had a feeling this was exactly what it sounded like: a fellow rancher, a decent man, worrying about a vulnerable woman.

Jed took a look around the galvanized tank to see Thayer standing in the same place, gazing off into space. Water level must have gotten really low.

"If you don't mind keeping your phone close," Jed said, "I can give you a call if I get pulled away during the night. It's been a few days since the rustlers have struck."

"I'll do that," Alex agreed. "I hope you get those sons of bitches. It's not just the cattle we lost. I knew Gary Webb. And I sure don't like to think about Linette alone right now."

"I don't either."

They ended the call, although Jed had a good idea what Linette would think if she'd overheard the two men worrying about her just because she was a woman. Well, she was wrong where he was concerned. There were other women ranchers in this county, some of whom lived alone. He wouldn't be staking out their places simply because their cattle might be stolen. Jed's intense worry was specific to one particular woman.

Without the distraction of the phone call, he grew increasingly antsy. He had to get out of here.

His chance came unexpectedly. Thayer suddenly had a phone to his ear. Talking, he left the hose where it was but walked over to the barn and bent to turn off the faucet, or so it appeared.

From there, he strode to his car, got in and slammed the door with unnecessary force, turned around and drove down the dirt track. As soon as he swung onto the two-lane country road out front, Jed ran for the fence.

Too much in a hurry, he was careless sliding between the two strands of tightly strung barbed wire. This time, the vicious little barbs ripped across his back. Tearing himself free, he rolled to the ground on the other side of the fence.

Knowing he was hidden in the long grass, he lay still for a few minutes, eyes closed. His heart slammed against the wall of his chest. A man with a conscience would consider this fitting punishment for breaking the law. He decided that was fair enough. There was a time he'd believed multiple tours as a sniper had killed his conscience along with what few softer emotions he had somehow held onto. Now...he thought he'd just been numb.

If this was the process of thawing...he wasn't enjoying it.

His phone let him know he had a text. He read it.

The neighbor to the north of Gary Webb's spread had called. His teenage son might have heard something that night.

He hoped the parents weren't the hovering type, in case the boy's hesitation in speaking out had to do with the trouble he feared he'd be in.

*****

As the day went on, Linette debated whether she should arm herself. Midday, while eating her sandwich, she went online to find out whether she could buy a rifle or shotgun without a waiting period in Oregon.

The answer was yes. Any background check only took a few minutes.

As a rancher, she should probably already own a rifle. She didn't like the idea of killing anything, but if a wolf or coyote were attacking a young foal…yeah, she'd shoot.

For self-protection, her stepfather had championed shotguns. He'd even taken Linette out a few times to shoot his.

"You don't have to be a good shot with this baby," he said. "Just let whoever is threatening you get close enough. When you pull the trigger, he's gonna be real sorry."

He'd also taught her moves to protect herself from pushy guys. What a surprise when she'd needed to use them on him.

Linette shook off dark memories.

A shotgun would be fine if she were up in her treehouse keeping watch. Sleeping in her bedroom…what was she supposed to do? Cuddle with it in bed? Wouldn't it be awfully clumsy – and slow – to lift into firing position? Alternatively, she could lean it up against the bed, and probably kick it over several times a night. She'd always been a restless sleeper.

A handgun was out. Her stepfather's revolver had been way too big for her hands. Just once, after Theo hurt her, she'd been desperate enough to stop by a gun store and range where she was allowed to try out several small pistols. After about ten minutes, she had fled to her car shaking. She'd been more scared of the explosive force in the gun she didn't know if she could control than she was of a violent man.

Even the shotgun – could she really pull the trigger when the moment came? Shoot and potentially kill a human being?

Undecided, she carried her baseball bat unobtrusively as she went about her chores, preferring that Troy not notice.

Thank goodness this had been one of his scheduled days. His mother didn't like him missing church services, but Linette had a feeling his eagerness to work on the Sabbath was a form of rebellion, and a pretty mild one at that. After seeing her bruised, swollen face, he did the hard work with alacrity and went so far as to suggest that he put in some extra hours this week.

"You don't have to pay me," he said awkwardly. He had trouble meeting her eyes. "I could just, like, help out. You know?"

"If you're willing, I'll accept gladly," she said. "Except you'll be paid."

He frowned. "You got someone to stay tonight? You shouldn't be alone."

Remembering the expression on Jed's face when she suggested Troy as her guardian, Linette smiled shakily and said, "I do have someone, but thank you. He'll be along a little later."

Apparently, she was a better liar than she'd thought, because after his six hour shift, her young employee waved goodbye in a friendly way and drove off in his sorry excuse for a pickup truck.

Even though the sun remained high in the sky, she felt a chill. No, she wasn't looking forward to a sleepless night on watch for that scum sucker who thought he'd scare her with some tricks and then steal from her. That didn't mean she wasn't up for it. Or that she'd let herself depend on a man who'd walked out on her so abruptly, she hadn't even had the forewarning to brace herself.

Alex Burke's offer had been nice, but what was she going to do? Flutter her eyelashes at him and sweetly thank him for protecting the little woman? It wasn't like they'd been long-time friends, or friends of any kind. There was no history of helping each other out. She'd have no way to reciprocate.

She set her jaw and started for the house. She'd sworn off men, thank you, and she hadn't only meant for sex. And maybe, if she were honest with herself, it wasn't only men. Her mother hadn't exactly proved herself to be a reliable prop, either. Linette's childhood wasn't as bad as Jed's, but her ability to trust was somewhere between fragile and nonexistent. She was better on her own, that's all. And she shouldn't have to keep reminding herself of something so basic.

Or was going it alone to face down danger beyond her capabilities just plain dumb? Pride goeth before the fall, etc.

Beyond her capabilities? There were other ways to combat evil than physical force. Women did it all the time, she thought with a trace of bitterness.

Late lunch, she decided, and last chores. For now, she wouldn't think about tonight's return to the treehouse, where she'd stand guard on the horses that meant everything to her.

*****

Jed stopped at his house to make a sandwich before he set out to talk to Brady Price.

While he ate, Jed took out his phone and scanned for Kiger Mustangs for sale.

Several sites came up, although he quickly discovered that most included half-Kigers, Appaloosas and any trail horse. He found a couple of Kiger ranches selling some stock, and was disconcerted by relatively low prices. Admittedly, the breed wasn't well known. Still, he had to wonder: did the piece of shit trying to steal a young foal from the LB Kiger Ranch know anything about the breed? Did he care? Had he surveyed the mares and foals during daylight and picked out a prime prospect, or did he just grab the first one he could get his hands on?

Jed leaned toward the latter. If somebody tried to sell a Kiger filly or colt, however promising, without bloodlines, he'd meet with low-ball offers. He might also encounter suspicion. Nobody sold a foal so young he should still be with his mother.

Jed didn't like thinking about what the guy had had in mind for that baby. Mutilation? Although if that were the case, why hadn't he committed the atrocity right there in the pasture? Or did he just not get a chance?

Jed wished his mind didn't turn so readily to hideous possibilities that wouldn't occur to most people.

And, damn it, how did Linette imagine she'd make a living if her horses weren't worth any more than that?

He sighed and pocketed his phone before rubbing a hand over his scratchy jaw. Only a day and a half from his last shave, and he already itched.

A ten minute drive took him through the open gates of the White Oak Ranch. He'd been here once before to talk to the boy's father, Nelson Price, about branding his calves. He immediately recognized the man who crossed the yard from the barn to meet him.

"Detective Dawson."

"Mr. Price. I understand your son recalls something that might interest me?"

"Hard to tell if it really will, but it seemed best to let you know. Brady's in the house. You're welcome to let yourself in, unless you'd rather I sat in on this talk."

"Doubt there's any need for that." Jed nodded and went to the house. The side door led through a utility room into the deserted kitchen. He called, "Brady? Your dad said you're in here."

The thud of feet on the stairs let him know he'd been heard.

A typically lanky boy appeared in the doorway. He wasn't a big kid, but still his feet and hands looked outsized. His wasn't the worst acne Jed had seen, but it wasn't good. The boy's gaze went to Jed's badge and weapon, and he said, "Um, officer..."

Jed held out a hand. "I'm Detective Jed Dawson."

Brady stared at it as if he wasn't sure what he was supposed to do. Then, cheeks flaring red, he held out his hand, too.

After they belatedly shook, Jed said, "Why don't we sit down."

"Oh, uh, sure." They both took chairs at one end of the farmhouse table. "I didn't know...I mean, I didn't expect...you know."

Jed hoped the boy wasn't always so incoherent. He knew he'd better proceed carefully if he wanted to mine any useful information from sixteen-year-old Brady Price.

"Relax," he said. "There's no pressure here. Your dad said you'd woken up and heard or saw something going on at the Webb place the night Gary was killed. Any little thing can turn out to be useful." He smiled. "Most interviews, I end up empty-handed, so don't worry if your father got excited and sent me on a wild goose chase, okay?"

The boy bobbed his head. "Sure...um, okay."

Jed suppressed a sigh. "So, thinking back to that Thursday night." Which was...nine days ago. He'd have to ask why the kid hadn't spoken up sooner. "Were you home during the evening?"

Brady looked surprised. "Well, yeah. I almost always am. I mean, I have to help with the stock. You know. And I usually have some school work."

Jed thought back to his years fostered by a ranch foreman. There'd always been an assumption that he'd set to work as soon as he got off the school bus, dumped his pack and had a snack. He'd let himself forget that was likely be the norm for ranch kids around here, too.

"How late did you stay up?"

"Not very late. I mean, the bus comes at, like six-thirty."

Jed winced. "That's early."

Brady shrugged in apparent resignation. "We're way out of town. Anyway, first bell is at seven-thirty."

Jed had sort of known that. He often saw the afternoon school buses dropping middle-school and high-school kids off before three o'clock. However, he was rarely up early enough to see the morning buses.

"What time did you fall asleep?"

The teenager eyed him warily, as if fearing he'd be chewed out if he stayed up too late. "Like, ten?" he said finally.

"Was your window open?"

He nodded.

"What woke you up?"

Brady frowned, actually appearing pensive. "I think it might have been a gunshot. I decided I must've imagined it, or...I guess I'd have woken Dad up. You know?"

Jed nodded encouragement.

Reassured, the boy seemed to gaze into space. "I heard shouting and cattle bawling."

"Vehicle engines?"

"I guess." He sounded doubtful on that point. "I sorta thought Mr. Webb woken 'cuz his herd got worked up. Like if there was a coyote in the pasture. It made sense that he'd have gone out and yelled to chase it away and maybe even taken a shot or two."

Brady was right; that did make sense – except for the engine sounds. The boy had presumably known about the cattle rustling problem, but maybe he'd been thinking like teenagers behind the wheel of a car did. Bad things didn't happen to them – or, in this case, to their families or neighbors.

"Any chance you made out any words when you heard the shouting?"

Seeing Brady's forehead crease again and the puzzlement in his eyes, Jed held his breath to keep from distracting the boy.

"This is weird," he said after a minute, "because I thought I heard someone yell, 'jeans'. Like pants or something. But that's dumb, isn't it?"

"You sure there was an S sound on the end?"

The boy gaped at Jed. "You mean…like the DNA stuff?" Then his eyes widened. "Or I heard a name? Gene?"

"What do you think? Is that possible?"

He nodded jerkily. "I must've just thought the jeans part. Like, why's that guy yelling about blue jeans? You know?"

"I do know." Jed leaned back in the counselor's chair and smiled. "Our brains make those leaps all the time. The leap makes sense of something illogical."

"I wish I'd heard more. Or…" He looked away, color rising again to his cheeks. "Woken up Dad. I've been feeling bad. If somebody found Mr. Webb sooner, maybe…"

However irrational the guilt, this was why he'd kept his mouth shut. Satisfied now that he knew, Jed shook his head. "From the injury he suffered, we know he died instantly. You couldn't have saved him by getting help."

"Really?"

"Really. I wouldn't lie to you about this."

Brady let out a whoosh of air. "I'm glad. I mean, not that Mr. Webb is dead, but, you know…"

"I do know." Jed rose to his feet as a signal and held out his hand again. "Thank you. You were an excellent witness."

Brady jumped up, knocking his chair back. He blushed again as he righted it and clumsily shook hands.

Jed let himself out of the house, his mouth quirking at the memory of how humiliating it had been to be so gangly, he didn't have adequate control of his too-big feet and hands.

That amusement faded quickly.

Gene. That lying sack of shit.

*****

It was aggravating to find herself having to consciously identify every night noise instead of being able to let her mind do so automatically. Casual assumptions didn't cut it tonight, though. This was too important.

Was that an owl hoot, or could it be a signal sent by a conspirator to another? The tap, followed by a hollow thud? Horse hoof on the wooden floor, or a man briefly stumbling as he crept through the barn? It went on and on, the quiet of the night filled with a myriad of small sounds. Normally she slept through them, while nocturnal creatures of all kinds came awake.

A squeak of alarm. Poor mouse.

A whisper in the grass. Snake?

Once again, Linette was reassured by the small plane passing overhead even if it hadn't done her any good the previous night. This time, the light played over her property. Patrol cars drove slowly by at something like hour intervals, too. No doubt ordered by Detective Dawson.

She ached fiercely at every passing thought of him. Seeing him again, waking to find him beside her bed, driven to protect her, that had complicated her feelings even if she'd buried her confusion under anger this morning.

Was guilt all he felt? His patience and tenderness argued otherwise. And then there was the fact that he had come to this rural county on the other side of the United States from his – and her – native Georgia. He *had* to have followed her. What other explanation could there be?

Anger reawakened as she reminded himself he'd then avoided her like the plague.

An annoying inner voice murmured, *Could he have been nervous about how you'd react to him?*

And then there was the shooting in which he'd been involved.

Linette scrunched up her face. *Involved?* Yeah, not the right word. He'd somehow moved into position without his prey ever seeing him, used his scope or maybe only his instincts to zero in a man's head, and pulled the trigger. What he'd done was use his sniper skills to kill again. Justifiably, but his nation, his officers, had believed that what they'd asked him to do in Iraq and Afghanistan and who knew where else was justified, too.

Thinking that filled her with renewed rage. No one should ever have asked that of a young man who'd never had the security of a real home, had no bedrock to hold him up when hideous memories came, as they inevitably would. When he was filled with self-loathing. It was no doubt unpatriotic of her, but Linette didn't expect to ever forgive the army in general and Jed's commanding officers in particular for what they'd done to a good man.

She snapped back to the present. Was that a car coming? No, it sounded more like a truck than a car, and was moving well below the speed limit. In fact, it almost stopped at the foot of her driveway.

She lifted her binoculars, despite their limited use in the dark, and saw the rack of lights atop a white SUV. Sagging in release from the burst of adrenaline, she rolled onto her back for a moment.

Staring up at the stars scattered over black velvet, the clarity so much greater than she'd ever seen before, Linette knew she'd been a fool to turn down help. What had made her think she could stay awake all night and still do her work during the day?

What if nothing happened tonight, or tomorrow night, or the one after that? Remember, there'd been days between the unpleasant pranks.

She needed help. And she knew who she wanted here, if only she could summon the beginnings of forgiveness.

There's the rub, she thought ruefully, then made an awful face. Really? She was quoting Hamlet?

The famous speech came as if she'd heard the tragedy performed yesterday.

To die, to sleep

To sleep perchance to dream:

Ay, there's the rub.

For in that sleep of death what dreams may come.

And oh, yes, she knew exactly why she had committed that particular speech to memory years before.

It always made her think about Jed.

CHAPTER EIGHT

Walking a semi-circle around Linette's property Sunday night while ensuring she didn't see him demanded Jed's full attention. What he'd give for night-vision goggles. As it was, with the moon barely a crescent, he moved slowly and was careful where to put his feet. The ranch fences were solidly constructed with boards, thank God; the long gash on his back from the barbed wire burned every time he bent forward, twisted or flexed nearby muscles. Linette's fences he easily climbed.

Still, dark shapes kept rearing from the darkness. Most turned out to be horses, but he found a water tank, a roofed structure that would offer protection from rain, snow or a glaring sun. The pastures were dotted with trees, too.

The one place he didn't venture was in front of her house and barn. If she was up in the treehouse, she'd see him and probably call 911.

After each lap he walked, he'd return to sitting in his truck parked in an overgrown turn-out presumably created to allow access to a pasture or field no longer cultivated. With grasses overgrown and sage brush taking over, it wasn't obvious at all. In fact, he'd found it yesterday only because he had walked the shoulder half a mile each direction from Linette's ranch in an attempt to figure out where the man trying to steal the foal had parked. It couldn't be too far; he wouldn't have wanted to be seen in the middle of the night leading a leggy, frightened colt along the road.

Recent days had been dry enough, Jed had failed. The horse trailer and truck had either been parked along the road – although he spotted no obvious tracks on the softer earth of the shoulder – or in a neighboring driveway.

He'd turned off the overhead light so he could leave the driver side door open and listen to a peaceful night.

Jed was left with too much time to think.

He tried to keep his mind on the investigation – although it was hard to be dispassionate now that Linette was part of it. He'd started by scanning voter rolls and the motor vehicle records for other people with the first name of Gene. Unfortunately, there were a number, and what if the ring of cattle rustlers were really Crook County or Grant County residents? And then it had belatedly occurred to him that Jeanne, whatever the spelling, was a reasonably common name for women. He shouldn't leap to assume no woman would be involved in the crimes. As he'd already noted, there were a number of women ranchers in the county, and that didn't count the women who helped their husbands to a greater or lesser extent.

His belief that Gene Baxter was his man didn't falter.

That got him to wondering again why any member of a so-far successful cattle rustling operation would take extra risks to steal a two-month-old foal not worth a staggering amount of money. Jed found himself shaking his head again. His gut said this was separate and had to do only with Linette – but he couldn't be sure.

Linette.

He'd met her just over five years ago when he went riding with Niall Callaghan, an army friend who boarded a quarter horse at a ranch less than an hour drive from Fort Benning. He'd wandered over, curious, to watch a woman working with what he'd immediately sensed was a dangerous horse. Seeming unafraid, she'd been infinitely patient yet firm, countering the animal's every attempt to rear or buck, encouraging obedience. Her voice, gentle and husky, had gotten his attention as fast as her slender, graceful body or the thick mass of maple brown hair and a face that was more pretty than beautiful – but had stunned him for reasons he never had nailed down.

Jed had asked her out, she'd accepted, and a month later he left his base housing to live with her. They had most of a year together until, as the date for him to leave on his next deployment neared, he had felt ice encasing him, a fraction of an inch at a time. He was a killer, a trained assassin. That made him something less than human. Linette deserved better than him. A thousand times better.

Almost a month before he was due to deploy, he packed his things and was waiting when she got home from work. He told her calmly, emotionlessly, that he wasn't good enough for her. No point in dragging this out for a few more weeks, he said. Jed remembered wishing the best for her, and climbing into his truck. He didn't let himself look back. As it was, he had never been able to forget her shattered expression.

Now, with a raw sound, he slipped out of his truck and into the night for another patrol. Unfortunately, his feet knew the way, freeing his thoughts to continue inexorably to a conclusion he knew, in one way, but hadn't wanted to accept.

Back then, he'd convinced himself he was being noble. Freeing her to find a truly good man, a white-picket-fence perfect life he could never give her.

A branch cracked under his feet. Cursing himself, he froze. Listened hard.

All he heard was a snuffling sound and a soft clop of a hoof. A moment later, one of those dark shapes materialized. He held out his hand for the velvet soft lips to touch his palm. Smiling crookedly, Jed stroked the horse's jaw and down the powerful arch of neck. The Kiger horses bore a remarkable resemblance to the Spanish Andalusians, for an obvious reason. This horse, dark enough he simply couldn't tell the color of the coat, had the exceptionally long mane and forelock that was one of the most noticeable features of the breed. Not just long: thick, too. When he walked on, the horse accompanied him. He was momentarily tempted to climb on and see what happened, although he was really too large a man for a horse that couldn't be over fifteen hands tall.

The horse lipped the brim of his Stetson, knocking it off. Jed caught the hat on its way down.

"Not a chance," he murmured to his new friend.

A whicker answered him.

Jed continued along the fence line. Five minutes later, the horse drifted away, there one moment, gone the next. He wouldn't be able to pick it out of Linette's herd in daylight.

Thinking her name brought a piercing pain in his chest.

He hadn't left her out of genuine nobility, he'd taken off like a terrified jackrabbit. What he felt for her was new to him. In retrospect, Jed didn't know if he'd doubted what those feelings really were, or only understood that she endangered him more than the Taliban and ISIS fighters put together.

He had loved her, and couldn't trust that she felt the same, that he could depend on her not to hurt him. It was as simple as that.

He had returned from that deployment not so much frozen solid as not present. His body went about his business, he spoke to people, played pool, sat on a bar stool and pretended to care whether the Atlanta Falcons had just gotten cheated out of a touchdown by the refs or not.

Six months after coming home, he'd thought about checking to be sure Linette was okay. Not to ask her to take him back, of course not. Just…to reassure himself.

He hadn't, telling himself he'd let her go. Following up now would almost be stalking. But Niall returned from his own deployment and let Jed know he'd seen her out at the ranch.

"She's living with a guy and seems fine," Niall said with a shrug.

Jed nodded. "That's good to hear." His tone was perfect, close to indifferent. He doubted Niall had noticed that he'd excused himself from the gathering less than five minutes later.

Tonight, he circled behind the barn and walked toward her house. He stayed in the darkness to the side where she couldn't possibly see him, but he could make out the oak tree where he knew she was.

Did this qualify as stalking? he wondered. Or was he excused because she'd let her stubbornness and pride turn her into an idiot?

Or was he wrong and that kid who worked for her had stayed? Troy could be up in the treehouse, Linette sleeping peacefully in her bedroom. She might have male friends he knew nothing about, too. He'd been careful not to look too closely into her life when he wasn't ready to try to step back into it. This minute, he regretted that. In fact, he regretted every mistake he'd ever made with her. His jaw clenched hard enough to break a tooth, but he made himself turn away and continue on his rounds.

Jed swore under his breath. He was still scared of what she could do to him, and that was the truth. But maybe what he felt was meaningless. If he'd seen even a glimmer in her eyes…but he hadn't.

Didn't mean he wouldn't do everything he could to keep her safe, whether she liked it or not.

*****

Jed drove through town on his way to the sheriff's department headquarters, intending to check in and then go home for a few hours sleep. He hoped he didn't encounter Jarman. He wasn't in the mood to deal with the jackass.

But before he even reached headquarters, his eye was caught by a crowd on the sidewalk outside Pronghorn Seed & Feed. All men, and from a block away he could see that tempers were hot.

He called Grant, who picked up on the first ring.

Jed explained and said, "Figured if I get lynched, someone should know why."

"Who's in the crowd?"

"'Bout what you'd expect. A bunch of ranchers who've been hit by losses. Austin Jackson, Frank Vanbeek, Dennis MacLeod..." He shook his head. "You'd think he'd be old enough to know better. Let's see, something Erickson."

"The older or the younger?"

"The son."

"Lars," Grant supplied. "Listen, I'm on my way."

Jed didn't argue. He still held some hope that the group of men were strategizing instead of whipping themselves into a rage that would allow them to do something really stupid, but the faces he could see didn't bolster that hope.

After parking at the curb only feet from the men, he climbed stiffly out of his pickup and circled the front of it. Voices fell silent and they all turned to look at him.

He nodded in greeting. "Gentlemen."

A few returned his nod grudgingly.

"Something happened I should know about?"

"We're just talking. That's not against the law, is it?"

That was Lars Erickson, the son who had hovered in the background while Jed talked to his father a few weeks ago.

"You know it isn't." He raised his eyebrows as he scanned the group. Eight...no, nine men. Jed let his voice harden. "I see some of you are carrying."

"That's not against the law either, last I knew." Erickson again.

Jed's gaze roved. A few met his eyes, while others in the crowd didn't want to.

"You're looking like a mob, which makes me uneasy." He was glad to see Grant's marked vehicle glide to a stop at the curb.

"You're acting like you think *we're* the ones who've done something wrong," Tim Brekhus said. He was one of many who had a spread small enough to make ranching a hobby rather than a serious attempt to make a living. He'd lost ten cows and calves, if Jed remembered right. Chances were good that hit him hard enough, he wouldn't be able to start over.

In fact, the serious ranchers weren't here, with the exception of Lars Erickson. Jed doubted his father, the actual owner of the Bar Double E, would approve of whatever was going on here.

Grant strolled up to join him, startling most of the idiots who hadn't noticed his arrival. "Fellows," he said with a nod that probably irritated them as much as Jed's had. Maybe it was the gray, sheriff's department Stetson both wore. Or the badges both displayed on their belts.

"We're just talking," Austin Jackson said hastily.

Right over the top of him, Lars snapped, "Doesn't seem like law enforcement has been a lot of help. *You* may not have a clue who these fuckers are, but we do."

Dylan Hardin sneered. "We don't have to stand by while—"

Jed interrupted. "What makes you think we don't have a clue?" He stared hard at them, focusing on one face at a time. And damn, he wished his head wasn't throbbing. "Unlike you, we need proof to satisfy the prosecutor and convince a jury. We don't have the luxury of turning on people we don't like, or who haven't been hit by the rustlers yet. For God's sake, use your heads! Some ranches have neighbors too near to make them good prospects. A couple of ranches that haven't had trouble yet are on dead end roads. Rancher wakes up, hears something going on, all he has to do is call us and those rustlers will run right into a roadblock. Frankly, they've shown some discrimination so far. They started with the best quality beef – Whitney's Wagyu calves, the Circle S's and Arrowhead Creek ranches' Herefords. Some small ranches – and I know damn well who you're thinking about – don't have the kind of cattle to justify the risk."

He could tell a few in this group were thinking now. Dennis McLeod was inching toward the glass doors into the feed and seed. Austin Jackson looked chagrined. He was mad, but also smart enough to hear the sense in what Jed was saying.

"I'm asking you to cooperate with the sheriff's department, not get in our way. Please don't put us in the position of having to arrest any of you. You hear me?"

He heard resentful mutters, but Jackson wasn't alone in showing signs of backing down.

"Yeah, but damn it, if I don't get my cattle back I'm done for," a guy named Blake Albaugh argued.

"Do you really think if you all roar on out to some local rancher's place you're going to find a bunch of stolen cattle there?" Jed shook his head. "I'm here to tell you that I and other members of this department are looking. You know we're doing flyovers."

There were nods.

"We're not finding the cattle. The pilot or the observer would have spotted an unexpectedly large herd or any size of herd where they shouldn't be. They're checking out federal land, too." He paused again to meet a few men's eyes. "I think the cattle have been taken out of the area. There's got to be a temporary holding area, but you know Nebraska and Oklahoma don't have brand inspectors to verify ownership. These guys can load a semi-truck, have your cattle two states away in no time."

He saw grief. Those with any sense had already known what he was telling them, they just hadn't wanted to admit it. The majority of these men hadn't carried insurance. Because of that, they'd lost the most.

Jed squared his shoulders to finish. "I'm glad to meet any of you individually or in a group. Feel free to call. Just know that we won't tolerate any vigilante acts."

After a little more back and forth, the crowd finally broke up, a couple of men going into the store, others circling around back to where they'd parked. Nobody lingered to talk to him right now.

Grant asked if he'd seen Chris Jarman recently.

"Yeah, he's pissed."

Grant's expression morphed into a scowl. "If he said anything—"

"Just expressed his feelings. Who was I to judge?"

"I almost hope he screws up again so I can fire him."

Forget the *almost*. Jed hoped the same. Jarman wasn't in law enforcement for the right reasons, but Jed wasn't worried. The guy's attitude said it all. No lesson had been learned. He'd make that career-ending mistake any day. It had just better not involve Linette.

Grant had been watching him. "And may I say you look like shit."

Jed let one side of his mouth curve. "Appreciate your honesty. I'm going home to sack out for a few hours."

Grant tipped the brim of his hat, grinned and walked back to his SUV.

*****

With a few hours of sleep clearing her head, Linette decided to spend the afternoon working with this spring's foals. She wasn't up to dealing with a frightened two- or three-year-old that outweighed her by a thousand pounds or so, however unlikely that was to happen.

She did her best to avoid ever presenting her horses with scary experiences. She touched the foals as soon as their dams seemed comfortable with it. Many trainers waited to halter-break foals until they were weaned, but she preferred to start them on a line really young so it was never shocking. She didn't begin seriously riding her horses until they were three-year-olds, but that didn't mean they couldn't be accustomed to a blanket and even a saddle on their backs long before that. Because she was a small woman, she sometimes eased herself onto their backs sooner. She avoided traumatizing her horses at all costs.

Linette had a six-week-old claybank filly named Paloma trotting happily around the small arena, obeying gentle commands, when she caught sight of a man watching.

She'd used sheets of plywood along the fence to eliminate outside distractions. Jed stood behind the gate, the one place he could see inside and be seen. His right foot rested on the lowest bar and he had crossed his arms on the top one. He wore western boots, jeans, a crisp white shirt and a gray Stetson.

He dipped his head. "Didn't mean to interrupt."

"Then I'll finish with this session."

He might have been there for a while; when she worked with any of her horses, she shut out everything else. Right now, she needed to stay aware of what Paloma was thinking, when she quit having fun. Better to end the session than let her became bored. Preventing herself from becoming distracted was crucial.

Of course, now she'd lost the magic, the feeling that the filly and she were communicating, as if the line stretching between them encapsulated a bundle of shared nerves alive with messages whisking back and forth. She was too self-conscious, even though Jed had watched plenty of other times while she worked with horses at the stable outside Atlanta.

Finally she conceded defeat and brought Paloma to a walk then gently drew her in and stroked her face and neck. "Good girl," she murmured.

The filly nibbled the pocket on Linette's shirt. She laughed and led her toward the gate, which Jed held open for them.

Studying Paloma, he said, "She's a beauty. Strong hindquarters."

"Yes, the Kiger aren't lanky at this age. In body type, they have more in common with a quarter horse than with a thoroughbred."

"I don't suppose there are many thoroughbreds in these parts."

She passed him without really looking at him. "You might be surprised. There's an Oregon thoroughbred owners and breeders association. I understand there's a circuit of racing at fairs in the summer."

"Huh."

She cross-tied Paloma in the barn aisle and started brushing her. The filly's sensitive skin rippled, and she occasionally leaned into an especially pleasurable stroke.

Jed laughed and said, "If you have another brush, I can do this side."

Linette found one and handed it over without saying a word, careful not to let her fingers brush his. Damn, she was invariably surprised anew at the crystal clarity of his blue eyes and the piercing quality of them.

"You get any sleep?" he asked after a minute.

"Some." She stole a look at his face and saw lines deeper than they should be. "You look tired."

"I caught a few hours this morning." He hesitated, distinctly wary. "I kept watch on your place last night."

Her hand stopped and she stared. "But…I told you I could take care of myself. You offered. I said no."

"Did I bother you?"

"Obviously not," she said stiffly, "or I'd have known you were around." She frowned. "Where were you?"

"Sat in my truck some of the time, walked a circuit through your pastures about every hour."

And she'd never heard or seen him. Although why that should surprise her, she didn't know. He had often caught her by surprise because he moved so silently. Gravel didn't dare crunch under his feet.

Irritation was only a thin layer atop Linette's stew of emotions. Somewhere beneath…there was undeniable comfort at knowing he'd been here if she had needed him. But also, she couldn't deny a skin-crawling awareness that if Jed had wandered around the ranch without her seeing him, so could someone else.

Determined he not see her confusion, she bent to pick up Paloma's dainty front hoof, then her back one. Both were clean and healthy.

Linette straightened. "You're so sure he'll come back." She couldn't quite make it a question, when she had no doubt of the answer. *He* – that dark, faceless threat.

"I am." Jed looked at her with a certain grimness. "Linette…the things happening to you seem personal. Do you have any idea at all who he could be?"

She opened her mouth…and closed it, pressing her lips together. No. She'd thought about this enough. Why, after so long, would Theo have come after her? He'd probably gone through several women since her.

Jed's eyes narrowed. She might have imagined the curl of his lip that suggested contempt, but she didn't think so.

"You're protecting someone."

"No. I wouldn't. It's not like that. I just can't imagine—" Clear as mud.

Jed shook his head and crouched to inspect Paloma's remaining hooves. Linette trusted him; he knew horses, and she'd never seen him treat one with anything but kindness.

"I was involved with someone after you," she made herself say, even as she fixed her gaze on the bright square where the double barn doors stood open. "It didn't end well, but I think he was glad to see the last of me."

"If you give me his name, I can check on his whereabouts. We can rule him out."

Panic swirled with humiliation. If she told him, he'd find out how low she'd sunk. She had fought hard since then to regain her self-respect. Jed would never respect her again, that was for sure. Which shouldn't matter…but did.

She shook her head. "There's not a reason in the world he'd be doing this stuff. I've been in Oregon for over three years now. And no, before you ask, there's been nobody since I got here. I've had it with men, present company included. I like my horses better."

Linette unclipped the line and led Paloma out to the pasture. Her dam, grazing in seeming unconcern, was also a claybank. Paloma's coat was currently lighter than her dam's, cream barely tinted with a hint of red. But like her mama, her mane, tail and legs were darker.

"Not many of us achieve our dreams," said Jed, behind her, his voice so gentle her knees momentarily wobbled.

She closed the gate and watched Paloma race toward a cluster of other foals, bucking and kicking, seemingly delighted when they joined her like a flock of starlings to tear around the pasture. Her smile was real, but her eyes stung.

With her peripheral vision, she saw that Jed had joined her at the fence. He stayed quiet, which he probably remembered was a more effective tactic with her than demanding answers.

"You want to know where I got the money."

He glanced at her, eyebrows raised.

She supposed there was no reason not to tell him. "My stepfather died."

"And left you his money."

"No, he left me my mother's money." She added grudgingly, "That was decent of him. He didn't have to. He had a son."

"Your mother didn't have it tied up to come to you?"

"No." Her mother had cut her off for her 'lies', but Linette didn't have to tell Jed that. This was something she didn't talk about. Still, she saw the speculation in his eyes.

But he surprised her with what he did say. "You never told me you came from a privileged background."

"Money, you mean," she said bitterly. "Well, we had that." She shrugged. "I almost gave it all away, but then I decided it should be mine. It gave me the chance to start over."

His mouth crooked just a little, giving his face the fleeting warmth she had once loved so much.

She walked past him, returning to the barn although she couldn't remember what task was next on her agenda.

"Where's Troy?" Jed asked.

"Lunch break. He usually sits on the front steps, but if you didn't see him, he might be in the kitchen."

"You let him in the house?"

Linette just shook her head. "He's a nice guy. Of course I let him put his lunch in my brand new refrigerator. I even make lunch for both of us sometimes."

Jed winced at her mention of the ridiculously expensive appliance. "Couldn't get the smell out?"

"No." Or maybe she'd only imagined the lingering odor. Didn't matter. "I'm thinking about buying a gun," she said.

He gave her a sharp look. "Do you know how to use one?"

"I practiced some with Lloyd's shotgun."

"How many years ago?"

"What, you think I should stick with the baseball bat?" she snapped.

"No, damn it." Jed leaned toward her, anger suffusing his face. "I think you should use *me*."

Linette stared at him, speechless…and oh, so tempted.

CHAPTER NINE

Jed hated the shock on her face. Hadn't she taken his offer to guard her seriously? Or was she only stunned because he hadn't gotten her message? To all appearances, Linette hated him and the ground he walked on. He couldn't blame her. He'd treated her like crap.

He heard again her scathing tone. *I've had it with men, present company included. I like my horses better.*

The only good part had been the preface. *And no, before you ask, there's been nobody since I got here.*

Her chin came up. "You don't owe me anything."

Oh, yeah, he did, but he knew better than to say so. "That's not what this is about."

She studied him, those green-gold eyes seeing deeper than Jed liked. Then she gave an odd half-laugh, tipping her head back to gaze toward the open beams above where he'd earlier spotted several sparrow nests.

"Last night," she said quietly, "I had an epiphany. Alex Burke called and offered to spend the night again. I said thanks but no thanks. When Troy offered, too, I lied and claimed I had a friend lined up."

Jed's throat felt so tight he doubted he could swallow.

"Then—" she stole a glance at him "—I climbed up in the tree and discovered I was scared. I found myself thinking stuff like 'pride goeth before the fall'. Oh, and cutting off my nose to spite my face."

Thankfulness and even a trace of humor eased his tension. "No need for original thought, I take it?"

Linette scrunched up her nose in a way that sent a painful pang through him. God, he'd missed her.

"I was working my way around to a point."

He let himself smile.

"If guarding the ranch and me will allow you to feel you've balanced the scale in some way, I can live with that."

His sense of satisfaction crashed and burned. In Linette's view, was this the same as when she'd accepted her mother's fortune? Because she was owed?

Well, fuck it. He *did* owe her. Besides, staying as long as she needed him gave him a foot in the door. A chance to show her he'd changed. Or maybe he should say, that he *could* change.

That he'd never leave her again.

You so sure? an inner voice mocked.

Yeah, he thought. He was. But whether he could be enough for her, that was another story.

"Fine," he said. "Expect me before dark." He turned and left her standing alone in the shadowy depths of the barn.

*****

Knowing Jed didn't like surprises, Niall Callaghan sat on the front porch steps so that he'd be seen right away. A dark SUV that shouted cop car slowed as it approached the house, finally drawing up to the curb. The man getting out eyed the unfamiliar truck before he noticed Niall. He relaxed subtly, probably on seeing the Georgia license plate.

Niall rose slowly to his feet. His face split into a grin. "If it isn't Jedediah Dawson himself."

Jed laughed. "Niall Callaghan. Damn."

They shared a back-slapping hug.

Drawing back, Jed asked, "What are you doing here? I thought you were settled back in Alabama." That's where Niall's mother and sister were, the Huntsville area. He felt guilty he hadn't made more effort to stay in touch with friends. He couldn't remember the last time he and Jed had talked or made contact online. Before Jed had inexplicably moved to Oregon, he knew that.

"Got tired of taking orders." Niall shrugged. "I'm traveling. Visiting old friends." Looking for something he couldn't name.

"I'm glad to see you." Jed sounded like he meant it. "I hope you'll stay for a while."

"Few days, anyway. Got a duffle in the truck."

"Bring it in."

Once Jed had put together sandwiches and poured them both coffee, they studied each other over the kitchen table. Seeing Jed again seemed unreal, especially in such a different context.

"Okay," Niall said, his southern drawl stronger than Jed's, "you have to explain why you moved to this godforsaken part of the world."

Jed didn't exactly squirm, but he came close, especially for a man who rarely betrayed emotions or his thoughts. Intrigued, Niall waited.

"Remember Linette Broussard?"

"How could I not? Never seen a guy fall so fast and so hard. *Boom!*"

"Fuck you," Jed said agreeably.

Niall was smiling again. "So you're back together?"

"No, it's not that simple. I, uh…" Jed planted his elbows on the table and yanked his hair. "She says she's done with men, me included. Sounds like she got into a crappy relationship after we split."

After Jed had walked.

The grimace suggested he was thinking the same thing. "She's in trouble now, though."

Niall's brows rose.

"Long story."

Jed told it in between bites, starting with a gang of what sounded like professional cattle rustlers, moving onto some nasty tricks played on Linette followed by an attempt to steal one of her foals that sent her to the hospital.

"She's finally agreed to let me stand guard nights. Daytimes, she has a young guy working with her at the ranch. Usually he's part-time, but he seems to be putting in extra hours for now."

Niall didn't hesitate. "I can help. You can't do your job and stay awake all night, too." This might be just what he needed: a mission. Like Jed, he had the experience to handle bodyguard duties. An army veteran, he'd served as an MP for a few years and a cop since he got out.

"The sheriff is cutting me some slack," Jed said. "I slept a few hours this morning." He paused, frowning. "If you hit on her, you're out of here."

Niall grinned wickedly. "Would I cut out a friend like that?"

"Not if you know what's good for you."

This time when Niall laughed, Jed joined him.

"Hell, she'll probably be glad to see you."

"Of course she will be. I'm a good guy. *I* didn't dump her."

"Yeah, you and Clarissa broke up not that much later."

Niall felt his jaw tightening. "I came back from my last deployment pretty messed up. She couldn't take it."

"I'm sorry."

"Couldn't blame her." Niall's shoulders jerked. "I hardly noticed when she left."

Jed would know the feeling. The intensity of the anger, the nightmares, the plunges into depression, made it hard to maintain any kind of relationship. A lot of marriages failed.

Niall didn't like failing at anything. Jed at least had a better excuse. He'd been messed up long before he joined the army.

Jed being Jed, he changed the subject. "I have to stop by headquarters. If you want to come along, I'll introduce you to the sheriff, Grant Holcomb. He's a good guy. Served a few years, too. Hey, he's desperate for deputies. He'd hire you in a minute."

Tension crawled up Niall's neck. "You know I signed on with the Madison County Sheriff's Office. Patrol for a while, then narcotics."

Jed grimaced. He'd known about the narcotics part. "Grant would think you're manna from heaven."

"Yeah, the thing is, I'd have to take orders. I meant it when I said I'm done."

"How about my orders?"

"Call 'em requests and we'll be fine."

"Deal."

They grinned at each other.

*****

Disgruntled after taking a call from Cassie letting him know she couldn't meet him for lunch, Grant decided to eat at his favorite Mexican restaurant anyway. It came as a surprise to see Harrison Seward, the Fort Halleck police chief, sitting alone at a booth. As far as Grant was concerned, Seward exemplified some of the worst of small town policing. Unfortunately, since Fort Halleck was the county seat and largest city, and the sheriff's department headquarters had been built on the outskirts, Grant couldn't avoid the man entirely. They'd worked together cooperatively a few times, butted heads more often.

A man in his late fifties, Seward looked up while Grant waited to be seated. With a phony smile, the chief gestured. "Why don't you join me?"

If Cassie had been here, Grant would have had an excuse. As it was, he did try to maintain as cordial a relationship as possible with his counterpart in the FHPD.

"Good to see you," he said insincerely, joining Seward. Scrutinizing him across the table, he could see why the guy's first name hadn't been relaxed to Harry. Not a big man, Seward seemed to have a Napoleon complex. Everything about him, including his flat-top haircut, bristled whenever Grant saw him. Maybe he was always that stiff. For his sake, Grant hoped not.

"Grant."

They shook hands.

Once Grant had ordered, the two men discussed administrative annoyances they both faced on a regular basis, as well as the difficulty in finding capable men or women to fill open positions. A Fort Halleck PD officer had been murdered back in February. During the investigation, Grant had had to fire one of his deputies.

Seward shook his head. "Guy I took on to replace Chad Norman? Let him go last week. There were rumors he was napping during his shift. Last straw was when I smelled booze on his breath when he came into the station to sign out."

"I'd have fired his ass, too." Apparently they did have some standards in common. "I have to say, I've been really happy with the woman I hired to replace Youngren. She was hands down the most impressive candidate who applied. People relax around her. She's doing extra training to be able to take over some of the basic crime scene jobs, too."

"I don't know." Seward dropped the subject while the waitress delivered his enchilada, resuming after she retreated. "Not sure I'm comfortable having a woman out there with a badge and gun. I've seen that little gal you hired. Not much to her. Now, you tell me how she's going to take on a belligerent drunk who weighs two or three times what she does."

Grant set down his soda. "Research shows that women cops don't have to physically confront aggressive men nearly as often as male cops do. They're better at defusing anger, settling everyone down so the situation doesn't turn violent."

"What you mean is, even drunks might have some qualms about punching a cute gal like your deputy."

No, that wasn't what he'd meant, but Grant doubted he'd get anywhere with this argument. Even so, he couldn't resist countering, "No, I think on average women are better at using their smarts and their words than the average man. But you have a point, too. Most men *are* likely to hesitate to attack a woman."

"Well, you let me know how it goes with her," Seward said, no give in his attitude.

Grant's lunch arrived and he started to eat. Seward asked about the cattle rustling and Gary Webb's murder, which carried them for a few minutes. That was fine until Grant got the uneasy feeling the police chief was a lot more interested in the subject than he would have expected.

"You have acreage yourself?" he asked casually.

Seward's hesitation increased Grant's curiosity. "I do," he said at last, surely realizing that Grant could easily find out where he lived. "Run some cattle, in fact. Brings in extra income."

"Do you? I don't think Detective Dawson has you on his list. How big a herd do you have?"

"On top of some steers I'm bulking up, I've got close to forty calves. And yes, I've branded them."

"Herefords?"

"Nope, I've got Red Angus and I'm moving into Charolais. I like the look of them, and their calves are big."

"Never seen one. Cream colored, aren't they?"

"In the dark, they look like ghosts moving out there in the pasture."

The man had more poetry in his soul than Grant would have guessed. Also shrewdness, and a reasonably successful sideline to his job in law enforcement.

It did cross Grant's mind that a herd of Charolais had been stolen, although he couldn't remember from which ranch. And had the calves been branded? He'd ask Jed.

Seward didn't seem happy with the turn of the conversation, or maybe he'd just recalled an obligation. Either way, he pushed away his plate, dropped some bills on the table and excused himself with surprising speed, his manner stiff again.

It was also possible he'd just remembered how much he disliked Grant. Word had it he disapproved of Grant's youth and thought he'd been offered the job as sheriff only because he'd been a high school football star, leading the Fort Halleck team to a state championship at their level.

Grant was fine with letting him think whatever he wanted to, as long as it didn't get in the way of their working relationship. Truth was, he didn't know whether Seward's territorial tendencies had anything to do with his feelings about Grant, or whether that was just his nature.

Seward's ranching operation wasn't huge, but it was bigger than a lot of the small-time ranchers in the county could boast. So why hadn't he come to any of the meetings Jed had held in cooperation with a bunch of separate agencies, including the Bureau of Land Management, the Oregon State Police, even the Oregon Department of Fish and Wildlife? The man was in law enforcement himself.

Not a cow had disappeared since Gary Webb's body had been discovered. Either the cattle rustlers had scared themselves, or the volunteer patrols and flyovers were having an impact. The sheriff's department had been able to reroute deputies to back country roads with the highway patrol stepping up on the highways in the county. Following the example of Malheur County, Jed had asked ranchers to note dates, times and license plates when they saw vehicles they didn't recognize in grazing areas, or on the roads at night, especially any pulling a stock trailer. Jed encouraged individual ranchers to set up security cameras if they could, too.

At this point, there wasn't a lot they could do that they weren't already doing. But murder had upped the stakes, Grant thought grimly. The Hayes County Sheriff's Department wasn't close to giving up.

*****

Jed's light rap on Grant's half-open office door brought an immediate, "Come in." When Grant saw the stranger accompanying Jed, he rose to his feet and looked inquiring.

"Niall Callaghan," Jed said. "Old army friend of mine who drifted into town."

Waving them to seats, Grant smiled at the description. "Planning to stay awhile?" he asked civilly.

"Longer than I intended," Niall said. "Seems Jed here needs help shoring up defenses out at Linette Broussard's place."

Jed hid his wince. He'd forgotten to tell Niall that his boss knew nothing about his history with Linette.

"That so," Grant said with interest. "What do you have in mind?"

"I've talked her into letting me stay out there nights," Jed said bluntly. "Niall may reinforce me for a few hours each night so I can get some sleep."

Grant transferred his gaze to Niall. "Are you armed?"

"I will be." His grin was effortlessly charming. "Didn't think I ought to walk in here carrying."

"Smart decision."

"Niall spent some of his time in the army as an MP," Jed explained. "He got stuck on protection details for visiting congressmen and the like. He's been a cop since he got out three years ago, too."

"I don't suppose—"

Niall laughed. "I've spent too many years taking orders, thank you."

Grant grimaced. "I was getting to that place myself. Now, Jed—" there was a smile in his eyes "—I rarely have to give him an order. For you, Mr. Callaghan, I suggest you find a small town that needs a police chief."

"That's...not a bad idea."

"Shame Seward isn't ready to retire," Jed said dryly.

"Speak of the devil—" Grant cut himself off.

Jed knew why. "Niall knows how to keep his mouth shut," he said quietly.

"High praise from the most close-mouthed man I know," his friend said, humor warming his face.

Grant nodded in easy acceptance of Jed's testimonial. Jed knew how lucky he'd been to find a man like him sheriff of the county.

"I had lunch with Harrison today," Grant said. "I was supposed to meet Cassie at Tia Maria's. She cancelled last minute, I found Chief Seward sitting alone."

Curious, Jed waited to see where this was going. He detested Seward, and knew Grant felt the same. The man wasn't so incompetent there was anything they could do about him, he was just so determined never to get showed up, he saw any offer of assistance as an insult. His sole detective was an idiot whose ideas of crime scene investigation were a century out of date. So what did Grant have on his mind?

"We tussled briefly on whether women should be cops." Grant's mouth twisted. "You can guess which side of the issue he came down on."

Jed had worked with women cops in Georgia, and he'd been impressed so far with Deputy Brown despite her youth. He still wasn't surprised to learn that Seward disapproved of her. There was a reason she was the first woman cop ever hired in Hayes County.

"Then things got interesting." Lines gathered on Grant's forehead. "Did you know he's a rancher, too?"

"Seward?" Jed hadn't seen that coming. He couldn't picture the guy in a saddle, never mind shoveling shit or wrestling with an animal that weighed two hundred pounds plus come time to brand, castrate and vaccinate.

"Not a huge operation, but it sounds more professional than some. He says he has Red Angus and is going into Charolais. He has something like forty calves this spring and some steers he'll be selling at the end of summer. I didn't get a chance to ask why he hasn't gotten in touch with you or come to any meetings. He didn't seem very comfortable talking about the ranching."

"That is interesting. You know Andy Ruckman lost some Charolais."

"I'd forgotten who it was, but yes."

With a sidelong glance, Jed saw how closely Niall was following the conversation. He must know what they were suggesting.

"Damn," Jed muttered. "I'd like to get a look at those brands."

"Were the calves branded?"

"No, but the cows were, of course." He made a humming sound. "I wouldn't want to get caught trespassing on the police chief's land."

Grant's laugh was short and sharp. "No, you would not. Or on anyone else's." He paused. "Is that a possibility?"

"A time or two," Jed conceded. "I was careful." He wasn't about to mention the close call when Thayer showed up unexpectedly.

"Well, you might want to talk to Seward. He won't be surprised after our lunch today."

They discussed what had been happening at Linette's place, including the early pranks, if that's what they were. Jed hadn't gotten that far with Niall earlier.

"I'll make sure any deputies patrolling her place know about Niall. Wouldn't want to get him shot."

"No." Grant frowned. "She doesn't have any idea who this could be."

"She says not." Jed's loyalties butted up against each other. He hadn't been sure, but Linette came first. He kept his mouth shut.

"She lived with a guy for awhile after you and she parted ways," Niall said.

The surprise on Grant's face wasn't more than a flicker. Apparently, he'd had his suspicions.

"Marlene hated his guts. Uh—" He glanced at Grant. "Marlene Harris owned the ranch where I stabled my horse. Linette trained horses for her, and Jed used to ride there, too." He looked at Jed, expression apologetic. "I thought it was better you didn't know." He shrugged. "Wasn't sure you'd be interested."

An ice pick arrowed straight in on Jed's heart. If he'd been told, what would he have done? He wished he knew for sure.

"Marlene saw some bruises, a more serious injury or two. She didn't like Linette's explanations and was real glad when Linette broke it off."

Jed discovered he was grinding his teeth. Was this why she hadn't wanted to give him the asshole's name?

It took willpower to loosen his jaw muscles and say without any obvious inflection, "When I interviewed her, Linette told me about him.

She said she hasn't heard from him since the split. There was no stalking, she's been here in Oregon for three plus years."

"He doesn't sound likely." Grant looked at Jed. "You get his name so you can check his background and whereabouts?"

"No."

The silence expressed the other two men's opinions – which Jed shared. Still, she was right; why *would* the guy show up here after that long?

"I didn't hear his name," Niall said. "I could call Marlene."

Man, he wanted that name, but Jed didn't like the idea of invading Linette's privacy to that extent.

"Let's hold off for now. There are other possibilities. One is that the attempted theft of the foal didn't have anything to do with the tricks somebody played on her."

He saw that Niall and Grant conceded his point, and continued. "A member of the cattle rustling gang might have been testing her security."

Grant locked his hands behind his head and leaned back. "I looked up Kiger horses. They aren't valuable the way a top thoroughbred is."

"The price for the foal would have been comparable to a calf, and potentially a lot more."

"With papers, sure."

Jed ignored that. "I mean to check out her employee. He could resent her for some reason – maybe thinks she should be paying him better, or she stiff-armed him when he made some kind of move on her."

"Or hasn't had the guts to make the move, but knows deep down he isn't in her league," Niall contributed.

Jed shrugged this time. "Has she fired anyone? Did she interview several people and one of them is pissed he didn't get the job? She claims she hasn't dated since she moved here."

I've had it with men, present company included. I like my horses better. Not words he intended to share.

"Doesn't mean men haven't asked her out," he continued, "or someone she's encountered at the feed store, the grocery store, the real estate office, who knows, hasn't gotten fixated on her."

"That's true." Niall kneaded the back of his neck. "We had a real ugly case—" His eyes met Jed's. "Sorry. I shouldn't have said that."

Jed's muscles had locked tight. He wasn't sure he was capable of saying anything.

"Linette's a beautiful woman," Niall said baldly. "Not a supermodel look, but I can't imagine a man not noticing her." Once again he sounded apologetic.

Jed's jaws and stomach muscles ached. It didn't help that Grant was clearly intrigued.

"I'll look forward to meeting her," the sheriff said mildly. "You sure you want to let your old friend anywhere near her?"

"No, I'm not." The too-quick response was raw, revealing more than he liked.

But Niall only smiled, almost gently. "You know me better than that."

Jed groaned. "Yeah. Yeah, I do. I'm sorry."

His friend slapped him on his back. "Happens to all of us."

Jed had sworn he wouldn't *let* this happen, but it seemed he no longer had a choice. He was sunk.

He stood, pushing back the chair. "Let's catch the SOB who is terrorizing her."

"Whatever you need," his boss said simply.

Jed already knew that Grant would have his back, which was lucky. If he were on his own, he'd have a problem finding adequate time and focus for the investigation into cattle rustling and Gary Webb's murder with Linette's problems added on top.

He reminded himself that the perpetrator could be one and the same, simplifying his life and job.

As the two men walked out to Jed's truck, he saw Erin getting out of her car. He almost waved her over, but Niall, as hyper-alert as Jed, saw and dismissed her. Jed didn't want to embarrass her, and saw no reason to warn Niall that Deputy Brown *was* a cop and therefore not as harmless as she appeared.

CHAPTER TEN

Linette was mucking out stalls when she heard the sound of a powerful engine out in front. She wasn't expecting any orders, there was no reason for Jed to come back until evening, and Troy was already here. His aging truck didn't sound like that, anyway.

Well, her unexpected visitor could just wait.

Hands protected by leather gloves, she steered the heavy, loaded wheelbarrow out to the manure pile, where she dumped the contents. After taking the wheelbarrow back into the barn, she wiped her forehead with the hem of her flannel shirt, looked down at herself ruefully, and headed out front.

There were two pickup trucks, Jed's gray one and a bright blue Ford F-150 pulled right up behind it. Jed and another man had walked over to the fence and were petting Maria Angela, a blue dun mare, whose four-week-old colt, Manrique del Rio, hovered a few feet from the fence.

Jed must have a sixth sense where she was concerned, because the moment Linette started toward them, his head turned. Having him watching her made Linette even more self-conscious. Her knee-high wellies were caked with shavings and manure, her jeans were ancient, and her flannel shirt sweat-soaked. Wisps of hair must be escaping her braid. Yes, this was her at her most attractive.

Doesn't matter, she told herself fiercely, but knew she lied.

"Jed," she said politely when she'd almost reached him. The other man turned and grinned. For an instant, Linette only stared. Then she said, "Niall? Oh, my God. It *is* you." Laughing, she rushed forward to hug him. He kissed her on the lips.

Jed didn't say a word.

Linette stepped back to look Niall over. Close to Jed's height, he was lean and long, not quite as broad although his shoulders were impressive. With dark brown, wavy hair, blue eyes and a wicked grin, he'd turn any woman's head. She might have been interested when they had first met, except he was married. Now? He wasn't Jed.

"You look so good," she declared. "But what are you doing here?"

"Traveling, seeing old friends, before I decide what I want to do next with my life."

"I heard you got divorced."

"Yeah, my fault. I wasn't in good shape when I finished that last deployment." Niall shrugged. "Lost some friends."

"I'm sorry," she said softly.

He nodded acknowledgement. "I got out of the army about six months after Jed did, so it's water under the bridge."

Like she'd buy that. But she smiled. "Well, I'm glad to see you. Welcome to the LB Kiger ranch."

"So modest," he teased.

Linette laughed. "Have to remind myself it's all mine somehow, don't I?"

"You look good, too."

"Liar. I'm not only filthy, I stink. But if you can stand me, I'll make you a cup of coffee."

"Won't turn that down."

Leading the way to her house, Linette finally noticed Jed's stone face. Was he mad? She couldn't imagine why. *He'd* brought Niall out here.

At the back door, she toed off her boots before continuing into the kitchen, where she scrubbed her hands and splashed water on her face as she and Niall continued to exchange tidbits about their recent histories. After starting the coffee, she joined them at the kitchen table.

"It's been a long time since the three of us were together."

"It has," Niall agreed. "Have you stayed in touch with Marlene? She'd love this place."

"We mostly email. She's really happy for me. I invited her out for a visit, but she can't stand to leave her horses."

"That deadbolt looks new," Jed asked brusquely. He was studying the back door.

"So much for chit chat," Niall said in amusement.

Cold blue eyes zeroed in on his friend. "That's not what we're here for."

And she shouldn't forget it, Linette thought. She stood, poured coffee and brought the cups to the table. "Cream, anyone?"

Both men declined. She was the only one to add sugar.

"I did replace the deadbolt on the front door and add this one on the back," she said, feeling renewed tension. "Until a month ago, I wasn't locking my doors during the day, and I didn't worry much. Really, I should replace this door. No lock will do any good if someone can just break the glass and reach in."

Lines formed across Jed's forehead, softening his expression. "I don't like reminding you—"

"Not as if I forget." All she had to do was look in a mirror at the colorful bruising on her face.

"Okay." Ignoring Niall, Jed pulled out a small notebook and pen. "You said you haven't dated since you moved here."

Just what she wanted to discuss with him. Out of the corner of her eye, she saw Niall's eyebrows climb.

"I haven't."

"I'm betting some men have asked you out, though."

Linette blinked, for a moment wondering why he was raising the subject. But she wasn't really that naïve. Men who felt rejected could become stalkers.

"Yes, but...I don't know how much help I can be. Even when they introduced themselves, I don't remember names."

He pressed, "None of them?"

"Well...a few." Wonderful, being put on the spot. "Let me think. Um, one was that police officer who was killed. Chad Norman."

Jed's jaw tightened, but he didn't bother writing down the name.

"A guy who works at the Shell station in town. Allen Bowman. Bowden. Something like that."

"Persistent?"

"I didn't give him a chance. I switched to buying my gas at Arco instead."

She offered a few other names. His expression never changed until she added, "Oh, and a guy named Rob Fullerton. That was the most recent. Maybe six months ago? We got talking at the coffee shop. He said he ranches."

Jed made an audible sound, as if she'd punched him. "You like him?"

"No, he reminded me too much of—" She bit her tongue, she stopped so suddenly.

"Theo," Niall contributed. "Wasn't that his name?"

Linette scowled at him. "It was. Is. How do you know about him?"

He shrugged apologetically. "Marlene."

Stung, Linette said, "She gossiped about me?"

"I asked about you, she said you were living with a guy."

Looking away from both men, she said, "I'll bet that isn't everything she said."

"No. I'm sorry. She worried."

Her laugh lacked any humor. "I'd like to say I can take care of myself, but it turns out I can't. You have no idea how much I hate that."

A flicker of some emotion passed across Jed's face too fast for her to identify. All he said was, "Niall has offered to help stake out your place. We plan to split the night shift."

Suddenly alarmed, she said, "So…what? You're both moving in?"

"I don't know about Niall. I plan to sleep here, on the couch if need be." His shoulders moved. "I will need to use the shower, keep something in your refrigerator for breakfast."

Niall set down his coffee cup. "Depends on the plan. If we aren't hiding our presence, I can stay at Jed's place and drive over here when I'm due to take over. If we're hoping to catch the guy in action, then I'll pretty well need to stay, too. Although, is there anywhere we can hide our vehicles?"

Her mind boggled at the idea of these two big men who exuded so much testosterone sharing her house. About the only way she could pretend they weren't here was to shut herself in her bedroom.

But she wouldn't have to be afraid. She could sleep.

"I have two extra bedrooms, but one of them is unfurnished. The other one is set up for guests. You can switch off in that bed it if you're okay with that, or lay down a pad and sleeping bag in the empty room. Or sleep on the sofa, which isn't a pull-out. Whatever you want."

"I have camping stuff with me," Niall said. "I don't mind sleeping on the floor."

"As for the pickups…" Linette hesitated. "You can't come in one?"

"If we do that, Niall will be stranded here when I head into work," Jed said.

"Why don't I help out here daytimes?" Niall suggested. "Look like a new employee. Take over mucking out stalls and the like."

"I really can't afford—"

He smiled gently. "Strictly as a volunteer. I don't need money."

Jed didn't look pleased, but he kept his mouth clamped shut.

Free labor. How could she turn that down? "Okay. Yes. For a few days anyway. If your pickup isn't here, you won't stand out if someone is watching the place."

Niall offered to load up on groceries, they decided he would come back when Jed did this afternoon. Jed thought his arrivals would be less likely to be noticed if he got here well before dark.

"He'd stand out if he were watching you in daylight."

Linette wanted to think he was right. "What do I tell Troy?"

"The truth. Niall is an old friend who might take advantage of your spare bedroom for a week or two."

If Troy thought they were sleeping together, so what? It wasn't any of his business, she decided.

In fact, she saw her employee when she was walking the two men out, and introduced him to Niall.

"My truck needs some work, so Jed is going to drop me off out here later today," Niall said easily. "I figure I can earn my keep. I'm sure Linette can come up with something for me to do."

If he really meant to work, he could start replacing a run-down stretch of fencing she hadn't yet gotten to. She had enough supplies to get him started.

Mumbling, "Ah, it's nice to meet you," Troy backed away. He'd already disappeared into the barn when both men turned their pickup trucks around and left, Jed taking up the rear this time.

She shouldn't stand here and watch them go, but she did anyway. Her life was being flipped on end, and the flutter in her chest that she labeled apprehension might be something else altogether.

Jed would be sleeping in her house tonight.

*****

Jed had learned that Baxter paid his bills by working for a roofing company. Maybe he'd been able to buy those shingles to re-roof his barn at cost. Rather than talk to him on a jobsite, Jed decided to tackle Fort Halleck Police Chief Harrison Seward first.

Seward wouldn't like Jed showing up at the police station, but Jed didn't let that stop him.

Dating to the 1920s, the building was classic government architecture, if on a modest scale. Imposing and unfriendly, it appeared dated rather than historical. The only exterior modernization was a ramp added to the side of the stairs to allow wheelchair access.

Inside, the waiting room had the air of police stations anywhere. There was even an underlying scent that reminded him of a locker room, albeit this sweat had been induced by nerves rather than exercise.

The desk sergeant had a thin comb-over and a huge beer belly. He looked astonished at Jed's request.

"Is Chief Seward expecting you?"

"We didn't have an appointment, but he's expecting me to drop by."

The sergeant called to the back. Hanging up, he said, "Chief says to send you back. Last door on the right."

Jed nodded his thanks and strolled back, taking in the offices, record room and bullpens on the way. Not much security here, if someone showed up who had a grudge against a cop. The sheriff's department at least had a locked steel door preventing anyone who hadn't been invited to get beyond the front counter.

Seward's was the corner office, of course, although the blinds were down but slanted to allow some light in. In the middle of downtown, his views wouldn't be anything special, and unless that was one-way glass he wouldn't have any privacy. He rose from behind his desk but didn't come around it, although he leaned forward and extended his hand. "Detective Dawson."

Jed shook. "Thanks for seeing me."

Impatience showed on the police chief's face as he resumed his seat. A little guy, he never came across as very friendly. "This about the cattle rustling?"

"It is." Jed sat in a straight-back wood chair, all that was available.

"As I told the sheriff," Seward said pointedly, "I've kept abreast of the news. I'm too busy to join in any volunteer patrols, but of course I've instructed my officers to watch for any suspicious behavior or vehicles, and to lend their assistance should you need it."

"Thank you. That's good to hear. Grant says you haven't been visited by our neighborhood cattle rustlers?" Jed now knew that Seward owned a couple of hundred acres out toward Tribulation, an unincorporated community in the southeast corner of the county. The property bordered a stream that joined Desperation Creek, which Jed would have called a small river. It ran right through town and was the reason a fort had been built here in the nineteenth century.

"Haven't had any losses. Don't think any of my near neighbors have, either."

The observation was interesting. Jed wondered if there were other clusters of ranches within the county that hadn't been hit, either. Was it chance that Seward's neighbors hadn't had trouble? Or were there factors that would have made the risk for the rustlers too high? He'd lay out a map when he got back to the office and give some thought to this.

"I hear you have some Charolais."

"What's that supposed to mean?" the chief snapped.

"Just curious. I've never seen one. Far as I know, Andy Ruckman's the only other rancher in the county who was trying out the breed. He got wiped out."

"Are you implying…?" Seward half-rose to his feet.

"Implying?" Jed let it hang.

"That *I* have this Ruckman's cattle?"

"Never crossed my mind," Jed lied. "Like I said, I'm just curious. We don't have a lot of Red Angus locally, either. I think that's what Jack Baker goes in for."

The effort it took Seward to make himself sit back down showed.

"Someone told me he ran some," he said stiffly. "I've met Jack. He's an old-timer. I'm sorry for his loss."

"I think the rustlers have to be local men and women. Not a single ranch in any neighboring county has so much as lost a calf during the past couple of months." He watched the police chief closely. "You've been in law enforcement in this county for quite some time."

"Thirty-six years," Seward agreed.

"Given that perspective, do you have any suspicion who might be involved with this rustling ring?"

Expressionless, Seward held his gaze. "If I did, I'd have given you a call."

Jed waited a minute, but had to give up. With a nod, he rose to his feet. "Thank you for your time, Chief Seward."

All the man said was a cool "I assume you can see yourself out."

Was 'You're welcome' too much to ask?

He was crossing the waiting room when he nailed down an oddity in the conversation.

Grant says you haven't been visited by our neighborhood cattle rustlers?

Strange. He'd expected something like, *Nope. Neither have my neighbors.*

Instead, Seward had taken a sideways step. *Haven't had any losses.* But the rustlers might have visited?

And then there was the added comment, *Don't think any of my neighbors have, either.* This man was a cop. He'd been kept informed about the surge in cattle rustling. And yet he hadn't spoken to his neighbors about it? Wouldn't you think he'd have wanted to know how close the rustlers had gotten to his ranch?

Jed thought he might have an interesting conversation with one or two of those neighbors.

*****

Baxter wasn't any happier to see him than the police chief had been. Fortunately, Jed had long since become inured to the antagonism he faced on a day-to-day basis.

This time, he parked at the curb in front of the tiny rental house Baxter had given as his mailing address instead of driving out to the ranch. Baxter might go straight out to check on his cattle, but it seemed likely he'd stop at home to grab a bite to eat first.

In fact, Jed hadn't been here fifteen minutes when Baxter's pickup, a ten-year-old Dodge, appeared around the corner at the end of the block, coming to a near-stop when the driver spotted the sheriff's department vehicle in front of his house. The guy was evidently smart enough to know that doing a U-turn and fleeing wouldn't look good. He pulled into his driveway in front of a single-car, detached garage too small for a modern-day pickup truck, got out and walked to meet Jed.

"You again," he said flatly.

"Get used to it," Jed advised. "Until I arrest every single man or woman involved in the cattle rustling operation, I'll keep coming back."

"You have no reason to suspect me."

"Most ranchers have welcomed me with open arms. They *want* me to catch these sons-of-bitches. They still have hope they might get some of their herd back. Most of the ones who haven't suffered a loss are welcoming, too. They're eager to participate in patrols. They invite me out to inspect their fences and see their herds."

Gene Baxter stared at him with growing alarm. For the first time, he had to understand how bad he'd screwed up.

Jed continued, "Then there's the handful of you who meet me with hostility. Who seem nervous at the idea I might look around their property."

"I called you out when my trailer was stolen," Baxter blurted.

"Sure you did. But me, I'm distrustful by nature. I couldn't help wondering whether you were afraid that trailer of yours had been seen hauling cattle that weren't yours. Might be a good idea if you made sure we wouldn't trace it to you."

"That's ridiculous." The protest came out sounding weaker than Baxter had undoubtedly intended.

"Just a thought." Jed shrugged. "Either way, we're looking for your missing trailer." He nodded, turned away then back. "Oh, something else. One of the Webb's neighbors heard some shouting the night Gary was killed. Interesting thing. The neighbor heard a name. Bet you can guess what that name was."

From the shock on Baxter's face, Jed could have been a rattlesnake coiled in the driveway. Tail rattling, head positioned to strike.

He nodded again. "Good day, Gene." He strolled to his vehicle, got in and drove away.

Baxter stayed unmoving, staring after him.

*****

Jed's phone rang before he could call Grant to report on his conversation with the police chief. He recognized the number, having spoken several times with the detective in Crook County.

Detective Frazier launched right in. "We got lucky. You know we were at a standstill with Oren Calderon."

Jed knew. Frazier had been more than cooperative when Jed asked for a favor, going right out to talk to the man, then returning again a week later to put some pressure on. Neither visit got him anywhere. Apparently he hadn't given up, for which Jed wouldn't have blamed him.

Feeling a buzz, he pulled off the road. "What happened?"

"The idiot had a break in his fence. Can you believe he'd be that careless? A fellow driving by had to slam on his brakes to keep from hitting a calf. He saw a few cows and calves had wandered out. Some were grazing on the road verge. A rancher himself, he saw that the calf carried Calderon's brand. But it ran back to its mommy, and *her* brand didn't match. He kept checking, found three unknown brands, but all the calves he could get close to bore Calderon's brand. Plus, the fence down was his. That passing rancher didn't like what he'd seen. He gave us a call, waited for me while I drove on out. Just got back, in fact. Took some pictures, then the two of us shooed the strays back into the pasture and propped up the fence. I'm waiting for my warrant, which we'll serve first thing tomorrow."

"You've made my day. We haven't had a recurrence of the rustling, which means the patrols and fly-overs are doing some good, but I'm not even close to making an arrest. Glad the guy driving by had sharp eyes. And that you were available."

"Oh, I'd have made myself available even if I'd been in the middle of a high-speed pursuit. And, like I said, Frank had heard about the troubles ranchers were having in your county. You're not that far from his place. He's steamed, and glad to keep his mouth shut until we get out there to secure the animals on Calderon's land."

"He could have bought already-branded cows."

"Check your email." Frazier sounded smug. "I sent the photos. Three of the brands matched ones you asked us to watch out for."

Jed gave an astonished laugh. "I never thought we'd get any of the cattle back." He frowned. "You have someone watching his place tonight?"

"Damn straight we will. Once we sort out the cattle and sit Mr. Calderon down, you want to join us?"

"There's nothing I'd like better."

A minute later, he called Grant with even more to report on than he'd expected.

*****

From the moment the men arrived, they took over Linette's house as if they belonged there. Niall deposited half a dozen bags of groceries in the kitchen before carrying his duffle and sleeping bag upstairs. She hadn't gotten halfway through putting away the groceries when he returned to shoo her out of the kitchen.

"I'll cook tonight."

Not sure what Jed was doing, Linette took refuge in the barn until he chased her down to say dinner was ready. As they walked back to the house, she saw how worn Jed's face was and that his usually clear eyes were bloodshot.

Once they sat down to eat beef stroganoff and asparagus, he said, "This is for your ears only."

She and Niall nodded.

He proceeded to tell them about what sounded like a big break in his investigation of the cattle rustling ring. They might even be getting back some of the stolen animals.

Feeling a rush of relief, Linette said, "You mean, this might be over?"

"You're talking about what's been going on here at your place?" When she nodded, he said, "No. For one thing, if we can't get this guy to talk, we'll be back at a standstill. For another... I'm not convinced your troubles are connected."

Linette wasn't sure what his expression meant. Was that pity she saw? Frustration? Or something else altogether?

Niall's gaze flicked from Jed's face to hers, then back again. "Did I tell you I apparently don't have a horse anymore?"

They both stared at him.

"Yeah, my youngest sister, Ginny, started riding Grendel." Grendel was his black quarter horse/morgan cross. "Next thing I knew, when I showed up at the boarding ranch to ride, I'd find out she already had him out. He's, man, I can't believe it, fourteen now. Anyway, I made it official when I set out on my cross-country jaunt."

"You love that horse."

"I love my sister, too." He smiled crookedly. "They're good together. Once I'm settled, I'll find a young horse."

After that, conversation at the dinner table flowed easily, for the most part. They shared enough history to give them something in common. Jed had seemingly gotten over his earlier dark mood, although he spoke less than Niall and she did. Which was nothing new; he'd always been quiet. Charm and a southern brand of good manners characterized Niall, although she suspected that both were a thin veneer protecting whatever demons lay beneath.

When Jed rose to start clearing the table, she took the dishes from his hands. "Have a cup of coffee and sit. Both of you. I'll clean up."

From the kitchen, she could hear them talking, but not make out what they were saying. When she rejoined them, she learned that Jed planned to stand his watch first. Linette thought about protesting. The few hours' of sleep he'd had this morning obviously hadn't been adequate, but she knew he wouldn't let her take his place.

When he rose to his feet, stretched until he touched the ceiling and said, "I'll go out the back," Linette jumped up, too.

She said, "I'll head to bed."

"I won't be far behind," Niall agreed. "I'll get the lights."

Linette thanked him and trailed Jed toward the kitchen. She should have stopped at the foot of the stairs. That she kept going had to be the result of some kind of compulsion. She watched as he turned off both the kitchen and outside lights and opened the back door.

"Be careful," she whispered.

"You know I will," he murmured, in a voice of deepest velvet.

She hadn't seen him move, but she felt a soft stroke on her cheek, his fingertips or knuckles. And then he slipped out, leaving the door open. By the time she peered out, he had already vanished from sight.

CHAPTER ELEVEN

Linette might be an early-to-bed, early-to-rise woman, but she was far from sleepy. Conveniently enough, she was in the middle of a really good British mystery, so she propped herself up with several pillows and settled in to read. As tired as she usually was at the end of a day, she had been making slow progress on the book. Having Troy here fulltime and now Niall working for a few days, too, she could indulge herself.

She heard Niall come up while her light was still on, so she called, "Goodnight," and he did the same.

A couple of hours after her usual bedtime, she turned off the light, readjusted the pillows, and declared herself ready to sleep. Unfortunately, the message didn't shut down her thoughts.

What was Jed doing right now? Sitting in the tree house? Patrolling her property the way he had last night? What if he got in trouble? Would she or Niall hear, too late, a shot from the far reaches of her land or a squeal of tires on the road out front?

The worry drove away what little drowsiness she'd dredged up.

She lay still, listening as hard as she could. Her screened window was open, but it looked westward, while most of her land lay north and east of the house. She'd left her door cracked, too, not liking the idea of being oblivious to whatever happened during the night.

Now, she punched her pillow into shape and rolled over. She was tired. She was. So why couldn't she sleep?

She knew herself better than to ask such a dumb question.

Eventually, she must have dozed, at least, but she didn't sleep through the faint squeak from the staircase. Oh, no. Consciously or not, she'd been waiting up for Jed. Unless this was Niall going downstairs for some reason? Had Jed called him? Body tense, she heard a low voice. Niall's, she thought. A light from the hall must be coming from the crack beneath the bathroom door. A soft exchange of voices didn't relax her. Jed was back safe.

Finally, the sixth step betrayed Niall heading downstairs.

After that, Linette didn't hear a thing. She lay still, staring toward the dark hall, unable to tell if Jed had paused outside her door or already gone into the bedroom to sleep. Finally, she couldn't help herself.

"Jed?" she whispered.

*****

Busted.

Jed stifled a groan. How had she seen him standing out here? He'd been asking for it, though. The knowledge that she lay in bed so close had rooted his feet in the hall right outside her door.

"Yeah? Did we wake you up?"

"I don't know," she said softly. "I wasn't sleeping well. Did anything happen?"

Still talking to the darkness, although he knew exactly where her bed was and that he was looking straight at her, he said, "Nope. Quiet as a mouse."

"Oh."

He waited, although he should say goodnight and go on to bed. God knows he was tired enough to fall asleep before he got his boots off.

"I was worried."

That she'd made the admission blew him away. He felt the rough edges of her anger every time they talked, but something else had been going on, too.

Unless first thing in the morning she told Niall, too, that she had worried.

He grimaced at the unjustified jealousy. As far as he knew, there'd never been any chemistry between the two of them, and Niall had as good as promised he'd keep his distance. Linette wasn't the kind of woman who'd come on to a friend of Jed's just to rub his nose in it, anyway.

"I'm good at this," he heard himself say. "Staying unseen."

"I know. Even so—" The silence formed a deep, dark pool. "I...paid attention to news, kept an ear out anytime people talked about casualties. I ran into Randy Ellroy. Remember him? He told me you were back, uninjured."

It was true Jed had been unscathed on the outside. Inside…his last remnants of humanity had been blasted to smithereens. He'd thought them dead and been genuinely astonished when he began to feel odd flickers of emotion.

"You moved away," he said.

"Why did you come here, and then never even say hello?" She sounded genuinely curious.

It was weird, having this conversation without any visual cues. But what the hell. He'd expected her to ask eventually.

"I was working up the courage." He backed up until he could lean on the opposite wall. "And then I had to kill a man."

"You saved a woman's life. Was there any other way?"

He closed his eyes. "No."

"Then?"

"I had to suit up." She'd know what he was talking about. He'd told her what a ghillie suit was. Showed her one. "Crawl forward. Get within range. See his face right before—" He'd shattered the guy's head, watched in living color.

"It took you back."

Of course Linette understood. He hadn't been open with her about his job, about the toll it took even as it saved the lives of American soldiers, but he'd always known she saw more than she should, understood him in a way nobody else did or ever had. That, he thought now, was part of why he'd fled.

"Yeah," he said huskily. He cleared his throat. "I wasn't in any shape to—"

"Hide what you were feeling from me?" she said sharply. "God forbid you talked about it. Let someone—" She didn't finish.

Let someone what? Hold him?

Maybe she *didn't* know him the way he'd been afraid she did. He'd feel pathetic if he said, *No one ever has before.* He still remembered the shock on Grant Holcomb's face when Jed had told him so bluntly that not everyone had any idea what having family meant.

"Forget it," Linette snapped. "It doesn't matter. Go to bed."

He hadn't answered soon enough. "It does matter." Jed didn't like the raw desperation in his voice.

"No. I was curious, that's all. I mean it, Jed. You need the sleep."

He did, of course, but, God, what he'd give to join her in that bed, wrap himself around her, comfort himself with her scent, her strength, her breath, the thick silk of her hair. Right now, he was tired enough to think he could be content with that, that he wouldn't fall on her like a starving man.

"Goodnight," he said quietly. "You need to sleep, too."

"Thank you for...being here."

"I wouldn't want to be anywhere else." And *that* was the most honest thing he'd said in a long time.

As he pushed himself away from the wall and started for the bedroom across the hall from hers, he heard her whispered, "Goodnight."

She hadn't said that to him in five long years. His fault.

*****

Linette heard Niall come in just after daybreak and go straight to the spare room to sack out. She rolled over and went back to sleep.

The next thing she knew, her alarm clock went off. Blearily, she thought, *Wait. I didn't set it.* No, that was her phone. She groped for it just as someone started pounding on the front door.

Jumping out of bed, she grabbed jeans and yanked them on even as she answered the phone.

"It's Troy!" He sounded distraught. "Horses are out, on the road."

"Joaquin—" His voice broke. "He got hit. He's...I think he's dead, Linette."

Pain compressed her ribcage. No, no, no! He'd jump up. He'd—

"I'm coming," she said hoarsely, dropped the phone, shoved her feet into her boots and pulled a sweatshirt over her head. Bleary-eyed, Niall stumbled into the hall, meeting her almost face-to-face.

"What?"

"Horses are out." She ran downstairs, where she found the front door open and Jed listening to Troy.

She tore past them, bounded down the stairs and ran for the road.

Jed yelled after her. "I'll bring flares!"

Troy... She didn't look back to see whether he was following her or not.

Out on the road, she saw a man already laying out flares. The other direction... Oh, God. A hundred yards away, a foal lay almost on one shoulder. An old pickup truck was parked not far past him.

Had anybody called the vet? She should do it— But she knew, even before, gasping for breath, she dropped to her knees beside the ten week old colt, that no veterinarian could help. A leg and shoulder were badly damaged, and where his ribcage had been was a...concavity. His big dark eyes were fixed, dull, filmed over.

Tears ran down her face as she gently touched him with a hand that trembled. How could this have happened? *How?* Some of the fences needed replacement, but not urgently so. She or Troy checked them regularly.

Her head came up at the clatter of hooves on the pavement. Imelda, a beautiful silver, sidled nervously toward her. She was Joaquin's dam, not understanding any better than Linette did why her colt didn't scramble up and run to her side.

"Ah, Christ." Jed crouched beside her, compassion written on his face. "I'm sorry, Linette."

She swiped her wet cheeks with her forearms. "Will you find out how they got out?"

His "yeah" was so rough, he had to clear his throat. "After we catch all of them."

Both of them turned their heads at the sound of a siren. "That'll scare the horses more!" she exclaimed, even as Imelda shied away, her hooves skidding on the pavement.

Jed ran toward the deputy's SUV pulling up. Tears still leaked, but Linette rose to her feet, feeling as stiff and ungainly as a newborn foal, watching as Jed spoke vehemently to the uniformed deputy.

Jarman, she realized, the jerk who'd responded to her first 911 call. He did lean in and shut off lights and siren.

Jed jogged back to her. "I'm sending him to find the break in the fence."

"Just so I don't have to talk to him." The mare was back, trying to nose her foal again. "Let me take the halter," Linette said. "She knows me." After taking halter and rope from Jed, she went directly to Joaquin's dam, who tossed her head but didn't try to evade her.

Linette gave her a little longer to nose her dead colt before leading her along the side of the road and up the driveway. Troy was already leading another mare into the barn, her foal following docilely. Jed was coaxing yet another mare.

They used stalls, paddocks, tied a few horses in the broad aisle.

At last Jed said, "I don't see any more horses. Can you tell if any are missing?"

"Rey!" she exclaimed.

Jed laid a hand on her shoulder. "That the stallion? I saw him. Was he in a different pasture?"

"Yes." She sagged. "Oh, thank God."

"All right." His eyes held the kind of tenderness she'd once dreamed of seeing but could no longer believe in. "The driver who hit the foal is waiting to talk to you. He put out flares and has been lending a hand rounding up the horses."

"Who is he?"

"Says his name is Curt Deeter. He works at the Arrowhead Creek Ranch. He was on his way to work."

Linette nodded dully. "I don't suppose it was his fault."

"No." Not a man who did a lot of touching out of bed, Jed seemed to be putting his hands on her a lot these days. Right now, he squeezed her upper arms and held her gaze. "He's pretty upset."

"He's not alone." She swallowed and backed up, saying sharply, "My foal was in the road. My fault."

"Stop and wash your face."

He sounded so damn kind, she wanted to cry again, but of course she wouldn't.

She did go outside to the trough right behind the barn and splash her face. She dried it on the hem of her sweatshirt as she walked back down the aisle. Beyond him, apparently waiting, stood Deputy Jarman. Linette didn't acknowledge him.

The guy Jed had told her about – Curt? – hovered right outside the entrance. Maybe mid-twenties, lean and wearing typical cowboy garb, he looked more than upset. His eyes were puffy and red-rimmed, which told her he'd cried. Shoulders hunched inside a denim jacket, he paced back and forth until he saw her.

"I'm—" He swallowed. "This your place?"

"I'm Linette Broussard." She held out a hand.

"Curt Deeter. I work at—"

"Jed told me."

He bobbed his head. "I'd give anything to have kept from hitting him, but I didn't even see him until he jumped the ditch and ran right out in front of my truck. I swerved, thinking he'd keep going, but he fell to his knees. I—" His voice broke and his eyes were wet. "Shit. I'm sorry. I, uh, never thought I'd kill a beautiful animal like that."

"No, I'm sorry." She laid a hand on his arm. "If it's anybody's fault, it's mine. You had no reason to think a horse would run across the road."

At the same time as she felt an inexplicable warmth at her back, Curt glanced past her before meeting her eyes again. "Other animals do sometimes. Pronghorn, rabbits, coyotes. You know. I try to drive carefully. I've never hit an animal before."

Jed wasn't touching her this time, just standing close behind her, but his presence helped. Stiffened her spine. "It can't be helped." She hesitated. "A man tried to steal a foal just a couple of days ago. I think this must be connected. We haven't gotten out to check yet, but somebody must have pulled down a fence."

"Niall called a minute ago," Jed said quietly. "That's probably why Jarman is waiting to talk to us. Niall says a gate was wide open. Padlock must have been cut. We don't know, because it's missing, the chain lying on the ground."

Forgetting both of the other men standing there, she looked at Jed. "During the night?"

"No." Hard and edged with angry, this was wasn't even his cop's voice. There was too much emotion in it. "Probably as soon as Niall came in. I'm betting the horses were lured out with feed, or even chased out."

That...made sense. Too many had been out. What were the odds they'd all wander out, when the pasture most of the mares and foals had been in was thirty acres? Despite being descended from mustangs, these weren't wild horses. At most they'd be skittish if a man, or men, approached them.

She made herself breathe through her own anger before she turned back to Curt Deeter. "Let me know if there's damage to your truck."

"I haven't looked. But...I carry insurance."

"The insurance company will come after me, anyway."

"Not if I said I hit a pronghorn or deer," he said stubbornly.

Linette shook her head. "Don't lie. I do carry insurance." With a big deductible, but this young ranch hand shouldn't suffer because of her problems.

He searched her face and finally nodded, then touched the brim of his hat. "I don't know if this has anything to do with what happened, but I heard a car or truck start and drive away." He gestured west. "Your ranch hand was running down the driveway, and I just didn't think about it."

Jed stepped forward. "Did you catch a glimpse of it? Or notice a vehicle earlier that was parked somewhere off the road?"

Deeter shook his head. "I'm sorry."

"Let me get your phone number."

He gave it readily before saying, "I'll be on my way, then. If there's anything I can do..."

Linette managed a smile that seemed to alarm him more than offer reassurance, but he did finally depart.

Once he was out of earshot, Linette moaned. "Now what?"

"Now Niall and I look for tracks. Had the guy not made his getaway yet, and was surprised when Deeter hit the foal? Waited until Deeter was distracted to run for it? Or was he hanging around for a reason?"

Stricken, she said, "For a chance to see me scared, tearing around trying to corral the horses?"

Jed was frowning. "I have another idea. Let me check something. I'll load the colt in the bed of my pickup at the same time. Get him off the road."

She didn't like the look on his face and felt new apprehension build in her chest. What was he going to check?

"I'll start digging a grave with my tractor," she offered.

He nodded, searching her face before he spoke briefly with Jarman. Linette couldn't hear what was said, but she saw a flash of intense anger on the deputy's face before he turned and walked down the driveway, apparently dismissed.

Jed called for Niall. As they drove away, she took the opportunity to dash inside and finish getting dressed. Specifically, stripped to put on a bra, panties and socks before pulling on the same jeans and sweatshirt.

Outside, she and Troy discussed where to dig the grave. They'd barely agreed on a location when Jed's pickup truck came back up the driveway.

His expression was grim when he got out. Out of the corner of her eye, she saw that Niall's was much the same.

"Linette, you need to see this," Jed said. He nodded toward the bed of the pickup.

Her feet didn't want to take her forward, but she made herself follow him around to the back, where he let down the tailgate. The minute it dropped, she saw.

A web of fine filaments – wire? – mixed with the coarse hairs in the dead foal's short, bushy tail. A small capsule with a sort of needle hung from his rump. Not far from it was a tiny, raw wound. Another of the capsules with a barbed tip dangled amidst the mess.

Linette knew that her mouth had dropped open. Beside her, Troy gaped, too.

She'd never seen anything like this before, but it wasn't hard to guess. "A taser?"

"Yep." Fury honed the edge in Jed's voice. "This is why that bastard hung around. To drive one of the horses out in front of the first vehicle that came down the road."

"Is it…a police taser?"

"No."

Linette felt her grief ball into something hard, ugly. "He murdered Joaquin."

"He did. We can charge him with animal cruelty on top of everything else."

"If you ever find him."

"Do you doubt me?" he said softly.

She met that cold gaze and shook her head. "No."

His face softened, just a little. "Give me a few minutes to look for anything he might have dropped, a decent footprint, tire marks, and I'll be back to help."

"Is Deputy Jarman gone?"

"Yes."

"Niall—"

"He can stay and help." He glanced from her to the other two men. "Did you have a spare padlock, Linette?"

Troy said, "I'll go get one."

"Thanks." Jed watched him go. "I'd suggest we replace that gate with fencing. You don't use it, do you?"

"No, I don't know why it's there at all."

He nodded. "After the burial, I want all of us to have a conference. You, me, Niall and Troy. But let's take care of first things first."

Linette's headache had kicked up more than a few notches. She hoped Jed couldn't tell. "I'll bring the tractor out here."

Jed's hand on her arm stopped her. His voice had softened. "Take some of your painkillers first."

She made what was probably a grumpy sound, mostly because he was right, and stomped up to the house. If only the prescription meds could treat her deeper pain.

CHAPTER TWELVE

Two hours later, Jed walked into the Crook County Jail, where he was met by Detective Ed Frazier. At a guess, the man was in his early forties. Medium height, lean and tough looking. He was bulked-up some by the vest he wore under his tan uniform shirt. Jed wore his, too, as he did every working day even in the heat in summer.

The two men shook hands, after which Jed took in their surroundings. The building had showed its age outside, but in here, the problems were more obvious. The ceiling had water damage, the walls were constructed of painted concrete bricks, and every space Jed had seen so far, from booking to a rec room, was cramped.

"Bet you're looking forward to the opening of that new jail," he remarked. He'd seen the plans online.

Frazier grimaced. "Supposed to be next month. Can hardly wait. You know we house more inmates at the Jefferson County Jail than we do here? Got to tell you, I'm sick of the drive back and forth."

"I can see why."

"We're sitting down with Oren in the visitors' room. Not ideal, but the best we can do without transporting him to our office. Fair warning – he's not a happy camper."

Jed grinned. "Haven't met one yet in a jail."

Frazier laughed, too, and showed him into a cramped room that had only three stations for family or attorneys to speak to inmates through glass panels. With none of them in use, the table would allow room for the three of them to sit – or four, if Oren already had an attorney.

Jed wasn't surprised to find that he had counsel with him. He had to be sharp enough to know he was in major trouble.

Calderon looked about the way Jed had expected. In his late sixties, he had a skinny body wizened by years and exposure to the elements. Gray hair cut in a flat-top reminded Jed of Police Chief Seward's.

Discontent had carved deep lines in the leathery skin on his face, and unhealthy looking reddish-purple color flooded his cheeks.

"What possible grounds can you have to arrest me?" he snapped the minute Jed and Detective Frazier walked in.

They both took their seats. Frazier said calmly, "As you know, Judge Linder approved the warrant we served this morning based on the brands observed on cattle that had wandered out through a break in your fence line."

"You mean, you cut the strands so you had an excuse to get closer to my herd!"

"Oren," his attorney murmured. "Let me handle this."

Either Oren didn't know how to keep his mouth shut, or he wasn't a man to allow anyone to speak for him. The attorney kept on with the remonstrations, Oren blasted responses to the detective's every question or comment.

He insisted he'd bought every single cow and calf on his land fair and square. How was he supposed to have known if they'd been stolen? If it was true they had been. His glare was meant to blister. "I've been a rancher in this damn county for going on forty years now, and to be accused of something like this now is outrageous!" He hammered a fist on the table.

"Mr. Calderon," Jed said, "Detective Frazier and other Crook County deputies will be searching your paper and computer files. It would help if you'd identify the individuals from whom you claim you bought these animals."

His face turned an even deeper shade of purple. "*Claim*? I bought the damn cattle! It's not my fault if—"

It continued in that vein until Jed lost patience. He'd left Linette reluctantly, and he could see this wasn't going anywhere.

He pushed back his chair and stood. "Mr. Calderon, you're wasting our time. We all know you provided pasture and possibly transportation to a stockyard for the men who have not only stolen those animals, they murdered a rancher in my county. Do you want to take the rap for the others? Be the only individual who goes to trial and is convicted on those charges? That includes murder, since cattle with the WBB brand were among those identified today on *your* land. Those stolen from Gary Webb the night he was shot dead." He stared at that choleric face, into eyes that showed fear and more defiance, but not regret, and shook his head. "Excuse me, Detective Frazier. I need to get back."

Frazier rose, too. "Mr. Marsh, I encourage you to help your client understand the gravity of these charges. We'll talk again."

He followed Jed out of the room and down the hall, nodding at the jail sergeant to let him know the inmate was alone with his attorney. Outside, Frazier said, "He'll break. Oren never thought it would come to this."

"I hear he's a whiner who thinks he deserved breaks that didn't come his way."

"That's his reputation. Once he understands he faces real time in prison?" The detective shook his head. "He'll crack. I see him as ultimately a coward."

"I hope you're right. Won't mind seeing Oren spend some time in prison, but I really want the SOB who gunned down a good man because he got in their way."

They parted with Frazier promising to keep the pressure on, Jed to share any other news from the investigation.

During the drive from Prineville to Fort Halleck, Jed felt stress gripping his neck muscles. In his last job, the victims had all been strangers. It would only get worse if he stayed in this rural county where, sooner or later, he'd know every resident.

And no, that wasn't his real problem. Her name was Linette Broussard. Vulnerable, and under assault for unknown reasons.

The woman he loved.

*****

Maybe she was foolish, but Linette said some silent words over the grave, raw ground smoothed level. Niall and Troy stood silently by. Knowing both were animal lovers, she suspected they might be doing the same. She hadn't decided whether to place a marker.

From there, they loaded a small trailer with materials to replace several sections of fencing while they were at it, and bumped in the tractor across the pasture to a stretch on the east end of her acreage.

This was her first look at the now-closed gate. She clambered off the tractor and studied it. She'd always wondered why it was there. The posts supporting it showed signs of rot and had needed replacing anyway.

"We need to look closer at the horses when we get back. See whether there's any sign they were whipped to drive them out." She couldn't swear there weren't marks even on the horses she'd led up from the road herself. They'd all been in such a hurry, distracted by the heartbreaking sight in the road.

Both men nodded.

Linette tried to help, but truthfully was grateful that Troy and Niall did most of the work. She still felt the effect from the assault that put her in the hospital. The headache was now duller, but her neck and shoulder hurt, too. The pain meds helped in one way, but also made her feel tired.

With only a few words here and there, Niall dug the holes to replace the posts in the worst shape, and he and Troy hammered boards into place, then strung barbed wire tautly across the top. From there, they walked in opposite directions to verify that there weren't any additional breaks.

When they were done, Niall turned in a slow circle, his eyes narrowed as he scanned every direction. Linette knew what he was thinking; one of Jed's suggestions was that they install surveillance cameras. She knew businesses often had them outdoors, but how would they work spread over her acreage?

When she asked, his answer hadn't helped a whole lot.

"Let me see what I can find."

Niall suggested a circuitous route back, both to check fences and, she knew, to plot placements for other cameras. The idea seemed absurd, with her sprawling, open land and small herd of horses. None of this made any *sense*, yet she couldn't deny that the cameras, if they proved possible, would make her feel a lot safer.

The attacks so far were devastating enough, but what would happen next?

And what would she have done without Jed and, now, Niall?

*****

Erin had listened to the call on the police radio regarding the loose horses at the LB Kiger Ranch, but Chris was covering that part of the county today so she continued on with a routine patrol. Eventually she heard him report that a gate had been open and, while the owner claimed – he added a distinct emphasis to the word – that it had been secured with a padlock, he'd found the chain that might have held the gate closed on the ground and no padlock in the vicinity. Since Detective Dawson was there, Chris had gotten back on the road.

Did he have any idea how much of an ass he sounded? Erin wondered. Anybody listening – and you knew the sheriff was – could tell he didn't like Ms. Broussard *or* Detective Dawson.

A couple of hours later, she stopped by headquarters to have lunch, the salad she'd prepared at home this morning. She was heading back to her car when she saw Chris Jarman walking toward his own pickup truck. He tossed something into the bed of his truck that landed with a muffled clunk, then turned toward the back door she'd just come out of.

Seeing her, he said with a curled lip, "What are you staring at?"

"I was going to say hello." She shrugged and walked past him. Once she'd unlocked her patrol car, she glanced back. The heavy steel door was just closing.

Unable to resist the jab of curiosity, she hurried over to his pickup. What had he had acquired out patrolling that he needed to leave in his truck?

A dirt bike lay on its side, and she saw a pickaxe and a shovel loose on the rubber-lined bed. Closest was a wad of cloth – a ratty old T-shirt, she thought. Sneaking another look to be sure no one was watching, she picked it up, immediately feeling the weight inside. What was—

It was a padlock that had been cut open. Feeling sick, she stared at it. Why would he have taken it? There was no reason on earth for *him* to cut it in the first place and let those horses loose. Unless he was mad enough at Ms. Broussard for having complained about him?

If he'd done it, he had taken a terrible risk. Why hadn't he just wiped it to be sure there were no fingerprints and left it behind?

Because somebody else had been near enough to see?

An uncomfortable tingling up her spine pushed her to make up her mind what to do before Chris roared out that back door.

Hating this terrible suspicion, Erin yanked the tail of her uniform shirt loose and dropped the padlock onto the sack she'd formed with it. She wadded up the old T-shirt again and placed it right where it had been. Then she hurried to her car, heaving a big breath of relief once she was behind the wheel and could dump the padlock on the passenger seat. She'd wait until she was a few blocks away, then stop and grab an evidence bag out of the trunk.

Tomorrow, when nobody was paying any attention, she'd fingerprint the padlock and send in whatever she found. If she couldn't get a good print or there was no match…well, so be it. But she'd have settled her mind.

*****

Jed's shopping expedition took another chunk out of his day. He wanted to drive straight back to Linette's ranch, but still had to do his job. He went into headquarters, checked messages and returned a few calls, then printed out the email from the Crook County detective, detailing the cows found with what brands. Every single one had a calf at her side.

Then he called Austin Jackson even though it was midday and he knew Jackson worked at the lumberyard. He answered his phone on the fourth ring, though.

"This is Detective Dawson." Jed leaned back in his desk chair. "I have good news for you. We've recovered some of the stolen cattle, and your herd is among them."

The silence all but vibrated. "My whole herd?"

"Looks like. We're going to have to figure out the logistics of transporting them, but I'm guessing we'll get them to you by the end of the week."

"I can't believe it." Jackson was crying. "I thought—"

"I know. Unfortunately, we've found only a portion of the animals that were stolen. I'm glad yours were among them. Most of the larger ranches did carry insurance."

"Can you tell me where they are?"

"I can't give you details at this point. They're not in this county. We've made one arrest, but we don't believe this individual is among the rustlers. We think he agreed to hide some of the cattle. So far, he's refusing to give names, but I think his stance will change once he really understands the charges we're filing on him."

Austin expressed his thanks in a thickened voice.

Jed said he'd keep him informed.

He called another rancher who would be glad to get back his stolen cows and calves, although he'd had them insured. If sales prices stayed up, he'd be better off recovering the animals; if they dropped, he might be sorry. The third rancher, Blair Greenough, had a lot in common with Austin Jackson. Blair, too, held an outside job and dreamed of expanding his ranch. Given the news, he was as emotional as Jackson had been.

"I'm sorry if we gave you a hard time that day. You know, at the feed store. I guess I never thought—"

"Understood," Jed said gently.

Finally, he spoke to Hayden Webb, who had gone back to his job after arranging for a part-time caretaker for his father's ranch. His subdued thanks was understandable. He admitted that he and his sister were talking about trying to sell the ranch, but didn't expect to get much for it if they succeeded.

Grant had strolled into Jed's office while he was on the phone with Webb's son. After ending the call, he gave his boss the latest news about the cattle rustling, then told him about that morning's events at the LB Kiger ranch.

"Son of a bitch," Grant growled. "Somebody *tasered* a foal?"

Jed picked up his phone and found one of the photos he'd taken of the colt's rump and the trailing taser wires.

Grant looked, swore some more, and scrolled forward and back through the other photos. His mouth was tight when he returned the phone.

"Sounds like you need twenty-four hour a day surveillance."

"I bought cameras to supplement what Niall and I can do. We'll install them this afternoon."

"Most wireless ones don't have much range."

"I bought the best I could find." He'd spent over three thousand dollars, but he wasn't telling anyone that. "Eight cameras, some range extender antennas, and an app so we can monitor the cameras from our phones."

"You're going all out."

Jed challenged his boss with a stare. "What's the alternative? The attacks are going to escalate. I'm not leaving Linette to deal with them on her own."

Grant's smile was faint but present. "She have anything to do with you taking the job here?"

Was there any point in denying it? "Yeah. I, uh, came looking for her."

"An ex?"

"We were together for about a year before my last deployment." Jed moved his shoulders uncomfortably. "I broke up with her. Stupidest thing I've ever done. I don't know that it's fixable, but the least I can do is keep her safe. This ranch, it was her dream."

Grant nodded. "If there's anything I can do, you let me know."

"I'm still working the rustling investigation, but unless I'm needed for something important, I may cut back on hours for a week or so until we nail this fucker's hide to a wall."

Rising to his feet, Grant looked down at him. "That's not cutting back on hours, it's working two investigations. Like I said, if you need backup or anything else I can provide, it's yours. I hope I get a chance to meet this woman."

Jed couldn't keep himself from smiling. "Linette has a lot in common with Cassie."

"Stubborn and independent?"

"Oh, yeah."

Grant laughed and walked out.

Jed stuck his phone in a pocket and decided to visit a couple of his suspects again, just to keep them nervous. He'd hope to find Rob Fullerton home, too, and see if he got any feel for how hard Fullerton had taken his rejection at Linette's hands.

Then back to the ranch to start installing the cameras.

*****

Apparently, a camera would be aimed at the aisle in the barn, which made sense. The horses had been turned out earlier once the work on the fence was done, which made it possible for the men to work in here. Linette saw Jed climbing a ladder while Niall handed up tools. For a second, she lingered, watching as he reached over his head to drive in screws to secure the camera in place. It was hard *not* to look, given a chance when he was unaware of her presence.

He was such a beautiful man, powerful muscles bunched in his back and arms, sweat soaking his shirt in places and probably trickling down his spine beneath the waistband of his worn jeans. Having him here was bittersweet, with more of the sweet than she'd expected.

When she realized Niall was grinning at her, she beat a retreat.

Troy left at his usual five. He had stepped up in a way she wouldn't have guessed he could. She'd have to tell him so.

Tonight, Linette did the cooking, making a triple batch of spaghetti sauce that might even feed them a second night.

When they all sat down to eat together, Niall detailed what they'd accomplished, supported by an occasional grunt or word from Jed.

They had set up one DVR in a stall, where it was best situated to receive signals from the four cameras that had come with it. A second DVR was in a rain/sun-shelter in the far pasture. The cameras that had come with it were aimed at fence lines.

"But what if something happens when it's too dark?" she asked.

Jed set down his fork, his blue eyes meeting hers. "The ones I bought have infrared night vision. Not military quality, but better than nothing. Motion detection, too. Good HD resolution." He explained about being able to monitor the system from the cloud, using their phones.

"I'll pay you back for whatever this cost. How much *was* it?"

He shook his head. "I took care of it."

"I can't let you—"

If he said he owed her, she might blow up.

Jed being Jed, he said, "This is a police operation. Not your responsibility."

She narrowed her eyes at him. "We'll talk about this again."

He gazed blandly back at her.

Ever the peacemaker, Niall jumped in. "The trick was to hide the cameras. Lucky you have some good-sized trees in key positions."

There was the military mindset at work.

"Then you'll both be able to sleep tonight?" she asked.

Jed shook his head again. "We'll still take shifts. We just have more eyes on the ground now."

Niall cleared the table tonight and poured the coffee, after which Jed told them more about Oren Calderon.

"Wonder what they're holding over him that makes him afraid to talk and cut a deal," Niall commented.

Obviously brooding, Jed shook his head. "I have a good idea who two or three of the local men involved are. None of them are the sharpest knives in the drawer. These guys tried to put together a militia awhile back to lash out at the feds on the land issues. It was all talk, no action. Originally, I believed the rustling ring was made up of outsiders. Professionals. It was all so smooth, until Gary Webb confronted them."

"You think there's a…a ringleader," Linette said.

His laser-sharp eyes met hers. "I do. Can't figure out who it could be, although…" He trailed off, his frown deepening.

Linette set down her coffee mug with a clunk. "You have a suspicion."

"I do, but it's not someone I can name." He rolled his shoulders. "May be way off track."

Niall stirred. "You talked to Holcomb about it?"

"No. I won't until I have something more to go on."

He wouldn't say any more, which left Linette speculating wildly. She hadn't socialized much since moving here, but she did read the County Courier. With a relatively depressed economy, who in Hayes County would have even Jed leery?

Niall told a few stories while Jed became preoccupied by his phone. When Linette went out near bedtime to check on the horses, he accompanied her. They didn't talk, but she couldn't deny how reassuring his presence was. Remembering the creepy feeling that had dogged her in past weeks, she wondered how long it would be before she felt safe again doing something as simple as walking alone from the barn to the house at night.

Please, she thought, *let Jed catch this guy so I can begin.*

Not until she'd closed the barn doors again did he break the silence. "I've checked out all the men who asked you out, the ones whose names you remember."

"Do they know you were looking at them?"

"Rob Fullerton is the only one I actually spoke to."

She stopped. "Why?"

The motion-activated light on the peak of the barn roof abruptly went off, plunging them into darkness but for the glow from the living room windows and porch light. The darkness made her more conscious of the texture of Jed's voice. Rough and yet soft at the same time, he could arouse her with a few words when he turned to her in the middle of the night.

"Fullerton has a bad temper. He had a dishonorable discharge from the army, if that gives you an idea."

Linette shuddered. She hadn't even considered agreeing to a date with Rob, but he was a good-looking guy and she might have if she hadn't written men off altogether. To find out he was so like Theo...

"You really don't think the cattle rustlers are behind what's been happening here." She hadn't known she was going to ask again until the words were out.

"No," Jed said flatly.

Was she being a fool not to tell him about Theo? It made no sense to think he'd come after her, but the casual cruelty displayed by the man who'd driven a foal – a *baby* – out in front of an on-coming vehicle to die was something she could see Theo doing. Lacking any conscience, as she had eventually realized, he had enjoyed small acts of cruelty, from a vicious word to a hard kick. She'd been in the relationship with him for a couple of months before she noticed he had no real friends, and that what he wanted most from her was complete obedience to gratify his irrational need for control.

No, she didn't like Jed finding out how many apologies she'd accepted from Theo before she gathered her courage to leave him, but...it would be good to know for sure that he was back in Atlanta where he belonged.

Probably abusing another woman.

Only then did she realize that she hadn't resumed movement, and that Jed waited patiently a few feet from her, so still she was reminded that blending into any environment was as natural to him as breathing was to her. He had some help just now, though, as she'd come to a stop in the darkest place in the yard, beneath one of the spreading oak trees.

"I think maybe you should look for Theo, the man I lived with for a while after…" After *you*. "I don't see him looking for me now. I told you, it's been years, except… I don't know, but I think he might be a genuine sociopath. Hurting people amused him."

Jed didn't appear to have moved a muscle, but her skin prickled as she felt his rage wash over her.

"What's his last name?"

His voice was so quiet, so uninflected, Linette knew she was right about his reaction.

"Theodore Darcy Willis. He lives…lived in Smyrna last I knew, but since he was in an apartment…" She shrugged.

"I'll find him," Jed said curtly.

"He was a mistake." She had to talk to his back, since he was walking away. Having to scurry after him because she was afraid to be out here in the pleasantly cool night air by herself made her mad at him all over again.

CHAPTER THIRTEEN

Hyper-aware of Linette in the kitchen, doing some last cleanup, Jed sat at the dining room table with his laptop to do the research.

Logging in and out of law enforcement databases, it didn't take Jed fifteen minutes to learn enough about Theo Willis to make him sick to his stomach.

He very carefully closed the laptop. Almost immediately, Linette appeared in the open doorway, her face pinched. Sounding tentative, she asked, "Did you find…?"

"He's on the run, Linette. Wanted for murder."

What little color her face had retained drained away. She gripped the doorframe. "Murder?"

Jed struggled to rein in his emotions. This wasn't time to tell her how he had felt, reading about the damage that asshole had done to *her*. To know now how much worse Theo Willis might have done. Or wanted to do now.

"I'll call the investigator in the morning." To his ears, he sounded eerily calm. "There was a domestic abuse call to his apartment one evening. The next day, his boss called him in to fire him. The two of them were alone in the construction trailer. He strangled her, went back to his apartment and killed the girlfriend, too, packed up and left. They've been unable to locate him."

"Oh, dear God." She stumbled forward and almost fell into a chair across the table from him. "I never dreamed—"

"Maybe you should have, Linette." Was it fear or fury that had leaked into his voice? "Did you ever think of calling me?"

Her spine visibly stiffened and her head came up. "Why would I have?"

"Because you must have known I could take care of that son-of-a-bitch," he snapped.

She stood, completely steady now. "You hurt me more than he ever did, Jed." After a pause, she said, "Goodnight," and walked out of the room. A moment later, he heard her footsteps on the stairs.

Jed didn't move for a long time.

*****

A cluster of young men walk down the road toward the village. They talk animatedly amongst themselves, gesturing. Dust kicks up with every footstep. They circle a crater that an IED had opened to one side of the road. One points and they all laugh.

Jed's finger tightens infinitesimally on the trigger. He knew two men who died in that explosion.

His attention is tugged to a woman – presumably a woman – trailing well behind the men. He can tell almost nothing about her, since she wears an niqab over an all-enveloping black abaya. Although much of her face is hidden by the veil, he might see her eyes if she weren't looking down. But she walks steadily, never lifting her gaze. None of the men look back. They are at the most arrogant of ages. A mere woman may be invisible to them.

He shifts his view through the rifle scope between the men and the woman. She makes him uneasy. She carries a bundle – probably food or clothing – but he can't tell. He and Barry debate, just above a whisper that is probably not necessary given that they are six hundred yards from the road and have excellent cover between two sandstone abutments. If someone knew to look with high-powered binoculars, they might be seen, although that is a risk they often take.

They have been here for four days now, with few breaks, trading between sniping and spotting. The sun beats relentlessly down on them. Now the tension rises because a convoy is to use this road today. Bombs and attacks have made this stretch exceptionally dangerous. Almost impassable. His operation order is very clear.

"Forty-five minutes," his spotter murmurs.

The young men break up when they reach the village, going their separate ways, all eventually disappearing into various mud-colored houses. None are armed, that he can see. They appear carefree, although that can be deceptive.

The woman's head lifts when she realizes she's alone. The narrow strip between the naqib that covers her lower face and the black cloth wrapping her head shows too little for him to be sure she isn't a man hiding a bomb beneath the abaya – or not hiding it at all, if it is wrapped in the bundle.

She now fills his field of view, eliminating any awareness of his sweat or stench or hunger. His mind already works through the engagement sequence because his subconscious has sent the message that she is a threat, though she hasn't yet presented as one.

Despite the muffling effect of the naqib, he shifts the crosshairs from her chest to her head. He prefers the kind of shot that will drop her in place, allowing her no time to trigger a device or even shout.

She stops. Sinks to her knees.

"Fuck." Barry.

Nobody likes shooting a woman.

She almost falls forward to all fours, seems to push the bundle toward a pothole. Nobody else is visible in either direction on the road.

"Take the shot." He isn't sure if that is Barry's voice, or if he is telling himself. Despite a sharp jab of uncertainty, he has zeroed in on the side of her head.

He pulls the trigger.

She drops.

Barry is already scrambling back, but he doesn't move even as people come running from the village. One of the first to arrive is another woman. She trips over the bundle, which falls apart and reveals itself to be nothing but clothing.

One of the men rolls her to her back. That is when he sees what her abaya hid.

His mouth opens in a shout—

*****

The light Linette had turned on in the hall let her see Jed sitting up in bed, the quilt pooled below his waist. He stared straight ahead, horror on his face. She wasn't sure he was awake.

"Jed."

He didn't move. He was naked from the waist up, every muscle standing out, locked in tension.

"Jed." She hurried to the bedside. "Wake up. Please. Wake up."

His head turned toward her, his eyes colorless and yet searing. Did he see her? Or only whatever monstrous memory had come to him in his sleep?

Stopping next to the bed, she started to reach out but was afraid to actually touch him.

"I...I heard you yell, and I wanted to be sure you're okay. Maybe you have nightmares all the time, but if it's because of what's happening here, I'm sorry." Oh God, she was babbling. "Um, will you say something? You're scaring me."

He blinked a couple of times, groaned and flopped back against the pillows. "Sorry," he mumbled. "I don't usually—"

"Have awful dreams?"

"Make any noise." He rolled his head, shoulders, relaxing his fingers with seeming deliberation.

She hadn't seen his bare chest in five years. If anything, he was now more perfectly sculpted, although she couldn't imagine him lifting weights in front of a mirror or anything like that. His muscles were purely functional, never intended for show.

She wasn't at his bedside to gawk, Linette told herself severely.

"You didn't use to have nightmares," she said.

His head turned. "I did. I never wanted you to know."

The reminder of the many ways he'd shut her out felt like a knife sliding between her ribs. She nodded.

"Don't look like that."

"Like what?" she asked, trying to school her expression.

"As if—" His mouth thinned, but he continued, "I hurt you."

"You didn't have to hide from me," she said honestly. "I would have loved all of you."

He flinched. "I…didn't believe that. I wasn't even sure—" He didn't stop quite soon enough.

"That you wanted me to," she finished, hoping her bitterness hadn't leaked into her voice. "I got that."

He scrubbed his hand over his face. "You don't understand."

Suddenly weary, she said, "It doesn't matter, Jed. What's done is done. I'll let you sleep—"

His hand caught hers before she could back away. "Wait."

Not moving at all, she whispered, "Wait for what?"

"I don't know. Will you stay for a minute? Maybe sit down?"

There was something in his voice she'd never heard. Not quite a plea, but…close? And…sit on the bed right beside him? He wouldn't be completely naked, would he? No, surely he'd wear at least boxer shorts in case something happened.

What had ever made her think she could resist Jed Dawson?

Hesitantly, she sat, tucking one foot under her so that she could face him. She wished she could see him better, but didn't reach for the lamp. He looked away for a minute as if he didn't know what to say.

But *he* was the one who'd asked her to stay. So she asked, "Are your nightmares always about things that happened when you were deployed?"

He surprised her by answering. "Mostly. I have recurring dreams." He frowned a little. "I always have."

"Really? And you remember them?"

The sound he made wasn't a laugh. It was too pained. "When you have the same one enough times, you remember."

"Was tonight's one of those?"

His chest rose and fell with a long breath. "Yeah."

"Will you tell me about it?"

His eyes were a darker blue than usual, clouded rather than piercing. "Why do you have to know?" He was trying to suppress his anger, but it seeped through.

Apparently, he could go only so far.

Still, she tried. "It might help if you talked about it." Then she felt dumb. "Well, you probably have with friends."

Time to go. She shifted her weight in preparation for standing up, but didn't get any further before his hand caught hers. "No," he said hoarsely. "We don't talk about what we did or saw. Nobody wants to."

Staying completely still, Linette absorbed that. Was it just a man thing? Or was living with bad memories easier if you never aired them out? *She* certainly didn't like thinking about her stepfather or, worse, her mother.

Jed's hand tightened. "What are you thinking?"

"That maybe I'm a hypocrite, because there's something I never talk about, either."

"Would it help if you did?"

She was the one to avert her face this time. "I doubt it."

Very quietly, he said, "I will if you will."

She gaped at him. "You mean that."

Voice low, he said haltingly, "I'm…trying, Linette."

Did he really want her back? Could she believe that? Had he changed enough… She didn't want to finish that thought.

Oh, why not tell him? It had happened a long time ago. This could be a sort of test. Would he really reciprocate?

"My stepfather sexually molested me." It wasn't so hard to say after all. "He was good to me until I started getting a figure. I was thirteen the first time he…touched me."

Good to me. She'd had to use *those* words?

"Son of a bitch." Jed's hand had tightened until it was nearly crushing hers. "Did he rape you?"

"Yes. Yes! Only a few times." She had to take a moment just to breathe. "I broke his nose, and then I ran away from home."

"You were a street kid?"

"Not for long," she said bitterly. "The police picked me up and brought me back. He never did it again, but I had to live four more years at home always thinking he would. Listening for sounds at night. For a long time, I braced a chair under my bedroom doorknob." The confidence she'd felt as an adult had evaporated all too quickly when she realized someone had been in her house while she slept.

"Jesus," Jed whispered. "The police officer didn't believe you?"

"I didn't tell him. The only person—" No, that was the worst part.

But of course Jed guessed. "You told your mother."

"She wouldn't even look me in the eye. She kept saying, 'I don't believe you. Why are you making this up? He's been *good* to you!'"

Of course Jed caught the repetition. He swore again. "I guessed there was something, but..." He shook his head. "No wonder you've given up on men." He sounded...sad.

Didn't he get it? It wasn't men she'd given up on, it was *everyone*. She had no basis for trust.

He had even less, she suspected. He'd admitted to having grown up in a series of foster homes. At least she'd had the early years. The memories of her father, faded but not completely forgotten, of the days when she had a child's certainty that her mother loved her. Yes, even the first few years when she'd seen how hard Lloyd was trying to gain her trust.

Some of that had proved to be untrue: her mother's love had limits, and Lloyd had likely been grooming her to be his victim. Or maybe not. She'd never know.

Still. She had a bedrock that Jed didn't.

"Your turn," she said flatly.

"God." He contemplated the ceiling. "I've killed a lot of people."

"I...assumed you had."

"Sometimes I had a specific target. All I had to do was identify him and—"

Blow his head off. That was what he didn't want to say, wasn't it?

"Sometimes it wasn't that clear-cut. We had to make snap judgements. I made mistakes. This nightmare..." He swallowed. For once, his usually impassive face held desolation. "I shot a woman in an abaya. Those are robes—"

"I know what they are."

"We couldn't always be sure that what we saw was really a woman. The robes made an effective disguise for a man carrying weapons or a bomb." He waited until she nodded. "This time, I thought she was placing an IED in a hole in the road. She knelt—" He did nothing but breathe for a minute. "One of our convoys was due in less than an hour to take that route." His fingers dug into her hand. Even in this light, the knotted muscles in his jaws showed. "I shot her." He said it as if he felt nothing. "As she fell, she dropped the bundle in her hands. It was just clothes. People came running from the village up the road. One of them rolled her onto her back." He hesitated. This had to be the bad part. "I saw her belly. I'd just shot and killed a pregnant woman. She must have been nearly due. Of course, I killed her baby, too."

"Oh, Jed," Linette whispered. She scooted nearer to him on the bed. "You were doing a job."

He grunted. "Is that an excuse? How am I supposed to forgive myself for that, Linette? Is it even possible?"

"Do you know how much I hated whoever decided to make you be a sniper?" she exclaimed passionately. "Were you chosen only because you were a good shot? Did they ever think about what they were doing to you?"

"We were at war. Soldiers kill. Why not me? Why pick someone else instead? I was good at what I did." He said that with loathing so terrible, it had to be the acid that ate at him from deep inside.

Linette's eyes burned. She wanted more than anything to wrap her arms around him and never let go. At that moment, she had an epiphany. He didn't have to change for her to love him.

Only...it would be smart to think about that before she said anything she'd regret.

"You must have saved lives," she said, almost a random.

He let out a ragged breath. "I did. Not so sure that balances the scales, though."

"You saved Cassie Ward's life."

Jed didn't look at her. "Killing from a distance should be cleaner than up close. It's not. Through my scope, I'm an arm's reach from my victim. I see his expression just before he dies. I see the spurt of blood. I can feel the heat of it spilling over my hands."

"No." Linette lifted his hand. "There's no blood here. You did a hard job. I've...I've read that some snipers keep a count. They can brag about how many kills they made."

"I kept a record. We all did. Had to note all the details to learn from what worked and what didn't."

"Why didn't you tell me all this, when we were together?"

He turned an almost blank expression on her. "I grew up on my own." He said that almost gently. "I learned early to stay guarded. Even now, with you...maybe especially with you," he amended, "I feel as if I've stripped. I'm standing naked in the cold, goosebumps all over, my cock shriveling. I can't defend myself, all I can do is wait."

Her heart cramped painfully. She'd demanded this from him? Was that love? But she had to ask.

"What are you waiting for?"

"How would I know?" he said simply.

"Oh, God, Jed." She threw herself at him, wrapped her arms around him as well as she could, laid her head on his shoulder. "I'm sorry! I'm sorry! I should never have—"

"Hush," he murmured, his mouth close to her ear. "It's okay. I shouldn't have said that. What you survived... I wish I'd known."

It would have made no difference. She knew that. More likely, he wouldn't have let himself get involved with her in the first place if he had suspected she, too, was damaged. Vulnerable. He'd have been so afraid of hurting her, he couldn't have let himself take anything from her.

He must feel her hot, salty tears on his neck and shoulder. Did they feel the same as blood? Horrible thought.

She cried silently even as she fought to regain control. He must hate having a weeping woman in his arms. But when she quit crying and tried to roll away, his strong arms didn't release her.

"Please," he whispered. "Will you just lie here with me? Let me hold you?"

She wanted so desperately to do that, her alarms screamed. Never again, remember? Even if he wanted to renew their relationship, how could she ever trust that he wouldn't again cut her off as if she didn't mean anything?

She couldn't.

"No!" She sounded frantic to her own ears as she struggled to escape his embrace. Once she'd sat up and scooted away, poised to jump off the bed, she said, "No. This is ridiculous. You just want to hold me? I'm supposed to be deeply touched? You already made it clear that you don't want me at all. I can't even imagine why you're—"

He sat up, his eyes blazing. "Not want you? You know better than that."

"You walked out on me!" Dear lord, she was screaming at him. "When you told me to have a good life, I got the message!"

Teeth bared, he shouted, "I never said anything like that!"

They stared at each other with quivering intensity Linette wanted to think was hostility.

"As for not wanting you," he said, the softness all the more effective given what came before, "I can demonstrate."

"Don't you dare." She inched back, but he moved faster than her, throwing back the covers and landing on his feet even as she flung herself off the bed.

He did wear gray knit boxer shorts. Somehow, they didn't do an awful lot to counteract the expanse of powerful chest dusted with gold.

"One kiss, Linette."

*****

It was his fault she wanted to flee. He had wounded her more than he'd known. How could he not have guessed that her physical shyness with him, coupled with the estrangement from her mother and stepfather, added up to a logical conclusion?

Jed knew better than to lay a hand on her now. Play-wrestling had been one thing when she'd trusted him, something else altogether now.

"That's all I'll ask tonight," he promised, voice hoarse.

As wide-eyed and cautious as a doe approaching a water hole and seeing an animal that might be a predator there before her, Linette didn't move.

Predator? Suddenly disgusted with himself, Jed took a step back. "I'm scaring you. That's the last thing I want to do. Go to bed, Linette."

Her chin came up. "I'm not scared of you. I'm angrier than I should be after all these years, but I know you're not like Theo or Lloyd. You'd never hurt me, or force me."

Christ. She'd been raped by one man and battered by another. And then there was what he'd done.

"Thank you for that," he said wryly. "I'm just the bastard who dumped you with no explanation. Forget what I said."

Her eyes searched his with an intensity he didn't entirely understand. "You moved here because of me."

Hadn't they already done this? He'd as much as admitted to being a gutless wonder. He'd been so near to her, but hadn't been able to take that last step.

"You know I did."

"Why?" Lines gathered between her eyebrows. "You came back from your deployment four years ago."

"I've been here almost a year."

"That leaves three years in between. Did you even give me a thought?"

"I asked Niall about you. He said you were living with a guy. What was I supposed to do?"

"You didn't consider just calling to say hello?"

"How could I, after the way I treated you?" Seeing his name displayed, she wouldn't have answered. He made himself say the rest. "I was really messed up. You deserved someone better than me."

Linette whispered, "Oh, Jed." Eyes dark and troubled, she stepped forward, cupped his jaw with her slim, calloused hands, and rose on tiptoe. She pressed her lips to his.

He froze under fire, although his heart accelerated its beat enough to make him dizzy.

After a second, she dropped back to her heels, and Jed saw that he'd blown it again.

"Linette." His voice was pure gravel. "I came after you because you're the one person who makes me *feel*." He took her hand and laid it over his heart. No way she'd miss the tumult inside. He tried again. "You scared me." Did she understand what he was saying?

"Oh, Jed," she murmured again. God, he hoped that wasn't pity on her face.

His hands shook, but he didn't let himself back away however desperately that's what he wanted to do. Instead, he bent his head slowly, giving her time to retreat. She went on tiptoe again to meet him.

He kissed her with blind ferocity, with, yeah, desperation. His hands sought every remembered curve and dip, her pulse at her throat, the thick silk of her hair. And damn, she kissed him back as if she felt the same. It went on and on – his tongue in her mouth, hers answering, chasing his. Her arms locked around his neck as if she needed him to keep her on her feet.

He had to pull his mouth from hers to breathe, but filled his lungs and dove deep again. This was even better than he remembered, a jolt of adrenaline and hope and the connection with her that had once scared the shit out of him.

Still did, a part of him knew, but this was a risk he had to take.

He started to move her toward the bed. She didn't seem to notice until the back of her legs came up against it, and then she stiffened in his arms.

Jed wrenched his mouth from hers and looked down at her. Her eyes were dilated, her cheeks scraped red by his morning beard, her lips noticeably swollen – and she was the most beautiful thing he'd ever seen.

Not sure he was verbal right now, he got out one word. "Yes?"

The pause was long enough to send a chill over his skin.

"No." She shook her head. "No. I didn't expect… I don't know if… I'm sorry." She tore herself away and bolted from the room and across the hall before he so much as turned to look after her.

At the sound of her bedroom door closing, he jerked.

No.

CHAPTER FOURTEEN

Just getting dressed was a task that felt like too much. Linette dragged herself out of bed, found clean clothes and did it anyway.

She also did a little praying. *Please let Jed be gone for the day*.

Halfway down the stairs, she smelled bacon and coffee. A moment later, the low murmur of two men's voices drifted up. Crap. Unless Troy had come in?

No, she knew the velvet deepness of Jed's voice. She would recognize it anywhere.

She hesitated, squared her shoulders and entered the kitchen. Both men turned immediately, although she'd swear she hadn't made a sound.

"Good morning, sunshine!" Niall said with a grin.

Jed… Well, she didn't let herself meet his gaze.

"I'm glad somebody is cheerful," she said grumpily. "Why aren't you tired?"

"I'm always cheerful. Hadn't you noticed?"

On the surface, he was.

Jed turned his back to her as he apparently stirred scrambled eggs. Bacon was draining on a paper towel on the counter beside him.

"I'm ready to get some more work in on that fence," Niall added. "Troy just checked for supplies and says he isn't finding the nails. I think we used up what we had yesterday. I'm supposed to ask you. He's afraid you guys forgot to get them. Do you have more stashed somewhere"

"Nails? Oh, crud. No, I guess I just assumed there were enough out there." She made a face. "I don't remember buying any recently." Although right this minute, she was so aware of Jed's silent presence, her memory wasn't as sharp as it could be.

Niall shrugged. "That's okay. One of us will run into town and pick some up. Won't take long. Only thing is, we'll have to borrow your truck. Troy's mother dropped him off half an hour ago. His wouldn't start."

"I'm not in any hurry this morning," Jed said. "Why don't you take mine? It's parked out front. Toast done?" he asked.

Niall hurried to butter two pieces that had popped up who knew how long ago. "Should we ask Troy if he wants to join us?"

Linette shook her head. "He always says no. He'll have had breakfast, and he's pretty shy, in case you haven't noticed." These two men seemed to intimidate him, besides.

Why did Jed want to linger? Fingers crossed it wasn't to talk to her. She hadn't come to terms with last night's epiphany – or her instinctive resistance.

Niall did most of the talking over the breakfast table, although Linette and Jed responded to direct questions. She had no doubt Niall noticed the tension between her and Jed, though.

Once they'd cleared their plates, Jed pulled out his keys and handed them to Niall, who nodded his thanks.

Linette pushed back her chair. "Put anything you buy on my account."

"Sure thing. I may send Troy and start hauling everything else out to the broken section. Damn, I'd love to run an electric wire."

She opened her mouth, but he grinned.

"No, I don't want to zap the horses, only the humans." He winked at Jed, who sat stolidly at the table sipping coffee, and departed.

Ignoring Jed, Linette stacked dirty dishes. After she'd finished loading the dishwasher and came back out, she found him still there.

"I need to get to work," she said.

"Will you sit down for a minute?"

She hesitated, then did.

"I got too pushy last night," he said gruffly. "I need to apologize."

She could say, *Thank you*, and scuttle outside, but that would leave him with the wrong impression. She didn't feel ready to talk to him about this, but hurting him didn't seem to be an option.

"No, it wasn't like that," she said. "*I* kissed you. I just, um, freaked out. I'd sworn I was done with you."

"And all other men."

"And all other men," she agreed. "Except I know you're trying to, I don't know, let me in. You've confused me, and I'm not sure what I want anymore, okay? I need time."

Outside, Troy or Niall started the truck and she was vaguely aware of the engine sound receding down the driveway.

As usual, she couldn't tell what Jed was thinking even though his eyes continued to meet hers.

After a minute, he said, "Take all the time you need, Linette. Just know—" He shook his head hard. "There I go again. I can wait."

The front door slammed open. "Jed!" Niall yelled. "Something happened down the road. Maybe an accident."

Between one heartbeat and the next, Jed's expression locked down. He leaped to his feet and ran, Linette right behind him. *Not Troy*, was all she could think.

Halfway to the barn, Jed spun. "I need your truck."

"I'll drive." Feeling sick, she raced for the shed where she parked. Despite hands that shook, she got the key in the ignition and accelerated out of the shed at an unsafe speed, slamming on the brakes when she reached the two men.

Jed leaped into the passenger side. "Go!"

She stepped on the gas even as she said, "Isn't Niall—?"

"He's sticking to be sure this isn't a diversion."

At the road, she glanced both ways out of habit, then turned toward town. Not fifty yards from her driveway, she entered the first curve.

Jed swore. "He's in a ditch."

Yet another pickup, this one old and battered, was parked on the far shoulder. A man was yanking at the driver's side door of Jed's charcoal gray truck.

His head turned when he heard them. "The man's hurt! Help me get him out!"

Oh, dear God. Linette set the emergency brake and put her gear shift into park before leaping out. Jed had already reached his own truck and the other man.

She didn't know the older guy beside Jed, but had waved at him in passing. He, too, must work at Arrowhead Creek.

Jed had his phone in his hand. Within seconds, he was talking on it urgently. Feeling queasy, Linette hurried.

He stopped her from getting too close with a hand on her arm. "He's been shot. An ambulance is on its way."

"Shot?" she echoed, feeling stupid. Why would anybody want to shoot a nineteen-year-old kid... "Someone thought it was you," she whispered, horrified by the glistening blood that made Troy's features unrecognizable.

Jed wasn't listening. Instead, he added his strength to the other man's and the door gave way with a metallic groan. The next moment, he bent inside the cab and examined Troy, slumped sideways, held up only by his seatbelt.

Dragging her attention from the two bullet holes forming odd spider webs through the windshield, she asked, "What can I do?"

"Open this." He grabbed a large metal box from behind the seat. "Get me some wipes and gauze pads."

She set the box on the road. When she struggled to unlatch it, the other man crouched and helped her. "Thank you," she said shakily.

"You folks have been having your problems."

She nodded distractedly. Ripping open a packet of wipes, she passed them to Jed, who was careful not to move Troy but used the wipes to find the damage. Eventually, he accepted the pads she held out and pressed a couple to the side of Troy's head.

Scared and sick, she felt helpless. Her phone. Did she have her phone? She'd have to call Troy's mother, tell her to meet her son at the clinic. He'd be evaluated there, and then likely sent on a Life Flight to the hospital in Madras.

If he lived long enough.

*****

A lengthy search turned up absolutely nothing. There were places on the higher ground to the north where a trained sniper or experienced hunter could have set up unseen, but if that was the case, he left no sign, and Jed had plenty of experience at finding that kind of evidence. He thought these shots had been taken from closer, anyway. Probably ten to twenty-five feet, and the shooter had still failed to make a definite kill shot.

Jed wasn't sure he'd have heard a car. Kirk Wise, the man who'd already been at the scene, insisted no vehicle had passed him in the last mile or so. There were driveways, though, and one intersection almost a mile from here. The shooter could have come that far on foot. Alternatively, if he was driving, he could have continued on toward the Arrowhead Creek Ranch, found someplace to duck out of sight.

Jed sent a deputy down the road to look.

He had to believe he'd been the intended target. Once the EMTs had eased Troy out of the truck and onto a gurney, Jed had seen Troy's bloody Stetson on the passenger side floor where it had fallen. Not exactly the same color as Jed's, but close enough. His truck, to all appearances his hat.

Me.

Guilt twisted in his gut. He'd had no reason to believe anybody was after him…but this wouldn't have happened if Troy had taken Linette's truck.

His suspicion turned to the obvious suspects: the cattle rustlers. They might believe that, if they eliminated him, the hunt would slow. They were wrong. Grant had been a detective in Arizona before coming home to Fort Halleck. Unlike FHPD chief Seward, he knew how to pursue an investigation. Making Grant angry wouldn't be smart. Besides which, killing a cop would bring other agencies down on the stupid SOBs.

He turned to see Linette hovering beside her pickup, fingers laced together, face betraying her anxiety. Her eyes never left him as he walked over to her.

"You haven't heard anything?"

Jed shook his head. "No news is good news. Someone would have called me if he died."

He knew she'd informed the boy's mother. The search had taken long enough, Troy was either on his way to the hospital or had already arrived. Jed would have been informed if the boy had regained consciousness, too. It was unlikely he'd be able to identify the shooter, but miracles happened.

Linette crossed her arms tightly. "You have to go, don't you?"

"In a minute." Much as he wanted to hold her, he was aware of the nearby deputies, one of whom was Jarman. He kept his voice low for the same reason. "Are you okay?"

"Yes." She lifted one shoulder, her expression wry. "Not really, but I'll manage."

Shit. He'd give a lot to stay with her. He wouldn't have left her if Niall hadn't been waiting for her.

"You need to take my truck, don't you?" she continued, uncrossing her arms so she could dig in the pocket of her jeans. "I can walk back—"

"No." He laid a hand on her arm, and she looked up. "I won't leave you two stranded. I'll hitch a ride." He nodded toward the deputies waiting for him. "Be careful today. Stay in the barn as much as you can."

"But it wasn't me—"

His fingers tightened. "No, but we can't be sure what the goal was. Does whoever pulled the trigger know Niall is here? This might have been an attempt to isolate you."

He would have regretted scaring her if he didn't believe that Theodore Darcy Willis had targeted her. Like most cops, Jed was highly suspicious of coincidences. Theo had murdered two women eleven weeks ago and then vanished. Another woman he'd once brutalized – a woman who'd not only called the cops on him but also walked away from him – was now living in fear after a number of incidences that ranged from puzzling through scary all the way to vicious. Sounded like his *modus operandi*.

Linette *needed* to be afraid.

She nodded. "I'm not stupid."

Jed's mouth curved. "No," he said softly. "Stubborn, though…"

She made a face at him. Then, solemn again, she said, "You be careful, too, Jed. Somebody tried to kill *you*. I wish I thought you'd stay safe in your office."

"You know I can't." He released her arm and took a step back. "I'm hard to kill, you know."

Resignation and something else he couldn't identify crossed her face. But all she said was, "Please keep me informed about Troy," and opened the door and hopped into her truck.

A minute later, that pickup disappeared around the curve.

*****

Jed's call confirmed what Grant had already heard over the police radio. Deeply disturbed by the news, Grant picked up his own phone. Chief Seward might have heard, but if not it was Grant's obligation to let him know that it appeared someone was, once again, shooting at local law enforcement officials.

As was too frequently the case, he had to wait on hold for several minutes before Seward picked up.

"We have reason to believe an attempt was made to kill Detective Dawson this morning," Grant told him. "Thought you should know."

After a pause, the police chief said, "He's annoyed more than his share of residents in this county."

Stunned not so much by the sentiment as by Seward's indiscretion in expressing it, Grant couldn't help noticing that any concern about whether Jed had survived the attempt was conspicuously lacking.

The chief added hastily, "That didn't come out the way I meant."

"Didn't it?"

"You have to admit, he's more aggressive than any of your other deputies." The tinge of dislike was unmistakable.

Grant said carefully, "A police detective's job is to look for the truth. To do that job well takes a certain attitude, don't you think?"

"Of course. Guess I'm just wondering if this was personal, or if it has to do with that cattle rustling investigation of his."

"I doubt it was personal. If I'd believed that, I wouldn't have called you. Since I assume this shooting has to do with Detective Dawson's job, I thought you might want to warn your officers to keep a sharp eye out."

"I'll do that. Ah…I hope he wasn't badly injured."

"A teenage boy who'd borrowed his pickup truck was shot instead."

This silence must have lasted thirty seconds. "A *boy*?" His shock was apparent. "Was he killed?"

"He's in critical condition."

"Why would Dawson let anyone drive his pickup?"

Given the strangeness of some of Chief Seward's responses, Grant wasn't sure he wanted to answer that question. He knew he wasn't going to name the victim. "I understand the loan was for a quick errand while the detective was having breakfast."

"I see. That's, ah, unfortunate."

That a boy had been shot? Or that Jed *hadn't* been shot?

"Yes, it is. Now, I have other calls to make…"

"Of course, of course. You'll keep us informed?"

Grant lied. He had no intention of sharing any more information with Harrison Seward. Damn, he wished Seward would retire and the city council and mayor would hire a truly competent replacement.

*****

Half of Jed's drive back to Fort Halleck from the hospital in Madras had been spent on the phone. He'd learned that the damage to his truck was limited to the right front fender and headlight as well as the windshield – and the tears and blood on the driver side headrest. Didn't mean fixing it wasn't going to cost, although insurance would cover all but the deductible. Donald Rooney, the owner of the auto body shop, had promised the pickup would be ready tomorrow morning.

Jed had been glad to be able to call Linette and let her know that Troy was awake and talking, that the bullet had ricocheted off his cranium. The MRI had showed some damage to the parietal bone, and there was swelling beneath, so the doctor intended to keep him for what might be several days.

He spoke to the Crook County detective, who was supervising as the stolen cattle were loaded for return to their owners. Oren Calderon had just paid bail and walked, still having refusing to name confederates. Apparently, it hadn't occurred to him that he might be safer in jail.

Between phone calls, Jed brooded. He was stuck on his own question. Now what? Make the rounds and lean on all his suspects again? Look for recent transplants to the county in hopes of unmasking Theo Willis? Ask sheriff's departments in neighboring counties to do the same, in case Willis had the brains not to be living here in Hayes County?

His instincts said Willis hadn't dared rent an apartment or house, and wasn't working, either. Either way, he'd be taking a big chance. Plus, with a relative small population, he'd risk being recognized if police flashed his picture around. More likely, he was staying outside the area – or had found someone he could use. Someone who was putting him up and asking no questions, very likely a woman who had no idea what a monster she'd taken in.

Jed did now have a photograph from Willis's last, and still unexpired, driver's license. After printing it out, he had stared at it for longer than he would want to admit.

He'd been uneasy to see parallels with him. They didn't share any resemblance in facial features or coloring, thank God, but their builds were similar. According to the driver's license, Willis had brown hair, although in the photo his head was shaved. He wore a close-cut beard in the currently popular style. Jed guessed the guy, now that he was on the run, had either grown out the beard as a disguise, or shaved his square jaw. Good bet that he'd let his hair grow, too, although it would still be short.

His eyes were brown, his nose a little crooked, as if it had been broken at some point, and his smile was closer to a sneer. His gaze had seemed to challenge the photographer, as if he resented having to submit to authority even in the form of the driver's licensing bureau.

Jed wanted to ask Linette how they'd met, why the guy had attracted her, why she'd let him treat her like shit before remembering she had a spine. But no, that last question wasn't one he'd ever ask. Given that she'd been sexually molested by a man she should have been able to trust, abandoned by another one – him – she might have been doomed to make bad choices where men were concerned.

In her mind – and he couldn't deny it – *he* was one of those bad choices.

Was it remotely possible she might give him another chance? Jed thought that's what she'd implied…but couldn't be sure. He knew he'd never forgive himself for walking out on her the way he had.

He pulled into the lot behind headquarters and turned off the engine, but sat for a minute trying to shake off his personal issues. He kept a wary eye out for Chris Jarman as he crossed the parking lot, knowing he might blow his top if the swaggering bastard said the wrong thing right now.

Inside, he saw Erin Brown coming out of the women's restroom.

"Hey," he said, nodding as he passed her.

"Detective?"

Jed stopped and turned around. "Something on your mind?"

She took a deep breath. "Normally I wouldn't tattle, but I heard something that bothered me."

Jed waited.

"Chris was talking on his cell phone. He didn't see me. What he was saying was probably all hot air, but…I didn't like it. I have no idea who he was talking to, but he said that you being buddy-buddy with the sheriff didn't make you untouchable."

"Untouchable," Jed echoed.

She nibbled nervously on her lower lip. "He sounded so angry, I had goosebumps rise on my arms."

"You're sure he didn't see you?"

Erin nodded.

"Then what I want is for you to do your best to stay away from him. He may associate you with his embarrassment because you're the one who did the follow-up with Ms. Broussard. I doubt he'll try to pull anything, but he obviously doesn't appreciate being corrected. I did discuss the incident with Sheriff Holcomb, who spoke to him. He didn't like it."

"Then he's even madder."

"That's possible." He smiled. "Like you said, he was probably just venting, and he'll get over it. But if he wants to take me on, that's fine by me."

"Okay." She hesitated. "I did something— Oh, it doesn't matter. Gosh, I'd better get back out on the road. Thanks."

"Stay safe."

He watched until she pushed through the heavy exterior door before continuing on his way. What had she done?

Once Grant waved him into his office, Jed shelved the question. He had trouble making himself sit, but he didn't want to give away how unsettled he felt by pacing.

His boss raised his eyebrows. "Do you have anything new?"

Jed shared his conversation with Detective Frazier in Crook County. "Calderon could be a flight risk." Or at risk of having his mouth shut permanently.

Grant grunted. He leaned forward, elbows on his desk. "I had a strange conversation with Chief Seward."

"I've never had anything but."

Grant reacted with a quick grin, then started talking. Jed listened intently. At the end, Jed said, "You thinking what I'm thinking?"

"Reluctantly."

"Seward's no dummy."

Grant's gaze sharpened. "Are you back to your theory that none of your suspects could possibly be the brains behind the organization?"

"Yeah." He tipped his head back for a minute, contemplating the ceiling. "I could take a quiet look at his place."

"He's got to have some employees."

Jed released a breath and met Grant's eyes. "I have another idea."

CHAPTER FIFTEEN

At the sound of a deep-throated engine outside the barn, Linette hurried to the open door. The unmarked black SUV had all the hallmarks of a law enforcement vehicle. Jed parked it and stepped out, his gaze finding her in the shadows just inside the barn as if she were jumping up and down, waving her hands.

A wave of relief washed away the unrelenting tension of the day. Just seeing him shouldn't have so powerful an effect, but how could she resist this tumble of emotion? Caught in the moment, she rushed out to meet him.

She hadn't intended to throw herself into his arms, but when he pulled her against him, she didn't resist him. It felt so good to lean on him, feel his strength, to wrap her arms around his solid torso.

He made a ragged sound. "This is what I wanted to do this morning. With the other deputies still there, though…"

"It's okay. I didn't expect to be comforted."

"You should have a right to expect it." He sounded…offended.

She lifted her head from that broad chest. "Why me?"

He frowned. "You're so determined not to need anyone."

"Aren't you, too?"

Unblinking, he held her gaze for so long, she gathered herself to step back. But then he spoke. "I have been, but I was wrong."

He meant…he would come to *her* when he needed to be held? To talk about something troubling? Her cynical side wondered if he meant it. She was stunned to discover that she believed he was being honest. The very fact that he looked unhappy was convincing. He would *hate* the idea of laying himself out there. Had he finally understood…?

If this was a con job, he would finally break her.

No. Just *no*. What she'd do was summon again the resolve that had allowed her to go on. To make a life free of emotional ties. She'd done it once, she could do it again.

His mouth tightened. "I don't like what you're thinking."

"Tough." Surprising even herself, she rose on tiptoes and pressed a kiss to his jaw. "I'm glad you're here, but right now, I left a horse cross-tied and wondering where I disappeared to."

Jed released her. She identified his expression as bemusement. Over her shoulder, she added, "Give me a minute, and I'll come in to put dinner on."

*****

Niall was just stepping out of the bathroom with a towel wrapped around his waist when he saw Jed at the foot of the stairs, frowning up at him.

Irritation obvious, Jed said, "You couldn't take your clothes in with you?"

Amused at his suspicion that Jed feared his girlfriend might fall into lust with him if she set eyes on his semi-naked body, Niall grinned. "Don't worry. Just wasn't thinking."

Still not sounding real warm and fuzzy, Jed said, "Dinner's ready. Biscuits might be gone if you don't get down here quick enough."

Niall yanked on sweats and a faded T-shirt. He didn't bother with shoes or combing his hair. If these biscuits were sourdough like his mother made, he didn't want to miss them.

In fact, once he got to the table, he saw that the biscuits smelled amazing and were golden brown. Oh, yeah, these were the real deal, sourdough biscuits from starter she kept going. He and Clarissa had gone to Linette and Jed's apartment a few times for dinner. He'd forgotten what a good cook she was.

As they dug into a really good stir fry, the conversation was a hundred percent produced by Niall and Linette. That wasn't unusual; if nothing said demanded Jed's participation, he didn't bother talking.

Of course, he might still be annoyed.

"Thank God Troy wasn't hurt worse." That was Linette.

"Hard head," Niall suggested.

She hoped the kid's mother remembered to pick up his truck from the mechanic.

Jed finally thought to tell them he'd bought the nails Troy had been on his way to the hardware store to buy. "Forgot I had them. I'll go out and grab 'em after dinner."

"Any chance you can take a couple of hours in the morning to help me with the fence?" Niall asked.

"I can—" Linette started to say.

"Planning to," Jed agreed.

She made a huffing sound. Niall would have grinned if she, too, wasn't already mad at him. In her case, she'd hinted that he cook tonight, and not been happy when he told her he wouldn't leave her alone at the barn.

Jed dished up a second helping for himself and grabbed two more biscuits, which he buttered. Then he set down his knife. "I have a proposition," he said to Niall.

Immediately wary, Niall asked, "What?"

"I'd like you to apply for the open position at the Fort Halleck P.D."

Niall dropped his fork and stared at him. "You're kidding me. You want me to do what I said I wouldn't, and oh, by the way, leave Linette alone all day, every day?"

Now they were both gaping at him. "I think the police chief is dirty," Jed said bluntly.

Eyes wide, Linette jumped to her feet. "If you two need to talk alone—"

He shook his head. "I know you won't gossip. Anyway, this may or may not be mixed up with your troubles."

Not, was the correct answer. Niall could tell that Linette read between the lines as well as he did.

"I'm wondering if he might be part of the cattle rustling ring," Jed continued. "Maybe even the boss."

"The police chief?" Obviously shocked, Linette sank back onto her chair.

Jed talked about getting some odd vibes when he interviewed the man, and about what Grant had told him about the most recent conversation.

"He'd be in a perfect position. Neither Grant nor I had any idea he owned a ranch. It would be interesting to learn if his officers knew. I think the stolen animals had to be taken somewhere nearby for the night, or for a few days, until they could be moved on unobtrusively. He hurried to mention he had some Charolais, which are cream colored and stand out. Said he'd been raising red Angus, too. A herd of each breed were stolen."

"You want me to go undercover." Intrigued now, Niall thought it over. This could be interesting.

Jed dipped his head. "Seward will hire you for sure. You can do the job with one hand tied behind your back. Meantime, you can make friends—"

Niall smirked. "With the idiot detective?"

Jed had complained about Oakley, who had bungled an investigation into the murder of a newspaper employee related to a case of Jed's.

"Even with him. If we're lucky, you might get a few minutes alone in the chief's office. If he considers his officers loyal to him, he may be indiscreet."

"He won't hire me if he knows we're friends."

"Fortunately, you weren't at my house long. Go with the truth. You're drifting around the country, haven't found anyplace you want to settle."

Niall mimed astonishment. "And I tell him I fell for Fort Halleck, Oregon?" He waited for Jed to claim this was the most beautiful place in the U.S., when in fact much of the dry landscape was butt-ugly and really Jed was only here because of Linette.

Jed didn't even try. He only shrugged. "Say you won't promise more than a year if the fit isn't right, but you'll guarantee to stay that long."

"Hmm." Niall picked up his fork again and ate a few bites of the cashew chicken stir fry before saying, "What about Linette?"

Her mouth opened, but Jed didn't give her a chance to assure them she'd be fine by herself.

"I talked to Alex Burke. He's going to lend us one of his ranch hands. They may rotate in and out, he may take a day or two himself, but he says he won't send anyone who doesn't know horses and isn't willing to carry and use a gun."

Linette closed her mouth.

"He seems like a good guy," Jed added.

Niall sensed his reluctance. Was Jed mostly worried because neither Burke nor the borrowed ranch hands were likely to have experience in protecting a vulnerable woman? That was a worry Niall shared.

But Jed looked at Linette and said bluntly, "You need the help, and the security of having a second person here. Burke already knows some of what's been going on. He offered to help, and he meant it. He can afford to loan you an employee."

Even though she held his gaze with hers, he wasn't sure how she'd react, but after a minute she nodded.

"Won't they wonder about Niall?"

"Burke didn't ask about him. The only time any of his employees would have seen him was the morning the horses were chased out on the road. But I did imply we think this has to do with the cattle rustling. His outfit was hit, you know. His cattle were insured, but he's still angry."

Showing perturbation, Linette said, "That was…a little deceptive."

"I can't always be honest." He hesitated. "Or tell you what I'm working on."

Her eyes dilated. The way the two stared at each other, Niall wished he could easily slip away.

But Jed flicked a glance at him, which broke whatever tension that stretched between him and Linette. No, Niall thought; all was still not well in that department.

She said softly, "I understand," before aiming a smile that looked a little forced on Niall. "Is this one of the reasons you turned in your badge?"

This was something he didn't talk about. Niall moved his shoulders uncomfortably. "Ah…no. Actually. After Clarissa, I didn't have any relationships I'd call serious, and I'm not sure my family ever realized how much I didn't tell them."

"People don't, do they?" Linette commented with a trace of sadness.

"You okay with this?" Jed asked her.

"Why are you asking *her*?" Niall complained. "I'm the one who has to go to work."

Linette laughed, as he'd intended, and said, "Yes. I'm fine with it."

"I'm game, too," Niall agreed. "That drifting thing was getting old. I assume this will still be home?"

Jed grimaced. "We sure don't want you seen living at my house."

"And if someone did notice me there and asks about it?"

"An army buddy gave you my name as someone who'd probably put you up for a night or two, might know about job openings."

"As you did."

In the ensuing pool of silence, Linette jumped up. "I have chocolate mint ice cream."

They both agreed they'd like a bowl.

The minute she disappeared to the kitchen with the now-empty ceramic serving bowl, Niall looked straight at Jed, his expression dead serious.

"I hope you mean whatever you've been telling her."

Jed's eyes iced over. "What's between us is nobody else's business. Got that?"

"Yeah. I got it."

*****

At seven-thirty a.m., a shiny black Ford F-250 pickup truck turned into the driveway. Burke himself.

Jed wanted to be sour about it, but he respected what he'd seen of the man. Even felt a degree of trust, which allowed him to leave for work after thanking Burke.

He hadn't reached town when his phone rang. Dispatch.

"A Mason Thayer called to report cattle were taken last night."

Now, this was a twist.

After establishing that nothing else of any urgency had happened, he let her know he'd go straight to Thayer's place.

Already scowling, Mason came out of his house the minute Jed pulled in. Jed got out of the SUV and rounded the hood to find the other man walking toward him.

His first words? "I can't believe this. I thought your damn patrols were supposed to stop it."

Jed said mildly, "The patrols could have covered more ground if all local ranchers had given some time."

"So this is *my* fault?"

Had this been kindergarten, Jed would have had a retort. As it was, he said only, "Show me how you think they got trucks onto your property."

The padlock on the gate near the barn had been cut. Unlike when the horses were chased out at Linette's ranch, the padlock and chain lay where they'd fallen. He'd take the padlock for Erin to fingerprint, but only to show due diligence. If the cows and calves had really been stolen, the rustlers had undoubtedly worn gloves. Mason Thayer's fingerprints would be on this padlock, and it wouldn't be unreasonable to find those of any of his buddies, too. The results wouldn't help Jed.

Given that the land was flat and devoid of trees, he could agree that there wasn't an animal left in the pasture. He turned on his heels and studied the barnyard for tire tracks, but the ground was predictably hard-packed after several weeks of dry weather.

"You didn't hear a thing."

Thayer glared. "I was in town until late. Should have looked around when I got home, but I didn't. I fell into bed, okay?"

"So you assume the cattle were already gone when you got home."

"'Course they were!"

If he'd fallen into bed because he was drunk, he might not have heard an elephant trumpeting outside his bedroom window. But there was no harm in agreeing.

"Seems likely." Jed put his left hand into his pocket but kept his right hand dangling casually not far from his weapon. "Where were you last night?"

Thayer took an aggressive step forward, fury – real or simulated – twisting his face. "I'm the victim, and you're investigating *me*? You've had it in for me from the start, haven't you?"

Jed made sure to sound calm and keep his expression unaltered. "You believe the theft happened when you were…wherever you were, making it reasonable to suppose someone saw you and made a call to give the go-ahead, wouldn't you say? If you remember who was in a position to do that, it would be helpful."

"Did you ask the *rich* fuckers where they were while their cattle were being stolen?"

Jed held his gaze. "I did. I certainly know where Gary Webb was."

Swearing, Thayer shook his head. "I wasted my time calling this in."

"You did if you won't cooperate with the investigation."

He glared, but finally bit out, "I was at a tavern. The Bar Double-D."

If Jed wasn't mistaken, that's where Cassie Ward had once gone in an effort to interview this very man. According to Grant, she could well have been gang-raped if he hadn't followed her there. The 'Double-D' part of the name served as a warning, since posters featuring topless women with huge breasts decorated the walls in back, around the pool table. Following a brawl, Jed had made several arrests there shortly after taking this job.

He took out his notebook and pencil. "And who did you recall seeing during the evening?"

Mason Thayer offered names, subtracted some, added a few back. He'd first listed his closest confederates, including Gene Baxter and Brian Warring. It must then have occurred to him that Jed would talk to the bartender. Somebody had certainly moved the cattle last night. Jed's money was on Baxter and Warring. Thayer wanted to give them an alibi, but hadn't thought through the pitfalls.

This crowd had been careful so far. They wouldn't have risked moving the cattle in daylight. Safer to do it after dark – while the ranch owner got conspicuously drunk in town. Of course, Thayer spent a lot of time at the tavern, so that wasn't uncommon.

"I'll talk to these people," Jed said, closing his notebook.

"You're not going to look around here?"

"Can't think what there'd be to see. If there were tire tracks, they've been obliterated—"

"Is that an accusation?"

The guy was a jackass. Jed had no idea what his problem was. He also couldn't figure why Thayer believed claiming to be a victim would remove him from the list of suspects. Baxter had a better excuse for taking this route, with an easily identifiable trailer. It would make more sense if the supposedly missing cattle had been insured. Mason could have double-dipped – collected on the insurance and sold the animals, too.

Jed's best guess was that he had just panicked. This was a guy who acted on impulse rather than reason, and who, giving him something in common with Oren Calderon, seemed driven by resentment because he hadn't had the success he was sure he deserved.

Shaking his head, Jed said, "You have a real chip on your shoulder, Thayer. Now, if you'll excuse me, I'll get on with tracking down these folks." He'd opened the driver side door when he turned back. "By the way, do you know Harrison Seward? The police chief? I hear he runs cattle, too."

A nerve jerked beneath Thayer's right eye. "The police chief? Why would I know him?"

Keeping it casual, Jed said, "Ranchers in these parts all seem to talk. Not that populous a county."

"I suppose I've met him. What of it?" he challenged.

Jed smiled. "Just making conversation." He swung himself into the cab, slammed the door and fired up the engine.

Mason retreated toward the barn without ever turning his back. Jed had long since known he had a gift for scaring people. Maybe the intense focus required of a sniper had burned itself into his irises, belying his every attempt to appear harmless or sympathetic.

He grimaced. Nobody had ever called him warm and friendly, even when he was a kid.

*****

Phone to her ear, Linette sat on a stump kept in the tack room to serve as a chair.

"I think they're letting me go Friday," Troy said. "I could come back to work, like, Saturday or Sunday."

"What did the doctor say?" she asked, suspicious.

"Oh, um, I don't know, he kind of said maybe next week, but—"

"Then next week it will be." He argued, but she interrupted again. "Troy, you got *shot*. It's...not very safe here right now. Jed and Niall are different because they're army veterans and cops. They carry guns and know how to use them. I'd never forgive myself if you were hurt again. I *know* your mother wouldn't forgive me."

"But...the horses."

"I have temporary help. The owner of the Arrowhead Creek Ranch insisted on lending me one of his employees every day until you come back." She didn't add that today's help was Alex Burke, the ranch owner himself, or that he was currently mucking out a stall with the ease of experience. "You wait until you're really healed, okay? And if you're worried about me replacing you, I won't. You're a great employee, and I want you back."

She'd barely slid the phone into a pocket when Niall drove up in that bright blue pickup truck, so much showier than Jed's. Was the bold color another part of Niall's veneer?

There'd be no hope of hiding the multiple vehicles tonight. For some reason, she'd assumed that he would lurk in town or something to avoid explaining to Alex that he was staying here.

In fact, the neighboring rancher, a tall, handsome man, came out of the barn the minute he heard the truck, his bodyguard duties obviously on his mind. His eyebrows lifted quizzically.

Niall went to meet him, hand extended, as Linette hurried to join them. Was she supposed to come up with an explanation for his presence?

But the two men shook, and Niall said, "I'm a friend of Jed's. I've worked in law enforcement, too. He asked if I'd stay out here nights so we can switch off sleeping. I'm asking you to keep that to yourself."

"I'll do that." Alex glanced at her. "Jed seems confident that there'll be another attack."

"He might be a little paranoid, but I'm sleeping better nights with the guys staying here," she admitted. "And I really appreciate you helping out, too. Oh!" She told both men that Troy was on the mend and would likely be back to work by early next week.

"That's good news," Alex said. "Seems like a nice kid."

"He is, and great with the horses."

The pleasantries completed, Alex went back to the stall.

Linette had been banned from working any horses on an obstacle course she'd created out of natural terrain on her land because Jed deemed it too exposed, but she could spend time in the enclosed ring with the foals. The minute she thought Alex was out of earshot, however, she asked, "How did it go?"

Niall grinned. "You need to ask? I'm now an FHPD officer. I'm to pick up a uniform in the morning and start work. They've already issued me a gun and badge. Want to see?"

She made a face at him. "No, I believe you. Did I ever mention I don't actually like guns?"

He sobered. "Jed's all about guns, you know."

Linette saw red. "Don't say that! I thought you were friends. There's so much more to him. I think he likes law enforcement, but I know he hopes he never has to shoot anyone again."

Apparently silenced by her vehement defense, Niall took a moment before responding. "You're right about that." His face wiped of expression, he said, "Since you're not alone, I'm going to catch a few hours of sleep. Besides, I've got to change out of my good clothes."

His 'good clothes' were stiff new blue jeans and a western style shirt with snap closures. Watching him walk toward the house, she recognized the boots, scuffed and worn but still suitable in these parts for a job interview.

She grabbed a miniature halter and a lead rope and ducked between fence rails to round up the first foal, trying to decide why she was so mad at Niall even as her own vehement defense of Jed alarmed her.

Had she made a decision without realizing it?

CHAPTER SIXTEEN

Linette's Thursday temp worker turned out to be Curt Deeter, the young guy who had hit and killed her colt with his truck. When Alex called, he'd asked if she would mind, and she was being honest when she said, "No, of course not." Curt had seemed like a nice guy, genuinely torn up about what happened.

Turned out he was a good worker, too, his ease with horses natural enough he even managed to stroke Rey, before the stallion realized he didn't know this man and shied away.

"At least he didn't bite my fingers off," Curt said cheerfully, when he noticed Linette watching.

She laughed. "He's been known to try."

Jed arrived at five-thirty, looking weary and grim. He and Curt exchanged a few words before Curt headed out in his old pickup, Linette calling after him, "Thanks for doing this."

"Happy to," he said, before slamming his door and starting the engine.

"Decent worker?" Jed asked her.

"Really good. I'd hire him any time."

He nodded. "Niall not back yet?"

"He didn't call you?"

"No."

"He's staying in town to have a burger and beer with some other officers. 'Undercover,' he said."

Jed's laugh sounded half-hearted. "Sounds like he's being accepted."

"Niall has a talent for making friends. Most people don't notice—" She stopped.

Jed's eyebrows rose.

It still felt weird to have to unlock her front door, but he watched in approval as she produced a key from her jeans' pocket.

Inside, he turned the deadbolt and followed her to the kitchen. "Don't notice?"

"Oh, that his good humor and charm are only skin deep." She didn't look at Jed, instead going to the sink to scrub her hands. Reaching for the dishtowel, she saw that he'd stopped in the doorway.

"You look really beat," she exclaimed. "You and Niall can't go on like this, barely sleeping four or five hours a night."

Jed smiled in that gentle way she didn't remember from the old days. "Sure we can," he said. "It won't be forever. We can sleep in this weekend."

She reached for a saucepan as an excuse to turn away to prevent him from seeing that she was on the verge of tears. Stupid. There was no reason, and yet her eyes burned. Once she'd put water on to boil for the noodles, she checked the chicken paprika she'd started in the crock pot that morning. Inhaling the spicy aroma helped. Feeling more herself, she said, "We need a vegetable."

"*You* may. I can live without."

Okay, now she was smiling, too, and the danger that she might actually cry had passed. "You're right. Who cares?"

"Let me go change," he said, and disappeared. Unlike when Niall went up and down stairs, she didn't hear Jed – except, apparently, when he wanted her to.

He returned in well-worn jeans, athletic shoes and a faded tan T-shirt that was probably a leftover from his army days. Niall had worn desert camo pants one day, but Jed never did. Tonight, he'd left his badge upstairs, but was still armed.

Jed's all about guns, you know, Niall seemed to whisper in her ear. Linette shook off the memory. Jed had never carried a weapon when he was off-base in the old days.

Once they sat down, she asked if he'd learned anything today.

"Not a damn thing." He sounded as tired as he looked. "I talk to the same people, over and over. Drive around the county looking for somewhere a stolen herd could be stashed." He shook his head. "It's been long enough now since the last episode, the lost animals may all be on their way to stockyards if they aren't already tenderloins."

"Do you really believe that?"

"No." He rolled his shoulders. "It would be safer for the rustlers to distribute the cattle as widely as possible. Go for a bunch of different stockyards and feedlots. Different states. Wouldn't hurt to put some weight on the calves, too. I have to wonder if they didn't steal too many cattle, too quickly, without having the capability to move them on right away. Transportation may be their bottleneck."

"And that Oren... Is that the right name?"

"Yeah, and if that's what you're asking, he's still got his mouth zipped tight. Right now, he's more afraid of his confederates than he is of us."

"You think that's because one of them is the police chief, don't you?"

Those vivid blue eyes met hers squarely. "That's my best guess."

"But how could they get at him— Oh. He's probably out on bail, isn't he?"

"Yep. I wonder if keeping his mouth shut will save him. Assuming he knows names, he's a threat to everyone else involved. The rustlers wouldn't have so much on the line if they hadn't killed Gary Webb. Now they're looking at murder charges no matter what. Gary's death also means these people have killed once, and so far gotten away with it. Why not do it again, if it'll shut Oren up once and for all?"

Her appetite flagged, but she kept eating determinedly. If she were to let Jed into her life, she had to get used to this kind of conversation over the dinner table. That, or a lot of silent meals because he couldn't talk about his work.

His openness demonstrated an astonishing change, she thought.

Trying to sound less disturbed than she was, she asked, "Is somebody keeping an eye on this Oren?"

"Crook County deputies, insofar as they can. They aren't any better funded than we are."

She knew what that meant. Quite often, only one or two deputies would be patrolling the entire county. If he – or, now that Erin Brown had been hired, she – was called to help someone in distress, a second caller might have a good, long wait. And yes, the population was sparse in this and other rural counties in much of eastern Oregon, but the distances were great.

Linette didn't know what else to say. And the minute they quit talking, she became aware of an undercurrent that had been there all along. Or maybe awareness was a better word. With realizing it, she had noticed every shift of expression on Jed's face, the crinkles beside his eyes, the way the bones and sinews stood out on the back of his big hands, his throat as he swallowed, the shape of his ears. She had loved to kiss and nibble her way down his neck.

Her plate was empty. He'd refilled his, but seemed to have lost interest in food. He focused his hungry attention on her.

"I never thought I'd sit down to a meal with you again," she heard herself say. "Just the two of us."

"No," he agreed, voice husky. "If I'd approached you when I first came to town, asked you out, what would you have said?"

She thought back. "I...don't know. When I first saw your photo in the Courier, I felt some hope. I didn't like it, but it was there. That you'd come after me..."

He winced.

"But when you never contacted me, first I was angry, and then I quit feeling anything at all."

"So you might have said yes."

"I really don't know," she repeated. She tore her gaze from his. "Have you been involved with anyone since me?"

"Involved? No." Creases formed on his forehead. "After I found out you were living with another guy, I was angry. Even then, I knew that was irrational." He paused. "There were some women. They were all...temporary."

Under the table, Linette squeezed her hands together until they hurt. She had no right to feel such outrage and hurt. *She* had gotten herself entangled with Theo. But she hated those women anyway, and didn't want, ever, to picture him with them.

"It's been a long time, though," he said after a minute. "Not since I've been here, and awhile before that." An internal battle showed before he cleared his throat. "No woman I saw was you."

Exhilarated, anguished, made mute, she could only stare at him.

*****

Hope was more painful than the emptiness he'd felt for so long. "Linette?"

Her mouth opened and closed, but nothing came out.

He could not make a move. Any decisions now had to be hers. Since he'd learned as a child how little he could control, he had never surrendered that grip. Maybe this was why he hadn't picked up the phone or stopped by the ranch, even after he'd moved to Fort Halleck. Feeling so powerless sucked.

After a moment, he said, "I'm pushing again, aren't I?"

"No." Her eyes teemed with emotions. "I never expected…"

"If…you'll let me in—" Jed's voice sounded as raw as he felt "—I will never walk away from you again." *God.* He felt like a captive waiting to be executed, wishing he had been blindfolded so he couldn't see the face of the woman who would pull the trigger. He felt compelled to keep talking, as if he'd magically find the right words. "I'm…not so easy to live with, I know that. I can't promise I won't…retreat. If you can be patient with me—"

Linette let out a cry, jumped up and rushed to him. He barely had time to push away from the table and hold out his arms before she threw herself onto his lap.

Jed heard himself talking and didn't even know what he was saying. He wrapped her tight in his arms, feeling hers close around his neck. She was here. She'd chosen— Damn, he'd choked up and had to swallow.

"Linette."

Their eyes met, held. Hers were stunningly beautiful. They also shimmered. Jed didn't want her to cry. Not ever again, not if he was to blame.

Desperate as he was for her, he needed to keep looking at her.

In these years apart, she'd changed, but not by much. Her skin was still pale and fine-pored, the dusting of freckles were as disarming as ever. Fine bones, a high forehead and a pretty mouth made her as beautiful in his eyes as ever – although he had a suspicion his heart didn't hammer like this because of her outward appearance. There was something more about her, and always had been.

He loosened one arm so he could slide his fingertips beneath her braid and up her nape. Silky skin, the delicate bumps of vertebrae. A vibration…because his hand was shaking.

"You didn't cut your hair," he murmured, the hoarseness something he couldn't help any more than the tremor in his hand.

"No." Her smile trembled, her eyes betraying nerves. "I almost did a few weeks ago. So if we happened to run into each other, you'd know that, well, you had nothing to do with my decisions anymore."

"But you didn't."

"I told myself I'd get to it. I was just too busy."

He closed his eyes momentarily. "After four and a half years, you'd decided to give up on me."

She rubbed her cheek against his jaw. "You deserved it."

"I did." He slid his hand down that fat braid until he reached the elastic, which he tugged off and dropped to the floor. Then he occupied himself unplaiting her gorgeous, thick mass of hair, reveling in the way it slid between his fingers, triggering a hundred memories. Yet another lump formed in his throat. "I need you."

"Oh, Jed." She stretched to press a clumsy kiss to his mouth. There and gone…except he couldn't let her go.

He brushed his lips over hers again, softly, then with more pressure. She nibbled, he licked, and the kiss went deep and hungry.

It felt amazing, so good he thought about sitting here, in this hard wooden chair, for the next half hour or so, doing nothing but kissing Linette and holding her close.

The hunger he'd suppressed for five long years didn't allow for that kind of patience, though. With a guttural sound, he rose to his feet, lifting her effortlessly. Even so, her arms tightened around his neck. Leaving the remnants of their meal on the table and the lights on, he strode toward the stairs.

"I can walk," she gasped.

He hated to let her go, but retained enough blood in his head to recognize that refusing to let her walk under her own power – make the conscious decision to go upstairs with him – would be a mistake.

Jaw clenched, Jed lowered her to her feet. The slide of her body against his made him groan. God. What if she changed her mind? Or hadn't meant to take this so far?

But she took his hand. "Jed?"

"I want you."

Cheeks pink, she said, "I noticed."

"Are you…okay with this?" He nodded upward.

Anxiety still brewed in her expressive eyes, but she whispered, "Yes. Please."

He gave a jerky nod and put his foot on the first step. Holding on as tight to his hand as he was to hers, Linette did the same.

They mounted the stairs together. He hesitated, but she didn't. She led him into her bedroom. Jed kicked the door shut, swung her up in his arms again, and set her on the bed.

*****

She might be crazy, but Linette had carried that earlier epiphany to its logical conclusion: if she loved this man, she had to love who he really was. Messed up, scarred, a novice at real intimacy. As he'd said himself, a man who might not be able to help sometimes retreating behind barriers erected when he was only a boy. She loved the boy as much as she did the confident, vulnerable, dominant man he'd become.

If he was a mess, so was she.

Watching Jed unbutton his shirt, she tore off her socks and tossed them before peeling her sweatshirt over her head. His eyes heated at the sight of her ridiculously pale belly and sturdy bra. Even as she laid her hands on his muscular chest, Linette knew she ought to shinny out of her own jeans so she could take the equally practical panties unseen with them.

Too late. His shirt gone, Jed unfastened her bra with one hand. The next second, she found herself on her back, his mouth on her breast. He had to remember how sensitive her breasts were, how she responded to the suction of his mouth. Linette whimpered and arched upward, gripping him with frantic hands.

He teased her other breast, then came back to her mouth. The kiss exploded as their tongues tangled. They wrestled, arms tangling as each tried to explore the other's body. He hadn't lost any muscle after leaving the army, that was for sure. His skin shivered at her every touch. A groan rumbled from his chest.

He lifted himself off her to tackle the button and zipper of her jeans. Rearing up, Linette went for his.

He retreated, heat blazed across his cheekbones. "Not this time."

"Not fair," she gasped, moaning as his fingers slid into her wet heat. "Hurry."

Swearing, Jed wrenched off her last clothing, tossing jeans and panties, too. He'd forgotten his boots, and had to sit on the edge of the bed to pry them off. Linette knelt behind him, pressing her breasts to his back, kissing and licking his neck.

Socks gone. He rose gingerly to finish undressing.

Linette stared at that beautiful body, long, lean, powerful. His chest hair was a dark gold that went with the glint of stubble on his hard jaw. Her gaze lowered, and her abdomen cramped at what she saw.

Jed eased her back and planted a knee between her thighs. He asked her something she couldn't parse, blinking at him when he gave her a shake.

"Are you on birth control?"

"Oh. No, but I bought some—" She turned her head toward her bedside table.

He showed her a wolfish grin as he reached for the drawer. "Lucky. I did, too, but they're in my bedroom."

Linette squirmed. She didn't want to wait.

He grabbed a packet, ripped it and rolled the condom on. At last, he came down on top of her, kissing her as if he'd hungered for this during the long years since they parted.

Her fingers found a scar she remembered, then one she didn't. She'd let herself care about it later. Right now, she was too desperate to feel him inside her.

They rolled, with her briefly on top and his fingers back between her legs, stroking, teasing, demanding. She saw his face, eyes glittering, skin pulled taut, teeth showing, just before he flipped her. Making noises she didn't even recognize, Linette parted her legs and lifted her knees to bracket his hips. Arching upwards, she was rewarded by the blunt tip of his penis pressing at her opening. With a ragged sound, he pushed forward, sliding deep, then holding himself there.

Linette opened her eyes to meet his. There was astonishment on his face along with the passion, and something else, too, that resonated with her own wild emotions. All she could think was, *He's home,* I'm *home,* before he resumed movement.

She lasted barely a minute, and he was with her.

*****

They made love one more time, only a little slower with Linette riding him, before Jed heard the sound of Niall's pickup truck turning into the driveway. Damn, damn, damn. He didn't want to let her go, have to get out of bed and dress. Conduct any kind of conversation with his friend, who would know the minute he looked at Jed or Linette what they'd been up to.

"Niall's here," he mumbled into the thick blanket of glossy brown hair that flowed over his face and chest. He slid one hand down the graceful line of her back, resting it on her hip and taut buttock. She fit him in every way. He'd forgotten how well.

Linette grumbled something incoherent that made him grin. Exhilaration swelled inside his chest. She'd forgiven him. After years of aching for her, they were twined together in her bed.

Stunned, he thought, *I'm happy*. When he should be getting his butt out of bed, he instead examined astonishing and unfamiliar feelings.

Hating to sour his mood, he reminded himself that they had problems aside from their personal relationship. Her enemy would come after her again, they both knew that. He might come after Jed again, too – or was that one of the cattle rustlers?

Groaning, he gently lifted her off his body so he could roll over and sit up. "I'll tell Niall you've gone to bed, if you want to stay here," he offered, voice gruff and raspy.

"No-o. I don't suppose he learned anything, but…" With a sigh, she stretched, momentarily paralyzing him.

Half-aroused again already, he forced himself to struggle into his boxer shorts and jeans. Sliding off the bed, Linette padded right in front of him to collect her own clothes.

He reached out and patted her ass. "Give me a break."

She laughed, sounding as happy as he felt. "I hear the front door."

"Crap." Jed winced and adjusted himself before he bent forward to locate his boots.

Linette hastily got dressed before disappearing to the bathroom. Where she'd look in the mirror and discover her cheeks were scraped red from his stubble, and that her lips were puffy.

Smiling, Jed went downstairs.

He found Niall in the dining room, contemplating the abandoned, half-finished meal. Seeing Jed, Niall raised his eyebrows.

"In a good mood, I see."

Jed tensed. "Yes, I am. But don't say a word to Linette."

"I wouldn't." Niall shook his head, his mouth curling up. "You're a lucky bastard. Don't blow it again."

"I won't." It felt like another vow – and not a good moment to realize that, for all their lovemaking, Linette hadn't said a word about her feelings. Of course, he hadn't, either – but he hadn't in the old days, either, yet that hadn't stopped her from often saying, "I love you." Words he'd told himself he didn't want to hear, even as he now knew he'd hugged them tight.

What if she'd softened toward him, wanted him, but couldn't risk loving him?

But for all his usual pessimism, Jed didn't believe it. The words would come…as long as he didn't screw up, and she stayed alive and well.

CHAPTER SEVENTEEN

Once Alex Burke showed up the next morning to take another shift at the ranch, Jed felt confident enough to leave. Curt Deeter seemed okay, but he looked to be in his early twenties. A kid. How would he stand up to a brutal, armed intruder?

During the drive, Jed would normally have focused on his day ahead. Shut out personal problems and shifted into the right mind-set. A distracted cop made mistakes.

Today…all he could think about was Linette. Sitting around the table drinking coffee with Niall last night had been awkward, but that wasn't Niall's fault. No surprise, he hadn't learned any earthshaking secrets about Chief Seward on his first day, but had discovered an atmosphere of intense loyalty to the guy, above and beyond what he'd expect even in a department where the officers respected their boss.

Jed's thoughts flicked back to where he'd begun. He had taken the first shift of the night. He walked Linette to the foot of the stairs when she announced her intention of going to bed – her face pink because they all knew she'd already been to bed. But she'd said quietly, "When Niall takes over, will you come to my bedroom?"

His heart had taken a hard beat. "You're sure? He might see me coming out of your room in the morning."

She rolled her eyes. "As if he doesn't already know we're sleeping together again."

Sleeping together. Not how he'd have described their reunion, but he'd take what he could get.

Indeed, at three-thirty in the morning he had slipped back into her bed, his cold body startling her awake. She'd warmed him nicely. He was smiling at the memory when he realized he'd arrived at work. He damn near drove right on by. So much for getting his head in the game.

He was barely in his office when dispatch buzzed him. An Irene Brown had asked to speak to him. Assuming this was the same woman,

Jed knew her. She owned a horse ranch in the southeast corner of the county, and had played a part in Grant finding the murdered body of a FHPD officer out in the boonies. The one, in fact, who had once asked Linette out.

Jed picked up the phone and poked the flashing red button. "Ms. Brown? This is Detective Jed Dawson. I believe we've met."

"I had my arms around you."

Jed laughed. "So you did." On a bitterly cold night, she'd ridden behind him on an ATV.

Now she asked, "Are you investigating the cattle rustling?"

His attention snapped into sharp focus. "I am."

"Oh, good. Well, I saw something…" She sounded more hesitant than seemed natural for the woman he remembered. "Except now I'm doubting myself. The cattle I saw are probably just loose to graze on leased land."

"Ma'am, why don't you tell me what you did see? Something about it made you uneasy."

"I called, so I might as well," she said more tartly. "I trailered my horse today over near Parson's Rimrock to take a ride. That's something I don't do more than a couple of times a year."

Parson's Rimrock. Jed automatically blocked out the memories the name summoned and reflected that it would be hard to hide anything on the bare, flat land between the highway and the columnar basalt wall, the most impressive in Hayes County.

"Did you ride up to the top?" he asked.

"Yes, I did, and that's where… Well, it's been as much as twenty years since I've seen cattle out that way. These were in the distance, but I saw cows and calves. A couple of hundred, maybe. So I thought—"

"You thought right," he said with satisfaction. "I'm glad you reported this. We'll check it out. Thank you very much, Ms. Brown."

"You're welcome. I've known Gary Webb for years."

She was gone before he could comment.

Jed pulled up a USGS map on his laptop and studied it. He'd been right in remembering that much of the area was federal or state land. However, some private land did lie beyond the rimrock. Jed had gotten a look at it some weeks back when he went up in a small plane to plan for the regular, night-time patrols. That one had been in daylight hours.

Using binoculars, he'd allowed his attention to be momentarily snagged by the top of Parson's Rimrock – called Butt Crack by local teens, a vulgar description of the substantial split separating one side from the other. He'd made his last kill there, wearing a ghillie suit to allow him to sneak up on another former army sniper determined to take out Grant Holcomb and his girlfriend, Cassie Ward. Jed had gotten him first. Killing the way he had threw Jed back into the shit he thought he'd crawled out of, but whatever the cost, he didn't regret pulling the trigger.

During that same flight, he'd noted some falling down ranch buildings and fences in bleak country on the edge of the county, but no cattle. Since that was a matter of weeks ago, he couldn't imagine that a newcomer had bought the long-abandoned ranch, repaired fences and barns, and jumped right into cattle ranching. And, damn it, had the flights since avoided that completely empty area?

Energized, he carried his laptop to Grant's office, giving a tap on the half-open door before entering. "We may have caught a break."

When Grant heard who the caller was, he laughed. "Nice woman. Brisk and practical. As frozen as I was that night, I appreciated her help."

He studied the maps, after which they debated whether to fly over or just drive in.

"Sneak in," Jed corrected himself. "If I can find even one cow there with a brand identifying it as stolen—"

"We could get a warrant."

Jed guessed his smile would scare most people. "Better yet. We can set up a trap. Somebody has to be checking on the herd, maybe tossing out hay, at least filling water troughs. Map doesn't indicate so much as a creek running through that land."

Grant's answering grin was equally predatory, his combat experience and years as a cop showing. "I like it. Getting in there without being seen might be tough, though."

"I'll start by determining who owns the land. Legally, it would be good to have permission from the owner."

"You still don't want to be seen."

"No." Jed pushed himself to his feet. "But I know how to become a ghost."

Grant didn't have to say a word.

*****

Jed didn't enjoy donning the ghillie suit he'd brought home from Afghanistan and had worn only the once since, but given long practice it didn't take twenty minutes for him to cut some fresh branches of sage and rabbitbrush to weave through the mesh.

He'd determined that the state of Oregon actually had bought out the previous owner of the deserted ranch, and had reached the appropriate individual at DSL – the Department of State Lands – to give him permission to search on any or all Oregon state public lands for evidence connected to the cattle rustling.

From a little-used road that cut cross-country from the highway, he spotted a dirt track near to being overgrown by the ubiquitous rabbitbrush that was more aggressive than the native sagebrush. He drove within half a mile of the fence line, parked in an unobtrusive spot and still covered the roof of his department SUV with a blanket constructed like his suit that he had last laid over his horse when he made the approach to Parson's Rimrock. Jed jogged twenty-five yards or so away and turned back to see that the vehicle had virtually disappeared.

Satisfied, he took out his binoculars and searched the landscape for movement, for any glint of metal, anything oddly shaped, but saw nothing. From then on, he moved in short bursts, bent over, pausing regularly to look again.

Not until Jed got close to the fence was he able to see that it had been reinforced with fresh strands of barbed wire. Acknowledging a moment of grim satisfaction, he felt sure DSL wouldn't appreciate illicit shoring up of structures or fences even if the purpose *wasn't* to hide stolen livestock.

Cattle were scattered across the land on the other side of the fence, grazing on the high desert bunchgrasses. Jed saw no vehicles even in the ranch yard, nor evidence of a human presence. Even so, he belly-crawled the last distance, cut a stretch of wire and rolled beneath the remaining strand.

He moved just as carefully until he reached a cluster of Black Angus – or were they Wagyu? – with a sole white-faced, red-brown Hereford cow and calf in the midst. They appeared not to notice him. Jed moved close enough to snap photos of brands. The black calves appeared to be unbranded, but the Hereford calf did have one. Jed waited until a butt swung toward him to get a picture of the brand on one of the black cows. And, damn, he recognized it right away. Had these idiots really held onto Walt Whitney's Wagyu herd this long, and not twenty miles from Whitney's ranch?

Sure they had – they'd wanted the calves to bulk up before being sold. These might be the most valuable cattle stolen.

No need to take the risk of trying to get close to any of the other animals.

After checking to be sure all the photos were clear, he belly-crawled back the way he'd come. Once on the other side of the fence, he pulled the wire toward the next post and did his best to anchor it with several rocks in hopes no one noticed it had been cut.

Halfway back to his ride, he heard the growl of a truck engine. After turning, he stretched out flat behind a sizeable sagebrush and adjusted his binoculars. The graying wood of the ramshackle ranch buildings came into sharp focus.

Black pickup truck. Two men climbing out, heads turning warily. Wide-brimmed hats hid their features. One was shorter, stocky, while the other appeared tall and lean. He was a stranger, Jed decided, but the shorter guy…he'd lay money that was Mason Thayer.

Jed lay still, waiting until they were fully occupied running a hose from a large tank in the bed of the truck to a steel stock tank. Then he cautiously moved, a little at a time, until he'd made it back to his SUV.

As he drove, he eyed the sun, already on its way down, and knew they wouldn't be able to move fast enough to set a trap this evening. The surprising appearance of the two men in broad daylight made him wonder if the rustlers were always this bold, or if these two had other plans for tonight. Surely they feared that regular traffic out here would draw attention. They'd pass better unnoticed at night, when fewer people were on the road.

Tomorrow night, he decided, before any cattle were shipped away.

*****

When he arrived home – at Linette's ranch, he corrected himself – he thanked Alex Burke, waiting until Burke left before following his directions to find Linette in the tack room. Head bent over her work, she was applying saddle soap to a leather line with a clip on end. Bridles were ranged around her, most appearing supple and glossy after treatment.

Hearing his footfall, she looked up with a shy smile. "You're early."

"Not much more I could accomplish today," he said. He looked around and found a seat on a burlap bag full of shavings. The concavity at the top suggested the bag had served the same purpose before.

"Did you accomplish anything?" she asked.

"Yeah." Even he heard the satisfaction infusing his voice. "Most cops will tell you that their keen insight into criminal thinking and their brilliance in tying the dots together explains why they're able to close investigations. I'm here to say that's a lie."

Linette laughed, as he'd hoped. He loved seeing her face when she was open and relaxed.

"Then how do you close cases, Detective Dawson?" she teased.

"Luck. Pure luck. I depend on other people seeing what I didn't." He told her about Irene Brown's phone call and his own reconnaissance. "Needless to say, don't mention this to anyone at all, but we plan to set up an ambush tomorrow evening. We'll probably nab only one or two of these guys, but they'll talk."

Hearing the steel in his voice, she raised her eyebrows. "Do you plan to pull out some fingernails or something?"

He grinned. "Tempting, but no. I already know who at least some of these men are. They're whiny and immature. Keeping their mouths shut means accepting sole responsibility. Since a second degree murder charge is part of the package, I feel sure they'll be eager to talk."

She studied him for longer than was comfortable, finally nodding and bending her head again over the line she was now buffing with a soft cloth to a sheen. Jed couldn't help wondering what she was thinking.

Then she told him.

"You've always claimed to be a loner. How is it you're so astute where other people are concerned?"

He dodged. "Forget astute. It's luck, remember?"

She pinned him with a look.

After a minute, he said, "You know I grew up in foster care."

Linette nodded, watching him with anxious solemnity.

"You learn to read intentions." He added reluctantly, "It's a survival instinct."

Seeing her shiver, he reached out to lay a hand on her arm. "I don't mean that literally." Actually, there had been a few times, but he didn't have to tell her everything. "You learn when to back off, when to stay quiet, when to—" Disappear before you took a fist to the face. "When to do what you're told to do," he substituted.

Her hands had gone still, her attention all on him. "How many different foster homes were you in?"

In the past, he'd shut her down when she asked these kind of questions. That was still his instinct – but she'd told him the most hurtful things from her childhood, and even he sensed there wouldn't be any balance until he did the same.

"Eight or ten." Seeing her expression, Jed said, "I really don't know. I was two when I went into the system. I have only scattered memories of the first few years."

"Nobody ever…wanted to, well, keep you?"

"Only once. I had a foster dad who was a foreman on a good-size cattle ranch. His name was Mitch Jones." Jed paused, remembering the wiry man with leathery skin who seemed to know everything about horses and cattle. He'd taught as much of it as he could to Jed, seeming to understand his foster son's frequent suspensions from school. "He was…a good guy," Jed said finally. "I was never sure why he'd decided to foster. I think I was his one and only. I stayed with him for three and a half years. Then…he got hurt. Kicked by a horse. When his leg didn't mend, the ranch owner let him go. Mitch…" Jed had to swallow. "He called social services and they came to get me." He had begged to stay with Mitch, who'd looked sorrowful and said, *Don't know where I'll go or how I'll keep myself, boy. You'll be better off with someone else.*

He hadn't been. The time with Mitch was the only stability Jed had known but for the army. His foster father wasn't demonstrative. If he had been, Jed would have rejected any overtures. Even so, he knew now that his years with Mitch had included deep affection.

"How old were you?" Linette asked quietly.

"Sixteen." He shrugged. "They placed me, I ran away. After a couple of repeats, I ended up in a group home. It wasn't that bad. My birthday is in June—" Had he ever told her that? "—so I graduated from high school and aged out of the foster care system at the same time. I enlisted right away."

Linette still studied him. "Did you ever try to find your foster dad?"

"Yeah." Jed cleared his throat. "After my first couple of deployments." He still wasn't sure what had motivated him, but guessed that, if he asked, Linette would be able to tell him. "He'd gotten as far as Arizona. Far as I could tell, he'd been living on disability. Six months before I went looking, Mitch was killed in a single car accident. He'd been drinking."

"I'm sorry," she whispered. She was the one to reach across the divide this time, giving his hand a quick squeeze. "I'm sorry I made you remember."

Jed had carried a hard knot in his chest for a lot of years. Now he became aware that the knot had softened, was maybe even dissolving. It was the strangest sensation. There'd been a time it would have panicked him. Knowing Linette could make him feel so much *had* panicked him. Now… Bemused, he smiled crookedly. "It's okay." More than okay. "Those were good years. I wish I'd looked for him sooner, except…maybe he needed to hold onto his dignity." He'd never know, but he couldn't change his hesitation, or Mitch's decision not to allow himself to lean on anyone, including his foster son.

Linette tipped her head. "You've changed."

"I've been telling you."

Her smile was tremulous. "I think I actually believe you."

"About damn time." He stood and pulled her to her feet. The lead line and rag dropped to the floor, Linette not seeming to care as she wrapped her arms around his neck and met his kiss.

Everything about her drew him, from her scent and taste to the way her body fitted against his. The small sounds she made, her curves and strength. And, man, he loved her hair. He wanted to free it from the braid…but the ever-vigilant side of him heard an approaching car or truck.

Niall, Jed realized.

Gentling Linette, easing back, he didn't feel quite as much frustration as he would have even a day ago. It was different now, because he'd be joining her later in her bed.

Something else he liked: the bewilderment on her face. Knowing she shut out everything and everyone else when she was in his arms kept at bay his edgy fear that she didn't feel as much as he did.

*****

Linette felt more enthusiasm for cooking these days than she had in years. The hungry, hopeful way both men eyed the serving dish in her hands told her why.

Apparently she'd missed the beginning of a conversation, because as Niall accepted the bowl from her and dished up a heaping pile of scalloped potatoes layered with ham, he said, "Nothing you can take to a judge yet."

"Are you still talking about undertones?" Jed asked. He helped himself to an equally ample serving before passing the bowl to Linette.

Lucky she had already learned the extent of their appetites.

"Mostly." Niall frowned, but took a few bites before he continued. "Our police chief has favorites. The other officers resent being shut out. A couple of those have begun complaining to me, but I get the feeling what they really all want is to be part of the in-crowd."

"High school all over again?" Linette said.

"Too damn close. You were right," he said to Jed. "Cattle rustling aside, this is a police department I wouldn't want to have to depend on. It needs to be gutted before it's rebuilt."

Linette couldn't help noticing a certain energy in his voice. Intrigued by it, she wondered if Niall had just plain been depressed when he showed up in Fort Halleck. That would make sense; his wife had left him, he quit his job and began drifting around the country. Maybe being rootless didn't suit him.

Jed had been watching Niall, too, but his eyes briefly met Linette's. She had the feeling he was thinking the same. In fact…had this been his plan when he sent Niall to work undercover? He clearly despised Police Chief Seward, FHPD's one and only detective, and maybe the officers he'd met, too.

After clearing half his plate, Niall continued. "Here's the thing. My informants believe the 'in' guys are somehow making extra bucks. Maybe working some kind of security for Seward, they don't know. But what kind of 'security' would he require?"

Jed's mouth curved, but his eyes were a particularly cold shade of blue. "We know the answer to that, don't we?"

"I'm itching to plant a listening device in his office—"

Jed shook his head. "You know you can't do that without a warrant. Getting the warrant is why you're there in the first place."

"Are you doing fly-overs of his ranch?" Linette asked.

Both men glanced at her. Jed answered. "Occasional. Remember that our pilots are all volunteers. It's a little tricky to say, 'We suspect our long-time police chief and want you to concentrate on his ranch.'"

Jed and Niall started talking again. Linette tuned them out as she examined the problem.

"Wait, I have an idea!" Belatedly, she realized she'd interrupted Niall. "I'm sorry—"

He smiled. "We were spinning our wheels."

Jed nodded in agreement. "What are you thinking?"

"Well…it's what you said, a while back, that none of the ranches in that quarter of the county have been hit by the rustlers. What if you tell the pilots you're afraid that with law enforcement focus elsewhere, that's where the rustlers will make their next move? Ask them to concentrate on the area – you could even mention that Chief Seward has a big ranch that would make a likely target. You're concerned."

Jed's eyebrows twitched. "That's good thinking."

Niall shifted his gaze to Jed. "Are they taking photos?"

"Usually only when there's an observer as well as the pilot, and then only when they see livestock trailers on the road at night, or any indication that cattle are being moved."

"You could ask for more photos, just to give you a better idea how many targets there are in that part of the county," Linette suggested. "The fly-over could even be during the day." She spread her hands in a gesture of innocence. "Who could object to that?"

Niall grinned at her. "You may have missed your calling."

"I agree." Jed's eyes had warmed this time when they met hers.

Niall said thoughtfully, "It will be interesting to see whether your net scoops up any of my fellow officers tomorrow night."

"Oh, yeah," Jed agreed.

It took restraint for Linette not to roll her eyes. Of course, they were both enjoying themselves when all *she* wanted was for this to be over. As long as Jed felt obligated to make up for the past by guarding her with the dedication of a highly-trained police dog with lots of sharp teeth, how could she be sure how he really felt about her?

CHAPTER EIGHTEEN

Beneath a quarter-moon, the old ranch buildings tilted drunkenly, while others displayed gaps like missing teeth where boards had fallen out. Washed with faint silver light and deep shadows, this could have been a ghost town. Tonight, it was occupied by the living, although Jed's troops were doing an admirable job of staying invisible.

He, on the other hand, struggled to remain still. Among his peers in the army, he'd been known for legendary patience. If they could know how restless he was tonight, they'd get a good laugh out of it. He'd already adjusted his stance half a dozen times in the past hour. Now he cautiously leaned a shoulder against the barn wall, wincing at the squeal as a rusty nail protested. The structure stayed upright, however, so he eventually relaxed.

Damn, what he'd give for night vision goggles or binoculars. He'd considered buying cheap ones, but couldn't make himself, not when the quality he was accustomed to ran five thousand dollars and up. Way up.

Something to talk to Grant about, Jed mused. The military occasionally offered surplus equipment and gear to police departments. This request from the Hayes County Sheriff's Department would sound modest compared to the armored vehicles some law enforcement agencies had been bagging.

Through the high-optic binoculars he did own, Jed searched the darkness toward the mile-long, rutted dirt lane that would carry any arrivals from the little-traveled county road. Nothing. A deputy had positioned himself that afternoon and early evening to watch the ranch. Nobody had come or gone, he reported.

Maybe the thieves didn't feel a need to check on their herd of stolen cattle every day, he brooded.

This could get expensive if they had to repeat it tomorrow night. Grant was here, crouched just inside the barn when Jed had last seen him. Three other deputies – Eddie Aguilar, Ben Fischer and Erin Brown – had found hides of their own. Details of the sting hadn't been shared with anyone but the participants, but everyone else in the department knew something big was going down, if only because the schedule had been readjusted so that the two oldest deputies handled routine duties. Deputy Numsen patrolled tonight, while Kitson – nearing retirement – was expected to be ready to act as backup.

One other deputy had been excluded from the plans: Chris Jarman. He'd worked the day shift today, which took him out of the building while they planned. Going off-shift, he realized something was up and begged to be included. When Grant said, "No, we need you ready to go, fresh, come morning," Jarman's response was telling.

With an ugly expression, he'd said, "It's Detective Dawson who wants me to be left out, isn't it?"

Jed had a feeling Jarman's employment would soon be terminated. Nothing about his attitude would recommend him to Grant.

Shaking off thoughts of the jackass, Jed touched his watch, which lit up with a green glow. After ten. He needed to get into the zone. They had agreed to stay until midnight, at least.

His phone vibrated on his hip. New text from Niall. *All well on the home front.* Jed tapped out, *No action here.*

Why were they all hiding? They could have held a barbeque while they waited. God knew, they could see anyone coming from a distance. Unless, of course, their prey came a back way, as Jed had. But why would they, when they'd driven in yesterday, cocky as could be?

Amusement lifted a corner of Jed's mouth. Niall was burned out on taking orders. That had never been Jed's problem; apparently what *he* wasn't very good at anymore was the endless waiting. He'd have to tell Linette—

A faint luminosity in the distance caught his eye. He lifted the binoculars, adjusting them until he was certain he was looking at oncoming headlights. Somebody was out on the road. Didn't mean they wouldn't shoot on by, although if so, this would be the first vehicle to pass in the two hours he'd been watching. The twin beams grew steadily brighter…until they abruptly winked out.

No, not entirely. As the vehicle turned into the dirt track leading into the ranch, he saw smaller running lights. They couldn't drive totally blind.

He murmured into his radio, "Company coming."

Soon he heard the engine, the sound of tires. Pickup truck, he bet, even before it appeared in the ranch yard not fifteen feet from his position. The engine was turned off. Both doors swung open. He faded back in case one of the two men who got out decided to sweep the surroundings with a flashlight.

"Let's get this done," one of them said in a low voice.

No response.

Jed eased back to look around the corner and saw that one was lowering the tailgate while the other stretched over the side for a coil of hose.

Wait. Wait.

The man at the back of the truck heaved a hay bale onto his shoulder.

Jed murmured into his radio, "Go." Then he walked forward, not ten feet from them when the first of the two men whirled. "Police! Hands up!"

*****

It hadn't taken a minute to have both pressed belly up to the cold metal sides of the pickup bed, hands cuffed behind their backs, being frisked, then read their rights.

Jed and Grant hung back, let their young officers have the fun of making the arrests. The entire time, Mason Thayer had glared at Jed. If looks could kill.

Ignoring him, Jed was struck by how anticlimactic this operation had turned out to be. And yes, it was only one step; he knew that. Theory was, these two would lead them to more participants, who would lead them to more, until they reached the top. That was important; Gary Webb's family deserved justice, and Jed was determined to get that for them.

What disturbed him, he realized once they were back at the station, was that he no longer believed this network of thieves had any connection to Linette's assailant. What he couldn't be sure was whether the attempt to kill him had to do with her, or the cattle rustlers.

Right this minute, he needed to put that question aside and do his job. He had to persuade these two fools to talk.

Thayer, who had demanded an attorney, was currently stashed in a holding room. The fellow Jed hadn't recognized had said, "I don't understand. Why would I need a lawyer?" As a result, he waited in the interrogation room.

Grant stood at Jed's side as they both gazed through the one-way glass. "I didn't recognize him out there, but damn. That's Jimmy Hinton."

Jed frowned, the name ringing a bell. Five foot ten or eleven, this guy was lean and possessed a limp Jed had noticed earlier. Short, light brown hair, skin weathered but not yet forming deep creases. At a guess, he was in his early thirties.

Grant said, "He's enough younger than me, I wouldn't have known him from the old days. I'm thinking he's around Cassie's age." His fiancée, owner and managing editor of the local newspaper since her father's death, had also grown up in Fort Halleck, but something like five years behind him.

"Then how do you— Wait, is he the rodeo star?"

"Yep. Jimmy Hinton rode bulls. He has at least a couple of national titles, from what I recall. Believe it or not, I kept up with the County Courier all those years. Hinton was a shining star by this town's standards. Lots of pictures." Grant shook his head. "Guess the success didn't hold up. I hadn't heard he was back in the area."

The table Hinton sat behind hid his belt buckle, but Jed had noticed earlier that it was big enough to demand attention. Wasn't that the rodeo version of a trophy? "The press will be all over this," he grumbled. "*Cassie* will be all over it."

"No shit." Grant did not look thrilled. He rolled his shoulders. "It'll make her day."

Jed muffled his laugh, but not soon enough. His boss shot a rueful sidelong glance his way.

"Have at it," Grant said, nodding toward the glass. "This is your investigation."

Jed started toward the door, but his phone rang. He'd have silenced it if he hadn't been worried about Linette. The caller was his Crook County colleague, Detective Frazier.

"I'm sorry to tell you that Oren Calderon was found dead early this morning. Supposed to look like suicide, but it didn't quite work. The medical examiner confirms my impression. He was murdered with his own gun, sitting in his living room."

Jed wished he was surprised. "Damn it," he growled. "They eliminated him as a threat."

"That's my take."

Jed updated him on what had been happening here, and Frazier promised to keep him in the loop. Pocketing his phone, Jed filled in the parts of the conversation Grant hadn't heard or figured out.

When Jed walked in to sit down with Jimmy Hinton, the guy glowered, the annoyance he projected that of an innocent man. "What is this? I was hired to help take care of some cattle. That's all I was doing."

All? Along with stealing cattle, the gang had now committed two murders.

Jed pulled out a chair directly across the table from his prisoner. "You didn't wonder why you had to sneak around at night to feed the cattle? Which, by the way, are being held illegally on state-owned land?"

"State-owned?" His surprise appeared genuine. "The people that hired me said they'd leased the land from the heirs of whoever used to ranch there. And we went out there at night because we both have day jobs."

On a Saturday?

"What is your day job, Mr. Hinton?"

His chin came up. "I'm a warehouse forklift operator."

"Your employer?"

Jed had to pry it out of him, but finally got the name of a small manufacturer and the name of Hinton's direct supervisor. He also learned that Hinton had only held the job for three months, and hadn't stayed in any job longer than six months since he had to give up bull riding after a serious injury over five years ago. He became increasingly sullen in his responses. He claimed that sometimes he'd discovered he couldn't do the work because of his chronic pain issues. Sometimes he got bored, or thought he was treated like shit or underpaid.

Up to a point, Jed understood. After a high-adrenaline lifestyle that had brought a man stardom, being able to do nothing but menial work had to be a blow to both the ego and the pocketbook. Jimmy Hinton had been ripe to be recruited for some kind of nefarious work. His skill set had been right, too; he knew how to herd and load and unload cattle and likely could competently drive a pickup hauling a fully-loaded livestock trailer. The under-the-table money would be a motivation, but the real engine for his decision to participate was probably his resentment at everything he'd lost.

"Who hired you for this job?" Jed asked bluntly.

His expression stayed stolid. "The guy I was with. Mason. I knew him back when. He's who hooked me up."

"Fair drive from Prineville," Jed remarked casually. "Hardly worth the trip, if all you were doing was throwing out some hay and refilling water tanks."

"I got friends up here."

"How long have you been working with Mason?"

"Like, a month? Easy job. You know. The grazing's good right now."

"Are you aware some of those cattle belong to Mason Thayer?"

Hinton accomplished a fair pretense at being surprised. "Yeah, sure. I helped move them. The boss gave him permission. His own pastures can rest a little."

"Interesting mix of breeds."

Real wariness appeared now. "Well…common ones. Hereford and Black and Red Angus."

"Not Black Angus. Wagyu."

Hinton's eyes widened with what might be outrage. "You sure?"

"I am." Jed contemplated him. "Guess you noticed the mix of brands, too."

"I didn't think about it. Might be like a bunch of small ranchers teaming up to compete with the big guys."

"Consortium is the word I think you're going for. And were you paid by check? I can contact the bank—"

"Ah...Mason was just giving me cash. Easier that way. You know."

Jed smiled thinly. "I'll need to inform the IRS, ask them to check that you paid taxes on these earnings."

The former rodeo cowboy straightened with a jolt. "The job was just temporary! I was going to file what I had to, but I figured I'd wait until they didn't need me no more."

"Uh huh. Well, I'll let you explain to them." Jed lifted an eyebrow. "Did your buddy Mason tell you he'd reported his cattle stolen?"

Jimmy Hinton stared. "No! Why would he do that?"

"I have a good idea." Although Mason had been a fool to do it. Jed paused. "Now, here's what you need to know. All of those cattle under your tender, loving care were stolen. You can't have missed reading or hearing about the cattle rustling happening here in the county."

His Adam's apple bobbed. "I—"

"So you're looking at some serious charges here, Mr. Hinton. Felony charges that will see you spending a few years in the penitentiary. And that's if your buddies don't point fingers at you for murder. Because some of you *are* going down for murdering two ranchers." Pictures flashed in his head: a good man left sprawled dead in the dirt, pajamas peeking out from under hastily donned clothing. The disbelief and grief on the face of Webb's son.

Hinton reared back. "Two? What are you talking about?"

"Oren Calderon was murdered last night."

"I never heard of him! I didn't have nothing to do with anything like that! I'm no killer."

"Were you there the night Gary Webb was shot?"

"Not me," he said hurriedly. "But I heard talk. You know. It was kind of an accident. Nobody meant to shoot anyone. It was just..."

"Inevitable."

A desperate gaze met Jed's. "I want a lawyer. I'm not saying nothing else until I have one."

Jed let his face go blank. "Very well. I'll see that you have a phone and a local phone book, if you need one." He pushed back his chair, rose and walked out.

Grant hadn't moved. His face was carved in granite, a reminder of his friendship with Gary Webb's son Hayden and thereby the whole family.

Jed glanced through the glass at a man who looked as if he'd shrunk in the past fifteen minutes. He was diminished, pale and scared.

"He's ready for a deal," Grant said.

Jed thought so, too.

One down, one to go.

*****

When Linette heard Jed's pickup truck out front, she dashed to the front door. He'd parked close enough to the house that she saw he wasn't alone. That was either a boy or a small woman— In the next moment, she recognized the woman. It was that deputy Jed had sent out to check up on her, the one who did fingerprinting.

"What the *hell*?" Niall said from right behind her. Of course he'd heard the door open and come running.

As he mounted the porch steps, Jed's eyes met hers, holding warmth and intimacy that others were unlikely to see.

You've changed.

I have.

"Jed." His name came out husky – or was that sultry? But Linette managed to switch her gaze to the young woman with him. "Deputy."

"Call me Erin," the petite cop said.

"Erin who?" Niall asked, raking the other woman with a look.

Linette understood his surprise. Even she'd had to blink a few times before she could quite picture Erin Brown as a cop rather than the teenager she especially appeared to be now in black jeans, athletic shoes and hoodie.

"Deputy Erin Brown," Jed told him, not seeming to notice his bemusement. He ushered her inside ahead of him. "Erin, meet Niall Callaghan."

"I've seen you." She studied him, forehead wrinkled. "You were in uniform. I thought you must be a new hire at FHPD."

"I am," he said stiffly, sending a glower Jed's way.

Jed opened his mouth and then closed it. Linette guessed he wasn't ready to confide his suspicions about the police chief to the young deputy. "I knew Niall in the army," he said after a minute. "I asked him to help.

He and I have been splitting the night, keeping an eye out for the creep who's giving Linette trouble." Somehow, he'd maneuvered without being noticeable until he was at Linette's side, his upper arm brushing her shoulder. "I'm beat," he said. "Come morning, I have to sit down with the two men we arrested tonight and their attorneys. I asked Erin if she could help out."

"I was off today," she explained. "Anyway, I'm still wired."

Niall shook his head in obvious disbelief. "You're kidding."

Jed frowned. "Why would I kid? You have to work in the morning, too. Erin doesn't."

"You're going to send her out in the middle of the night to check camera feed and walk the property line."

Erin bristled. "Why would you have a problem with that? I'm a cop. Or is it that you don't think women *should* be cops?"

Niall looked right over the top of her head at Jed. "I don't care if she went through the police academy. We know the asshole who went after Linette is a big guy. What if this little girl meets up with him out on the far end of the property?"

"I'm armed—"

"You gonna have that on your conscience?" Niall snapped, still ignoring Erin as if she hadn't spoken. Wasn't there.

"I can't believe we're having this discussion." Jed looked thoroughly annoyed. "Erin may be young, but she has good instincts. I never expected you to be biased."

Linette stood very still, shocked in one way that this scene had blown up, yet also not. Niall had a sharpness about him she had glimpsed on rare occasions in their earlier acquaintance. These past days, she'd seen flashes of anger that seemed out of proportion. Very likely he suffered from PTSD...but did that explain his complete dismissal of another police officer's competence? No, not just Erin's competence – he hadn't so much as looked at her since his first scathing evaluation.

"You're being a jerk," Linette told him. "Get over it."

The flare of real anger in his eyes took her aback. A sidelong look told her Jed hadn't seen it, or he would have reacted.

"Fine," Niall snapped. "Guess it's none of my business. I'm going to bed." With that, he strode toward the staircase.

They all heard him stomp upstairs.

Brows knit in perplexity or something stronger, Jed gazed after him. He let out a long breath before saying to Erin, "Forget him. I'll make the rounds once with you, then hit the sack if you're still up to handling a few hours."

She squared her shoulders. "You bet."

"Good." Jed touched Linette's hand lightly. "Why don't you get to bed. Shouldn't take me a half hour, and I'll be in, too."

Message received. Linette nodded, resisted the temptation to lift her hand to his bristly jaw, and thanked Erin. "After this is all over, if you're interested in riding, give me a call."

"Really? I'd love that!"

Unsure if they could become friends or not, Linette found she was willing to try. She hadn't done that in a good long while. She smiled and echoed Jed. "Good."

Upstairs, she saw Niall's door was closed. She almost knocked, but refrained. Whatever burr had bit into him, he could deal with it himself.

As tired as she was, Linette decided to read until Jed came to bed. She might have to re-read these pages tomorrow, but at least she stayed awake until she heard the rushing sound of water moving through the pipes. Several minutes later, Jed quietly opened her door and slipped in. He'd shaved, she saw, which served as another message. Or maybe reinforcement of the first one.

Linette lifted the covers for him and watched in silent appreciation as he stripped. Not until he slid into bed beside her did she switch off the lamp and reach for him even as he gathered her close.

CHAPTER NINETEEN

Midmorning, Jed walked out of a conference with Mason Thayer and his attorney, a local man named Rodney Wallace, to find Grant waiting.

Grant let his gaze move coolly over Mason before he asked in a quiet aside for Jed, "A word with you?" He did greet the attorney.

Mason had paid bail, the source of which wasn't clear, so Jed couldn't stop him from leaving. Would he bolt? Jed thought it was a possibility.

Watching the two men cross the parking lot outside the double glass doors, Grant said, "Get anywhere?"

"Not as far as I'd like. Mason stumbled over his idiocy in reporting his own cattle stolen, and finally admitted he was involved with stealing other ranchers' animals, but not for money."

Grant gave a short, disbelieving laugh.

Jed continued, "All those rich ranchers deserved to find out what it's like to face *real* trouble. His rage just poured out. Even the attorney couldn't shut him up."

"Did you point out that the really rich ranchers carried insurance and he hasn't hurt them all that much?"

They started down the long hall that took them from the county's prison into sheriff's department headquarters. "I did, but he kept ranting. A lot of years of anger stored up there."

"He wouldn't give you any names?"

"Interestingly, only one. Rob Fullerton."

Grant's eyebrows climbed. "Fullerton's name does keep cropping up."

"The spite makes me doubt Fullerton is involved at all." Except, if Jed was wrong about that and Fullerton *also* held a grudge against Linette for resisting his advances, the crimes would all be linked again. Jed could rule out Theo Willis, who scared him a lot more than Rob Fullerton ever could.

"You ask him about Calderon?" Grant asked.

"He and Hinton both claim they don't know the man, have never heard his name. I believe Hinton but not Thayer."

Grant didn't raise the subject that had sent him in pursuit of Jed until they entered his office and closed the door.

"Chief Seward heard we set up a sting last night and made some arrests," he reported, as he circled his desk and sank into his big leather chair. "He doesn't understand why he was kept out of the loop. Aren't we working together?"

"Because he's been so deeply involved?" Sitting seemed like a really good idea. If there'd been a cot or bedroll in here, Jed wouldn't have been able to resist it. Exhaustion had become his chronic norm. *I'm getting old*, he thought, settling for a chair. Of course, if he could resist making love with Linette when he crawled into bed with her, he'd get more sleep.

"You tell him who we arrested?"

"No reason not to. He went kind of quiet."

"I swear he's dirty." Jed thought. "Did he comment on yesterday's flyover?"

"Not a word."

Had the bastard not dared, knowing a complaint would be an ill fit with his sudden burst of brotherhood, law enforcement style?

"Damn, I've been too busy to look at any footage Bernie sent." Jed had only met Bernie Strotz in person once. An energetic, older guy with white hair that made Jed think of a dandelion puff, Bernie had let his son take over his well-drilling business. Instead of retiring, he and his wife started a lavender and herb farm on his acreage. He farmed, she distilled oils and oversaw the retail part of the business. An ardent photographer, Bernie sold some of his work to the County Courier. He'd eagerly volunteered to help when word got out about the patrols. The guy seemed tireless.

Jed wished he was.

"Let me grab my laptop."

He came back only minutes later, pulled up a chair to Grant's desk and logged in. Three emails from Bernie, the 'observer' Jed had personally requested for last night's flight, appeared immediately, all three with attachments.

Using detailed maps, he had labeled batches of photos by location. Jed skimmed through until he found those taken in Seward's sector. He flipped through…to find he was looking at empty roads, some fence lines, and finally one photo of the large, modern home and ranch buildings.

Swearing, he said, "Apparently Seward is untouchable."

Grant stood and circled the desk to look over Jed's shoulder at the handful of photos. He bumped Jed's hand aside and skimmed through the more helpful images showing nearby ranches, before venting his own curse. "Maybe Bernie and Seward are friends."

"Close enough friends that Bernie volunteered in the first place so that he could nudge pilots to take safe routes when he was along?"

They stared at each other in dismay. Grant muttered something under his breath as he returned to his own chair.

"Getting a warrant for Seward's place will be tricky, anyway."

Jed quit grinding his teeth to say, "Politics?"

"Not sure that's the right word for it. Seward has been the Fort Halleck Police Chief for a lot of years now. He knows everybody. You and I seem to be the only people who have noticed that he stinks at the job."

Jed told him about Niall's observations. "Cops who work together should be tight. We have to trust each other. But Niall thought this was more of a…clique, I guess. There's a secretive inner circle. Those in favor get some kind of…well, favor. The outsiders aren't sure what that is."

Grant nodded. "We don't have a lot of judges in this county, and even though I grew up here, I'm still the new boy compared to Seward. They're not going to want to believe anything like this about him. Bernie Strotz may be an honest man who thought he was being respectful. Show us access to the ranch but not intrude on the police chief's privacy."

"I want to find a pilot who'll take me up *now*." Screw Seward's privacy. Jed would do it if he didn't also know how it could backfire.

Grant's grimace suggested sympathy. But he was shaking his head at the same time. "Even if we find some nugget of information that gets us a warrant, what happens if he's involved but not holding stolen cattle? We'd end up with egg on our faces, and that would be the end of any inter-agency cooperation at all."

Jed gusted a sigh. "What do we have to do to *get* a warrant?" He hadn't hidden his frustration, which stemmed from a lot of causes.

Grant stared into space for a minute that drew on. Finally, he shook his head. "We'll know it when we see it. In the meantime, I need to figure out who best to approach for that warrant."

"What if Seward panics because of the arrests? Damn, I don't want to give him time to move the cattle off his place."

"No, but will he? If he were suddenly pulled over in the middle of the night hauling a big stock trailer, full up, *that* would look bad." Grant's eyes met Jed's. "I can find room in the budget to add patrols for the next couple of nights so we're not so stretched. I'll have a deputy linger in the vicinity of Seward's property each night unless they're pulled away by a call."

"Good." Jed closed the laptop and rose to his feet. "Any of those judges long-time friends of Gary Webb?"

Grant's expression changed. "Don't know, but I'll see what I can find out."

"I'm meeting with Hinton and his attorney at two. That gives me time to talk to Rob Fullerton first."

"Don't come back with a black eye."

Jed snorted and left.

*****

Mid-afternoon, Linette happened to glance out of the barn to see an older black pickup truck pulling a four-horse trailer pass by on the road out front, seemingly heading toward town. It was loaded, giving her a glimpse of horses' heads. Probably, it was coming from the Arrowhead Creek ranch – they did both sell horses and train cutting horses for outside owners – but the rigs she usually saw passing were gleaming and pristine. Their animals and services didn't come cheap. Analyzing her uneasiness, she felt sure she'd recognized the thick mane of one of the horses, with silver and black mixed while the head was a silver-gray. No other breeds seen locally had such long manes, either.

Her sudden certainty shifted into fear, making her stomach knot.

Jed had asked her to stay close to the barn. Actually, *ordered* was probably a better word. She wished she'd downloaded the app that would allow her to check camera images onto her phone. She suspected that he hadn't suggested it because he didn't *want* her to charge out to confront an intruder.

But that meant her only way to check all the cameras was to walk or ride out to the open shed in the back pasture where the second receiver had been set up. Or call Niall or Jed and have them take who knew how long from their work shifts to view images from at least four of the cameras.

No, this was something she could do. If the horses in that trailer were hers, it meant Theo – or whoever else had stolen them – was long-gone. And she did have backup of sorts.

She started thinking she'd have been happier to have Alex Burke as her helper today, but made a face. He had too much in common with Jed and Niall. He'd insist on going instead, once he'd locked her into the house for safety.

Okay, maybe it was a good thing that a young man named Ken Fields had showed up this morning. Long and skinny, he had also proved to be quiet. When she told him what to do, he nodded and went off to do it. Tempting as it was to leave him out of this altogether, she didn't want to do anything really foolish, either. So she asked him to accompany her out to check fences.

"You know we've had trouble."

He nodded. "Curt felt real bad."

"It wasn't his fault."

She chose a nimble-footed three-year-old gelding she intended to sell in the next year for Ken to ride, and a mare for herself. Ken briefly disappeared into the barn, returning with a Remington rifle he'd apparently kept close today. That was comforting, Linette discovered, but her unease didn't relent as they swung onto the horses' backs and rode across the pasture that held mares and foals. The gate into the far pasture was padlocked, for what good that did. Linette reined Felicidad close enough to allow her to unlock and drape the chain over the fence before opening the gate.

A sparse grove of trees, ponderosa and – she was told – lodge pole pines along with some western larch covered the rising land to the north here. None were very large – her ranch apparently straddled the boundary between high country desert and forest. A few quaking aspens followed the small stream that bisected the ranch, and had been the deciding factor when she bought this land instead of any of the other ranches she'd seriously considered.

Because of the trees, as they approached the three-sided shelter where Jed and Niall had stashed the receiver, she couldn't see most of the fence that defined the eastern edge of her property. She dismounted in front of the shelter, leaving Ken holding Felicidad's reins, and pulled a tattered piece of gunny sack off the receiver. Calling up current views from the nearest cameras, she frowned. Was that—? A slip-knot around her chest tightened. She wanted to race for the cut stretch of fence, but more important was seeing what had happened.

Going back in time, she found images stopped and started, since the cameras were motion-activated. Niall and Jed had both grumbled that, between the horses and the wildlife, they were activated often.

She continued until she reached a time-stamp that showed almost an hour ago. A black-clad man with his face shadowed by the brim of his hat strolled beside the fence until he found whatever he'd been looking for and dropped a pile of – *something* – to the ground beside him. He then used a mallet and his booted feet to break the three boards that formed the fence between two solid posts. He clearly wore work gloves when he wrenched the broken boards out of the way. Even if the boards had provided a smooth enough surface, there wouldn't be any fingerprints.

She squinted, but the details didn't sharpen. Maybe Jed or Niall could do something to bring his face into focus. Heart in her throat, she saw the man pick up what she immediately identified as a halter and rope and enter the pasture, going out of view from the camera. He reemerged a minute later leading a horse on a lead-line. Sickened, she saw that it – he – was almost silver, with darker mane and tail – a blue dun. Ramón, almost three years old. Before all this started, she had just started riding him.

Hate almost choked her as she watched the unknown man lead Ramón along the other side of the fence, and out of sight. He must have parked the trailer there.

Unknown? That wasn't true. The walk, the breadth of shoulders, the way he carried himself...all triggered memories. Denial had been soothing, but she had to let it go now. This was Theo.

He reappeared, led away a second horse, a third, a fourth.

He'd stolen them. Would he even have a place to pasture them, or did he intend— Her stomach lurched. It wasn't too late. He might still be on the road.

Her phone was in her hand without her having consciously taken it from her pocket. She touched Jed's name, and it rang.

"Linette?" he said sharply.

"He's been back. Theo. I'm sure now. He broke down a stretch of fence and stole four horses. I came out here to check the video after I saw an old pickup go by pulling a four-horse trailer. It's been—" She had no sense of time. "Half an hour? Can you look for him? Please, please."

"Of course we will. Tell me what you know."

Grateful he'd skipped any lecture about her personal security, she did: black pickup and white trailer that had both showed their ages. Only one man.

"You're certain this was Theo?"

She swallowed, made herself take a mental step back. Had she seen what she thought she should, or what she feared? "Not a hundred percent," she admitted. "Let's say ninety percent. I couldn't see his face. But...the way he moved, his height and bulk... Yes, I think it's Theo."

Jed swore. "I'll get the word out, to our deputies and to FHPD officers. Neighboring counties, too."

"Maybe I should go out looking." She had to do *something*, not just wait.

"No." He sounded harsh. "Go back to the barn—"

"I have to fix the break in the fence." She didn't even know where that came from, but it was true.

"You have someone helping you out today, don't you?"

"Yes, a young guy you haven't met."

"Send him out to do it. That son-of-a-bitch could unhitch the trailer and come back for you."

"I'm scared. And so angry." Yes. Her voice shook, and so did the hand holding the phone. "He owned guns. He didn't even bother to lock them up. Why didn't I kill him the last time he hit me?"

"He didn't try to prevent you from walking away." Jed's was the voice of reason, but also tender. "How could you have known, Linette?"

"I couldn't, but— Oh…hurry, Jed!" She ended the call. What had she rattled on for? Why had he let her? But the exchange couldn't have taken as long as it felt.

After explaining to Ken, she mounted and led him straight to the break. They propped up pieces to prevent any of the remaining horses from wandering out, then cantered back to the barn. They loaded his pickup. He thought he could figure out where Theo had parked. The intervals between him passing out of sight and reappearing told them the trailer hadn't been far away from the break.

She watched his pickup recede down her driveway and take the turn. Left standing there, she thought, *My fault*, even though she knew better. But right this minute— *If I'd left him sooner. If I'd never told him my dream of raising horses.* If she hadn't waxed lyrical about the joy of being in tune with her mount, to the point where they seemingly read each other's minds.

It *was* her fault that she had freely handed him the knowledge of how to hurt her the most.

No. She couldn't blame herself for Theo, any more than she'd been responsible for her stepfather's depredations. Or Jed's desertion. She had *sworn* she was done with self-blame.

And with trusting.

Hands clenching into fists, fingernails biting into her palms, she wished she'd bought a gun when she had first considered it. Maybe then she wouldn't feel so helpless now.

*****

Sitting in his department SUV out front of Rob Fullerton's house, Jed got on the radio and made calls, too. He feared that Willis had had plenty of time to go to ground. He'd have had a place ready. As Jed had reason to know, there were any number of rural properties in this county for sale or rent, or simply vacant, like the ranch lands they had raided yesterday evening, and that was if he wasn't living with a credulous woman, who would believe him when he said he'd bought the horses.

Once Jed had done what he could from a distance, he barely cast a glance at Fullerton's house before pulling away from the curb. He'd never made it out of his vehicle, but Rob could wait.

Jed drove almost as far as the LB Kiger Ranch before turning around. It was nearly a mile closer to town before there were houses near enough to the road to be worth canvassing.

As he asked questions and received in reply only shakes of the head, he mulled over the strangeness of this theft. Four days ago Willis – and Jed had no reason to doubt Linette's identification – had let loose a bunch of horses for no other apparent purpose than to make sure at least one was killed. He'd made no attempt to steal any. Did he even *like* horses? Know how to ride? Jed would have to ask Linette – and hope she had some insight into Theo's behavior.

Jed was disturbed at how repetitive this theft seemed. The scumbag had been escalating from petty tricks to tasering a young foal and watching it die. Did he intend to do something spectacular and horrific with the four horses he'd gotten away with?

Had Willis watched Jed and Niall installing the cameras, or spotted one? If so, he might have savored the knowledge that Linette would watch footage sooner or later. But Jed shook his head. Willis couldn't have seen more than one camera, or he'd have guessed footage was being streamed. He'd taken his time coming and going until he filled his trailer, displaying no concern that someone might be watching *right that minute* – and might be waiting at his rig to arrest him.

Having exhausted any hope from the canvassing, Jed called Grant. "I didn't get a chance to talk to Fullerton. Can you do it? Lights were on at his house, before I got pulled away."

"No problem. Anything you especially want me to ask?" They discussed tactics for a few minutes. "You going to make it back to sit down with Hinton and his attorney?"

"I'll let you know," Jed promised. "Worse comes to worst, I can put that off. Don't suppose Hinton would mind."

Grant made a sound Jed took as amused. "No, I feel sure he wouldn't. In the meantime, good luck hunting down this SOB who has it in for Linette."

"Thanks."

He called Linette every hour or so all afternoon to keep her up to date with the search – which had failed to find any trace of Willis. Jed had personally sought out every security camera he knew about, most of which were downtown, but none had captured a black pickup pulling a white, four-horse trailer. Clearly Theo was smart enough not to have driven at a meandering pace right down Fort Halleck's main drag, being erratically stopped by the half dozen stoplights – the only ones in the county – while the horses craned their necks to see out, and be seen.

Linette urged him to keep the appointment with Hinton and the attorney himself. "It's important, too," she said, despite the strain in her voice.

Jed sat across the table from the two in the conference room and asked for acknowledgement that they knew the conversation was being recorded. Then he said, "Ms. Todd, I hope you've encouraged Mr. Hinton to cooperate. As he and Mr. Mason have both admitted to having roles in the cattle rustling ring, they will also be charged with second degree murder in the shooting death of Gary Webb." It was unlikely that either man would be charged with Calderon's murder, given that both had been in jail when it was committed. "That raises the stakes considerably."

"We want a deal," she said. A tall woman with wild blonde curls controlled by some combs, Vanessa Todd looked to be in her early thirties. He hadn't encountered her before, which made him wonder whether she might be new in town.

"If Mr. Hinton agrees to name everyone he knows is involved, I can call the deputy district attorney to discuss what kind of deal we're willing to cut with him."

She turned her gaze on Jimmy, who nodded.

Jed excused himself to go out of the room to call Bruce Baldwin, a man Jed had worked with before and respected.

They agreed right away that, if they could confirm that Jimmy Hinton hadn't been there the night Webb was killed, they could withdraw that charge. Baldwin suggested a reasonably light sentence they could both live with, and Jed went back into the conference room to negotiate with Ms. Todd.

Jimmy pushed back his chair and lurched to his feet when he realized he'd have to plead guilty to felony charges. "Fuck that! I'll never get a job again!"

Jed felt no sympathy. "You should have thought of that before you started stealing tens of thousands of dollars worth of beef on the hoof."

"Tens of thousands of— But I only made a couple of thousand!"

"Why did you take so little?" Jed asked reasonably.

Hinton's mouth opened and closed a few times. He dropped back on the hard wooden chair with a thump. "I never thought—"

A common failing.

CHAPTER TWENTY

Jed left Hinton and his attorney alone again to confer. For what good it did, he kept an eye on the discussion through the glass. From her gesticulations, he had the idea that Ms. Todd was giving Hinton an earful. Unfortunately, she knew to keep her back to the window so he couldn't lip-read.

He had just propped himself up against the wall outside the room when his phone rang. Calling Linette again would have to wait.

Grant, he saw, and answered.

"Talked to Rob Fullerton," his boss said. "Goes without saying, he was pissed, and I don't blame him. First we suspect him of being a serial killer, then stalking Linette, and now being a cattle rustler."

Jed winced. He'd have been mad, too.

"He denies having anything to do with the cattle rustling. He runs a few of his own, but he also makes decent money as a long-haul trucker. He admits to having a temper, but says he doesn't steal. According to him, he and Mason have always butted heads. He showed me his record of truck runs, and he's been gone even more than usual this past month. I verified some of the trips, and I believe him."

"I'll take your word for it. Mason sounded spiteful."

"How's it going with Hinton?"

"He and his attorney are talking right now about what they're willing to offer and what deal they expect in return."

"Good," Grant said.

The attorney still seemed to be doing all the talking, her client looking cowed. Jed seized the chance to call Linette. "Just have a couple of minutes here," he said. "Question for you. Back home, did Theo go out to the ranch with you and ride? Today he looked competent handling the horses."

"Supposedly he'd done some riding when he was a kid, and he did come to the ranch with me a few times. I don't think he was all that interested in horses, though, and I had the feeling he didn't like not feeling like the expert."

"There you were, showing him up."

"Stupid me, I was trying to share an enthusiasm, but...he probably saw it that way."

"Not stupid," Jed said sternly.

After a moment, she said, "Okay."

"Why do you think he came back today to steal horses? He tried to steal the foal the first time, when you jumped him, then let a bunch of horses loose the second time but apparently didn't make even an attempt to get away with any of them." He told her his thoughts on the escalation of attacks, which wouldn't be news to her. Why repeat himself here?"

"Because I'm so well guarded. He can't get at me." Her voice was soft, almost...broken. "That's making him angry. If he's the one who shot Troy, he'll be mad that he made a mistake. His self-esteem demanded that he send the message that we can't stop him."

"And he failed to make a kill shot." Jed squeezed tight neck muscles with his free hand. Damn, he wanted—

Out of the corner of his eye, he saw the attorney signal for him. "I have to go," he said. "Stay safe, okay?"

"You, too."

"Yeah." He cleared his throat, wished she'd said, *I love you*, the way she once would have. His "See you soon" came out gruff.

Doing his best to ignore the now ever-present ache beneath his breast bone, he entered the conference room.

Ms. Todd said straight out, "We agree to your terms. Mr. Hinton was involved only in some of the cattle rustling incidents. He can tell you which. He does not countenance murder."

Jimmy started with obvious reluctance and a backpack full of excuses. Jed had heard them all before. But it became evident that the ex-bull rider hadn't thought through how much the stolen cattle were worth and was starting to realize he'd been robbed, too. A couple of thousand dollars had sounded like a lot initially, but as a percent of the total take, was miniscule.

"I already told you it was Mason asked me if I wanted to join them," he said. "I don't know all the guys. I only, uh, helped out three or, no, I guess four times. I mean, actually driving cattle through a fence break or loading them into a stock trailer. You know."

"Actually stealing them," Jed said.

He ducked his head and hunched like a turtle, but mumbled, "Yeah. That."

He explained the particular incidents he'd been involved in, and swore again that he wasn't there the night the rancher was shot. Looking Jed in the eye, he said, "I can prove it, too. I have a girlfriend, see, and the tenth was her birthday. We had a party that went on half the night, and I never left her place."

He offered the name of his girlfriend and several of his buddies along with phone numbers.

"You said earlier that you heard afterward about the shooting. I think you know who did it."

"It was…way I heard it, he didn't mean to do nothing like that."

"He."

Another mumble, indecipherable.

Jed waited.

"Gene." Jimmy sneaked a look at him. "Gene Baxter. He just kinda freaked out when he saw the old guy with a rifle. It's…he said it was self-defense."

Jed just shook his head. "Who else do you know who was part of this gang?"

He had four more names. Two, Jed didn't recognize. Two he did.

Brian Warring…and Jeremy Horner. An FHPD officer.

Now *there* was a string Jed looked forward to pulling.

*****

Anxiety crawled under Linette's skin like stinging ants. Working with any of the foals or horses was out of the question with fear rising until it nearly choked her. All the same, she went back to doing her chores, because what else could she do?

What was Theo doing to her horses, sweet-natured and willing because she'd handled them from birth, taught them to trust. They'd never had *reason* to fear. She felt as if she'd betrayed them.

Both Niall and Jed called to let her know they were running late, which meant she had to cook tonight. She let Ken Fields know when she was going in to start dinner, and he nodded as he continued to spread straw in a stall. She thanked him for fixing the fence today and working so hard. He nodded again.

Once she reached the kitchen, she stood still for a long minute to remember why she was here. Oh, lord – what should she make?

Steaks and baked potatoes would be easiest, she decided. She couldn't imagine wanting to eat, but she owed it to Jed and Niall to cook anyway. The two men seemed to need vast amounts of food to fuel their bodies.

Jed arrived first. She knew his footsteps even before he reached the kitchen. He held out his arms, and she flung herself into the haven of his embrace.

"Damn, Linette," he murmured, his cheek against her head. "I'm so sorry. I should have been here."

"No." Swallowing, she pulled herself together enough to wipe the few tears she'd shed on his shirt and lift her head. "You have to do your job."

"Right now—" He broke off. "Sounds like Niall made it."

She let herself rest against him for another minute, hands fisted in his shirt. Then, with a sigh, she straightened and stepped away, calling hello to Niall.

His appearance was her signal to put on the steaks to broil, giving both men a chance to go upstairs and change clothes. Jed returned in time to ferry some of the food to the table. Once she deposited the huge platter of meat in the middle, she pulled out her own chair as the men both did the same.

Niall looked directly at her, his expression pained. "I heard about your horses. I'm sorry. I wish I'd been here."

Jed paused in the act of dishing up to study her.

Did he guess what she'd think?

It was true that if Niall had been here, if he hadn't taken the job at Jed's urging, he would have been monitoring the camera feed. Chances were good he'd have seen Theo before he got away with the horses. Even so, she couldn't resent Jed's choice, not when the cattle rustlers had murdered a man as well as wiping out a lot of small ranchers. She and Troy had been casualties of her assailant – Jed speak – but both were recovering just fine. He was making the best decisions he could. Besides – she could have insisted on adding that darned app to her phone, whether Jed liked it or not, and kept an eye on the camera feed herself.

She hadn't.

So she managed a smile. "You can only do so much, and that's been a lot." Given Jed's scrutiny, this was a good time to push her food around on her plate in hopes he'd think she was eating. Whatever else he felt for her, being protective was part of it, and going without what he considered adequate food or sleep would fall under that category.

Niall accepted the serving bowl with fresh peas from Jed. "I heard some talk today that might be relevant," he said, his voice becoming more animated. "Rumor has it that Chief Seward put a lot of money in one investment and lost it all."

Niall had Jed's full attention.

"That is interesting. Did this rumor say what he invested in?"

"Something to do with electrical power, is all I know."

"Ah. I'll bet it was that projected wind farm." Seeing that Linette looked as blank as Niall did, Jed elaborated. "This happened before I moved here. Maybe three years ago?"

"Wait." Linette set down her fork. "I did read about that. Supposedly this group was buying up large swaths of land, and leasing more from the state for a forest of those giant wind towers. Or is it turbines?" She gave her head a quick shake. "That corner of the county was supposed to be ideal because the wind roars through with no ridges or even hills to slow it down. I remember the project being a huge source of controversy. It could bring some real money into the area, but the people who lived where they'd have to look at it were kicking and screaming."

Jed nodded. "Right. The group announced they'd incorporated, they solicited investments, and then one day, they up and disappeared. Turned out there was no incorporation, they hadn't purchased any land, and the state denied ever being approached about leases. People bought what the scam artists were selling without doing their research."

Niall smiled, not nicely. "Including Chief Harrison Seward."

Jed had an answering glint in his eyes. "The question of why he'd risk losing everything he spent a lifetime building has been a stumbling block for me. If his savings are gone…well, the ranch can't be very profitable, given that he has a full-time job and has to pay other people to do a lot of the work for him. And let's face it, retirement from a government job won't let him live high."

"And what if part of his investment was money he borrowed against his retirement?" Linette suggested. She made herself put a bite in her mouth and chew, whether she wanted to swallow or not.

"What if," Jed echoed. A slow smile spread on his face. "Yeah, that's a useful bit of gossip." He nodded at Niall, who appeared satisfied.

As they continued to eat, Jed first told them about Calderon's murder, then updated Niall on his day, including his research on the two unfamiliar names Jimmy Hinton had given him, and his frustration at still having no warrant to bring in Gene Baxter or so much as look at his bank records.

Linette listened, but had trouble taking in everything they said. What she'd seen on the camera footage ran in a loop in her mind. She wanted Jed and Niall to be talking about how to get her horses back, how to find Theo and arrest him. Instead, they talked about everything *but*.

"Grant likes a Judge Donald Yeatman, who is not only out of town for the weekend, he didn't answer his cell phone." Jed's jaw muscles spasmed. "We then approached Judge Arthur Bascomb. He wasn't happy that we'd bothered him late on a Saturday afternoon. He told us to come back Monday morning, and he hoped we'd have more evidence than the dubious word of a man desperate for a deal."

"How quick will Thayer call his friend to warn him?" Niall asked.

"Oh, I think Mason called his good buddy Gene the minute he walked out of the holding cell this morning." In his quiet way, Linette decided, Jed was furious. "We're trying to keep an eye on him, in case he decides to run, but our budget doesn't allow a twenty-four/seven stake-out. It's complicated further by the fact that he has a small house in town as well as the ranch, which means both places have to be watched." Looking at Niall, he said, "I'd get you involved, except it might blow your cover."

"I can stay with Linette if you need to fill in anywhere."

To her relief, Jed shook his head. "The others will manage. Even if Baxter does take off, he's not sophisticated enough to stay hidden."

The knowledge that he didn't intend to leave her calmed Linette. To contribute, she said, "You can't do a stake-out on a suspect inside the city limits, anyway, can you?"

He caught her hand for a quick squeeze under the table, telling her that he had guessed at her stress and tangled emotions. "Actually, we can," he answered. "The FHPD is confined by the city limits, but it doesn't work the other way around. Normally we avoid stepping on the police department's toes, but the sheriff's department has jurisdiction over the entire county."

Niall gave a slow smile. "Seward's head will explode if he finds out you're operating inside *his* territory."

Once it became apparent both men had finished eating, Linette hustled to the kitchen to scrape off her plate into the garbage. Niall followed her and said, "Let me clean up tonight."

She almost insisted on doing it. She needed every distraction, but couldn't turn down the opportunity to cuddle with Jed on the sofa and talk – or not.

When they first went to bed that night, they didn't make love. They held each other, Linette struck by a sense of unreality. She trusted him, turned to him in her need, everything she'd sworn she would never do again. She felt a deep pang of a different fear, this one that she'd succumbed to a few seemingly sincere words but no commitment on Jed's part. But the solidity of his body stretched out beside her, the comforting circle of his arm, the strong beat of his heart beneath her hand, the way he sometimes looked at her, all offered reassurance. He was being the man she needed, not saying words she wouldn't have believed anyway.

If he'd knocked on her door out of the blue, before this all started, and said, "I missed you. I love you. Please take me back," she'd have slammed the door in his face. And really, could she imagine Jed doing that? Had he even *thought* the word 'love'?

Strangely, she believed he had. Wasn't that what he'd been saying, when he said things like, "Use *me*."

Her breath hitched and her eyes burned. He stroked her back and shoulder as he lifted his head from the pillow. "Linette?"

She said urgently, "I want you."

As she scrambled higher in the bed to reach his mouth, he rolled to half-pin her beneath him. What he did was make love to her, with astonishing tenderness and intense focus on what he thought *she* needed.

No, he didn't have to say the words.

*****

Sunday crawled, as far as Jed was concerned. They were all in limbo, Linette most of all. He'd have given just about anything to be able to say, *We've spotted the truck and trailer, and what looks like your horses in a corral. SWAT is surrounding the property right now.* Instead, Theo Willis appeared to have driven off the edge of the world with her horses.

The real problem was the size of the county versus the few sheriff's deputies patrolling it. There were miles and miles of seemingly empty country, countless dirt or gravel lanes leading to distant farmhouses and barns. Theo could have driven right into a barn and pulled the double doors closed behind him. The horses could have been unloaded into stalls, paddocks, let loose in a pasture with other animals. Up close, the Kiger were distinctive, but not from a distance – say a plane flying overhead.

After breakfast, Linette and Niall went out to the barn to take care of the rest of her herd. With a grim sense of purpose, Jed stayed in to work. He continued learning what he could about the two other members of the rustling gang named by Hinton.

One had grown up here in Fort Halleck, attending school a couple of years behind Thayer and Baxter. Jed talked to Grant, who said, "Lee Graafstra? The name rings a bell." The pause suggested he was thinking. "I vaguely remember his older sister. Jenni? Jenna? Pretty sure she was a year ahead of me, though, so we didn't have classes together."

The other guy, Ross Alford, had drifted from his native Idaho through Montana, Nevada, Arizona and Northern California, working as a ranch hand, never staying on any job for more than a few months. Jed had the disquieting thought that Russ Alford was what he might have become if he hadn't joined the army – or if his foster father had dragged him along instead of insisting he stay where he could finish high school. This Alford seemed a natural to have been sucked into the cattle rustling gang:

perpetually broke, rootless, feeling no loyalty to any employer. He'd probably thought, *Why not?*

Like Mason Thayer, he was currently working at the Circle S, Karen Steagall's place. Unlike Mason, Ross probably bunked there, too. Had the two so much as thought twice about stealing from her, a widow desperate to hold onto the land for her young son? Jed would enjoy arresting this SOB, too.

It occurred to him that he hadn't called Karen to let her know about Mason, but he'd wait until he'd made the second arrest, too.

He moved on to search for any and every nugget of information online about Harrison Seward and Theodore Darcy Willis. In neither case did he find anything new.

He put together lunch, wishing his phone would ring. Vibrate. Something. He craved an update. When Linette came in, gaze fastened on his, he had to shake his head. *No news.*

A yearling named Alita Esperanza had a limp that worried Linette. Niall and she debated whether to call the vet, ultimately deciding to wait until morning in hopes she improved. Otherwise, they scarcely spoke as they drank soup from mugs and ate hefty sandwiches.

Linette only nibbled at half her sandwich, but did finish her soup. Jed swore her face looked thinner than it had yesterday, but told himself he was imagining things. Fasting was supposed to be good for you, wasn't it?

After lunch, he went out to work, too, hoping some hard physical labor would wear him out enough to sleep tonight. He rebuilt some older paddock fencing, keeping an eye on Linette when he could. It occurred to him that she almost had to be feeling cabin fever. When was the last time – besides her fun overnight stay in the hospital – that she'd left the ranch? Ten days? Two weeks? The only time she'd even ridden out on her own land was yesterday to check the camera feed. He'd seen the obstacle course she'd constructed on a hillside to work her horses in difficult terrain and response to her signals, but had banned that, too. Ditto for the large outdoor arena. In her shoes, he'd have been going stark raving mad by now. Maybe it was the years of lying stretched out in one spot for days on end, waiting, waiting. His body responded to the memory with a nerve tic below his right eye. No, he'd have a hard time now being constrained or confined in any way. Linette was handling it with grace – although he wondered how often she had chosen to leave the ranch when she lived here alone.

Did she prefer being alone? Feel crowded with his and Niall's presence? He hated to think that, but knew eventually he'd have to ask. This house, the ranch, already felt like home to him. What if, in the end, she didn't want him to stay?

Up in the barn loft to toss down a bale of hay, he huffed a laugh that didn't hold all that much amusement. There'd been a time when he had possessed the ability to wait with limitless patience. No more.

Knowing he'd be sleeping with Linette tonight…that helped.

*****

Jed was aware that Linette had hoped Troy would be back today, but the kid had called last night to let her know he'd have to take a few more days.

"I'm having pretty bad headaches," he had told her. Mumbled, according to Linette.

Poor guy had probably been eager to escape his mother's solicitous care, Jed thought.

The young guy who'd been here Saturday returned today. Ken something. Linette reported that he was even quieter than Troy, but a hard worker. Jed lifted a hand at him when he turned his truck around and started down the driveway.

In the rearview mirror, he saw Linette halfway between the house and barn, watching him go. His gut suddenly twisted and his foot moved to the brake. He didn't want to go anywhere. The reluctance that hit him was so powerful, he didn't know where it had come from. She wouldn't be alone, and he was in the middle of tying up his investigation of cattle rustlers. If they kept falling like dominoes, he'd be cuffing Harrison Seward in no time.

Examining his feelings, he clenched his teeth. No, he didn't actually believe in presentiments, despite his recent outbreaks.

Jed didn't let himself brake until he reached the road, and then only briefly.

Halfway to town, he groped for his ringing telephone.

"We have the warrant for Gene Baxter," Grant told him. "I've already sent it to you."

Jed had ignored a couple of buzzes. Surprised, he said, "Judge Bascomb?"

"Yeatman."

"Does it cover both the ranch and his house in town?"

"It does, and bank accounts, too."

"I wonder if he went to work today."

"Fischer says not. He's still in front of the house. He'll wait to provide backup for you."

Deputy Ben Fischer was young, but solid.

Ten minutes later, Jed rolled to a stop at the curb behind Fischer's patrol car. The neighborhood appeared quiet; kids were probably off to school, parents to their jobs. At the moment, there was no traffic, nobody on foot or bicycle within a couple of blocks. The timing was ideal to make the arrest.

He switched to studying the house, noting that the front blinds were pulled. Didn't mean he wasn't being watched.

After taking a minute to silence his phone and unsnap his holster, Jed got out. Fischer did the same. Their eyes met, and they fell into step going up the driveway.

Jed said quietly, "I need you to cover the back."

The young deputy nodded his understanding. As Jed turned on the narrow concrete walkway that led to the front door, Fischer eased around the side of the clapboard house.

Baxter didn't seem the type to struggle or pull a weapon, but you never knew. As he invariably did, Jed stood to one side of the front door when he rang the bell. A gong sounded from within, but he didn't hear any footsteps. After a minute, he knocked hard and called, "Police! Open the door, Gene!"

Still nothing. He reached for the doorknob, tried to turn it. Locked.

That's when a shout came from the backyard.

CHAPTER TWENTY-ONE

Before going to the locker room, Niall paused to check incident reports from the weekend, BOLOs, anything else that might help him do his job, however temporary that job was. He'd seen only three other officers doing the same. The rest swaggered in, went straight to the locker room, and swaggered out to their cars. The lack of discipline and training in the department infuriated Niall. He'd registered Jed's disapproval, but the atmosphere and morale here were even worse than he'd expected.

He was buckling his belt and running a mental checklist on what he'd need today before closing his locker when he heard a man's voice he recognized. Despite being hushed, it still carried.

"Chief wants us out there right away. Says daytime's safer—"

Bill Wheeler, a ten-year officer who had so far ignored Niall. He entered the locker room, saw Niall, and cut off what he'd been saying. Entering behind him was Jeremy Horner, the officer the ex-rodeo guy had named as a fellow cattle rustler.

Niall nodded at the pair. "Morning."

Horner nodded back. Wheeler grunted, looking suspicious.

As he should be, Niall thought, shutting his locker. On the way out of the building, he greeted a few other people. Once he was behind the wheel of his assigned cruiser, he drove out of the parking lot, circled two blocks and pulled to the curb behind another car in the shade of a big oak, where he could see any other vehicles leaving the station parking lot.

He offered a mental apology to the good citizens of Fort Halleck. Rather than sticking to the city limits and following his patrol route, being prepared to protect and defend those citizens, he intended to follow Officers Horner and Wheeler. He was a lot more interested in finding out just what the sheriff wanted them to do today than he was in ticketing speeders.

*****

Relieved that Alita's limp was scarcely noticeable this morning, Linette led another yearling into the plywood-enclosed arena Jed deemed to be safe. She'd be an idiot to argue about the limitations he'd set in place, but that didn't mean she didn't chafe at them.

The trouble was, her chores in the barn took only a small slice of her typical day, relatively speaking. Usually she spent as many hours as possible on horseback, working the horses on lead changes, staying straight and collected, lateral control, stops…and any particular issues each animal might have. She took longer to achieve outward results than some trainers, because her goal was to ensure that her horses never felt defensive or threatened. Linette aimed for calmness and trust. That was why she had the reputation she did as trainer.

Last year, for the first time since moving out west, she'd taken on some horses to work with on a temporary basis. The money had been a help, but this year she'd been saying no to callers. She had so many young horses of her own needing attention. She could only be grateful right now that she didn't have responsibility for anyone else's animals. Gee, a silver lining.

Having Jed in her life again might be another one. With her trust issues, she wasn't sure yet.

She couldn't even make herself look at the chart on the wall in the tack room tracking each horse's progress and what needed doing next. She had lost almost two weeks now, which wasn't a lot – but already she knew she'd see backsliding with the younger horses especially.

She looked around at the high plywood walls and couldn't decide if she felt safe…or penned in.

At her signal, Luis Alfonso circled widely around her on his lead. He was a true dun, his black markings distinct against his lighter coat. He moved well, stayed responsive when she asked him to trot, canter, walk, change directions.

She was the one to become distracted when she heard an odd coughing sound. Was that one of the horses? Or had Ken inhaled something awful? She didn't hear anything else, but with her focus lost, she drew in the dun colt and led him to the gate. They'd done enough for today.

Just before turning him out to pasture, she removed the halter. He tossed his head hard, sending his mane flying, and trotted away. For a moment she continued to watch, enjoying his springy steps.

After closing gates, Linette walked down the wide aisle of the barn. Alita snorted and stamped in her stall, and a sparrow darted from above out the open doors. The barn was otherwise quieter than usual. Admittedly, she'd yet to hear Ken singing, talking to a horse, dropping something and swearing… It wasn't late enough for him to have taken a lunch break, was it?

Linette glanced into stalls, but hadn't yet reached the tack room when she heard a footfall behind her. Unnerved, she started to spin – but a muscular arm clamped around her body just above her breasts.

"Hello, Linnie," Theo said. "Been waiting for you. Are you glad to see me?"

Through the terror, she asked, "What are you doing here?"

He pressed the sharp tip of a knife into the side of her neck hard enough that she felt a sting…and what she thought might be a trickle of warm blood.

"Have to teach you a lesson."

*****

Once they left town, Niall let an increasing distance open between him and the police car ahead. The country roads were too damn empty, running straight for miles on end. He caught only occasional glimpses of his quarry, not much more than ant-size, but believed he'd know pretty quickly when they turned off. Since he already suspected their destination, he didn't really need to see them anyway, and his route on the GPS confirmed it. They were heading for Chief Harrison Seward's ranch.

His suspicion, of course, was that they and perhaps any working hands here today were going to move stolen cattle. That was smart of Seward in one way. He had to be worried that one of the men who'd been arrested would roll on him. He knew about the regular air patrols at night. Livestock trailers or trucks would be more visible during the day, but his land was near the county line. Some of the smaller ranchers around him would be occupied with their day jobs. Others, if they even noticed cattle being moved, wouldn't think a thing about it. Hey, he was the long-time, trusted police chief of the county's largest city, and any rancher sent some animals to market now and again.

A prickle on the back of his neck had Niall snatching quick looks at his rearview mirror. What if the two officers ahead of him weren't the only ones Seward had sent? If they closed in on him, he could be in deep shit.

Should have brought backup.

He still didn't *know* what was going to happen – but this would be a smart time to call Jed.

The call went straight to voice mail. Perfect. He had entered Sheriff Grant Holcomb's phone number early on, so he tried that next. Same thing. Had Grant joined Jed to arrest Gene Baxter? Last year's serial killer aside, murder wasn't a common crime in Hayes County, so the sheriff might want to be involved.

He still hadn't caught sight of a single vehicle in his rearview mirror, but his unease hadn't lessened.

911? He should have asked questions about local dispatch. Who took the calls? How were they routed? He didn't want to risk this call catching the attention of anybody in his own department.

Crap. At Jed's insistence, Niall had one other number – for the absolute last person he wanted as backup.

*****

Erin was just about to get out on the road when her phone rang. Pulling it out, she was surprised to see the caller's name. Then she felt a jolt of alarm. There was only one reason he'd be calling her.

"Officer Callaghan?"

"Deputy Brown," he returned with a hint of sarcasm. "I can't reach either Jed or Grant. Do you know where they are?"

"No. Hold on, I'm at the station—" She rushed down the hall. "Neither are here. Is there anything I can do?"

"You're involved in the cattle rustling investigation?"

"Yes."

Silence. Finally, he said, "I'm following two FHPD officers out to Chief Seward's ranch."

"Out to *where*?"

Pause. "Jed always was close-mouthed."

She grappled with what he was implying. "He suspects the *police chief...*?"

"That's why I took the job here." He sounded impatient. "Thing is, I overheard one of them saying the chief wanted them 'out there' right away, that daytime's safer. I'm following them, hanging well back. I can watch what happens from a distance, but it would be helpful to have some backup if I need it. Can you track Jed down?"

"I'll try," she said doubtfully, "but I think he's making an arrest. If he silenced his phone..."

Niall swore.

"Who is with Linette?" she asked suddenly.

"Some young hand from the Arrowhead Creek Ranch." He paused. "What are you thinking?"

What she was thinking was that she hadn't heard back on the fingerprints she'd submitted from the padlock. The thought had vaguely crossed her mind a couple of times, but it hadn't been *that* long. She'd assumed they either hadn't popped, or there'd been a partial match that was being pursued. But what if—

"I need to follow up on something," she said. "I'll send someone out. Ben Fischer...no, he's probably with Jed. Uh...Eddie Aguilar is working today. Do you know him?"

"No. Damn it."

Despite the sense of urgency grabbing her, she asked, "Would you rather I come?"

"No!"

"I kind of guessed that," she said dryly, ignoring the burn. Not like he was the first sexist cop she'd met. "Then I'll give Aguilar your number, and keep trying to get in touch with Jed or the sheriff."

"Thanks." He was gone.

She first called Eddie and explained the situation. Currently out on patrol, he thought he wasn't more than fifteen minutes away from Niall's destination. "I'll talk to Officer Callaghan," he agreed.

Duty done, Erin hustled to her desk, where she'd left her laptop open. Calling up her email didn't take long. Still nothing. Thinking about how often her computer was unattended while she ate lunch or was talking to someone, she took a look at deleted emails. Nothing there, either. Erin wanted to be relieved, but wasn't quite.

Then she sent a quick inquiry, and sat staring at the monitor, fingers tapping an impatient rhythm on her desk.

Jed and Niall were closing in on the cattle rustlers, so she couldn't figure out why she had such a very bad feeling about Linette. It would be awfully coincidental if she were attacked right now…unless her assailant had a way of knowing what else was going on.

Reluctantly, she faced her fear. Chris Jarman wouldn't have any way of knowing what Niall was doing right now – she was almost sure – but he was working today. In fact, he'd probably been part of the surveillance on Gene Baxter. Which meant he'd know Jed and maybe Sheriff Holcomb would be tied up this morning. If he really had somehow connected with Linette's stalker, who had asked him to grab the padlock…

A new email sprang into her inbox.

The results of her submission had been returned to her Thursday – four days ago – but here they were again. One partial fingerprint from the padlock appeared not to be in the system, but the second one had come back with a match to a man named Theodore Darcy Willis.

Erin stared at in shock. This was the first conclusive evidence that he was in Hayes County – and there was only one reason he'd be here.

Linette Broussard.

And Erin already knew who had left the second print on the padlock picked up from the ground the morning Linette's horses had been driven out of the pasture and onto the road.

Dashing out to her car, Erin left urgent messages for Jed and Grant. Maybe she should inform Niall, too…but he was fully occupied.

As she accelerated out of the parking lot, she almost wished she *hadn't* left those messages. If she found Linette feeding grain to her horses, and some young cowboy keeping an eye on her, Erin was going to feel like a drama queen.

She was pretty sure guilt was at the root of this sense of foreboding. If something happened because she hadn't followed up sooner on the fingerprints, nobody would ever trust her again.

*****

Theo pulled her tighter against his body. At the feel of his arousal, Linette shuddered with repugnance almost worse than the fear.

Should she ask about Ken? But what if Theo had disregarded the pickup in front of the barn and wasn't aware that anyone else was here? No. If he'd been watching the ranch, and she felt sure he had, he wouldn't make that mistake. Jed or Niall might be able to shield her from Theo, but Curt Deeter? Ken Fields? All she'd done was endanger them by accepting their help.

Theo bent his head to brush his mouth against her ear.

Her flinch was completely involuntary.

When he snapped, "Time to go," he sounded angrier.

Had he really thought she'd *welcome* his touch? Dear God, was he going to rape her?

Linette closed her eyes. Of course he was. Suddenly, she was weirdly calm. Jed would come roaring to the rescue too late. She thought of him with pain, then dismissed the image of his agonized expression. Of his face at all. She was on her own, as she'd been for most of her life. One big difference: this time she'd do anything at all to keep Theo from winning. From humiliating, degrading and hurting her. She'd let him once. Never again.

He abruptly lowered the arm that had enclosed her and instead gripped her braid right at her nape. He must have lowered the knife, too, because she couldn't see it even out of the corner of her eye. He shoved her hard, only his hold on her hair keeping her from falling.

"Get your ass moving," he growled.

She complied, knowing him. Eventually, he'd get complacent. Think he had her back under his thumb, that she'd cower. She'd finally worked up the courage to leave him, but she hadn't ever fought back, a source of shame that burned like acid in her esophagus.

That could work to her advantage. If she was outwardly docile, he'd believe she wasn't capable of fighting back.

Lure him into making a mistake.

He suddenly wrenched her head to one side so that she looked into the tack room. Ken lay sprawled on his face, blood caking the back of his head. In that one, shattering glimpse, Linette couldn't tell if he was breathing.

"You're a monster," she whispered.

Theo laughed. "Kill one, might as well kill 'em all. And believe me—" his voice lowered to a snarl "—I *will* kill Jedediah Dawson. And you," he added carelessly.

He pushed her forward again, sent her stumbling toward Ken's older but shiny pickup truck. Theo yanked open the passenger side door, and forcing her in, twisting her so that she ended up on her knees in the foot well, bent over the seat. In a move so fast she didn't see it coming, he wrenched her arms behind her and snapped on handcuffs.

She turned her face from him.

He said, "Try to escape, and you'll die a little sooner," and slammed the door.

Theo got in the driver's side before Linette had a chance to straighten up. He put a key in the ignition, started the engine and said, "You're a lucky bitch that you don't have to walk back to my truck."

*****

Erin drove faster than was safe considering she wasn't using either lights or siren. Fortunately, once she flew over the Depression era bridge spanning Desperation Creek, the road opened up and half a mile out of town, no other vehicles were in sight.

Eventually an extended cab pickup with a pearlescent paint job and the Arrowhead Creek Ranch logo on the driver door did pass on its way into town. She saw an older, black pickup coming down a long, two-run driveway from a cluster of buildings. No trailer.

In the weird way the brain worked at moments like this, she thought how tiresome it was that practically all men and plenty of women in these parts drove pickup trucks, whether they had any real use for them or not.

That included every other member of the sheriff's department, from the sheriff down. Oh, and FHPD officer Niall Callaghan. That was a given, with his macho attitude.

Personally, she owned a bright yellow, restored, vintage Volkswagen Beetle.

She took the turn into the LB Kiger Ranch drive way too fast, sliding initially and kicking up gravel and dirt. Seconds later, Erin braked in front of the barn. She saw Linette's pickup immediately, but no second vehicle. Instantly wary, she told herself Linette's usual ranch hand might have been dropped off by his mother. Or ditto for a fill-in.

Unconvinced, she stepped out of her car, staying behind its bulk when she called, "Linette? Anyone here?"

The silence was deafening.

She thought about going up to the house, but this wasn't even mid-morning. Her sense of urgency redoubled. Hesitating only a minute, Erin pulled her Glock, lifted it into firing position braced with both hands, and circled the car and ran to the barn. She pressed her back to the ride-side door, open and hooked to the wall. There she held her breath and listened. A whuffling sound and thud she thought might be a hoof against a stall door or wall were all she heard.

She'd never searched what she feared could be a crime scene on her own before, but even assuming she could reach someone, she wasn't about to wait.

Realizing that she still wasn't breathing, she sucked in some air. Slow and deep. Twice. Then she stepped cautiously into the dim interior of the barn. A horse whinnied. No voice answered.

The stalls to her left appeared to be empty, but somebody could be crouched behind the door of one. She eased up to the first, looking over the top. Definitely empty. So were the next three.

To her right, she could see at an angle into the tack room. Hyper alert, putting down each foot as quietly as she could, Erin began to cross the broad aisle to reach that open doorway. She tried to stay vigilant for any movement in the shadows deeper inside the barn, of the faintest sound outside.

Two steps more, and she saw a pair of worn boots lying pointed-toes down on the floor with jean-clad legs attached. Weapon still extended,

Erin reached the doorway – and took in the sight of a man lying, unmoving, on the wood plank floor. Too much blood soaked his hair. Certain the room was otherwise deserted, she rushed to his side and laid her fingertips to his throat.

Her own heart hammered so hard, it took her a minute to feel the pulse, strong and steady. She pulled out her phone and called for an ambulance before, with risky speed, searching the rest of the barn.

Then she ran for the house, banged on the front door, raced around to the kitchen door, where she did the same but saw no one inside.

Linette had been abducted.

At the moment, the only deputy free and even conceivably nearby was Chris Jarman, the last person she could call.

Suddenly, as if a snapshot had appeared before her, Erin remembered that older black pickup, coming down an overgrown driveway bordered by scruffy fields that hadn't been grazed in eons.

She ran for her car, even knowing too much time had passed.

*****

Jed took out his phone before he'd gotten out the door of the interrogation room. It had buzzed half a dozen times or more while he was in there wearing down a frightened Gene Baxter.

The first message was from Grant. His mother had had what appeared to be a stroke and had been transported to the hospital in Madras. In his rush, Grant had left his phone behind. He could be reached via the switchboard at the hospital.

Number two had to do with another investigation of Jed's.

Then Niall came on, explaining tersely what he'd overheard in the locker room at the police station, that he was following the two officers in question, and with it now apparent they were on their way to Chief Seward's ranch, he could use some backup. "I'll find someone," he concluded.

Niall's message had been left an hour and a half ago. Damn it.

Erin Brown's voice came next. She was talking really fast. "You've probably gotten a message from Officer Callaghan by now, so I won't repeat that. He was going to call Eddie Aguilar. The thing is—" she drew a noticeable breath "—I forgot to tell you last week that right after all the horses were let loose at Linette's place, I saw Chris – Chris Jarman, you know – get out of his patrol car at the station and toss something in the bed of his pickup truck. It sort of clunked. I waited until he'd gone inside and checked to see what it was."

Jed froze between one stride and the next.

"It was a padlock that had been cut," she said in a hurry. "I got a couple of fingerprints off it and then put it back. I thought results had just been delayed, and, well, other stuff has been happening. But this morning, I thought 'what if', so I asked for results again. Either I didn't get them, or somebody wiped them off my computer. Anyway, there is an unidentified print, and one that came back as belonging to Theodore Willis. So I'm heading out to Linette's ranch, in case Chris and this Willis have somehow hooked up, because Chris would know you're tied up this morning and it might be a good window of time to…well. I'll let you know."

As scared as he'd ever been, Jed ran for his truck even as he heard a beep in his ear followed by Niall's voice again.

CHAPTER TWENTY-TWO

At the outskirts of town, Jed saw the approaching patrol car. He signaled and turned into the park where the remnants of the original fort could be seen on the banks of Desperation Creek. Erin pulled up next to him, and both jumped out, meeting in front of the vehicles.

She vibrated with anger and the sense of urgency he shared. "You got my second message?"

"I did." That poor kid had taken a tire iron to the back of his head. He was already being transported to the hospital when the second responding deputy – Chris Jarman – had found the tire iron in a stall where Willis must have tossed it. The blood on it had been starting to dry. It was just possible to distinguish it from the rusted metal.

Savagely angry, Jed wondered why Jarman hadn't hidden the damn thing. Maybe he thought the metal was too rough to hold a fingerprint.

Had Willis brought the tire iron with him? Or taken one from Linette's truck, or even Ken's? Jed shook off questions that weren't important right now.

"If I'd slowed to get a better look at the pickup…" Erin said miserably.

Would she have recognized Willis? If she pursued the truck instead of continuing on to the ranch, Ken Fields might have died because medical intervention had been delayed. Jed couldn't see how directing his rage and terror at this inexperienced young deputy would help. Particularly since she'd done something smart in the first place – wondered what a fellow deputy, coming directly from Linette's ranch, had had in his patrol car that he had to transfer to his own pickup truck.

Jed asked questions calmly despite the agony of emotions that spun viciously like a tornado inside him. She described the route she'd taken in pursuit, and they agreed that Willis must have turned off at some point. He asked her to lead him to where she'd seen the pickup.

He already had the county-owned search and rescue helicopter in the air, but knew it would be a miracle if it happened to be in the right place at the right time. No, he had to narrow down the possibilities.

As he drove behind Erin's patrol car, Jed checked messages. Grant's mother was stable and he was on his way back to Fort Halleck.

Jed's boss finished, "If there's anything at all I can do, let me know."

Jed might have been moved by the support, by the fact that he knew Grant really meant what he said, if only he'd had space inside his ribcage for anything but terror.

The second message was from Niall. "Thanks for the call to the Oregon State Police. They've sent reinforcements. I've been watching as a crew loaded a huge stock trailer. We'll close in on it the minute it leaves Seward's property." Pause. "Wish you'd call. Erin and Grant aren't returning calls, either. Makes me think something went south."

Because it did.

No word on the kid found unconscious in Linette's tack room. Jed hoped Alex Burke would let him know about any change in the young man's condition.

Two innocents severely injured at her ranch, and the possibility seemed real that this one might die. Jed knew how hard Linette would take that.

If she lived that long.

He felt as if he had razors beneath his skin. With every twitch, they sliced deeper. He couldn't let himself think about what Theo Willis was doing to Linette right this minute. No—he had to focus on finding her. Fast.

Ahead of him, Erin turned into an overgrown drive leading to a weather-beaten house and barn with a sagging roof. Jed was surprised. This seemed too far from Linette's ranch to be convenient for Theo to have watched her or mounted his assaults, but when Jed got out and asked about it, Erin was firm.

"This was it. I'm positive."

Jed strode to the barn and shoved open a sagging door that groaned at the movement. Inside, he saw Ken Fields's pickup truck, the one that had been parked at Linette's this morning. Already on the phone, he walked around it. No sign of the keys.

He shouldn't touch anything until the CSI crew he'd just summoned did their thing, but Jed didn't let that stop him. Fingerprints and any trace evidence might help convict Willis, but were useless in helping Jed find Linette, and that's all he cared about. He took latex gloves from his pocket and put them on.

From behind him, Erin asked, "What do you want me to do?"

"Touch as little as you can, but search the passenger side." If Linette had already been hurt, had bled, he didn't want to see her blood.

The truck was old enough, the driver door opened stiffly. An insulated travel mug nested in an old-fashioned cup holder. Had to be Ken's. That wasn't something Theo would have carried on his walk.

Feeling desperate, Jed first inspected the gap between the door and the seat. Easy to drop something down there. Nothing. He slid his fingers through the crack at the rear of the seat. Erin did the same on her side. Neither came up with anything.

His heart cramped so hard, he had to blink against dizziness. *Fuck. Fuck.* Without a clue, they'd never find her in time.

Floorboards. Beneath the gas pedal. He laid his cheek on the rubber mat to see under the seat. Not feeling much hope, he swept out everything he saw, from an empty cigarette packet that had been right in front to a crushed energy drink can, several crumpled napkins and one leather glove that had gone stiff.

Jed zeroed in on the cigarette pack. He hadn't caught so much as a whiff of cigarette smoke around Ken. The empty pack could have fallen out when Theo removed the key from his pocket. A tiny, wadded slip of paper tangled with the cellophane revealed itself to be a receipt when Jed pressed it flat.

Gas, paid for in cash, along with two six-packs of beer, a hot dog and a couple of candy bars. Jed knew the combined gas station/convenience store. It was on state highway 380, not a mile from the Crook County line. Ken might have had reason to stop there at some point, but he was unlikely to live out that way. He might even bunk at Arrowhead Creek Ranch.

Focusing the search on what could be misleading evidence could be a terrible mistake, but Jed had to make a decision. He made the call.

*****

Whoever was driving the crew-cab, dually pickup truck pulling the stock trailer knew what he was doing. He took his time coming out of the ranch driveway and turning onto a narrow two-lane county road that didn't have much in the way of shoulders. Slow and careful it went. Niall wouldn't have wanted to be the one behind the wheel even though he'd done some towing in his time.

Using his binoculars, Niall saw through the slotted sides of the trailer. If he wasn't mistaken, there were cattle of several different colorations.

While the driver was still maneuvering, Niall shifted the binoculars to watch another, somewhat smaller trailer being loaded via a chute into a pasture. Mounted men pressed the cattle forward. There went the Charolais.

Back to the first stock trailer, finally straightening out on the road, the dually pickup carefully accelerating. That's when two police cars, one county, one state, burst from concealment with lights flashing, sirens screaming. A second state patroller braked to block the driveway.

And that's how it's done.

Relaxing, Niall watched the action, and waited for the phone call.

Damn. Maybe he did still enjoy the job.

*****

Her instinct was to fight, but when Theo lifted her off the floor of the pickup cab, Linette made herself stay limp. He dropped her as if she were trash and kicked the door shut.

Face in the dirt, Linette bit her lip so hard she tasted blood to keep from crying out. With her hands cuffed behind her back, her knees and head had taken all her weight when she crashed down. Her neck hurt, but, oh, she hoped no tears had escaped. She didn't want to give him the satisfaction. Theo enjoyed seeing other people's pain, especially when he'd caused it.

She saw only his booted feet when he walked around her.

"Bet you wish you'd never left me," he taunted.

"You hurt me," she whispered.

"Do shit the way you're supposed to, it would've never happened," he snapped.

Linette kept her mouth shut.

"Wonder if you could stay on a horse with no hands," he mused.

But for her determination, she would have begged. *Please give me a chance. See how fast I'd be gone.*

Out of the corner of her eye, she saw a barn, any trace of paint long gone, the wood bone dry and cracking. The doors were closed and latched, but not locked. She'd be willing to bet the four-horse trailer was in that barn.

"Lemme see you crawl," he said, in a raw voice she had grown to hate. "Come on, bitch. You look good down in the dirt." He jabbed her with the pointed toe of his boot. "No, squirm like a snake. I might even take a picture of that."

Obedience, she told herself. Jed and Niall wouldn't find out she'd been taken until near six o'clock tonight. Even if Ken wasn't dead, he wouldn't be regaining consciousness and leaping to his feet to call 911 anytime soon. Giving Theo what he wanted would improve his mood and maybe buy her a chance to fight back. It would kill time, too...but time was on his side, not hers.

The burning coal of hate she'd carried for so long burst into flame, burning away her fear. She wanted him to know what it felt like when a fist smashed his cheekbone, when his arm broke, when shame and cowardice curdled in his belly. She wanted to hurt *him*.

Linette twisted enough to get some of her weight onto her shoulder and squirmed forward. Only inches, but Theo slapped her butt and said, "Just like that, baby! Yee haw!"

She drew her knees up under her and pushed forward again. Her shoulder already ached, not helped by the unnatural way her arms were pulled back.

She did it again, and again. When she lifted up on her shoulder, she glimpsed the peeling white paint and concrete foundation of a house. Her cheek blazed from being scraped on the ground.

If she lashed out with her legs, she might be able to bring him down, but he had the knife and probably a handgun.

Wait. Wait.

She heard...something. A buzzing. Maybe the engine of a passing car? But that wasn't quite right. It grew in volume, until Linette knew. A helicopter.

"What the *fuck*?" Theo reached down and grabbed her.

She kicked his knee, his shin, squirmed and fought. He roared with rage. *Please let the helicopter come right overhead. Please let somebody see.*

He slugged her, snapping her head back, then flung her over his shoulder. Even as pain exploded in her face, she flailed, legs thrashing, trying to connect with his balls.

The roar grew until she knew the thing had to be almost directly above. The view might still be blocked by the woods along the road. If so... No, she wouldn't let herself think anything so final.

Theo bounded up the two porch steps as if she weighed nothing, wrenched open a door and flung her inside. Linette skidded across linoleum, crying out when a peeled seam tore at her arm. Lying on her cuffed arms, she saw Theo snatch up a rifle from the counter. He took up a stance in the middle of the kitchen floor with the rifle at his shoulder. Waiting.

She couldn't do anything right now but lie where she was, rocked to one side to take some pressure from her shoulders, and listen. The sound of the spinning blades began to diminish, puncturing her hope. Only...it didn't *keep* diminishing. It must be staying close by, maybe flying over other nearby properties.

Theo spun toward her, his face contorted in fury that made him as ugly as he was inside. He gave her a hard kick aimed at her side that she twisted to take on her hip to protect her kidney.

"This is all your fault, you fucking bitch!" he snarled. "But you'll pay."

He shoved her over onto her face and unlocked one of the cuffs. Then he dragged her a few feet by the arm, yanked her into a sitting position, and she heard the snap of the cuff closing.

"Grab a few things," he muttered, seemingly to himself.

A second later, the heavy thud of booted feet on stairs came to her.

Dazed, Linette looked around. Everything seemed distorted, and she realized one eye must be swelling shut from that last blow. That side of her face hurt fiercely, as did her hip, shoulders, knees…just about all of her.

Concentrate.

Old kitchen, peeling linoleum and torn, battered cupboards. He had left the rifle on the countertop, where she had no chance of getting to it, not with her cuffed to the handle on the refrigerator. Left alone long enough, she might have been able to wrench the handle from the refrigerator door, given the age of the appliance, but a couple of tentative tugs didn't loosen it. She had this awful image of the refrigerator toppling onto her.

Theo must believe he could make a successful getaway. Why else did he need 'things'? Would he take her with him…or rape her now and kill her before he left?

Just for this single moment, she let herself remember the look in Jed's blue eyes when he'd awakened this morning and smiled at her. So impossibly tender. The painful emotions washed through her again. She didn't want to die, but almost worse, she hated the idea of leaving him alone. If he found her, saw her body… Linette was afraid it would break him. To finally let himself love someone and then lose her in such a hideous way would be bad enough, but he'd also believe he was to blame. He'd vowed to keep her safe. She couldn't imagine him surviving that failure.

Swallowing, trying to force back tears that burned behind her eyes and in her sinuses, Linette dug deep in search of resolve. Theo couldn't remain vigilant forever. She had to believe she'd have an opportunity to get away.

*****

The pickup truck met Erin's and Linette's description. Jed rifled the glove compartment and found a registration under an unfamiliar name. He slammed the passenger door and looked around.

Jed had driven here like a madman after getting a message relayed from the helicopter pilot that he'd seen a man and woman struggling near a black pickup. The woman, the pilot thought, might have been handcuffed. The entire way, Jed had feared the lead would prove to be false. What if this turned out to be the scene of an outbreak of domestic violence between some other couple?

Still tense, he heard a whinny. He didn't see any horses, but jogged around the barn. Behind a rusting barbed wire fence, he saw a horse with a silver coat and distinctive markings that always made him think of a zebra. A blue dun, Linette would have said. The horse's mane fell almost to its knees and the lush tail brushed the ground.

A couple of other horses rested under some trees, and he felt sure the fourth one was here somewhere. His relief was profound, weakening him until he bent over and braced his hands on his thighs. No mistake – *this* was where Willis had brought Linette.

And once he found her – and he wouldn't let himself believe he wouldn't – he'd be able to tell Linette her horses were safe.

Another patrol car had pulled in by the time he circled the barn again. Ben Fischer, who must have driven more moderately.

He gestured to his fellow deputy, who nodded and went around the house to the back.

Jed gave him a minute, then reached for the doorknob. It turned easily under his hand. Not locked. Simultaneously, he heard the crack as the young deputy kicked in the back door. Jed scanned the kitchen, then moved swiftly, gun in a two-handed firing position. He stopped momentarily at the sight of blood on the kitchen floor. Streaks only. He avoided it as he edged toward a hall. Bathroom. Bedroom. Linen closet, long unused. He turned to see Fischer waiting for him. Jed pointed toward the staircase. Fischer nod acknowledgement and Jed raced upwards, two steps at a time.

Once he saw the short, empty hall, he waved for the other deputy to join him in clearing the two rooms up here. Both had dusty floors showing no footprints. Nobody had crawled between the sheets on those beds in decades.

Jed lowered his Glock. Shit, shit, shit. He'd made a bad call when he asked the helicopter to back off.

Or maybe not. At the very least, a cornered Theo Willis would use Linette as a hostage. Worst case, he'd kill her quick. And why not? He was a fucking nutcase who'd come after a woman he hadn't so much as set eyes on in nearly four years. Besides, he had to know he was wanted for two brutal murders already. Freeing Linette wouldn't save him from the charges facing him back in Georgia.

"They're on foot," he said aloud.

His fellow deputy didn't comment. The helicopter had hovered near enough to watch for any traffic coming or going from this property. There hadn't been any. Therefore, if Willis and Linette weren't in the house or the barn – which Erin Brown and Deputy Numsen were clearing – Willis had to have run, forcing Linette to accompany him.

Downstairs, Jed calmed himself enough to take a careful look around. Food in the refrigerator suggested this was where Theo had been living. The trash can under the sink overflowed with plastic trays from microwave meals, crumpled bags that had held corn chips and the like, and beer cans. In the living room, crushed beer cans were scattered beside the sofa. The dregs of muddy looking coffee in a mug had been left on a scarred end table. Jed glanced up when Fischer flicked on an old television set, expecting static but surprised to see a grainy picture. Local channel. He hadn't noticed it, but there must be an antennae on the roof. Not likely Theo had subscribed to cable. Probably irrelevant, but it meant he could have followed the news.

Jed walked back through the kitchen, refusing to let himself fixate on the blood. The amount wasn't life-threatening. Outside, he scanned the woods.

There might be somebody else in the department with tracking skills, but Jed intended to rely on his own. There'd been times he'd tracked an assigned target for days before he could take him out. The dry, gritty soil wasn't so different than the lands where he'd served.

He drew to a stop, barely acknowledging the two deputies who walked out of the barn shaking their heads. No, damn it – he wasn't using his head. There was a much faster way to find Theo Willis.

*****

Grant bounded up the granite steps and strolled into the police station. The duty sergeant behind the long counter gave him a startled look. He must know something was happening, if not what.

"Sheriff?"

"Chief Seward expects me." Grant didn't ask; he told.

"I...yes, sir." This was one of the old-timers, arthritis making his knuckles knobby. He made the call, presumably using an internal line, but the phone rang and rang.

Grant got a sudden, sick feeling in his gut. He shouldn't have called and offered Seward the chance to come to down to the sheriff's headquarters to talk, not when the man must know he'd be sentenced to what amounted to the rest of his life in prison – and that as a cop, he'd face either solitary confinement or a good chance of a fellow inmate slipping a shiv between his ribs into his heart.

And this was a man with access to a buffet of weapons.

Dawning fear in the desk sergeant's eyes decided Grant, who shoved open the half door at the end of the counter and ran down the hall.

The office door was locked.

Hammering on it, Grant called, "Seward? Harrison? Open the door. We can talk."

He recognized the depth of that silence.

Voice shaking, the sergeant said, "I have a key."

Grant checked his immediate intention of breaking the door in and waited what felt like an eternity but probably wasn't more than a minute. Hand shaking, the sergeant handed over a key on a ring along with an identifying tab. Grant inserted the key, turned it and opened the door.

The smell hit him first, and he realized he'd already breathed in the tang. It hadn't been just the silence that had the hair rising on the back of his neck.

"Son of a bitch," he muttered.

Gazing at the body slumped in the desk chair, Grant hoped the Oregon State Police Department was having a slow day. His own resources were stretched far enough to snap. Three major crime scenes were more than a department the size of his could handle, especially since they didn't yet know which FHPD officers were implicated in the cattle rustling.

He needed help, and was hurt further by not being able to call on one of his already too-few deputies. Hindsight being what it was, Grant wished like hell he'd already fired Chris Jarman, although it occurred to him that at least now he knew where to find him. Grant's jaw tightened.

They didn't yet have useable evidence to convict Jarman, but he was going down along with Theo Willis. Grant only prayed the charge didn't end up being for the murder of Linette Broussard.

*****

When he heard the rumble of a diesel engine approaching the house, Jed looked up. He had quickly found scuff marks in the soil, but used his diminishing supply of willpower to wait.

Thank God, Dr. Knappe had been at home when Jed called, and had gotten here with startling speed. Since only one deputy was patrolling the county today – assuming that piece of shit, Chris Jarman, wasn't actually out here somewhere with a plan to aid Theo – the veterinarian had had next to no chance of getting pulled over for speeding.

Lean and dressed in boots, cargo pants and a denim shirt with sleeves rolled up, he jumped out of his truck, his yellow lab following a second later. They came straight toward Jed, who met them halfway.

"I have a second S and R volunteer on her way with her dog, in case we need help," Knapp said. "Do you have something of the woman's that will give Snoopy the scent?"

"Not of Linette's, although I sent a deputy to her ranch to grab an item of clothing in case we need it." Erin. "The man who abducted her has been staying in this house, though. I think this T-shirt is his." He held it out.

Jed had found it on the floor almost under the bed. It reeked of sweat.

Dr. Knappe took the shirt and presented it to his dog, who buried her snout in it and took a good, long sniff. Snoopy then lowered her sensitive nose to the ground…and without hesitation headed toward those scuff marks.

She moved so fast, she'd have left them behind if her handler hadn't had her on a leash. A man in his late fifties, Knappe had no trouble keeping up. Jed's heart drummed as he stayed on their heels. He was afraid of coming on Theo and Linette too suddenly, but it had now been an hour and a half since the helicopter pilot had spotted them. Linette would have hampered Theo, who'd have had to keep her under control. Still, Jed didn't like to think of how far they could have gotten in that length of time.

Mostly, he and Knappe jogged, slowing or stopping only occasionally when Snoopy paused as if momentarily uncertain. She always caught the scent again quickly, and took off with unmistakable eagerness.

They'd been moving for forty-five minutes when the vet pulled his dog to a stop.

"Cabin," he murmured to Jed, who came to his side.

The clearing in front of them was substantial – close to an acre, he thought. The cabin was newish, the lawn a week or two late for a mowing. Either Theo had known this place was empty and kept it in mind as a bolt hole – or he'd been prepared to kill anyone in his way.

The small-paned windows in the cabin were smaller than Jed would have liked, and from here he didn't see any not covered by curtains or blinds. He couldn't assume Willis and Linette were inside – this could be a decoy, if they'd continued on – but it made sense Theo would make a stand here. The log walls were solid. It would take a howitzer to rip through them.

Jed eyed the surroundings, focused on the slight rise behind the cabin where he'd set up.

Crack.

Fuck! A chip of bark from a tree not a foot from him barely missed his eye.

He dove towards the veterinarian, tackling him to the ground.

Crack. Crack.

With a whine, Snoopy scuttled back to huddle with them.

Eyes on the cabin, watching for any movement, Jed pulled out his phone. He'd get this place surrounded, then go for his own rifle. Sooner or later, Theo Willis would pass in front of a window.

Jed wouldn't hesitate to blow off his head.

CHAPTER TWENTY-THREE

"Somebody is out there." Theo sounded disbelieving. "I'll fix that!"

He was almost out of sight, but Linette heard him unlocking the front door. He must have cracked it open, because she could see his right shoulder and the butt of the rifle as he lifted it and fired. Once, twice, three times.

Linette winced with each explosive sound.

He must have shut the door and locked. The next thing she knew, he'd rushed to another window and peered between blinds. "How did the fuck did they find us so fast?" He spun toward her with that shocking speed he'd always possessed. "You have GPS on you, don't you?" His voice rose. "Where is it?"

"I don't!" Linette instinctively shrank from the huge, enraged man advancing on her. The too-familiar sight snapped her into a flashback. It flickered like a double exposure; one second she was here, the next she saw another time and place. His fist would be descending. She felt the phantom pain…

No. Abruptly, she was back to the present. She hurt because he had already hit her. If his last blow had cracked her cheekbone, what would this one do?

I'm not the same person. I'm stronger.

For what good that did her now. Unfortunately, she couldn't retreat very far, since he had cuffed her to the handle of the refrigerator here, too.

Nor could she keep herself from hunching into a small ball when his enormous hands reached for her. He groped his way over her body, thighs, between her legs, hips and finally breasts, which he squeezed painfully before he straightened and glared at her.

"Where's your phone?"

"I…don't know." She'd had it in the back pocket of her jeans while she worked in the barn this morning, hadn't she? That seemed like an eternity ago. She could tell he didn't believe her, but his search would have found the phone if she had it.

"Maybe whoever lives here was coming home," she suggested timidly.

"They're supposed to be away," he snapped.

He raced back to the living room to look out of the window.

What if he'd killed someone who had had an innocent reason for turning into this driveway or walking up to the house? The owner, a neighbor, a UPS driver.

The odds weren't good that whoever was out there was looking for *her*.

Linette grappled for understanding. Why had the helicopter been here in the first place? This couldn't be much more than midday. Jed had no way to know she'd been kidnapped, unless... No, even if by chance someone had stopped at her ranch and found Ken, how could Jed possibly have guessed where to send aerial reconnaissance?

Probably a child was missing or something like that. Or – had the helicopter been up watching for some cattle being moved?

A shout came from another room.

Unless Theo's paranoia had become so exaggerated he was seeing things, it seemed the cabin was being surrounded. She'd been wrong; somehow she and Theo had been tracked. But how?

After fleeing the old house where he'd first taken her, they could have gone in any direction. As Theo dragged her through the woods, she had wished desperately that Jed, or anyone else, was right behind them. Was it remotely possible someone *had* been trailing them, moving like a ghost between the boles of the pines? Or had more time passed than she thought? Her vision was still funny, and her head throbbed, but she didn't think she'd passed out. She peered toward the nearest window, but through filmy white curtains she couldn't see the angle of the sun.

Going very still, she realized she also couldn't see Theo. On that thought, she looked frantically around. She should have already done that. Unless she planned to crouch here waiting for him to murder her, she needed to use her head, whether it throbbed or not.

The refrigerator was located at one end of the kitchen counter and cabinets. A doorway leading into a utility room was on the other side of the fridge. Theo and she had come in that door. It didn't have an inset window, as such doors often did. Remembering the solid sound it had made closing behind them, Linette thought it was a steel door. She distinctly recalled Theo turning a deadbolt lock, too. There was a window in there, though, she could tell from the quality of the light.

She started to wonder how he'd gotten a key – or had the door been unlocked? – when she pulled herself back. Not important. So focus. What could she reach that had the potential to be a weapon?

She heard the footsteps just before Theo reappeared. Linette took care to round her shoulders and stay on her knees, trying to look cowed. It must have worked, because all he did was rake her with a disparaging glance on his way to...maybe a dining room?

A wooden block holding a selection of knives taunted her from the far end of the counter. Otherwise, a set of red glazed ceramic canisters were the only things on the counter, and they were almost as far away. But she could reach one set of cupboard doors and at least two of a stack of three drawers. She prayed they didn't hold waxed paper and aluminum foil, or tablecloths and napkins.

Theo passed by again, trailing invectives. Rage and, she thought, fear contorted his face. This time she heard him bounding up a staircase.

Cupboard first. A toaster. A waffle iron. A blender. A few pans, none cast-iron. Damn. *Quiet, quiet, quiet.* Linette eased the cabinet door shut. Hiding a cast-iron frying pan behind her back would have been a challenge anyway.

Still no sound of Theo coming back down.

First drawer held silverware. A butter knife didn't make much of a weapon. A fork...well, maybe, if she didn't find anything else. What she'd give for a hoof pick.

Feet thudded on the stairs again.

"I don't see anybody in back," he growled, coming straight to her. "We need to get out of here."

She made a point of cowering. "But, what if someone shoots at us?"

His mouth curled. "Yeah, you'll make a good shield."

Why hadn't she noticed back then that he never really smiled or laughed? What passed for a smile on Theo's face was closer to a jeer, derision, a sneer. If he was happy, a smirk.

Never violent, right this minute Linette would take pleasure in swinging the longed-for cast-iron frying pan at his face.

Lacking that…she stood passively while he unlocked the cuff from the refrigerator handle and jerked her toward the utility room and the back door.

*****

Erin crouched at one end of a large propane tank tucked beneath the eaves behind the cabin. She was confident she couldn't be seen from any window, and she had a narrow view between the tank and the log walls of the cabin to the back door. She, and all the other deputies now ringing the cabin, had orders to keep Theo trapped inside.

Erin had only her handgun, which felt huge in her small hands right now. She practiced regularly at the range, and was a competent shot. Not satisfied with competent, she put in more hours facing down the bull's-eye than did any of the other deputies. None of that practice helped right this minute. She'd been in tense situations before, but had never had time to think, *I may have to shoot and kill a man today*. She closed her eyes momentarily. God forbid anyone else ever guess she'd suffered a case of nerves like this.

And…that wasn't all wrong with her. She kept dwelling on why she hadn't followed up on those fingerprints sooner. If she had, Linette might never have been abducted. That young ranch hand might not be battling for his life at this very minute. She'd let something drop, and the consequences were dire.

If either Linette or Ken Fields died, Erin didn't know how she'd live with it. Maybe Niall Callaghan wasn't a jerk. Maybe he was *right*, that she didn't have what it took to do this job well.

She gave her head a hard shake. She couldn't afford this now. *Do what you have to do, indulge in guilt later.*

Oh, and while she was at it? She silently begged Jed to hurry. Call her a coward, but she didn't want to have to confront a vicious thug wanted for murder on her own.

At a scraping sound that had to be the deadbolt sliding in the steel door not twenty feet from her position, Erin's heartbeat jumped and wobbled, but she also murmured into her radio and steadied her grip on her weapon.

*****

By the time Jed made it back to the cabin where Linette was being held captive, he'd been updated on several fronts. He might as well be in another dimension, his world narrowed until he heard and understood what was said even as none of it touched him. He recognized the ice that encased him, that allowed him to do a deadly job. At least the calls coming in on his cell phone distracted him from the inner core of pain he couldn't let cripple him.

Harrison Seward had seen his downfall coming and swallowed a gun, one with a suppressor that had cut down on the sound so that, combined with thick walls in the old police station, no one heard the shot. He had likely been dead for half an hour or more before Grant discovered him.

A dozen cattle rustlers had been arrested, four of them police officers. These were the "in" crowd Niall had mentioned. For the moment, the cattle that had been loaded into two stock trailers were released on Seward's land again. A search of Seward's records would have to wait; most sheriff's deputies were out at the cabin preventing Theo Willis from taking off. The state patrol had really come through for the Hayes County Sheriff's Department today.

At this moment, Jed couldn't even think about the rustling investigation, the number of compromised law enforcement officers or the shocking end for a man who'd been respected by the citizens of this county during a long career in Fort Halleck. All Jed could think about was Linette. How frightened she was, whether she'd been hurt, whether that scum had raped her.

Whether she was still alive.

He pulled up behind a row of police vehicles at the foot of the driveway leading to a cabin that belonged to a local bank president, currently in Cancun, Mexico. Jed had spoken to him. The distraught man hadn't had the least idea that anyone was living at the old farmhouse a quarter of a mile past his place. He did admit to keeping a hideout key under a planter on the front porch. It worked for both the front and back doors.

"Nobody in the neighborhood has had a break in," he mumbled.

He had talked Jed through the layout of the interior. It was conceivable they'd have to go in, but that would be a last resort. The risk to Linette – he had to believe she was alive – would be too great.

Willis might be smart. He was quick to turn violent, seemingly lacked any conscience, and he'd killed before, possibly more than the twice that they knew about. What he hadn't done was serve in the military. There was no indication he'd ever belonged to a gang. He wasn't a career criminal. All of which meant it was unlikely he'd spent much time handling his guns – although that shot earlier had come closer to Jed's head than he liked. Even so, Theo would have no idea how to protect himself from a man who knew what Jed did, who'd spent years as a government-sanctioned assassin.

Mostly, Theo Willis reserved his anger for women. Lacking any control over his temper, he lashed out viciously, taking advantage of his size. And he'd had Linette in his complete control now for almost four hours.

Tiny cracks weakened the ice containing Jed's emotions. He'd never been this scared in his life.

Carrying his rifle and a duffle with any accessories he might conceivably need, he jogged up the driveway. Melting into the trees just before he would have emerged into the clearing, he immediately saw Ben Fischer waiting for him.

"What's been happening?" Jed asked.

The excitement mixed with nerves he'd expect from an officer as young as Fischer showed on his face, but his report was concise and steady. "A few minutes ago, he opened the back door. Deputy Brown is back there. She yelled, 'Police.' Ordered him to lay down his weapons. He shot at her."

The muscles in Jed's jaw spasmed.

"Bullet pinged off the propane tank behind the house. She shot back, he retreated inside. She doesn't think she got him. Nothing since."

"Okay." He thought about what the homeowner had told him. "I understand there's an upstairs window in back with no blinds or curtains, and another window on the ground floor with blinds that may have been left open."

"Yeah, the utility room. Can't see into the kitchen through it, so unless he's standing by the washer and dryer—" He shrugged.

"Has anyone actually seen him well enough to identify him?"

"The upstairs window, once," Fischer said confidently. "Kittson is back there in the woods."

Jed hoped his wince didn't show. Ned Kittson was pot-bellied, in his sixties and a year from retirement. But that was the current sheriff's department: the young and the old. Jed and Grant were the only two with experience under their belt, but not too many years. Jed wished Grant were here, but understood that he had to take control of the police chief's apparent suicide and the rest of the mess there, especially determining whether the officers who hadn't already been arrested were law-abiding, or just hadn't happened to be caught red-handed today.

"I'll set up in back," he said. "Let me know if Willis shows up clearly at any other window. Hold your fire unless he's clearly alone or comes out shooting. He might be using Ms. Broussard as a shield."

"Yes, sir." Fischer restrained his hand before he saluted. Barely.

At the sound of an approaching vehicle, Jed eased behind the thick bole of a pine. If this wasn't Grant, it almost had to be...

The engine cut off, and a door slammed. Sure enough, Chris Jarman stormed up the driveway. In this situation, the deputies had had to revert to using their radios, so he'd have heard what was happening here, if not at the other two crime scenes currently being processed.

Maybe Jarman was here to protest being left out of the action, but it was also possible he thought he could help Willis, or just screw with Jed because he was pissed.

And damn, Jed did not want to deal with this piece of shit, not now when Linette's life might hang on him getting set up to shoot, but Jarman had to be incapacitated.

"You're my backup," Jed murmured to Ben Fischer.

He swallowed hard, but nodded.

Jed stepped in front of the new arrival. "Put your hands on the tree."

Looking shocked, the jackass started to obey.

"You are under arrest for aiding and abetting a killer," Jed said grimly. "I'll be taking your weapon—"

Even as Jarman said, "What the fuck? I don't know what you're—" he turned to face Jed, his hand dropping toward the butt of his gun.

Jed had his Glock in his hand and pointed before this asshole had the chance to be even stupider. Fischer was only a beat slower.

Jarman flushed purple with fury. "You can't do this."

"Face the tree. Let me see your hands on it."

"You have no goddamn right—" He must have been able to tell Jed was the wrong person for him to argue with, because he flung himself around and obeyed.

When Jed said with surface calm, "Take his gun," Deputy Fischer stepped forward and gingerly removed Jarman's weapon from the holster. Looking shaken, he laid it on the ground a distance away, then on Jed's order cuffed his fellow deputy. A minute later, they searched and found a backup gun at his ankle. Confident he had no other weapons, Jed had Fischer put Jarman in the cage in the marked vehicle he had just arrived in.

Jarman was screaming for an attorney when they shut the door and walked away. He had good reason. The arrest wasn't legally justifiable, given that the only solid evidence was the padlock – which Erin had removed from Jarman's personal vehicle without a warrant. Since she'd put it back, it couldn't serve as any kind of evidence. Right this minute, Jed didn't give a shit.

"Let the sheriff know," Jed said tersely.

Fischer stole a look at him. "Yes, sir."

Jed wondered if any of them realized that he had no intention of arresting Theodore Darcy Willis. He was going to execute him.

*****

Once again cuffed to the refrigerator, Linette quelled the instinct that wanted her to crouch to make a smaller target. Instead, she stayed on her feet, the better to be able to stretch to reach the second drawer.

Theo backed away, but hate glittered in his eyes. "Every goddamn thing I've had to do is on you. If you hadn't called the cops… If you hadn't left…"

Oh, it was hard to keep pretending she'd take anything he threw at her. But reason never had worked with him. So she acted as if her life depended on it – as it did – and gazed at him fearfully. "I haven't seen you in four years. I don't understand."

"Doesn't matter if you—" His head turned sharply.

Linette, too, heard muffled yelling. Theo hurried into the living room.

She waited until he swore, the sound distant enough she knew he was at one of the front windows. Then she stretched, prayed and pulled out the drawer. Which, thank God, glided smoothly.

This drawer was filled with kitchen implements. Everything but knives. The usual variety of spoons for stirring, pancake turners, whisks, a can opener and a corkscrew. Shish kebab skewers. Linette gazed at the jumble, heartbeat racing like she'd never felt before. When she heard Theo stomping in this direction, Linette's hand shot out and snatched up a skewer before she nudged the drawer shut and slipped the sharp, thin stainless steel implement behind her back. She was pretty sure she got it into her jeans – at least, nothing metallic landed at her feet. When Theo appeared, she was dizzy with the stress. Oh God – if only she had the butcher knife instead.

His eyes narrowed as he crossed the kitchen. "You're up to something."

She sat down, her legs shaky enough turn her descent into a collapse. At least she didn't skewer herself. "What am I supposed to be up to? Digging for food in the refrigerator?"

"Good idea." He reached over her head for the handle.

She scooted as far sideways as she could. "There's not much in there but mustard and ketchup. They cleaned it out."

He stared disbelieving at the brightly lit bare shelves, closed the door and lashed out with his booted foot. Pain burst on her thigh. She gasped and tried to scrunch into a smaller ball yet, even as she assessed distances and whether she'd be able to get the skewer from her waistband and thrust it into his belly or chest fast enough – and with enough force to do serious damage.

He kicked her a second time and walked away.

*****

Rifle resting on a bipod, Jed lay on his belly, crushing some forest understory plants like the common creeping Oregon grape to release pungent odors. Taller native plants like serviceberry and snowberry helped screen him from sight. He'd changed into camouflage, including a billed cap. Trying to force himself to relax – which wasn't going well, but it would come - breathing slowly, he gazed through the scope, shifting his field of view gradually from one window of the cabin to another. The windows were smallish, as was typical of a log cabin, but at less than a hundred yards, he could hit a target the size of a dime.

The only other person he'd so far seen was Erin, still crouched at one rounded end of the propane tank. Her gaze had shifted to him when he first appeared and chose a spot offering the optimum line of sight as well as decent cover, but she hadn't looked at him in a while.

Knowing Linette was inside, potentially suffering, possibly already dead, clawed at him. The option of going in tempted him. If they could get their hands on that hideout key, Jed might have gone for it.

As it was, while they were breaking down a door, Theo would have plenty of time to kill Linette and himself.

He had to believe she was still alive.

Murmurs came from the radio. The deputies circling the cabin reported seeing blinds twitching, which meant Theo was constantly on the move, watching. Twice, Jed saw a subtle shift of blinds, too, but couldn't make out who was behind them – or whether Theo might be using Linette as body armor.

He had yet to appear in either of the uncovered windows here on the back and north side of the cabin. One, according to the homeowner, was above the washer and dryer in the utility room. Theo wouldn't be able to get close enough to the window to use it for reconnaissance. He'd have no reason to go in there, after the last time he'd tried opening the back door. That left the upstairs window in a home office as Jed's best bet.

Increasingly, he worried that Theo had to know that if he managed to walk out of the cabin alive, he faced life in prison if not the death penalty.

Letting Linette go wouldn't save him. He was just crazy enough to be getting ready to end this the way he may well have intended from the beginning: kill her, kill himself. If he'd rather commit suicide by cop, Jed would be happy to oblige.

He gave up on the possibility of relaxing. Breathing, that he could do. Having already adjusted for a slight breeze and zeroed his rifle for what would be a cold barrel shot, he visualized the bullet's path. The only acceptable outcome was a head shot that would drop this monster dead before he knew it had happened – and before he could lift his own weapon.

One moment of carelessness. That's all Jed asked for.

CHAPTER TWENTY-FOUR

"I wonder if I could toss you out an upper window. Bet that'd cause enough excitement, nobody would see me taking off. Hey, you can be naked. Yeah, that would give 'em all excited."

Color feverish, Theo paced the kitchen. Back and forth. Back and forth. He'd developed a nervous tic below his left eye. His free hand balled into a fist, loosened, did it again.

Occasionally he made the rounds to look outside, but less often. He hadn't gone upstairs in a while. He was never gone long enough for her to open the drawer again and see if there were better options than the thin skewer.

If Linette had been scared before, that was nothing. Seeing him falling apart and knowing what the outcome would be...*that* was terrifying.

I willingly had sex with this man, once upon a time. There was a horrifying thought. How could she not have seen what he was really like?

She knew, *knew*, that Jed was out there waiting, his eye to his rifle scope, his finger resting on the trigger. What would it do to him to kill again? What had it already done to him, preparing to shoot Theo? Had he slid back into the remote man he'd been, as had happened after he used his sniper skills to save Cassie Ward and the sheriff? When he was done, would he lay down his rifle and see himself again as a killer, unworthy of any woman's love?

Linette hated Theo most of all for what he was doing to Jed. She desperately wanted to live, she did, but not if Jed paid the price. Only...if she died because he failed, that would destroy him, too.

Her mind jumped back to the shish kebab skewer. Could she get a solid enough grip to allow her to drive the thin piece of steel through a cotton shirt, skin and the hard, muscled wall of Theo's torso? The handle wasn't made for anything like that.

Could she stab even Theo?

And what's the alternative here?

She breathed deeply. For Jed. For him, she had to at least try. Soon. It could become too late any minute.

She moved to get one foot under her, as if she was going to stand up. Her legs tingled and she was dismayed to discover that one foot felt numb. She wriggled the toes madly, trying to bring life back into them. He watched with dark, burning eyes, then returned to his pacing.

Once his back was briefly turned, she wiped her hand in case it was sweaty, pulled out the skewer and held it against her thigh. "Theo?" She tried to sound timid. "Do you think they'll come in after you? Like, break windows or..." Her shudder wasn't entirely pretend.

She could do this. She could.

"They'll probably try." He walked toward her, as she'd hoped. *My only chance.* "But you'll already be dead, won't you?"

"Why?" Under the circumstances, it wasn't all that hard to produce a whimper. "I still don't understand."

He leaned over her, hate twisting his face into something ugly. "Because of *you*, everything went wrong. *That's* why." His hand started to rise, the one holding the gun.

Now.

Linette sprang to her feet, using her momentum to drive the skewer into his belly and upward. It went deep before hitting something hard. The gun fired painfully close to her ear, so close to her head she quit hearing, but the bullet hadn't hit her. Crimson blossomed on his belly. Feeling sick, she had to let go of the skewer. As Theo staggered back toward the utility room, he tried to raise the gun again, but this shot hit the floor. He never took his eyes from hers, bewilderment transforming his hard, angry face. When the gun fell from his hand, she whimpered in earnest and watched him collapse against the washing machine. Under his weight, it slid into the dryer with a clang.

And then the window shattered and Theo just...dropped. She saw his death before he hit the floor.

*****

Jed ran toward the cabin. He had to get to Linette.

He bellowed her name even as he threw himself uselessly against the steel door. The knob did not miraculously turn under his hand.

He backed away. He could break out one of the front windows.

Erin was beside him saying something. As frantic as he felt, he made himself listen.

"If you hoist me up, I think I can get in the window you just shot out."

All he could do was nod and circle the corner of the house. He used the barrel of his handgun to knock shards of glass from the frame, holstered it again and bent with his hands clasped. It was just like tossing a woman into the saddle.

Straightening was easy, Erin a featherweight. She pushed herself halfway through before stopping. "He's, um, right here. Dead."

"Keep going." His heart was about to fucking beat it's way out of his chest.

That's when he heard Linette.

"Jed? Erin, is that you?"

"Yes—"

He drowned her out. "Linette? Are you hurt?"

"Not that bad." She sounded uncertain. "I...I can't let you in."

Because she couldn't even crawl as far as the door to unlock it? He didn't let himself ask.

"We'll be right there."

Erin squirmed forward until her feet left his hands and she descended inside to a metallic sound. She was on top of the washer or dryer, he realized, probably denting it. He hurried back around the corner. A second later, the deadbolt scraped and the door swung open.

Jed took in the sight of the very dead man, pausing briefly on what almost looked like a thick wire that stuck out of his belly at an angle. Then he vaulted the blood and the body, landing in a doorway leading to the kitchen.

When he saw Linette sitting in front of the refrigerator with her legs splayed and one hand cuffed to the refrigerator, he stopped. Rage flooded him again. He had to breathe through it before he could kneel beside her, cup her lividly bruised and swollen face in his hands, and say, not quite lightly, "You might scare the horses this time."

Her eyes burned, but her lips wobbled into a smile. "Jed."

*****

Niall had been the one to pick Linette up once the ER doctor decided to release her. Linette understood why Jed couldn't; he had crime scenes to oversee. From what Niall told her, the county was rife with them. Theo wasn't the only one to die today.

Niall came straight from the Fort Halleck police station, where he'd taken over from Sheriff Holcomb so that Grant could go out to assist Jed. The city council, Niall told her, had made him a very temporary acting police chief, since he was the one and only officer who came with guarantees. He'd be interviewing the few remaining members of the department tomorrow, with authority to arrest or fire as necessary.

"Sheriff's department will patrol within the city limits as well as out in the county until we get things together," he had added.

He also told her that the stolen horses were safe. Jed had seen them in a pasture near the house where Theo had apparently been living. Linette tried to wipe away her tears before Niall could see them.

He had no idea whether Chris Jarman was still on the job, or fired. Or whether they'd be able to prove he had assisted Theo. There were plenty of loose ends, too, like identifying who had killed Oren Calderon, but that, she suspected was normal.

Right now, Linette didn't much care about any of that. Against all expectations, she had survived. The way Jed had touched her, back in the cabin, gave her hope.

Declining anything to eat or drink, she plodded up the stairs, one step at a time, Niall hovering just behind her in case she collapsed. She tried not to let him see what a close call it was. In the bathroom, she stripped to survey her multiple, spectacular bruises, shuddered and ran a hot bath.

Once the water cooled, she pulled on flannel pajama pants and a baggy T-shirt, then snuggled into bed even though she doubted she would actually be able to nap. Remnants of fear kept zapping her with adrenaline. Having done something so gruesome to another human being would haunt her, too, as would the expression on Theo's face as he stumbled back.

A weight on the mattress woke her up. It was Jed, looking down at her with emotions so naked, she was afraid she was actually dreaming. But the setting sun had changed the quality of the light coming in the window. She must have slept after all.

In that golden light, she saw the man he might be in twenty years: lines carved too deeply in his cheeks and forehead, hair so pale it could be silver, darkness dimming the clarity of his blue eyes, as if she was seeing a total eclipse of the moon.

"Jed?" Scared anew, Linette struggled to free her arm from the bedding. He helped, and engulfed her hand in a warm clasp. She searched his haggard face. "Are you…all right?"

"No," he said roughly. "I'm having trouble believing you're here." He swallowed. "Alive."

"But I am."

"Yeah. Can I hold you?"

"Yes. Oh, yes!"

She started to sit up, but he kicked off his boots, pulled back the covers and got under them with her. He wrapped his arms around her, pressed his cheek against the top of her head, and shook.

All she could do was hold him, too. She tangled her bare legs with his, and gathered up a handful of his shirt, wishing he wasn't wearing it.

"I'm fine. You were there when I needed you. It's all over, Jed." She kept talking, unsure if she was getting through to him, but feeling his muscles loosen slowly, one by one.

That was when she whispered, "I killed him, didn't I?"

Jed was quiet for a long moment. Finally, his hand stroked up and down her back, soothing. "I think we both killed him. What in hell *was* that you stuck him with?"

She told him.

"A shish kebab skewer," he repeated slowly. "Jesus, Linette. What if it had bent?"

"It…didn't." Would she ever forget the sensation of shoving a weapon deep into a man's body?

"No." His arms tightened again. "The medical examiner thinks he'll find that it pierced his heart. He would have died. I just finished him off a little faster."

"Oh." Part of her wanted to see his face, part of her didn't.

Maybe he felt the same, because he didn't say anything else for a long while. And then he did.

"I've never told you I love you." He still sounded hoarse. "Today, I thought I'd never have the chance."

She froze. Had he really said the words she'd never believed he would? Needing to see him, she pushed herself up. His face was still naked in a way that thrilled her, even as it also horrified her. Could he survive without his defenses? How could she tell him she didn't need that from him, only his love?

Raggedly, she said, "I love you, too. You know that, don't you?"

"Yeah." He closed his eyes. "I've been hanging on by my fingernails. I kept thinking— I don't know."

"I'm here. I'm safe." She drew a deep breath. "I was afraid for *you*. I didn't want you to have to kill anyone for me."

He shook his head, incredulity chasing away some of the desperation. "I'd do damn near anything for you. To save your life—" he seemed to choke on it "—I'd condemn myself to hell."

"No!" She tried to shake him, without effect. "That's what I was afraid you'd do."

"You thought I'd pull away."

Linette wasn't a crier, but tears were very closer. "Yes."

"It's too late for that." The deep velvet of his voice was back, as was the whisper of a southern accent. "I need you. I want you to marry me, so I can know you'll always be here. That I can come home to you."

"Yes." Hot tears overflowed and ran down her cheeks. "Of course I will. Just don't—" She hadn't meant to say that.

"Leave you?" The darkness had retreated. His eyes, vivid blue, held hers. "Never. I swear."

"Okay." When she smiled, she tasted the salty wetness of her tears. They stung the small contusions on her face, too. One plopped onto his stubbled cheek. And for the first time since she was a small child, she knew complete happiness.

About The Author

Janice Kay Johnson is the author of more than ninety books for children and adults. Her first four published romance novels were coauthored with her mother Norma Tadlock Johnson, also a writer who has since published mysteries and children's books on her own. These were "sweet" romance novels, the author hastens to add; she isn't sure they'd have felt comfortable coauthoring passionate love scenes!

Janice graduated from Whitman College with a B.A. in history and then received a master's degree in library science from the University of Washington. She was a branch librarian for a public library system until she began selling her own writing.

She has written six novels for young adults and one picture book for the read-aloud crowd. ROSAMUND was the outgrowth of all those hours spent reading to her own daughters, and of her passion for growing old roses. Two more of her favorite books were the historical novels: WINTER OF THE RAVEN and THE ISLAND SNATCHERS, written for Tor/Forge and now available in ebook format for the first time. The research was pure indulgence for someone who set out intending to be a historian.

Janice raised her two daughters in a small, rural town north of Seattle, Washington. She spent many years as an active volunteer and board member for Purrfect Pals, a no-kill cat shelter, and foster kittens often enlivened a household that typically includes a few more cats than she wants to admit to.

Janice loves writing books about both love and family — about the way generations connect and the power our earliest experiences have on us throughout life. Her Superromance novels are frequent finalists for Romance Writers of America RITA awards, and she won the 2008 RITA for Best Contemporary Series Romance for SNOWBOUND.

Visit her website at www.JaniceKayJohnson.com.

A Note from the Author:

Thank you so much for purchasing my book. If you enjoyed the book, I hope you will take a moment to help me get the word out to others by posting a review on Amazon or Goodreads - or "like" my Author Page on Facebook to get future updates.

I also love to hear from readers, so please feel free to contact me on Facebook or via my website at www.JaniceKayJohnson.com.

Turn the page for a sneak peek at Cassie & Grant's story, the first book in the Desperation Creek series HOME DEADLY HOME.

Known for delivering stories that combine strong, realistic characters, compelling mysteries and deeply emotional romances, RITA award winning and USA Today bestselling author Janice Kay Johnson introduces her new romantic suspense series Desperation Creek with HOME DEADLY HOME, a gripping tale of murder, love…and the ominous shadow cast by the past.

The eerie voice of a killer…

Desperation Creek winds through stark, high desert country once known for cattle ranching. But a dying way of life means police are spread too thin, empty roads are bordered only by rusting barbed wire fences and sagebrush, and memories of the glory days barely keep desperation at bay.

After her painful childhood spent in Fort Halleck, Oregon, Cassie Ward longed to escape. Yet when her father needs her after he has a stroke, she reluctantly returns to take over the county's weekly newspaper. An anonymous caller promises her a "real" story if she'll go see a cattle rancher…who has been brutally murdered. Cassie complies when Sheriff Grant Holcomb demands she hold back horrific details from her reporting, but when the body count rises, she becomes determined to uncover the truth – whether the sheriff likes her involvement or not.

Grant had been grateful to return home after a seventeen year absence. He's seen too much death overseas and as a big city cop, but times have changed even here. He's falling in love with a woman who is not only still desperate to escape the town he sees as home, she has a dangerous connection with a madman using her to ensure headlines for his killing spree.

Are the deaths part of a battle for leadership of the revolt against federal control of large swaths of western lands? Or is this killer motivated by long-boiling resentment that overflowed once, like Cassie and Grant, he came home again? And if so, what part will they play in his deadly plan?

HOME DEADLY HOME

(A Desperation Creek Novel, Book 1)

PROLOGUE

One shot, one kill.

Satisfied, he took a last look at the effect. Dead man, smiles all around.

He'd wait until he was back at his truck to make that call to hurry things along. Of course, he'd toss this phone after, so he didn't have to worry about the GPS being traced. He didn't make a habit of carelessness. Never had, never would.

Tempting as it was to linger, enjoy that first shock and dismay, then watch the cops bumbling around, he'd hear all about it later. Maybe he'd get lucky this time, and either the local football star aka the sheriff himself or that new young detective would prove halfway competent and give him a real chase. That was the fun. The kill? It was almost too easy for a man with his skill and imagination.

Still – he was pleased to have proved once again that he was as sharp as ever, even when it mattered as never before.

Packing up his rifle, he smiled. Excellent beginning.

CHAPTER ONE

Cassie Ward ignored the first few rings of the phone. Finally, annoyed, she glanced up to see Helen's desk empty. Like everyone else working at this weekly newspaper, Helen multi-tasked, in her case as receptionist and phone person as well as filling in anywhere else needed. Last time Cassie had surfaced, Helen had been putting together the community calendar before she moved on to classifieds. She'd probably taken a restroom or coffee break.

No choice but to grab the phone. "Managing editor."

"Would you be Cassandra?" Low and slightly muffled, a man's voice. He sounded as if he was savoring her full name, a creepy notion.

He had her full attention. "I am."

"A newspaper reporter who will never be believed." He chuckled.

Cassie stiffened. She'd heard the joke before - her name did have a certain irony – but never in a tone that raised her hackles.

Did this guy know her? She wanted to feel sure the voice wasn't familiar, but couldn't. He was altering it somehow.

"Who is this? What can I do for you?" she asked briskly.

"It's more what I can do for you. If you want some *real* news, I suggest you go see Curt Steagall. Out at the—"

"Circle S. I know it."

"Front page," he murmured.

"Sir?" But she was talking to herself. He'd cut her off. Cassie muttered a few choice words under her breath. Andy Sloane was off working on something else, and she still had a ton to do to get the paper ready to send to the printer tonight. Even so, she couldn't ignore what he'd said, little as that was. Her current front page lead had to do with a construction project impacting businesses on Main Street. What she considered real news was undeniably thin on the ground hereabouts.

The caller might well be a nutcase. They got those. He could also be some regular guy who thought it was funny to get her stirred up. Or, hey, this was a real tip, delivered with unnecessary drama.

There was another alternative, she realized: a nutcase who had called to deliver a real tip. Now, *there* was an unwelcome notion.

After a minute, she sighed, dug through a drawer until she found the local phone directory, an even skimpier book than it used to be, and looked up the Steagall's number. If they had only cell phones… Nope, there it was. She dialed.

"Circle S," a woman said. "Karen speaking."

Cassie vaguely remembered Curtis Steagall from school. He'd been three or four years ahead of her, and therefore scarcely on her radar, or she on his. His father ran the ranch in those days, she did know that. Dad had probably told her whether Roger Steagall had died or retired or what, but she must not have paid attention.

Cattle ranching had been the dominant industry in this rural, eastern Oregon county until the past four or five decades, when raising beef cattle had become less profitable, and giant ranches owned by agri-businesses had increasingly driven small ranchers into selling out. Half a dozen local ranches still made it, though, and a good number of other local citizens ran some cattle and called themselves ranchers even though they held other jobs to pay the bills. The Circle S was a good size spread.

"Karen, this is Cassie Ward from the Hayes County Courier. I wonder if I could speak to Curt."

"Well, not right this minute, you can't. He's out feeding stock."

Sun high in the sky, of course he was. A crisp, cold day like this would be ideal for spreading hay. After a white Christmas, snow had lingered, thin and spotty, the earth frozen solid. His herd would be able to lip up most of the hay before they trampled the ground into a mucky mess.

Without prompting, Karen added, "I expect him back in the next half hour, give or take a little. He'll be hungry."

"Do you mind if I come out to the ranch?"

"Of course not, but…is there something I can help you with?"

"I wish I knew," Cassie said with complete honesty, "but since Curt's name was the one I was given, I'd like to start with him."

"All right, then."

*****

Wasn't that a strange phone call? Karen shook her head as she cut thick slabs of roast beef for sandwiches. What could a reporter want with Curt?

Maybe just a comment for some article about the ranchers butting heads with the BLM. The bureaucracy, or the incompetence, or the intentions of the federal Bureau of Land Management were part of plenty of conversations in ranch country, here in Oregon and across the west. Newspaper editorials, too. The BLM and the Forest Service and the soil conservation people and what not. The supposed experts were like ants on spilled sugar. The woman might just be looking for confirmation of information she'd gotten elsewhere. Even though that mess down at Malheur Wildlife Refuge when some angry ranchers staged a revolt had happened awhile back, it did still have people talking, and Curt had spoken out at the time.

Karen settled as she slapped mustard on the bread. That had to be it.

As she started warming soup, she tried to remember what she knew about Cassie Ward, who'd taken over Hayes County's only newspaper from her father after he had a stroke two or three months ago. She'd been told Cassie was a local girl, but one who went away to college and never came back except for visits. Dixie Percell said Cassie had been working for the Oregonian, over in Portland.

Nobody argued she didn't know what she was doing, managing the paper. She grew up at her daddy's elbow, Karen had heard. But the Oregonian leaned a lot further left than folks this side of the mountains liked.

Well, they'd see, wouldn't they?

The soup bubbled, and she turned off the burner, taking a look out the window above the sink even though she'd have heard the tractor if Curt were back.

She didn't see it even in the distance. This time of year, the landscape was bleak, no denying it. Brown pasture where it showed through snow. Beyond, more brown along with gray and white, at last a few tinges of dark green where the land started to rise and the first small junipers found footholds among the sagebrush.

No reason to worry; Curt had to finish what he set out to do, and they were getting close enough to calving season he might have been waylaid if he spotted a cow giving birth. This was only January 11, awfully early since usually that didn't happen until February at least. By then he'd have moved the pregnant cows in closer, where they could be monitored more easily. Still, you never knew, and that would hold him up for sure. Could have noticed damage to a fence, too. There were all kinds of possibilities.

She reached for her phone, but before she could try him, the doorbell rang.

Karen turned on a lamp in the living room before she opened the door to a woman bundled up against the cold. Her breath puffed out in a cloud.

"Come in! Here, let me take your coat."

The door shut behind Cassie Ward, she unpeeled her scarf, removed a fleece hat to reveal – yes, rumor had it right – a purple streak in short, dark red hair. Parka next. One glove fell out of her pocket and she bent to pick it up.

Karen draped everything over a coat tree, then led the way to the kitchen. "Curt's not back yet, but at least you can be comfortable while you wait. Can I get you a cup of coffee?"

"If it's easy," the reporter said. No, managing editor, that's what she was called.

Karen poured the coffee, then said, "Why don't I call him to find out what's holding him up?"

His phone rang, and kept ringing. He had it set on eight rings before it went to voice mail. At the least, he had to fumble off a heavy glove to answer.

She hesitated, but instead of leaving a voicemail, called again. Eight more rings. Finally setting the phone on the counter, she turned to the visitor. "He's likely to call back in the next few minutes." On the rare occasions when Curt was out of earshot, he checked for missed calls as soon as he could, since he worried about her alone at the ranch house. Especially now, with her pregnant although most people didn't know yet.

This Cassie Ward sure was a little thing, maybe five foot two or three inches at most. She'd taken a seat at the table, added sugar and cream to her coffee, and sipped it while watching Karen.

"Who was it gave you Curt's name?" Karen asked abruptly.

A few creases formed on the reporter's forehead. "That's the thing. I don't know." She shrugged, dismissing whatever had bothered her. "We get anonymous tips. People don't always want their names known."

Karen understood that. A real private person herself, she wouldn't have married a rancher if she couldn't be content living out in the middle of nowhere, not a neighboring house in sight.

She asked about Cassie's father, and got an update on his condition. Yes, for now Cassie was staying with him.

"He grumbles about his physical therapy – they work him hard – but we're all looking to the day when he can take over the newspaper again. It's been his life," she added.

Two women without much in common, they labored for another few minutes to make conversation. Karen couldn't relax enough to sit down. At a pause, she snatched up the phone and tried calling Curt again, with no more luck.

By now, she had a rock in the pit of her stomach. Accidents happened. With tractors, never mind animals that considerably outweighed her husband and were none too smart. He could have stepped in a hole and broken a leg. Too many things could go wrong.

"I'm going out there," she decided. "If you want to wait—"

Cassie shook her head. "I'll go with you. You might need a hand."

Karen hesitated, knowing the other woman was still looking for her story, but there was room for two on the four-wheeler, and she was just a little relieved not to be heading out alone. She nodded. "We'd best bundle up, then."

*****

Cassie held onto the woman in front of her as they followed in the tracks left by a tractor. Despite the freezing temperatures, the distinctive scent of sagebrush tingled in her nostrils. In between visits home, she forgot how different it smelled out in the high desert country on the east side of the Cascade mountains. Mostly the sagebrush, but also the juniper and maybe even the volcanic soil. The dry air and biting cold didn't have much in common with Portland's seasonal rain and forty degree temps, either.

The ATV was too noisy to allow for talking, which was just as well. Cassie had no idea what she was doing here, and she was afraid she was the cause of the tension she'd seen on Karen Steagall's face. Didn't sound as if Curt was usually late, and for it to happen just when a reporter got a tip to talk to him?

Cassie didn't like the coincidence. What about this could be a 'real' story? As they bounced across winter-dead pasture, she kept hearing the eerie way the caller said her name.

Karen had told her that the cattle were out in the northeast corner of the ranch right now. When the ATV came to a stop, Cassie hopped off to open a gate. The ground beyond was mucky, with strands of hay mixed into the frozen mud. Curt must have tossed the hay over the fence here more than a few times.

The tracks left by the tractor were clear. They headed off into more emptiness. The worried way the other woman stared now stretched Cassie's nerves, too.

Once Karen had driven through and Cassie closed the gate, Karen said, loud enough for her to hear, "We ought to be able to see the tractor."

The moment Cassie climbed back on, Karen accelerated to a speed that had the ATV bouncing over the uneven terrain.

The cold had a bite today. Bank in town said the thermometer read eight degrees. This had been a bitter winter even by local standards, hitting record lows. Cassie tucked her chin deeper in the collar of her parka and debated letting go with one hand to wrap the scarf around her face but decided she didn't dare.

Karen called something over her shoulder, and Cassie leaned to the side to see around her shoulder to where a big green tractor and trailer sat parked alongside a barbed wire fence that likely marked the back boundary of the Circle S. Only the tractor's height left it visible; a vast herd of red-brown cattle with white faces jostled for position around it. From here, she couldn't see the driver. Stacked hay bales on the trailer blocked any view of the other side. Why would Curt have boxed himself in like this? It made no sense to spread hay here.

Apprehension had been buzzing under her skin, but the sight of the neat rectangle of hay bales filled her with dread. If he'd been out here all morning, why hadn't he already fed his herd? How long had he been sitting here? Or had he ducked through the fence onto federal land because he saw something he needed to check out?

Instead of slowing down, Karen accelerated. The icy air whipped Cassie's face. The herd parted to let them through, closing back around them. A sudden stop flung them both forward. The engine shut off, letting them hear the unhappy complaints of hungry animals.

For an instant, Karen didn't move. "I don't see him."

Cassie sucked in that frigid air scented now with manure. "He might just be out of sight."

Neither woman believed it. Karen nodded, anyway, but still made no effort to dismount until Cassie climbed stiffly off the ATV, almost falling when a big head butted her. Once Karen joined her, the two women pushed their way toward the front of the tractor.

Cassie stopped before circling all the way around the front of it, her eye caught by something so out of place, she could only gape. A bright yellow balloon filled with helium floated above the barbed wire fence, a long yellow ribbon anchoring it to the wire. And...was that a face on the front of the balloon?

She took another step into the narrow space between tractor and fence. Two. And then her heart took a hard thump. The balloon had a smiley face, the cheeriness so bizarre she had to blink a couple of times before she could tear her gaze away to where the bulk of a man lay sprawled beside the fence. No, his arm was snagged on it, as if he'd grabbed for support on his way down. His head...

Bile rising to her throat, she backed up. Oh, dear God – she'd never imagined she'd see anything like this again except in her nightmares. Whirling, she found Karen on her heels. "No," she said. "You don't want to see this."

The other woman elbowed right by her. A terrible cry spilled from her throat. Cassie pulled Karen back around, holding her tight to keep her from rushing to her husband's side. At last the taller woman quit fighting and stiffened, her eyes fixed as if she was still staring at the worst thing she'd ever seen, even if her back was now to it.

The balloon bobbed as a cow got pushed against the fence at the back of the trailer, unable to squeeze into the narrow space but barely three feet from the body.

Uneasy thoughts crept into Cassie's head, sending prickles up her nape.

The caller hadn't said she should go talk to Curt Steagall. He'd said she should go *see* him. Which meant...

If he'd used a cell phone, he might still be here. Watching. Someone who'd seen what happened but didn't want to be named as a witness.

But remembering what could have been amusement when he said, "A newspaper reporter who will never be believed," she knew. He'd done a lot more than *see*. The balloon was commentary. Mockery.

Rage overcame her nausea and the echo of older horrors, and she fumbled with a gloved hand for her phone.

*****

The Quarter Horse moved easily under Grant Holcomb, maintaining a steady lope. Even seemed as if he knew where to go, once Grant had pointed him in the general direction. He'd saddled the first likely looking animal in the Circle S barn, since the two women had taken the ranch's only ATV. The reason he was out here took away from what otherwise would have been the pleasure of being on horseback on a clear, crisp day like this, quiet but for the creak of leather and the thud of hoofbeats.

As always, he reserved judgment, but if this was murder versus an accidental death, he'd have to deal with the difficulty of getting a crime scene unit way the hell out here. The body would most likely need to be transported by helicopter. All smaller counties in Oregon borrowed crime scene investigators from the state police. Come to think of it, they were bound to have a plan for deaths in the middle of empty country, not a problem he'd had in his last job with an urban police force.

The ground rose gradually, until the horse topped what Grant hadn't even realized was a low hill that had kept his sightline limited. The gelding, a gleaming chestnut, probably saw the tractor before he did, because their course shifted without any signal from him. Grant lifted a hand to his fleece hat – his Stetson sat on the passenger seat of the police SUV he'd driven – to tug it more securely over his ears. The cold burned his face.

Looking toward him, two women huddled beside an ATV. They disappeared from sight as the bellowing herd shifted while crowding the trailer and tractor beyond. Even bundled up, they had to be freezing.

He slowed the gelding to a trot, then a walk. Grant started dismounting before the horse came to a complete stop.

"Ladies." He took in their pinched faces. The taller one appeared shell-shocked, the smaller woman furious. That made her the one he'd spoken to. Raising his voice to be heard about the din, he introduced himself. "I'm Sheriff Holcomb."

"So we got the big gun," the little one said tartly.

Under other circumstances he'd have smiled. "A county with a skimpy population like this, I don't have a lot of minions. Now, I need to take a look around."

She held out a gloved hand for the reins. Nodding his thanks, he fought his way through the shifting herd toward the trailer. If not for the nonstop lowing, he'd have heard a slurp with every step, the ever-moving cattle having created a mud hole while depositing steaming manure piles. They were miserable, not understanding why they weren't being fed. The ones closest to the trailer were trying to pull strands from bales too tight to let them get much. He surely did hope Curt Steagall had either fallen on the far side of the fence, or that the corridor between tractor and fence was too narrow for even a small cow to push her way in. Otherwise, the body was being trampled beneath cloven hooves.

Rounding the front of the tractor, his gaze stuck on the balloon despite his awareness of the body sprawled on the ground below it – not trampled. *Jesus*. Cassie Ward had mentioned the damned balloon, but the impact still stunned him. A bright yellow, smiley face right above a dead man – now, that was an obscenity.

Without getting any closer than he had to, Grant crouched to study the body, lying face down with arms and legs at awkward angles. What he could see of the head was a bloody mess. That had to be the entrance wound, with extensive lacerations around it forming a star pattern, the bullet hole in the center. Grant's military tours allowed him to recognize the horrific result of a high-caliber bullet. The victim's head had connected with the split-wood fence post on his way down, doing more damage and leaving blood behind that could be hiding any stippling or fouling – although Grant didn't expect there to be any. He'd swear this shot had been taken from a distance. The exit wound wouldn't be visible until the body was moved.

The wound wasn't fresh; blood and brain matter had congealed and frozen. So – several hours. Could the victim have been shot while still in the tractor seat, and tumbled down? Grant considered the angles, and ended up doubtful.

He swiveled on his heels. Assuming there was an exit wound, the bullet had ended up somewhere. If Curt Steagall had been on his feet, it could have pinged off the tractor, but from here Grant couldn't see any obvious dents the right size and shape. If it had had enough force after passing through a human skull… Shit. Odds put it inside one of those bales of hay.

First time in his life he'd had to search for an almost literal needle in a haystack.

He rose to his feet again. He could be wrong; he couldn't be positive the shot hadn't been taken up close and personal. Say, two men arguing across the fence, the shooter on federal land. He sure as hell hadn't shoved his way through the herd to get his shot.

The balloon ruled out any possibility of an argument having accelerated into a shooting, anyway. The killer had brought the damn thing out here, already full of helium. Grant couldn't think of any reason for him to do that, except as an F-you to the dead man – or to the police who would investigate the death.

Teeth clenched, Grant scanned for a footprint on the other side of the fence, but couldn't pick out anything on the frozen ground. He swept the landscape for a likely hide. Once he got everything else started, he'd find it. Even most hunters couldn't make a shot that accurate from very far out. Grant had a crawling sensation up his spine when he realized that the only cover within a hundred yards or so was sagebrush. You'd think Curt would have seen someone lying in wait that close. Unless the killer had waved a greeting at him and been approaching, holding the rifle in a relaxed way. Could well have been someone he knew. Then...*bang*.

Grant's gut said this had been an ambush. Hard to make that shot if the gunman had been on his feet, moving. If he'd stopped and raised the barrel, wouldn't Curt have dived for cover?

Either way, the killer had had to walk right up to the body to tie that damn balloon in place. Couldn't get much more callous than that.

Still scanning the colorless landscape, Grant asked himself what had drawn Curt to this spot. He wouldn't have fed his herd here, boxing himself in. Had he seen someone he knew? Or the balloon, already tied on the fence?

Grant fought his way back to the women. He hated to ask, needed to be certain. He hadn't been able to see the victim's face very well. "Mrs. Steagall, did you get a good enough look to be certain that's your husband?"

Her face crumpled, but she nodded.

He made himself utter the formal words. "I'm sorry for your loss." With her face buried in her hands, she didn't respond. Damn. Tears would freeze on her face.

He shifted his attention to the woman beside her. "Ms. Ward, can you drive the ATV?"

"Yes. My dad runs cattle and has used one for years."

"All right. I'm thinking the two of you need to get out of the cold. Especially Mrs. Steagall, given her shock."

She nodded. He wished he could see her face better, but didn't blame her for using a purple fleece scarf as a shemagh. Not much showed but her eyes, big and brown with some gold striations.

"Persuade her to drink something hot – tea with a lot of sugar, cocoa."

"I'll take care of her."

"What got the two of you worried enough to come out here? Was it just the phone call?"

"Just?" she said sharply.

"Poor choice of words," he acknowledged. "I should say, were there any additional reasons for concern?"

"Karen expected Curt for lunch," she explained. "He was late. Me showing up with questions made Karen uneasy, too, so she tried repeatedly to call him. When he didn't pick up or call back, I could tell she started to really worry."

"Okay. I'll have to ask you to stay at the ranch house until I can get free to talk to you both." He laid a hand on Mrs. Steagall's arm, waiting until she at least tried to focus on him, her face wet. "Can you tell me when Curt headed out here?"

It took her a minute to dredge up an answer. "He had to load the hay. Between eight and nine?"

"Thank you. Mrs. Steagall, Ms. Ward is going to drive you back to the house. I need you both to wait there for me. All right?"

Incomprehension.

He helped steer her to the four-wheeler, and half-lifted her on. A belated thought had him extending a hand to stop Cassie before she could climb on in turn.

"I need to ask whether you took any pictures."

She eyed him for a minute. "I'm a reporter. Of course I did."

"Then I have to ask for your phone."

She snorted. "You think I'll hand it over? In your dreams. Besides, you're too late. I sent them off."

"To?"

"My email at the newspaper."

Of course she had.

"They're saved in the cloud, anyway," she added.

"You could really screw up this investigation," he said in a hard voice. "Don't you want us to find out who murdered Curt?"

The eyes narrowed to slits and she tried to get right up in his face. Which she couldn't pull off since he was a foot taller than her. "Were you *born* thinking most people are scum you're forced to wipe off your boots?"

He didn't know how to take that, but it didn't make him any less mad. "In my experience, reporters and editors think first about circulation, or getting a story picked up by larger outlets. The people along the way…" He shrugged dismissively.

She made a disgusted sound and yanked her arm free from his grip. "For your information, Sheriff, I took a picture of the balloon with the landscape beyond it. I plan to pause on the way back long enough to get a shot of the tractor and trailer surrounded by the herd. I did not photograph the dead man or anything else."

She swung herself up on the ATV, started it with a roar, and after saying something quiet over her shoulder to her passenger, made a U-turn maneuvering through the shifting herd, and headed back toward the ranch house.

Grant was left with the rueful knowledge that he'd put his horns down and charged before she whipped out any red cape. Good job – alienate a critical witness first thing.

Shaking his head, he started making calls.

Also Available from Janice Kay Johnson

Cape Trouble, a tiny Oregon Coast town, was named for the dangerous off-shore reefs. But some of its citizens seek refuge from their own troubles…which have a way of following them.

SHROUD OF FOG (Cape Trouble, Book 1)

The secrets of the past haunt the present…

Sophie Thomsen's life had a Before and an After – marked by the terrifying morning when she found her mother dead in the foggy sand dunes, an apparent suicide. Now, twenty years later, Sophie returns to Cape Trouble, only to find her aunt brutally murdered. Although she swore never to set foot again on Misty Beach, Sophie takes over her aunt's crusade to save the falling-down Misty Beach Resort and its wild sand dunes and beach from development. But Sophie's memories threaten a killer…who doesn't dare let her remember too much.

Having come to Cape Trouble to heal his own wounds, Police Chief Daniel Colburn investigates the present day murder, but begins to suspect Sophie's mother was another murder victim, not a suicide. Everything he learns increases his fear for the woman he is coming to love.

Sophie's fate may be to die in a shroud of fog, just like her mother before her, unless she can trust Daniel to help her uncover her past in time.

Also in the series:
SEE HOW SHE RUNS (Cape Trouble, Book 2)
TWISTED THREADS (Cape Trouble, Book 3)
WHISPER OF REVENGE (Cape Trouble, Book 4)
TRIGGER WORDS (Cape Trouble, Book 5)

What people are saying about the romantic suspense novels of Janice Kay Johnson:

• *"If you are in the mood for a wonderful romantic suspense story that will have you so engrossed in it that you lose track of the time, than look no further."*

- Night Owl Reviews (on <u>Shroud of Fog</u>)

• *"SHROUD OF FOG will immerse the reader in a world of suspense and intrigue. Elements of romance throughout this captivating read will capture your heart. I kept guessing as to whom the killer was up until the very end. Janice Kay Johnson has penned a deeply satisfying story that is appealing to mystery lovers as well as romance aficionados. If you are looking for a tale that has plenty of plot twists and amazing characters that will remain with you, then you should rush out and get a copy of SHROUD OF FOG!"*

- Romance Junkies

• *"[G]uaranteed to have you looking over your shoulder more than once in this explosive, fast-paced thriller."*
- Linda Silverstein, ROMANTIC TIMES (on <u>Dangerous Waters</u>)

• *"Studded with tension and skillfully riveting, [it] will capture you from the first page and won't let go until the end."*
- Kay Gragg, AFFAIRE DE COEUR (on <u>Dangerous Waters</u>)

• *"I've never read Ms. Johnson's work before and all I can say is I will be finding everything else she's ever written. This story is so masterful it takes you inside this small town and really makes you think you are there."*
- Sara HJ, HARLEQUIN JUNKIES (on <u>Everywhere She Goes</u>)

www.ingramcontent.com/pod-product-compliance
Lightning Source LLC
Chambersburg PA
CBHW030236200626
46816CB00002BA/386